ALL HER FAULT

www.penguin.co.uk

ALL HER FAULT

Andrea Mara

BANTAM PRESS

TRANSWORLD PUBLISHERS
Penguin Random House, One Embassy Gardens,
8 Viaduct Gardens, London SW11 7BW
www.penguin.co.uk

Transworld is part of the Penguin Random House group of companies
whose addresses can be found at global.penguinrandomhouse.com

Penguin
Random House
UK

First published in Great Britain in 2021 by Bantam Press
an imprint of Transworld Publishers

A CIP catalogue record for this book
is available from the British Library.

ISBNs 9781787634497 (cased)
9781787634503 (tpb)

Typeset in 11.5/15.5 pt ITC Giovanni by Jouve (UK), Milton Keynes
Printed and bound in Great Britain by Clays Ltd, Elcograf S.p.A.

The authorized representative in the EEA is Penguin Random House Ireland,
Morrison Chambers, 32 Nassau Street, Dublin D02 YH68.

Penguin Random House is committed to a sustainable
future for our business, our readers and our planet. This book
is made from Forest Stewardship Council® certified paper.

To Nicola, with love

PART 1

November 2018

1

Marissa
Friday

THE HOUSE LOOKED LIKE any other house and the door looked like any other door. Normal. A bit generic. Not what Marissa was expecting. She pressed the bell and stood back. What *had* she been expecting? Something a little grander, perhaps. Jenny had looked so groomed at the school social, and Marissa realized she'd built up an image that didn't quite tally with this very ordinary-looking house and its very ordinary-looking door.

As she waited, her mind ran over everything they had planned for the weekend. She'd have to pop into the office at some point – the audit was only weeks away, and she needed to go over the Fenelon file again. Then there was her tennis match, book club – and dammit, she still hadn't finished the book.

Footsteps. And a shadow through the glass panel as Jenny approached and opened the door. Only it wasn't Jenny. The woman was short with a mass of unruly brown curls, and a tea towel in her hand. The nanny perhaps? Though she didn't look much like the nannies and au pairs Marissa saw when she dropped Milo to school each morning.

'Hi, I'm Marissa, I'm here to pick up my son, Milo?' she said to the woman.

'Ah, you must have the wrong house, there's nobody called Milo here.'

'Oh!' Marissa said, fishing her phone from her handbag. 'I'm so sorry, let me just check . . .' She clicked into the message from Jenny and read aloud.

'14 Tudor Grove . . .' She looked up at the woman. 'Sorry, what number is this?'

'This is fourteen, but there's no Milo here. It's just me.'

Marissa shook her head, looking down again at the text, as though it might have somehow changed in the intervening seconds. She held it up to the woman.

'I'm not going mad, am I, this does say 14 Tudor Grove?'

The woman nodded. 'Someone must have given you the wrong address. Sure, give them a ring and see?'

She started to close the door, and that's when the first pang of unease hit. It felt like it did last weekend when she couldn't find Milo in the playground – he was there somewhere, of course he was, but she couldn't relax until she had eyes on him. And seconds later, she did. But she had no eyes on him now. Now, he was in Jenny's house and the woman who was not Jenny was closing the door.

'Wait! Sorry, do you mind if I stay here while I ring, in case there's been some mix-up?'

The woman's kind brown eyes suggested she had no idea what kind of mix-up Marissa meant, but she kept the door open. Marissa hit the Call button on Jenny's text and waited for the ringtone. There was none. Just an automated message.

The number you have called is not recognized.

Unease slipped into mild panic.

'It's not working,' Marissa said to the woman, her voice hoarse.

'Come in,' the woman said, pulling the door wide. 'We'll figure it out. Some kind of glitch with the phone company, no doubt.'

She chattered on as Marissa followed her through to her kitchen, still trying to phone Jenny. But the message was the same each time.

The number you have called is not recognized.

'Now, this person you're trying to phone – who is she?'

'Jenny. A mum from the school. My son Milo is on a playdate with her son Jacob. This is the address she sent me for pick-up.' The words came in short, breathless bursts.

She showed the woman Jenny's message.

The address is 14 Tudor Grove – if I'm not home from work when you get there, my nanny Carrie will be there with the boys.

The woman tilted her head, looking puzzled.

'It doesn't make sense,' Marissa continued. 'If this is her address, why is she not here?' Her breath got shorter, faster. 'Why is Milo not here?'

'And you've never been to her house before?'

'No, no – Milo just started school this year, and this is his first playdate with Jacob.' She swallowed, gulped at the air and tried to slow her breathing. 'I met Jenny at the school social, and she was lovely – I don't understand what's going on. How would she get her own address wrong?'

'Do you have numbers for other parents in the class, could you call one of them to get the right address?'

Of course. That's what she needed to do. Sarah Rayburn would definitely have a number for Jenny – Sarah knew everyone. There would be a simple explanation. Marissa pulled up Sarah's number and dialled. Sarah picked up, sounding surprised.

'Marissa, how are you?' she said, in a voice that meant, *Why are you calling me at half five on a Friday?*

5

'Sarah, do you have a number for Jenny Kennedy? Milo is on a playdate with Jacob, but somehow Jenny sent me the wrong address and now I've no idea where to get him!' Marissa laughed, but it came out sounding hysterical.

'Marissa, there must be some mistake. Did you get your dates mixed up?'

'What do you mean?'

'Milo can't be on a playdate with Jacob – Jacob is here in our house.'

That's when Marissa's limbs went loose. As the phone dropped from her hand, she sagged against the wall and stared at the woman.

'I don't know where my son is,' she whispered, and slipped to the stranger's floor.

2

ESTHER WAS HER NAME – the woman who owned the house that wasn't Jenny's – Marissa half heard her say it when she picked the phone off the floor and took over speaking to Sarah.

'I'm here with your friend, she's had a bit of a turn.' Esther was talking into the phone as she hunkered beside Marissa. 'Now – Sarah, is it? Would you have the right number for this woman Jenny?'

She went over to the table and, with the phone clutched between her shoulder and her ear, she wrote something on the back of an envelope.

'Lovely. We'll give her a call. So Jenny's little boy is in your house? You're sure of that? Of course, I understand. Yes, we'll let you know. Bye now. Bye.'

Esther looked over at Marissa as she disconnected the call.

'Will I do it for you – phone your friend?'

Marissa nodded again. Only Jenny wasn't her friend, was she? They'd met once, that night at the school social. They hit it off when they realized they were wearing the same dress – *we either avoid each other all night or have a laugh and take selfies*, Marissa had said to Jenny, a shy woman from Cork who seemed good

7

fun beneath the quiet exterior. So when Jenny had texted to invite Milo on a playdate, Marissa didn't think twice – they'd *met*, for God's sake, it wasn't like sending your child off with a stranger. Was it? Jesus Christ, *was it*?

There was something in Esther's expression as she waited, phone to her ear, eyes fixed on Marissa. Then her face changed.

'Hello, Jenny? You don't know me but I'm here with your friend Marissa. From your son's school? Yes. She thought her son was in your house today, there seems to be some confusion. I'm going to put you on speaker now.' She set the phone on the kitchen table.

'Hiya, sorry, I'm away with work – I'm in France,' said the voice on the phone. 'I didn't have any playdates organized in our house today – Jacob is at Sarah Rayburn's?'

'But you texted me about it?' Marissa said. 'You sent me a message to arrange it?'

'No, I didn't send any message . . . I'm not sure what happened there – isn't there another Jacob in the class, could that be it?'

Esther raised her eyebrows at Marissa – could that be what happened?

Of course! Jacob . . . Wilcox? That must be it. God, she was such an idiot, causing all this fuss. She started to get up, then paused. That only made sense if the other mother was also called Jenny. And it still didn't explain why she gave the wrong address.

Marissa stood and picked the phone off the table.

'Jenny, could you send the number for Jacob Wilcox's mother?'

When the contact pinged through seconds later, Esther and Marissa looked at it, saying nothing. The mother's name wasn't Jenny – of course it wasn't. But there could be some explanation, something that would make sense when they spoke to her.

Esther pressed Call and put the phone on speaker again.

After what seemed like for ever, the call was answered.

'Hello? Sorry, let me pop outside,' came the tinny voice, 'it's hard to hear in the bar – hello?'

Esther looked at Marissa and opened her mouth to speak.

'Hi, this is a friend of Marissa Irvine's – her son Milo is in your son Jacob's class, and we were wondering if Milo is in your house today?'

'No, Jacob's with my mother-in-law. Sorry, I'm at a work do, it's hard to hear. What made you think he was in our house?'

'Just a bit of confusion, thanks for your time,' Esther said, and disconnected. She looked at Marissa. 'What about Milo's dad – maybe he picked him up from school and forgot to tell you?'

Peter. That could be it. Premature relief flooded through Marissa as she dialled her husband's number.

'I know, I know, pizza night!' he said when he answered. 'I just have one final set of documents to send out, then I'll head home. Did Milo-Mouse enjoy his playdate?'

'Peter, is he not with you?'

'Milo? No, I'm still at work – did something happen? Why isn't he with you?'

'He was on a playdate and when I came to pick him up, he wasn't there, but it was the wrong house, the mum gave me the wrong address,' she said, all in one panicked breath.

'Can you ring her,' he said, 'get the address?'

'I did, but it wasn't her.' She knew she was making no sense. 'The person who arranged the playdate signed off "Jenny", but it wasn't the Jenny I know. And the number is out of service.'

'But surely you called the mother to confirm the playdate?'

'No, we arranged everything by text.' Oh God, she should have called. Why hadn't she called?

'OK, I'm leaving the office – we need to call the police, can you do that? And then start phoning every parent from the class. I'll meet you at home.'

She hung up and dialled 999.

In the end, Esther drove Marissa home, so that she could focus on making calls. Marissa wasn't sure she could have driven the car anyway. Her hands shook as she dialled each number, getting the same answer every time – *no, he's not here, can I help in some way, it's probably a mix-up.* Worried voices tinged with relief – *thank God it's not my child* beneath every *keep us posted* goodbye. As Esther pulled into the driveway, Marissa jumped out, suddenly certain Milo would be there – sitting in the doorway, somehow having made his way home from school on his own. She called his name, again and again, checking around both sides of the house, wondering if he could scale the side gate and get through to the back garden. Inside the house, she ran through to the back door, hands fumbling as she unlocked it, then out to the garden, still calling his name. Nothing. Nobody.

Esther had followed her in and was standing in the kitchen.

'There's a police car outside, and two gardaí getting out of it. They'll sort it out now, don't worry. Sit down there,' she said, patting a stool at the breakfast bar. Marissa didn't sit. She took her phone from her pocket and dialled the next number, but it was one she'd already called. She was losing track and running out of names. Were there parents she didn't have in her phone? Would Ana know? Wait, could this have something to do with Ana, maybe she wasn't away after all?

The doorbell rang though the front door was open – Marissa could see the two officers on the step and beckoned them in.

'I need to phone Ana – my au pair,' she said, before either one of them had the chance to speak. 'She's gone away for the

weekend and took today off, but maybe I mixed up the weekends –
maybe she collected Milo . . .'

She hit Ana's number and waited as it rang, pressing the
phone to her ear so hard it hurt. No answer. She tried again.
Still nothing.

'Mrs Irvine,' one of the gardaí said, a fair-haired woman in
her thirties who looked stern but not unkind. 'I'm Detective
Sergeant McConville and this is Detective Garda Breen.' She
nodded towards her colleague; a tall, thin man with a slightly
bored expression. 'Can you tell us what happened?'

And she did, while Esther made tea, and the guard called
Breen took notes. She paused every few minutes to try Ana
again, but it rang out each time. She tried the number in the
text from 'Jenny', then passed it to the gardaí to take a look.

'It's out of service, but I don't know what that means.'

The gardaí didn't look at one another but Marissa sensed an
unspoken exchange. Whatever way you thought about it, an
out-of-service number was not a good thing.

'How old is your son, Mrs Irvine?'

'He's only four,' Marissa replied, her voice breaking, as she
tried Ana's number again.

The sound of a key in the door made her jump up and run to
the hall. Peter walked in, but alone – no Milo trotting behind
him. Little by little, the straws were slipping from her grasp.

'Peter, where is he?' she said, burying her head in his
chest. His arms circled her, his face in her hair.

'It'll be OK, I promise, we'll find him. Are the guards in the
kitchen?'

She nodded and led him through to meet McConville and
Breen, and Esther too, explaining that she was the real occu-
pant of 14 Tudor Grove.

Breen, who with his light blond hair and high colour looked

like he was just out of training college, was in the corner on his phone. Looking for the owner of the 'Jenny' number maybe? Marissa tried to hear but his voice was little more than a murmur.

'Could Ana know something?' Peter asked.

'I can't get her on the phone. She's meant to be in Galway with her boyfriend, and for whatever reason she's not answering.'

They stared at each other, lost for words.

McConville cleared her throat, her wide, grey eyes still serious, but sympathetic too.

'I wonder if you could give me a recent photo of Milo?'

That's when reality hit Marissa like a millstone to the chest. It wasn't just a mix-up. Her son was officially missing.

3

Marissa
Friday

Everything moved blindingly fast from that moment on, but Marissa watched it in slow motion, numb, rubbing the scar on her chin. Peter sat at the table, scrolling through his phone for a photo of Milo. Esther made more tea. McConville was busy on her phone, trying to get a number for Milo's teacher, Mr Williams. He would surely remember who had collected Milo, wouldn't he? Marissa tried to picture the school pick-up line – the teacher walking across the yard to the waiting parents, handing over the Junior Infants, child by child. They had to raise a hand when they saw their parent or minder; the teacher never let them go without checking. But lots of kids were collected by a mix of parents, nannies and grandparents, varying from one day to the next – if a child raised a hand, would the teacher really look to see who was picking up?

Breen was looking at Milo's photo on Peter's phone and making notes.

'What was Milo wearing today?'

'His school tracksuit. Oh, and his favourite raincoat. It's bright green, silver dinosaurs on it. He loves that coat.'

'And does Milo have any distinguishing features?' he asked.

Did he? Did the freckle on his foot count, or the dimple on his chin? Fear and shock smothered her again as she thought about his tiny foot, his bright blond head.

'No, none,' Peter was saying. 'Though his hair might stand out – it's a bit longer than most of the other boys', and bright blond. He's small for his age too.'

'Any medical issues?'

'He's intolerant to dairy,' Marissa whispered, 'and he doesn't eat shellfish because we think he might be allergic but we don't know.'

Breen looked confused. She tried again.

'Peter is allergic to shellfish so we never have shellfish in the house – we're planning to get Milo tested, just to be sure. He had an odd reaction to paracetamol once so we don't give him that, and he's intolerant to soap, it brings him out in hives.'

Breen looked at her sceptically. Maybe he didn't believe in allergies and intolerances.

'Right. Anything else about him that stands out?'

'He's unusually bright for his age. He's super smart with numbers and he's obsessed with colours – he's always talking about the colour of things, even things we can't see, like letters and numbers. It might help someone notice him if they heard him talking . . .' Marissa trailed off, stemmed by Breen's raised eyebrows. This wasn't the kind of thing he needed to know; it wasn't going to help.

McConville walked towards them, her hand over the phone.

'I've tracked down Mr Williams's number, calling him now,' she told them.

Peter took Marissa's hand.

'He'd surely have phoned if nobody turned up to collect Milo – teachers don't just take kids home when that happens.'

'I know, I know,' Marissa said, her voice low and tight. Of course teachers didn't take kids home. Unless they became suddenly unhinged. And Mr Williams – a paunchy, middle-aged man with an easy smile – didn't seem like that kind of person. But then what does an unhinged person look like?

'Mr Williams? This is Detective Sergeant McConville of Blackrock Garda station. I'm calling in relation to a child in your class – do you remember who collected Milo Irvine from school today?'

Marissa and Peter sat forward simultaneously, straining to hear.

'Right, are you certain?' McConville said, glancing over at them. 'And nothing stood out? OK, we might need to talk to you again this evening – we'll phone to check you're back before we come over.'

'What is it – who?' Marissa said, before McConville had time to hang up.

'He says the minder picked Milo up. Can you give me her number and full name?'

Relief flooded through Marissa.

'It's Ana Garcia. Maybe the playdate was cancelled or she realized there was some mix-up. I'll try her again.'

Marissa dialled the number, but again it rang out. She passed her phone to McConville, who saved the number in her own phone, and called the station again, walking through to the hallway to speak.

Peter stood, running his fingers through his hair.

'But isn't she meant to be off? Didn't she go to Galway?'

Marissa threw up her hands.

'I don't know, Peter! I'm doing my best to piece this together. As soon as we get through to her, we'll know what happened – the main thing is, she's the one who picked him up.'

McConville came back to the kitchen and looked from one to the other.

'How long have you known your nanny?'

'Oh my God, what is it?' Marissa asked, as Peter sank into a chair.

'We just need to cover all the bases. Do you know her well?'

'Of course!' Marissa said. 'She's been minding Milo for over a year now, she's brilliant with him.'

'Does she have any ties here – any family in Ireland?'

'No family here, they're all in Peru, but she has a boyfriend. He's Peruvian too, working in a call centre in town or in Sandyford Industrial Estate maybe, I can't remember now.'

'Where do they live?'

'She's in a house-share in Dún Laoghaire, they don't live together.'

Peter interrupted.

'No, they do – he's one of the lads in the house-share, that's how they met.'

Marissa looked over at him. How had Ana never mentioned that? But then they didn't talk much about her personal life – it was mostly about Milo and what he'd done that day.

'Either way, we trust her implicitly. If she picked Milo up today, everything is fine.'

Breen looked at McConville and slid a notebook and pen across the table to Marissa.

'Could you write down her address, and we'll send someone around to the house since she's still not answering the phone?'

Marissa picked up the pen, her hand shaking.

'I don't know her address actually . . .' She looked over at Peter. 'Do you know it? Somewhere off Tivoli Road, isn't it?'

'Or is it up near the Glenageary Roundabout . . . hang on,' he said, 'I should have her CV in an email still.'

As he clicked and scrolled on his phone, four sets of eyes watched and waited in silence.

'Dammit,' he said under his breath after a minute. He looked up. 'The address is the one she had when she first applied for the job – a flat in the city centre. She moved out to Dún Laoghaire after we hired her. I don't seem to have that address.'

'That's OK,' said Breen, though it clearly wasn't. 'Would you have her boyfriend's name and we'll try to locate him?'

'Seb,' Marissa said. 'Seb . . . I don't know his surname. I mean, people don't tell you surnames, do they?' She turned to Peter and to Esther, looking for reassurance.

'I don't know it either,' Peter said, 'I didn't really see Ana much – it was mostly Marissa's territory.'

Marissa picked up her phone and tried Ana's number again.

'Can you locate her via GPS or something?' she asked, as it rang out.

McConville nodded. 'As long as the phone is still switched on, that's a good sign.'

The attempt at reassurance left Marissa with a cold knot in her stomach. A good sign of what? That her nanny hadn't inexplicably disappeared with her child? She shook her head. It just didn't make sense. Ana was lovely, so good to Milo, and so *easy* – she slotted right in as soon as they hired her. It had to be a misunderstanding.

'Do you have a photo of Ana?' McConville asked.

'Yes, hang on,' Marissa said, scrolling through her phone. Ana was always sending photos during the day – Milo in the playground, Milo in the garden, smiling selfies of the two of them on Dún Laoghaire Pier. She found one from a few weeks back – Ana's long dark hair glinting in the sunlight, her wide smile, sunglasses hiding deep brown eyes. Milo beside her, heads together, his smile just as wide, his shoulder-length blond hair lighter than usual under the sun. Marissa passed her phone to Breen.

This was surreal. An hour earlier she'd been making her way to pick up her son from a playdate, now the police were asking for photos of her nanny.

'Thanks. I'll message it to my phone now and we'll get it over to the station.'

McConville's phone rang and she got up to take it in the hall. Marissa stood too.

'We need to go out there and look for them.'

Breen shook his head.

'We need you to stay here in case Ana turns up, and we need to keep going over all of it with you, getting as many details as we can. We have gardaí out searching now. You're of much better use here.'

The tears came then, the panicky gulping sobs she'd been holding in for the last hour. Peter stood and wound his arms around her.

'It'll be OK. Ana absolutely adores Milo, you said so yourself. She'll be back any minute, mortified at all the trouble she's caused. And then you'll be mortified for doubting her, am I right?' He leaned back and cupped her chin, attempting a smile. 'In the meantime, let's call all the parents again. Maybe one of them was talking to Ana today at pick-up.'

Marissa nodded and sat back down.

'Do you have numbers for all the parents?' Breen asked.

'Yes, there's an Excel sheet in an email somewhere . . .' Marissa searched through her phone until she found it. 'I think there's about twenty on this, there were a few who never signed up to it.'

'OK, let's split it between us and start calling,' Peter said, leaning over her shoulder. Breen nodded. Maybe because it was

genuinely useful, or perhaps to give them something to do –
Marissa didn't care; she couldn't just sit there waiting.

'I'll help too,' Esther said, pulling out her own phone. And as
the guards got up and down to make and take calls from the
station, there they sat, Marissa, Peter and Esther, phoning every
Junior Infant parent in Kerryglen National School, to ask if
anyone had seen Milo Irvine.

4

Jenny
Friday

JENNY GRIMACED AT HER reflection in the mirror, taking in the black dress and the heels and the stripe of red lipstick. Was it all a bit much? She was never sure how fancy these work dinners might be. She turned to the side. The straps of the dress were a bit thin, maybe. She pulled on a blazer. Better. Better for a work dinner, anyway. Would she have worried like this before that night in Nantes, or if Mark wasn't coming? On cue, her phone beeped. Mark. She put on her glasses to read the message.

> Some of the London office meeting for drinks before restaurant, Irish bar just off Champs Elysées (is that how you spell it . . .) – near restaurant. Are you on for it?

She typed a reply.
I need to check in at home – I'll see you at the restaurant. Then she changed it slightly. *I'll see you all at the restaurant.* Little words mattered, and so did wrong impressions. Or not. Maybe she was overthinking it again.

She checked the time – just before seven, so almost six at home, Richie should be back from collecting Jacob. She pressed his number and waited, winding a strand of hair around her finger. Suddenly she really wanted to talk to Jacob.

'Hi.' Richie couldn't have sounded less interested in her call. How had they got here, with this distance between them? She brushed it off. Fighting on the phone never ended well.

'Hiya. I'm heading out for dinner soon. Another night of trying and failing to make interesting small talk about investment banking – why aren't there training courses for this?' She laughed self-consciously, cringing at how she couldn't even make small talk with her own husband any more. 'But anyway, I wanted to say hello to you guys – how's Jacob?'

'I haven't picked him up yet, I'm going now.'

'Oh, Richie! Playdate pick-up is normally five o'clock!'

'He's fine, he's probably delighted to have someone to play with.'

There it was. The dig. As if having another baby would fix things.

'Can you go get him now, and I'll text Sarah to say you're on your way? She'll be wondering.'

'Relax. You're the one who comes up with all these rules in your head – other people don't worry about every little thing.'

She bit her lip. Richie clearly didn't get that being an outsider at a school where all the parents seemed to know each other was hard enough, without annoying people by being late for pick-up.

'Will you call me when you guys get home? It's just . . . there was this weird thing earlier. Marissa Irvine thought her son was in our house, on a playdate with Jacob. I'm sure it's fine now, but I keep thinking about it – imagining what it would be like to not know where your child is. You know?'

Silence. Then the sound of the front door and the rattle of keys.

21

'Richie? Are you still there?'

'Yeah, I'm getting in the car now, I'll call you when we're back.'

He hung up, and she sat on the end of the hotel bed, staring at her phone. On impulse, she searched for Sarah Rayburn's number and hit Call.

'Hiya, it's Jenny, I'm so sorry Jacob is still there – I'm away with work, and I just checked in with Richie, he's on his way.'

'No probs. They're happy here watching TV. I wouldn't usually put it on during a playdate but I needed to get my youngest up the stairs – it was way past her bathtime.'

Crap. 'Oh God, sorry. Richie will be there any minute.'

'It's fine, don't worry. I better get her into her pyjamas now . . .'

'Listen, before I go, I got a funny call from Marissa Irvine earlier, she thought Milo was in my house? She said she was on to you as well?'

'I *know*, so odd!' Sarah suddenly sounded more enthusiastic about chatting. 'She was looking for your number, and when I told her Jacob was here she nearly *died*. There was just this silence then – I don't think I've ever heard Marissa Irvine go quiet. She's so, well, *confident* normally.'

'I suppose . . .' Jenny said, wondering what that had to do with anything. 'Do you know if it's all OK now – did they figure out where Milo was?'

'I don't think so. I just got another call from Peter, the husband – they're phoning all the parents in the class now to see if anyone saw who collected him. Can you *imagine*!'

Jenny couldn't. Once, she'd lost sight of Jacob at the beach and she could still remember the panic as she searched for him. It couldn't have been more than two minutes, but she'd never forgotten it.

'God, it's awful.'

'Yes, and especially when Marissa's so *precious* about Milo – you know how she's always saying he's gifted and special.'

Jenny had only met Marissa once and wasn't sure if this was true, but either way, it didn't seem like the right time for veiled digs.

'Well, I suppose he's her only child . . .' she said.

'This is it. Precious firstborn for ever. Hard not to spoil an only child. Oops, sorry, no offence, I'm sure you don't spoil Jacob! Anyway, when he rang, Peter asked me if I'd seen their minder, Ana, at pick-up,' Sarah said. 'Apparently they can't reach her. Sounds a bit dodge, doesn't it? She was meant to be off this afternoon but now they think she might have been at the school after all.' Sarah managed to put heavy implication into the last sentence.

'I suppose they're just trying to put the pieces together. Carrie – our minder – turned up for pick-up on her day off once, she just got her days mixed up. It happens, I guess.'

'Mmm, it sounded like there was more to it. It makes you think, doesn't it?'

'Yeah . . .' Jenny said, though she had no idea what Sarah meant.

'I know it's not politically correct,' Sarah went on, 'but I just don't know if I'd hire a foreign nanny. They're brought up so differently over there, aren't they.'

'They are?'

'Well, what do we know about how someone from Peru thinks? I just couldn't hire someone from a completely different culture.'

Jenny blinked in disbelief and tried to think of something to say. Later, as usual, several perfect responses came to mind, but at that moment, she had nothing. Sarah filled the gap.

'I'm sure that sounds OTT to someone like you but it's just the way it is around here.'

Jenny was officially baffled. 'Someone like me?'

'From the sticks, I mean. I'm sure in the country everyone knows everyone and people leave doors unlocked, and nobody even has a nanny. It's different in Dublin. Especially in Kerryglen.'

Jenny's eyes widened. 'I'm from Cork though, and I've been living in Dublin for fifteen years. I've never lived in the countryside. But even—'

Sarah cut across. 'Anyway, the point is, something dodge with the nanny or not, Milo still hasn't turned up.'

'God, poor Marissa. I won't bother her now but maybe you could drop me a text when they find him, just so I know he's OK?'

'Of course,' Sarah said, to the background noise of toddler squeals. 'And there's the bell, probably your hubby, I better go.'

They said a quick goodbye and Jenny was left in the silence of her hotel room, feeling weirdly out of everything. At least Richie was there now and Jacob was fine. Was *she* fine though? Was Richie fine? That part wasn't clear at all.

5

Marissa
Friday

MARISSA'S HAND HURT FROM squeezing the phone to her ear, praying each time that the next one would be different – that instead of, *No, sorry, I didn't see him* she'd hear, *Yes! He's safe and sound.* But nobody told her that. She heard fear and curiosity and empathy and – once or twice – a lilt of something else: the buzz of anticipation for drama on an otherwise dreary November night. Every few minutes, she tried Ana again, but still the phone rang out. Esther made more tea that nobody wanted but everyone drank, and Peter said half-heartedly that she should go home. Not at all, she told them, she had nothing planned for the evening and she couldn't leave without knowing the little boy was safe.

Detective Sergeant McConville was out in the hall again, murmuring on her phone, and when she came back, her expression said something had changed.

'What is it?' Marissa asked, standing up.

'No news on Milo I'm afraid, but we did track down Ana Garcia's address and talked to her housemates. None of them saw her today – she was asleep when they left this morning – but we got her boyfriend's number from them and we're trying that now. His phone is switched off but we'll keep trying. One of the housemates said he thought Ana was planning to head into town around three this afternoon to meet him – the boyfriend – at his office to take a train to Galway.'

'School ends at twenty past two. So maybe she was picking up Milo and then going into the city centre straight after,' Marissa said. 'But why on earth would she bring him to Galway?'

Four empty faces looked back at her. None of it made any sense.

'I need air,' Marissa whispered, moving to the French doors and opening one. 'I'll keep calling Ana.'

Outside, she stood for a moment breathing in the frosty night. Milo had to be with Ana. It was the only explanation that made sense. Mr Williams said she had collected him. Maybe Ana had told them she wanted to take Milo to Galway and they'd some-how missed it – one of those half-listening conversations at the end of a long day. She tried the number again, willing it to answer.

That's when she heard it.

Coming from the end of the garden, down beside the huge oak, the one with the swing.

Running across the dark grass, her own phone still clutched to her ear, she zoned in on the tree, and on the knothole, the one she'd seen Ana use when pushing Milo on the swing. And there it was, a light in the dark, its ringing so loud it seemed impossible she hadn't heard it before.

Ana's phone.

Back inside the kitchen, breathless and shaking, Marissa pushed the phone into McConville's hands.

'It's Ana's. That's why there was no answer – she left it here. It's not the first time she's forgotten it – I should have thought of that! But it has to be a good thing that her phone is here – it's not that she's ignoring our calls, she just *couldn't* answer. See?'

Peter nodded, but his eyes said something else.

'What?'

'Nothing. Look, let's keep going over everything we know about Ana – maybe we can figure out where she's staying in Galway.'

McConville left the room with Ana's phone, while Breen flipped a page on his notebook and waited, pen poised. Marissa sagged into a chair. Peter was right. They'd already told the police everything they knew about Ana, but going over it couldn't hurt. And they'd run out of parents to call.

'OK,' Breen said, 'can you go through her typical day?'

'She picks Milo up at two-twenty and brings him here, does his homework with him, then plays with him in the garden or takes him to the playground if it's not too cold. She gets dinner for him and has him in pyjamas by the time we get home from work. She gets the bus home. That's it. It's not much help . . . I'm sorry.'

'It's all useful. What does she do before she comes to your house?'

Marissa looked at Breen, then over at Peter. He made a tiny shrugging motion.

'I don't really know,' Marissa said, turning back to Breen. 'We chit-chat when I get in from work but it's always about Milo's day. Ana doesn't say much about the rest of her day and I don't ask her.' Marissa shifted in her chair. Breen said nothing.

'Well, of course you don't,' Esther said, rescuing the awkward silence. 'She's your employee and you don't want to be nosy.'

'That's it,' Marissa said, turning to Esther. 'I mean, she's here to look after Milo, so that's our focus.'

'Did you get references when you hired her?' Breen asked, eyebrows up.

'Of course! My God, we'd hardly hire someone to look after our child without reference checks. She worked in a school in

27

Peru before she came here, and there was a glowing reference from them. We hired her through a nanny agency, so she was vetted by them, but we still checked her references.'

Breen wrote something and looked back at her, his pale blue eyes scrutinizing her. Judging her?

'Did you speak to them?'

'Absolutely. They said she was excellent at her job.'

'Where did you get their number?'

'From the written reference.'

'The one she gave you? Did you cross-check the number?'

'What do you mean?'

'I mean, did you check online to make sure that the number on the written reference was real? How do you know you were speaking to someone in a school and not a friend of Ana's back home?'

Marissa's mouth went dry. She tried to think back to the conversation with the school – it was with an older-sounding woman and her English was flawless. Marissa had asked lots of questions and the woman patiently answered all of them. And then when Marissa ran out of questions, the woman had thrown in additional information – Ana was a non-smoker, non-drinker, and one of the most reliable employees they'd ever had, never late, never sick. That had been music to Marissa's ears – everyone said the one big problem with nannies and au pairs was sick days. What do you do if they don't turn up for work? But Marissa wanted Milo looked after in his own home, with his own toys, and this never-sick Peruvian girl was too good to turn down. Only now she wondered, was she too good to be true?

6

Jenny
Friday

JENNY FLICKED THROUGH THE French channels on the giant TV and checked the time; half an hour since Richie had picked up Jacob but still no call. She didn't want to phone while he was driving, but surely they'd be home by now? He probably just forgot.

Richie picked up the second time she tried a video call, his sallow face pale in the glare of the kitchen light, his eyes tired behind his glasses.

'Sorry, I meant to phone you but I'm getting his tea.'

'No worries. I think he ate at Sarah's anyway.'

'Yes, she said you called. There was no need to make a fuss – it makes me look like I forgot to pick him up.'

'Oh no, that's not why I called!' Jenny said, twisting her hair. 'It was about the missing child. I wanted to see if there was any news. Can you imagine? If that was Jacob?'

Richie's face softened. 'I know. Nightmare.'

'Is there any update?'

'Not that I've heard, but I saw it on social media, the guards have put out an alert with a photo of Milo and one of their nanny. It seems she picked him up from school.'

'Does Jacob know about it?'

'No, though I suppose they'll all hear on Monday at school.'

God, imagine if he was still missing on Monday. Jenny shivered.

'Anyway, how's Jacob doing? Will you tell him when I see him tomorrow, we'll build the new Ninjago LEGO together?'

'It's done,' Richie said. 'Carrie did it with him earlier this week.'

'Oh! I'd made a plan to do it with him. That's a pity.'

'Well, Carrie was here and he wanted to do it – it's not really fair to penalize him just because you're at work.'

Penalize him? Where was this coming from? Richie was spending too much time listening to his mother.

'No, of course I don't mean that. It's great that Carrie did it with him. Anyway, put him on to me, will you?'

Three minutes of one-sided conversation later ('So what did you do at school today?' 'What did you play in yard?') Richie took the phone back.

'I'll see you around lunchtime,' she said. 'I'll get a cab from the airport.'

'OK. We're going to Mum's for brunch, and we might not be back by the time you get in.'

She suppressed a sigh and instead said brightly, 'OK grand, enjoy, love you both.'

'Bye.'

Great, a whole morning listening to his mother's list of things they were doing wrong. Top of the list, always: *Jenny is never at home.* Which wasn't even true; she was home way more than she would have been ten years ago – the upper levels in investment banking were surprisingly flexible, and in her new role as Head of Business Development, nobody cared if she left early to take over from Carrie once or twice a week as long as she was doing her job.

But of course, Adeline Furlong-Kennedy didn't see it that way.

Her grandson needed his mother at home, just like she'd been at home for Richie and his siblings, and that was that. No middle ground, no acknowledgement that things had changed in the forty years since she'd had her children. And now she'd have a whole morning to unleash her pronouncements on Richie.

Once upon a time, they used to leave Adeline's house laughing together at his mother's rants. Her claim that the tearooms in the village had gone downhill now that nobody spoke proper English. Her worries about the gay marriage debate – she was all for equal rights and all that, but what if children heard the discussion and decided to be gay? Jenny used to ask Richie how he turned out so normal, and he'd shake his head and tell her she better watch out – he might morph into his mother someday. Now those huddled laughs were a distant memory, and she had no idea why. Were they just growing apart the way couples did? Though it was more of a pulling apart, with Richie doing the pulling. Sighing, Jenny slipped a key card in her clutch, put on her coat, and headed out into the rainy Paris night.

By the time she reached Rue de Ponthieu, everyone had left the bar and arrived at the restaurant. Mark was waving at her – he'd kept her a seat.

'I'm saving you from sitting beside Pierre,' he whispered with a grin as she hung her coat on the back of the chair. 'You can buy me a drink later.'

Jenny smiled back as she wiped raindrops from her glasses. 'Thanks. After the evening I've had, I don't think I could face making small talk with the boss all night.'

'Oh – everything OK?'

'Everything's fine – just typical domestic stuff, you know.'

He nodded, though of course he didn't really know. He didn't have a cranky spouse at home or any kind of spouse at all, and nobody was making him feel bad for leaving a small child while he went on a business trip.

From across the table, her boss nodded at her.

'Jenny, welcome. I was also holding a seat for you – I thought we might talk about the new KPIs. But no matter. We will speak later, yes?'

Oh God. Key performance indicators on a Friday night. And she used to think business trips would be glamorous. She smiled at Pierre.

'Of course, later sounds good.'

'Ah Pierre, give her a break,' Mark said. 'She's too polite to say it herself but she's escaped the domestic grind for a Friday night in Paris, the last thing she wants to talk about is work!'

'Ah yes – how many children do you have, Jenny?'

'Just one,' she said, waiting for the inevitable response. Everyone had an opinion on Jacob's only-child status. *Wouldn't he love a little brother or sister to play with?* Or *Must be time to go again!* Or Adeline's favourite: *It's hardly fair on the child to leave him on his own like that.*

But Pierre just nodded. 'The same for us. But my son is I think older than yours, he is already fourteen. Does your son look like you – he has your red hair maybe?'

Jenny smiled. 'He does, his hair is red like mine, but he escaped my pale skin – he's dark like his dad and has his dad's brown eyes.' She fizzed inside, thinking about getting home to Jacob, hugging him, snuggling up in pyjamas to watch a Saturday-night film together.

'And who is looking after him when you are here with us in Paris?'

'My husband's with him now – he's a secondary school teacher so he's home earlier than me most evenings – and our childminder Carrie has him the rest of the time. It works pretty well,' she said, wondering who she was trying to convince.

'And you, Mark,' Pierre said. 'You have children too?'

'No, God no, I'm resolutely single.'

'You like your freedom too much?'

'Well, I'd happily give up my freedom for the right woman, but she'd have to want to give up everything too, I suppose – that's the tricky bit,' he said, glancing at Jenny.

Jenny reddened, silently cursing the giveaway flush that let her down every single time. Thank God for low lighting. And Mark hardly meant *her*, she was reading too much into it. But that night in Nantes, there was no doubt about it, he definitely meant her. Did he even remember? They'd had so much red wine, then moved on to absinthe, a terrible idea in any situation, but especially on an overnight trip with a work colleague. A work colleague who was getting flirtier by the glass and seemed to have trouble remembering she was married. Luckily, *she* remembered she was married – just about – and went back to her room alone despite Mark's suggestion to walk her up and her brief, *very* brief, instinct to say yes.

'Maybe tonight you will meet a beautiful French woman and she will seduce you to move to our country,' Pierre said. 'You can transfer to the Paris office!'

'Ah, I'm too much of a home bird for that. If I ever do settle down, it'll be in Ireland, with a brood of kids kicking a football around the field behind the house.'

Jenny had a sudden image of Mark doing exactly that – his long legs in jeans instead of the usual work suit, a beanie pulled down over his dark, curly hair, hands in pockets as he kicked the ball, familiar grin on his face. He'd be brilliant with Jacob. *Jesus*, what was she doing? She took a big swallow of wine and glanced over to find Mark smiling at her, which only made her cheeks hotter.

A vibration from the clutch at her feet gave her the escape she needed.

'Sorry, I need to take this,' she mumbled, though she had no idea whose number it was.

Outside in the cool Paris air, she answered. The caller explained he was from Blackrock Garda station. He was aware Jenny hadn't arranged for Milo to come to her house that afternoon but needed to go over it with her directly. Had she sent any message to Marissa? Did she know who had? No, Jenny told him, she had never arranged a playdate and didn't know who had sent the messages. When the call ended, she stood for a moment, her back against the restaurant wall. She shivered, watching Paris twinkle behind a sheet of misty rain, wishing she was home with Jacob. Not because there was anything to worry about, she reassured herself – he was as safe with Richie as he was with her. But there was something deeply unnerving about all of it, especially the message arranging the playdate. Was she just a random name, plucked from the class list? And if not – what did that mean, why would whoever sent the text choose *her*?

7

One week earlier

MARISSA KISSED MILO'S HEAD and shooed him in the door to school. As she turned to walk back to the car, she heard little footsteps behind her.

'Mummy, can I have a boy in my class over soon? Alex Smith is going to Josh Quinn's house on Friday. Everyone in my class is doing playdates 'cept me.'

She hunkered down to talk to him at eye level.

'We'll do it soon, don't worry, now go on in.' She kissed him and shooed him again, and this time he went.

'Nothing like an everyone-in-the-class guilt trip,' said Grace Loftus, falling into step with Marissa. 'I can't do playdates at all – mine are in after-school care – so you're definitely not the only one.'

'It's a little like "everyone in the class gets biscuits in their lunchbox",' Marissa agreed. 'In fairness, I *could* do playdates, I just haven't got around to it yet. I probably should, I don't think he's really paired up with anyone in the class.'

'Don't worry, they're very young still,' Grace said, as they passed a group of chattering au pairs. 'Plenty of time for playdates.'

Marissa wondered if Grace was right, or just reassuring herself because of her own incapacity to host visiting children.

Milo seemed to be doing fine in school, but maybe he could do with a buddy at this stage. She resolved to do something about it, to go through the list of classmate names and organize for one to come over. Then she pushed it to the back of her mind, waved goodbye to Grace, and clicked into her work diary as she slid into her car. She needed a clear head and a clear morning if she was going to figure out the remaining kinks before the looming prospect of the audit.

That night, over a beef stir-fry, she told Peter she was going to find a friend for Milo.

'Isn't he perfectly capable of finding friends for himself? Is this another one of your pet projects?' Peter asked, grinning.

She threw a napkin at him, though he had a point. Last month's project was a family yoga class (Peter had politely but firmly declined). Before that she'd looked into starting a vege-table patch in the garden – until she realized it was the wrong time of year and involved a bit more dirt than she'd antici-pated. And in the spring, when she might have tried growing vegetables, she was busy signing up for a marathon.

You'll wear yourself out with your projects, Peter always said.

Wonder Woman! the mothers at tennis used to say, one or two with barely suppressed irritation.

She paid no heed. Marissa Irvine never worried about what other people thought.

'It's not a pet project. It'll take ten minutes max to go through the class list and pick someone for a playdate.'

'Why don't you just invite that kid whose house he went to – Josh?'

'Because Josh spent half the afternoon throwing conkers at his head and Milo doesn't want to have him back.' She looked over at her husband. 'I want friends for him but only nice ones.'

'Nice ones with nice parents too, right?' He grinned. She ignored him. Sometimes he knew her too well.

As she clicked into her phone to find the class list, a text popped through.

> Hi Marissa, it's Jenny here, Jacob's mother. I was wondering, would Milo like to come over for a playdate after school next Friday?

'Ta da!' Marissa said, holding up her phone to show Peter. 'I am *actually* Wonder Woman – I've managed to find him a friend without doing anything at all.'

Peter laughed, spearing a beef strip from her plate. She slapped his hand away and typed a reply.

> That would be terrific! Let me know time and address for pick-up?

Seconds later, two more messages pinged through.

> Fantastic! Jacob will be thrilled.

And then:

> The address is 14 Tudor Grove – if I'm not home from work when you get there, my nanny Carrie will be there with the boys.

Marissa sent a thumbs up emoji, and put down her phone to finish her stir-fry before Peter could steal any more.

'So, who's the kid – Milo's new best friend you've arranged for him without consulting him?' Peter teased.

'Jacob. I met his mum at the school social – we turned up wearing the same dress. Remember I told you?'

Peter nodded, a vague look on his face. He definitely didn't remember.

'Jenny's her name, seemed a little timid at first but actually very nice; we bonded over our mutual dislike of a group she christened the Coven.'

'The Coven?'

'Peter, do you listen to anything I tell you? Grace, Sarah and Victor. The resident school-gate experts with a side of bitchiness.'

'So you were bitching with this woman Jenny about the people who are bitchy?'

He was laughing at her again.

'Not bitching. *Bonding*. She was good fun, and' – she winked – 'she has great taste in dresses. Actually I think we could be friends. You should meet her husband, we could have them over for drinks!'

Peter rolled his eyes and got up to clear the table. 'Oh God, save me from another project.'

She swiped at him with her napkin again but this time she missed. He could laugh all he wanted, but if Jenny's husband was as nice as Jenny, they'd make a perfect foursome. She got up to help clear the table, nodding to herself. Because Marissa Irvine was never wrong about anything.

8

Marissa
Friday

'IF ANA'S PHONE IS here, and the phone used to arrange the playdate is out of service, does that mean it's some kind of . . . kidnap? Like, not an opportunistic thing or a mix-up, but an actual kidnap?' Peter's voice was shaking.

'We're looking into all avenues,' McConville said.

Marissa put her hand on Peter's. 'It's *Ana* we're talking about. Ana who we know and love and see every day. Ana has not kidnapped Milo. If she has him, he'll be OK. Ana is like family.'

And that's when they heard the doorbell. Marissa jumped up and ran to the hall, with Peter just behind. In the porch, she didn't stop to look through the peephole or the glass panels on either side – she yanked open the front door, and there was Ana, red-eyed and pale.

'Oh Ana, thank God – where is he, what happened?' Marissa said, looking past her, searching.

'What . . . I don't understand?'

'Ana, where is Milo?'

'What do you mean? He was on playdate with his friend, no?'

'No!' Marissa wasn't sure but she thought she might be screaming now.

'Didn't you collect him from school?'

'No, I was not working today, remember? I was going to Galway with Seb, but then we had a fight and now I come to get my phone. I forgot it.'

'You didn't collect him? But the teacher said you did!'

Ana shook her head and started to cry. 'Milo is missing?'

Everything went loud and quiet all at once as Marissa's legs buckled and she leaned against the open door. The final straw slipped from her grasp.

'We're going to interview the teacher,' McConville said, putting down her phone. 'He's just arrived home. We'll come back here as soon as we speak to him.'

'I'm going too,' Marissa said.

'Mrs Irvine, I think you'd be better here in case someone brings Milo back.'

'Peter can do that. I need to be there to understand what happened. Whatever his teacher says will make more sense to me than it does to you, because I know the school and the pick-up routine and some of the parents and minders.'

McConville looked like she was going to say no, but then seemed to change her mind. She nodded.

Mr Williams lived in a three-storey townhouse in a new development at the far end of Kerryglen village. He answered the door in running shorts and a Hard Rock Cafe t-shirt, looking very different from the man Marissa was used to seeing at pick-up: at school he favoured sleeveless knits and bow-ties.

He led them through to a cramped sitting room and switched off the TV, gesturing for them to sit.

McConville started to go through the details with him but Marissa cut across.

'You said Ana collected him but she says she didn't – which is it?'

Mr Williams rubbed his short beard, looking worried.

'Milo put his hand up to show me he'd seen someone, I glanced over and saw one of the minders, and said goodbye to him. That's how we do it, that's school policy.'

'Hang on, when you say *one of the minders*, what do you mean?'

'I know it was a childminder. Like, not a mother – the nannies and au pairs are all younger, that's how we know.' He smiled sheepishly. 'It was definitely a minder he went with, not a mother.'

'Yes,' Marissa said, her voice tight, 'but you keep saying *a* minder. Like a random nanny, not necessarily ours?'

Williams sat up straight and folded his arms. 'It's impossible to keep track – as long as they're going with someone we know, that's following school policy. On Fridays they're all on playdates, going home with each other's parents and minders.' He turned to McConville. 'Milo is a smart kid, gifted I'd say, as Mrs Irvine may have told you. He'd know not to walk off with a stranger.'

'Can you describe the person he went with?' McConville asked.

'Yes,' he said, relaxing back in his seat. 'Red hair, long, kind of hanging around her face. Pale, usually wears check shirts. Actually . . .'

'Yes?'

41

'I'm pretty sure she's Jacob Kennedy's childminder. But Jacob went home with one of the other kids today, so I'm not sure why his minder was there at all . . .'

'Carrie. Jacob's nanny is called Carrie,' Marissa said, letting out a shaky breath. 'Carrie has taken Milo.'

9

Jenny
Friday

JENNY WENT THROUGH THE motions for the rest of the meal –
smiling and nodding and playing with the almost-raw meat
she'd accidentally ordered, pushing it around her plate. Her
mind was hundreds of miles away in Dublin, on Jacob and
Milo and the unexplained text. She kept her phone on her lap,
checking it discreetly every couple of minutes. Her boss didn't
seem to notice, but Mark did.

'Everything OK? You're even quieter than usual since you
came back in after that call.'

'Sorry, I'm distracted. A problem with a child in Jacob's class.
I'm sure it's grand but . . . ah, I just feel a bit weird sitting here in
this nice restaurant in Paris when there's stuff going on at home.'

'Look.' He nodded towards Pierre, who had moved table to
talk to the head of funds. 'He's going to be there talking the
hind legs off Elaine for the rest of the night. Why don't you go
back to the hotel, and I'll tell him you had a headache? He won't
even notice.'

Jenny looked over at Pierre. He was leaning forward, deep in
animated conversation. Mark was right, she could slip away.

'OK, I'm going, thank you for being a rock of sense,' she

43

whispered, although nobody could hear anyway in the din of restaurant noise.

'I'll get you a cab,' Mark said, pushing back his chair.

'No, no, you stay here, there's a taxi rank just outside.'

Before he could argue, she picked up her coat and made for the door.

She was back in her hotel room when the call came.

'Jenny, everything is fine with Jacob, but the police are here.' Richie sounded breathless. 'They're saying it was Carrie. They think she took the missing boy.'

Jenny sank to the hotel bed, phone clamped to her ear.

'What?'

'The teacher says it was Carrie who collected Milo today. And nobody knows where either of them is. The police are searching Carrie's room, they've asked me loads of questions, they want to talk to you too. Jesus. I can't believe it.'

Jenny put her hand to her forehead. There had to be some mistake.

'Jacob's OK?'

'Of course he's OK. He was with me when you FaceTimed us earlier, remember?'

'And Carrie – was she in our house before pick-up time?'

'No, I haven't seen her since this morning. I gave her the afternoon off because Jacob was on the playdate.'

'Maybe something's happened to her? An accident?'

Silence.

'Richie?'

'I suppose anything is possible. But there's no reason for her to collect someone else's child. And the way the guards asked the questions . . . they didn't outright say it, but it felt to me like they're dealing with a kidnap.'

Jenny closed her eyes. Carrie? It just didn't make sense.

'They were asking me for a photo of Carrie, but I don't have any. Would you have any on your phone?'

'I think so, I'll send it to you. God, I can't get my head around this.'

'They're coming back downstairs, I better go. They might call you tonight though, OK?'

'OK.'

She sat, long after the call ended, with the phone pressed to her ear, rocking back and forth on the hotel bed. It couldn't be true. And yet, that seemed to be what they were saying: Carrie – quiet, shy Carrie – who lived in her house and looked after her son, had kidnapped Milo Irvine.

10

Irene
Saturday – one day missing

IRENE WOULD NEVER FORGET it. Frank was sitting up in bed, scrolling through his phone, no doubt hoping she'd go down to make the tea. She was pretending to be asleep, willing him to make the first move towards the kitchen.

'Holy . . . Irene, is that your Caroline? The surname is "Finch", but it looks just like her.'

Irene sat up and took the phone from him. And there she was, larger than life, all that straggly hair hanging around her face as usual. Caroline.

'God, it is! What is it – what's she done?'

'Irene, it says she's missing. Look,' he said, clicking through to the story. 'It says a four-year-old boy is missing too. And . . .' He read on, his eyes running across the screen, murmuring under his breath. 'Well, it sounds like maybe she kidnapped him.'

'What?' Irene sat up properly and took the phone again.

'See here,' Frank pointed, 'it says she's to contact Blackrock Garda station, and that she's not in trouble. That's the kind of thing they say to reel someone in, isn't it?'

Irene stared at the phone. Nine years since she'd last looked at her daughter's face, but she hadn't changed much. The same pale features, the same angry blue eyes. The red hair she got from her dad – if only that was all she got from him.

'Well, she's done it now. I always knew I'd be seeing her on the news someday, but I didn't think she'd do something like this. Mother of Jesus, what was she thinking?'

Frank shrugged. 'I'm guessing the guards will want to hear from us – should we phone them or go down to the station?'

'They'll find us if they want to talk to us, there's no reason for us to go doing their job for them.'

Frank looked like he wanted to argue, but he kept his mouth shut and swung his legs out of the bed. 'I'll make the tea.'

Irene leaned against the pillow and read the story again. Caroline – or Carrie, as they were calling her – was last seen at Kerryglen National School, where she normally picked up Jacob Kennedy, a child she looked after for his parents Jenny and Richie Kennedy. She'd been at the school as usual yesterday, but for reasons not yet clear, she'd collected Milo Irvine, a classmate of Jacob's, instead. Irene pursed her lips. She was probably off her head on drugs and had mixed up the children. How did they even hire someone like Caroline to look after kids in the first place? Parents who didn't bother looking after their own children, happy to let any old person take their place. That was one thing she'd got right – she'd never worked when Caroline was small.

Frank arrived up the stairs with two mugs of tea, and after placing one on each bedside locker, he climbed back into bed. His cold foot touched off her leg and she shifted away.

'What do you think is going on with her?' he asked.

'I don't know, but you know Caroline. Always up to something. Remember that time she took the money from my purse?'

'Ah, this is different, Irene. She was – what, thirteen then? What we're talking about here' – he pointed at the news story on the phone – 'is kidnapping.'

Irene took a sip of tea.

'That's how it starts though. Stealing money at thirteen, drugs at fifteen, running away at sixteen – she was always destined for trouble, just like her father. It's in the genes.'

Frank winced. He always did when she mentioned Caroline's father. Who could blame him – the nice house and the two shiny cars and the respectable job in the bank didn't really tally with playing stepfather to the child of an ex-con.

'Has he – has Rob been in touch at all in recent years?'

'Christ no, not since the day I told him I was expecting. You know that, and I'd hardly keep it to myself if he contacted me.' She looked Frank in the eye. He'd said once he always knew his ex-wife was lying when she wouldn't look him in the eye. 'I swear to God, I reckon I can take credit for him going straight. He was so scared of being tied down to a baby, he ran off to London like his arse was on fire and stayed under the radar ever since.'

'And what about Caroline, has he really never wanted to meet her?'

'Never. I've told you all this before, I don't know why you can't get your head round it. He's not the first father to want nothing to do with his kid. And she doesn't know a thing about him either. I always said her dad was a sailor. So no, we're not in touch. If it wasn't for Rob's sister sending me news every now and then, I'd think he was dead.'

'Have you heard from his sister then?'

'Kathy?'

'Yes, Irene. Kathy.' He knew she was stalling now.

'Sure, you know I have. Still sending cards twice a year, feeling guilty about her brother, I suppose. She sent a note with my birthday card a few months ago, said something about him moving back to Ireland.'

Frank sat up straighter.

'Really? You never said.'

'It's no big deal, he's moving down to Cork to be near Kathy and her kids, he won't be anywhere near us. Too busy with his latest blonde to be thinking about me or Caroline. This one is half his age apparently, a barmaid from his local pub. *Sienna* her name is.' She rolled her eyes to show Frank just how little she cared for Rob's new tramp and her fancy London name. 'So no, Rob won't be coming anywhere near us.'

'Poor Caroline. Not easy growing up never knowing your father.'

'Poor me, you mean! You can't miss what you never had – she didn't suffer for not having a dad. But I had to do everything on my own, with no help from anyone.'

Frank didn't say anything.

'I did my best for her, you know – you saw what she was like when you met me.'

He patted her hand. 'I know you did your best, love. It wasn't easy.'

It bloody wasn't. Frank was the best thing that had happened to either of them, and Caroline knew that, but it didn't stop her acting out. At first, Frank liked Caroline. But slowly, he started to see what she was really like. Moody. Rude. Sulky. Oh, she could be all sweetness and light when she wanted to be. Like when she needed money or a lift somewhere. Then, bam. Back to sulky-brat mode, as though the world owed her something, and everything was always someone else's fault.

Is there something wrong with her? Frank used to ask. *No, that's just Caroline being Caroline*, she told him.

She and Caroline fought a lot after they moved in with him – well, no more than they had beforehand really, but the look on Frank's face soon made her realize it wasn't normal. She'd pulled Caroline aside one morning when Frank went to work and told her so. *We need to try harder,* she'd warned, *we need this to work out. Do you want to be back in our crummy old house with the crap central heating?* Caroline said she didn't care either way. But Irene knew she did. She saw how she ran her hands across the cream leather sofa and sank her feet into the deep pile carpet. She saw her eyes widen at the huge TV, and her grin when Frank asked her if she needed money for her trip into town. No, Caroline didn't want to give up their new life any more than Irene did, but she wasn't going to admit that to her mother.

11

Jenny
Saturday – one day missing

TWO THINGS HAD SURPRISED Jenny when she arrived back from the airport at lunchtime on Saturday: there was a journalist on her doorstep, looking for a comment from what he called the 'kidnapper's boss', and there was nobody at all inside the house. According to a note on the counter, Richie and Jacob had gone to Adeline's for brunch as planned, despite everything that had happened.

And before she had a chance to lug her suitcase upstairs, two gardaí were ringing her doorbell, displacing the disappointed journalist. Detective Sergeant McConville and Detective Garda Breen took seats in her living room and turned down Jenny's offer of tea. She brought a jug of water and three glasses instead, her hand shaking as she poured.

'We've spoken with your husband already,' McConville explained, 'and we've searched Ms Finch's bedroom here, but we wanted to speak to you too.'

'Of course, anything I can do. Was the photo helpful – the one I sent Richie last night? I wasn't sure if a photo from a phone would be any use but it's the only one I have. Carrie always avoids photos if she can help it, she's really shy. I took that one when she was out in the garden with Jacob one day. You can't see her face very well, but hopefully it helps.' She was babbling now. She stopped, waiting as McConville's cool eyes appraised her.

'Thanks, it was just what we needed, we don't have any other pictures of her at all. She's not on social media and we know nothing yet about her family, so that's the photo we're using. We cropped your son out, of course.'

'Thank you.' Jenny stopped again. 'Sorry, I'm still in shock – I don't know what to think. You really believe Carrie has taken Milo?'

'It looks that way. Can you tell us about her? The more we know, the better.'

Jenny perched on the edge of her armchair and took a gulp of water.

'Absolutely. Her name is Carrie Finch, she's twenty-five years old, and she's been with us since June. She's a live-in ch—nanny. I always say childminder but apparently nanny is the proper term.' She stopped and rubbed her hands on her work trousers, wishing she'd had the chance to change out of her too-tight heels. 'Sorry, of course you know she lives here if you've searched her room.'

'Keep going, just tell us everything, even if you think we already know. What about her background?'

'She grew up in a house in the Wicklow countryside. They had horses. Um, let me think . . . she's quiet and doesn't have a lot of friends – sometimes I think she likes horses more than humans.' Jenny smiled nervously. Why was she so on edge?

Breen was taking notes. McConville nodded at her to continue.

'I think she had a happy childhood, she talked about it a little. Kind of wistfully, but that's because she's lost both her parents.

She was a teen when they died – within six months of each other, she said. First her mother, then her dad. Cancer then a heart attack, though she said her father died of a broken heart.'

Breen scribbled; McConville never took her eyes off Jenny.

'OK, what about her time before she started work here?'

'She'd been in Australia, taking time out after school and her parents' deaths. She wants to be a vet so decided to become an au pair for a few years to save up for college. She worked for a family in Galway before she came here.'

'Do you have their details?'

'A family called Drake, I can get her CV off my laptop – that'll have their phone number.'

'Thanks. And she wanted to live-in here, rather than commute from her family home?'

'Yes, too many sad memories, she said. Anyway, it suited us – we both leave early in the morning so it's good she's already here to do breakfast with Jacob.' Jenny caught herself. 'Well, not that good in hindsight. God, this is unreal. Is there any chance it's a mistake?'

'I'm afraid not. She went to the school yesterday and collected Milo Irvine – as agreed with Marissa Irvine because of a text that claimed to be from you, but you didn't send the text so . . .'

'And you think Carrie sent it, pretending to be me?'

'Yes, and now that phone is out of service.'

'So Carrie was planning it?'

McConville nodded. 'Did anything out of the ordinary happen recently – was she acting out of character?'

Jenny shook her head, only then becoming conscious she was winding her hair too tightly around her finger.

'I've been going over it and over it, but there's nothing. She brought Jacob to school every morning – she uses Richie's car because he can walk to work – picked him up every afternoon, and they were here when Richie got in from work every evening. Just the usual.'

'And did you see her, when you came home?'

'I get home later than Richie so I don't see her every night. Sometimes she stays in her room, reading. Other times she sits with us to watch TV. Herself and Richie both like those home makeover shows. I'm usually on my laptop getting through my inbox. The odd time when Richie is out, we chat over a bottle of wine. It can be a bit one-sided though – she's not much of a talker, but that's when she opened up about her parents.'

'Does she have any siblings?'

'Three brothers, all abroad – one in Boston, one in California and one in somewhere like Alabama. All older than her, and they'd moved out before her parents died. I got the feeling she had to do a lot of the organizing for the funerals by herself. I can't even imagine what that would be like as a teenager.' Jenny looked from Breen to McConville. 'Do you think that had something to do with it – losing her parents and being left to fend for herself warped her in some way?'

McConville blinked but said nothing. Breen was still taking notes and didn't look up.

'Does she have a boyfriend?'

'Not any more. She has an ex called Kyle who still phones from time to time. They broke up before she went to Australia, and I get the feeling she wasn't completely against the idea of getting back with him but didn't want to rush it.'

'OK, great – do you have any more information about him? His surname?'

'Kyle . . .' Jenny closed her eyes to remember. Carrie had used it once when he phoned, in mock annoyance or so it seemed. The name had reminded her of someone in a TV show. 'Kyle

Bird. That's his name. Kind of unusual – might be easy enough to find?'

McConville and Breen thought so too, it seemed – Breen got up to make a phone call from the kitchen.

'That's great, Mrs Kennedy. Would you know the brothers' names?'

'I do actually – they stuck in my mind because they're unusual – Caleb, Scott and Cole.'

'Great. Now,' McConville scrutinized her, as though weighing something up, 'was there ever a time when she seemed in any way unbalanced?'

'No! I'd never have let her mind Jacob if she did.'

'And did she ever hurt Jacob?'

About to say *no, of course not!* Jenny stopped.

'Mrs Kennedy?'

'It's probably not relevant, but there was this one time when I thought she was about to hit him. I shrieked at her, and she nearly died of fright. I was just so *shocked* – she was lovely to Jacob and when I saw her suddenly raise her hand, I let a roar out of me.'

'So, she did at least attempt to hit your son in one instance?' McConville asked, her face neutral. God, did she really think she'd keep on a minder who'd tried to hurt Jacob?

'No, that's just it. She was swatting a fly. Jacob had been whingeing and I was on my way out to the garden to see what was going on, and next thing her hand was up and . . . look, it was awful. I said something like, "Don't you dare hit him!" and grabbed him into my arms. She looked shocked, and she was still swiping at this giant bluebottle and even before she said it, it was clear what really happened. I was mortified.'

'And what did she say?'

'She was stung – who could blame her? She went all red and

she looked so cross. I was apologizing and at first she said nothing, but then after a hundred *I'm sorries* from me, she smiled and said it was all right.'

McConville tilted her head, examining Jenny, waiting.

'I know how it sounds in hindsight, but I'm a hundred per cent sure she actually was swatting a fly. I think if I was a childminder and someone reacted that way with me, I'd leave. She's a lot more forgiving than I am.'

'Yes.'

The word sat between them, as Jenny wondered why she was speaking up for someone who had just kidnapped a child.

'Well, this has been very useful, especially the information about her ex-boyfriend and her family,' McConville said, standing up. 'You wouldn't have the address of the old family home, would you?'

'No, but she told me it's a big white double-fronted house with a green door, on the old road between Bray and Enniskerry.'

'Good. We'll be off now, but we'll be back in touch as more questions come up.'

'No problem, anything I can do to help find poor Milo. God, what those parents are going through . . .'

She saw the guards out, noted with relief that the journalist was gone, and closed the front door. Leaning against it, she slid to the floor and sat with her head in her hands. There was no way to get around it. If she hadn't hired Carrie Finch, Milo would be safe at home with his parents.

12

CARRIE WONDERED WHAT IT would be like inside the house, this how-the-other-half-live house, and it did not disappoint. Neat. Shiny. Irritating. Just like its owner, people-pleaser Jenny. So smiley. So eager to be nice as she awkwardly broached the subject of pay. How much do you pay someone to mind your child? How do you put a price on that? Fifteen euro an hour, it turned out, the going rate in Kerryglen. Lush, green, smiley Kerryglen.

'Would you like tea? Coffee? Water?' Jenny had asked, hovering, nervous, twisting her hair.

'Water, please,' Carrie had said, because Carrie Finch was more of a water drinker. Clean-living, quiet, shy. No cappuccino-culture for this girl from the middle of nowhere and the back of beyond.

Jenny brought sparkling water without asking if that's what Carrie wanted, and halfway through the interview Carrie saw her eyeing up the untouched glass. She watched Jenny's eyes as she debated asking if it was OK. She sat answering her prospective employer's questions as Jenny decided maybe Carrie just wasn't thirsty after all.

Jenny's husband, the handsome but humourless Richie, was a little more relaxed. Not so much relaxed as detached. Oh, he

57

went through the motions all right, asking Carrie if she smoked and if she could drive, but there was something disengaged about it.

'I travel a bit for work,' the wife said, 'but Richie would always be here, we wouldn't be away at the same time. Does that sound OK?'

Carrie smiled and nodded, wondering what exactly she meant. Was Jenny asking if Carrie was concerned about being alone with her husband? Carrie glanced over at him. Good-looking, yes, but not her type. Not that she really had a type. Kyle wasn't so much a *type* as a habit. But still, at least he'd seen a bit of the real world, got his hands dirty. This Richie with his soft skin and smooth hands and serious glasses – far too preppy. Too teachery. On the other hand, perhaps he was Carrie Finch's type? But no, that's not where she wanted to go. She needed the job. She didn't need Jenny Kennedy worrying that her new nanny couldn't be left alone with her husband. And honestly, Carrie didn't think for a second – as Jenny smiled across at the pale, stringy-haired interview candidate – that the thought ever crossed her mind.

13

Jenny

Saturday – one day missing

IT WAS ALMOST THREE o'clock before Richie arrived home from his mother's. Jenny ran to take Jacob from his seat, hugging him close, resisting the instinct to ask Richie what had taken them so long. *Adeline* was what had taken so long. Once she got going with one of her monologues, there was no stopping her. Richie didn't say either way – he went into the house after a half-greeting, and she followed with Jacob's hand in hers.

'Can you believe it?' she said to Richie, once Jacob was in the playroom. 'Carrie? I don't know what to think.'

'I know. I keep waiting to hear it's some kind of mistake,' he said, sitting beside her at the kitchen table, suddenly sounding like the old Richie. It felt like for ever since he'd last answered with anything other than a prickly, curt response. Maybe the drama would bring them closer. She shook herself. God, what was she thinking – a child was missing. Taken by *their* childminder.

'If we hadn't hired her, none of this would have happened. I feel awful, Richie.'

'Don't make it about us, it's not our fault.' He swivelled in his chair to look at her. 'Don't start, Jenny.'

So much for the drama bringing them closer. She kept her tone even.

'I just mean if we hadn't hired her, she'd never have had access to kids at the school – she wouldn't have kidnapped Milo.'

'If she wanted to kidnap someone, she'd have found a way – someone else would have hired her if we hadn't.' He got up to boil the kettle and stood staring at it, his back to her. He was feeling as guilty as she was, Jenny realized, and arguing now for the sake of arguing.

She got up too and joined him, reaching out to rub his shoulder. He turned, discreetly dislodging her hand in the process.

'I think I left my phone in the car, will you make tea when that boils?' he said, walking out of the kitchen. She nodded at his back, and on autopilot took out two mugs. The pristine white cupboards and slate countertops mocked her as she waited by the kettle. Turns out new kitchens couldn't fix cold marriages.

She walked through to the playroom to check on Jacob. He was lying on his front on the wooden floor, his teddy under his arm, busy drawing – oblivious to the unfolding drama and his missing friend.

'What's the picture?' she asked, looking down.

'A monster who eats childrens . . .' He paused, putting a crayon in his mouth, and she smiled at his 'childrens' but less so at the murderous theme.

'Oh! Is that not a bit scary?'

He looked up at her, opening his mouth so the crayon dropped to the floor.

'A monster who eats children's vegetables for them.'

He got back to it. She smiled and walked over to the chalkboard on the wall. The top two thirds, where Jacob couldn't reach, were blank. The lower part was full of his chalk doodles – wobbly stick men, mostly – and words and names in his fledgling writing.

Jacob K. With two Jacobs in the class, he'd be Jacob K for the next eight years.

Aleks Smit. She smiled. There was something ridiculously cute about phonetic spelling. 'Is Alex a boy in your class?' No answer. She turned back to the board.

Andru Murfe. That took her a second. Murphy.

Shan Otool.

Milo Rvin. Milo Irvine. She stiffened. What the hell were they going to tell the kids on Monday?

Dani Von.

Kari. Carrie. Bloody Carrie. She reached over, rubbed out the name with the heel of her hand, and walked back to the kitchen.

Richie returned, patting his pockets. 'It's not in here, is it?'

'Your phone? I don't see it,' Jenny replied.

'I must have left it at Mum's – I'll go back over.'

'Well, have your tea first,' Jenny said, taking out teabags.

'Ah, I need it, I'll go now.'

God, was he that desperate to escape? Maybe it was time to bite the bullet and insist he tell her what was going on, even if every other time she'd brought it up, he'd said he was 'just tired'. She was sucking in a breath, readying herself for a show-down, when the doorbell rang. Saved by the bell.

Richie went to answer, and as the door opened, Jenny heard the unmistakable sound of her mother-in-law. Oh good God, even a discussion of their marital problems was preferable to a visit from Adeline Furlong-Kennedy.

'Jenny. You're home! I thought you were in Paris, living it up,' she said, wafting into the kitchen in a cloud of far too much Christian Dior Poison – her 'signature scent', as she liked to call it. 'Are you making tea? I came to drop Richie's phone back. We'll have the tea in the sitting room, shall we?'

With that, she pulled off the fur coat she had no compunction about wearing, and handed it to Jenny, following it with her cloche hat. She shook her silver-blonde bob free, smoothing it down with a glance at the oven door, and glided through to the sitting room.

Richie and Jenny looked at one another, resigned half-smiles on both faces. But just as quickly Richie's was gone. 'You go in. I'll bring tea.'

She wanted to argue but could think of no reasonable excuse, so followed her mother-in-law into the sitting room.

'Sit down and tell me everything about this ghastly business with your nanny,' Adeline said, smiling like a wolf. So that's why she was there – first-hand gossip.

'Yeah, I'm walking around with a knot in my stomach since I got the call last night. That poor little boy.'

'And of course, it's *your* nanny. That's not helping the knot, I'm sure. Where did you find this woman, Jenny?'

Suddenly it felt like being questioned by the police all over again.

'Oh – an online agency.'

'Ah. The internet.' Adeline managed to inject a world of suspicion in three small words.

Jenny rushed to explain. 'That's how people hire childminders – if you don't get someone through word of mouth, searching online is the next best thing.'

'Next best. Mmm.'

Oh God, would Richie ever hurry up with the tea?

'I suppose everything is online now, Adeline – you know, firms advertising when they're hiring – and it's the same thing; we were hiring so we looked online.'

'Only it's not quite the same, is it, Jenny? Hiring a nanny to look after your child isn't the same as hiring someone to do your accounts or some such.' Adeline loved saying 'some such' – she'd picked it up from an American soap and used it as often as she could. 'I told Richie from the start he needed to talk to you about it. You just don't know who you're letting into your house when you hand over your mothering to someone else.'

Oh, sweet mother of God. If Richie didn't get in there quick, Jenny would finally say something she could never take back.

'Ah, I don't really see it as handing over mothering – just getting help with childcare when both parents work. I suppose things have changed since your children were small,' she said, more gently than Adeline deserved.

Adeline's pale eyes met hers.

'I don't think things have changed that much, Jenny, dear. A mother is still the most important influence in her child's life.'

Much to the detriment of *your* children, Jenny wanted to say, but of course she didn't. And anyway, some of Adeline's six children had turned out OK. Richie – until recently anyway – was the most down to earth, emotionally intelligent, relaxed man she'd ever met.

'Didn't you have help when Richie was born?' Jenny asked, remembering photographs of a stout older woman with a no-nonsense look on her face.

'Rose was a home help, because I had six children and a big house to run. I didn't hand over the reins to her, I was at home with the children. There when she was there.'

As far as Jenny had heard from Richie, it was Rose who raised him while Adeline played tennis and met friends for lunch, but she didn't bring it up. There was nothing to gain from an argument with her mother-in-law, and it certainly wouldn't help the current cold impasse with Richie.

'I'll just see if Richie needs a hand,' Jenny said, standing up.

'Do, dear. He looks tired. It's not easy teaching all week then looking after Jacob at the weekend.'

Jenny bit her lip so hard it hurt and walked through to the kitchen. Richie was standing by the kettle, scrolling through his phone.

'Is the tea ready?'

'What? Yes, I'll bring it in.'

'Your mother is in flying form,' she risked saying, winking at him to soften it. But he didn't return her look or respond. A heavy stone lodged in her stomach. How had he become so unreachable? She followed him to the sitting room and watched as he placed a tea on the coffee table in front of his mother. Adeline sat forward, smoothing down her stiff houndstooth dress.

'I was just saying, Richie, hiring a nanny from the internet wasn't Jenny's best move. I'm sure she's better at her office job or she'd be fired by now, wouldn't she?'

Jenny's mouth dropped open. She turned to Richie. *She* might not feel comfortable standing up to Adeline, but Richie always knew when it was time to step in. Except this time, he didn't. This time, he drank his tea, glanced distractedly at his phone, and said nothing at all.

Jenny blinked back unexpected tears, and Adeline carried on, seemingly oblivious.

'Do you think we should search Carrie's room?' she said, eyes wide with anticipation.

Jenny cleared her throat.

'I don't think we should, Adeline. The guards have been up there already and no doubt they'll be back. And there could be an entirely innocent explanation. It wouldn't be nice to go through her private things.' It felt good to be the gatekeeper.

Adeline looked like she wanted to say something else, but instead she raised her tea to her lips and sipped quietly. After a moment, she stood and picked up her handbag.

'I'm just going upstairs to use the facilities.'

As soon as she left the room, Jenny turned to Richie. 'You don't think she'll go to Carrie's room, do you?' she whispered.

'I'm sure she's just going to the bathroom,' Richie whispered back, though he didn't look sure at all. 'I'll make more tea.'

Jenny looked at her still-hot, still-full cup but said nothing, as Richie went out to the kitchen.

Ten minutes went by before Adeline arrived back in the living room, a pleased look on her face, just as Richie returned with a pot of tea.

'Sit down, Richie love, you look pale – are you getting enough sleep?' She glanced at Jenny then back to her son. 'You must be exhausted after minding Jacob on your own.'

As soon as Adeline was gone ('Call over during the week, Richie love, if you need a rest, lots of peace and quiet in our house'), Jenny told Richie she needed to unpack and took her suitcase upstairs. Leaving the case at her bedroom door, she slipped down the landing to the last room on the right – Carrie's room.

She pushed open the door, not sure what to expect – she hadn't been in there since the day Carrie moved in. It looked different. The plain white duvet cover had been replaced with a floral print, and a small cream rug sat on the wooden floor. The white bookcase was full of books – mostly about horses, the kind Jenny used to read when she was a kid. A framed photo of two people she assumed were Carrie's parents sat on the top of the bookcase, along with a Claddagh ring and a beaded bracelet. Was it odd she'd gone without the ring? Jenny had seen her wear it sometimes – the heart turned outwards to show Carrie's single status – but it wasn't something she wore all the time. So, maybe not odd.

Feeling just a tiny bit uncomfortable about snooping, Jenny opened the wardrobe door. The rail was almost empty, with just two check shirts and a dozen redundant hangers. That didn't mean anything though – Carrie mostly wore shirts or hoodies with jeans, Jenny had never seen her in a dress. The shelves beside the rail were full of folded jeans, t-shirts and jumpers, all looking a bit haphazard. Carrie's mess, or a result of the garda search? Jenny couldn't tell. At floor level, there were two pairs of Converse, one navy, one red. What other footwear had Carrie worn? Just her Dr Martens boots, and she was probably wearing them now. Wherever she was.

As she was about to close the wardrobe door, Jenny's eye fell on something familiar. Reaching to the bottom of a pile of t-shirts, she pulled out a sparkly black top and stared at it. She turned it over in her hands and looked at the label. AllSaints. The top she'd picked up in London last January, missing for months. What was it doing in Carrie's wardrobe? It was nothing like the t-shirts Carrie normally wore – she had no reason to take Jenny's clothes. She left it on top of the stack of t-shirts. Somehow, she didn't want it back.

What else? Beyond the bed, the bookcase and the wardrobe, there was nothing much in the room at all; Carrie seemed to have very few personal belongings. Jenny lifted the edge of the duvet to look under the bed – nothing there but dust. As she put the duvet back down, she felt something crinkle inside the corner. Undoing the buttons at the end of the duvet cover, she slipped her hand inside and pulled out a photo. A Polaroid of a man. A boy really – he looked about eighteen. Pale face, a reddish tinge to his eyes that suggested lack of sleep or air, brown hair cut very short, dark stubble on a cleft chin. He was wearing a grey sweatshirt and a wary look on his face, as though he wasn't quite sure why someone was taking his photo. There was something familiar about him, though she was sure she'd never met him. Could he be Kyle Bird? Had the police seen it? Presumably not, if it was still inside the duvet cover. She pulled her phone from her back pocket and sat on the bed, chewing her lip as she typed 'Kyle Bird' into the search bar. A number of results came up, but nobody who looked anything like the man in the photo. She sat for a moment thinking back to the telephone conversation she'd overheard. Carrie had been pretending to be cross, but it sounded more like teasing. *Kyle Bird, you better not leave it so long next time!* Jenny was sure she had the name right – could there be another spelling? She tried Kyle Byrd with no success, then Kyle Byrde. That's when she hit gold – a full page of articles on Kyle Byrde. Jenny clicked through with a rising sense of horror. Assault. Burglary. Prison. Release. Possession. Possession with intent to sell. Another assault. Another prison sentence. A due-for-release date. Then nothing. Accompanying each article were various photos of Kyle Byrde, all unmistakably the man in the Polaroid. Dear God, what kind of person was her childminder hanging out with? But maybe this thing with Milo was all down to him – could he have forced Carrie to get involved with a kidnapping? Either way, the police needed to know about the photo.

Richie was watching TV with Jacob when she motioned for him to come into the kitchen.

'Look at this – I found it hidden in Carrie's duvet. I've let the guards know, they're coming to pick it up.'

'I thought I heard you telling my mother it would be completely inappropriate to search Carrie's room?' Richie said with a wry smile, and her heart broke for that old to-and-fro they used to have so easily.

She smiled back sheepishly. 'Fair point. But listen, I think we should get in touch with Marissa and her husband. I feel awful about all this, we can't just stand back and say nothing when it's *our* childminder.'

Richie's grin slipped away. 'The last thing they need is us turning up on their doorstep. And anyway, we don't want to indicate that . . .' He stopped.

'What?'

'You know – we don't want to signal that we're in some way responsible. I think we should steer clear for now. What if they think we're somehow negligent for hiring Carrie?'

'Richie, are you serious? Their four-year-old son is missing, and the only thing you're worried about is distancing yourself from any blame?'

'But we're not to blame.'

'I know that. Carrie is to blame. Or maybe this Kyle Byrde guy. But it doesn't mean we can put our heads in the sand. We need to take some ownership here, and at the very least get in touch with them, hard as that will be.'

'There's not much point in this discussion, is there, you're not going to listen. Why do you even bother asking?'

'Because you're my husband and I still care what you think, even if you don't care much for what I think any more,' she said sadly, taking the keys from the counter, and walking out the door.

14

Jenny
Saturday – one day missing

JENNY PULLED IN TO the side of the road when Google Maps told her she'd reached Maple Lodge. *You can do this*, she told herself, as she took in her surroundings. *And no matter what Richie says, it's the right thing to do.*

The Irvines lived about ten minutes from her, in the nicest part of town, on possibly the most upmarket road in Dublin. Trees lined either side, hiding huge houses, all set apart from each other and well back from the road. The gates to Maple Lodge were open, but it seemed less intrusive to leave the car outside, so Jenny got out and went on foot through the gateway and up the drive. Ahead stood a detached Edwardian house, the kind she'd ogled on property websites when she and Richie were house-hunting last year – spacious and full of character, but with price tags way out of their reach. Maple Lodge was a million miles from her own nice-but-nothing-like-this semi-d. To the right of the main house stood a second, smaller house. Marissa and her husband must be doing well – as far as she remembered, Marissa was a partner in a local solicitor's practice, which was obviously more lucrative than Jenny had realized. Or maybe Marissa's husband was the big earner; he did something with finance. She swallowed, her stomach churning. This wasn't going to be easy.

She rang the bell and took a step back, immediately deciding she should have called first. Too late. The inner porch door opened, and she could see Marissa peering out through the glass. Jenny started to smile on instinct, then stopped. Marissa opened the front door, red-eyed and dazed; her chestnut hair, so perfectly groomed at the school social, unwashed and unbrushed. Unsurprisingly. She was wearing workout clothes and trainers, the standard downtime uniform of the Kerryglen mothers. Her face was pale, free of make-up, and streaked with tears.

'Hi, I'm Jenny Kennedy – we met at the school social.' It came out in a half-whisper but she kept going. 'I'm so sorry for what you're going through.'

Marissa stared, saying nothing, her index finger fluttering to a small scar on her chin.

This was a mistake. Jenny tried again.

'I don't know what to say – obviously we had no idea Carrie would ever do something like this. If there's anything I can do to help, please let me know.'

To her horror, Jenny realized she was close to tears.

'Who is it?' came a voice from the background – Marissa's husband presumably.

Marissa looked at Jenny, focusing properly for the first time.

'It's a friend, checking in on us,' she called over her shoulder, then turned back to Jenny. 'Thank you for thinking of us, please come in.'

Jenny followed Marissa through to the huge kitchen, where a giant breakfast bar had a double sink and what looked like a built-in hotplate for making pancakes. She had a sudden image of Milo sitting on one of the high stools, looking on while Marissa or Peter made pancakes for him. *Milo.* God.

'We're just home a few minutes,' Marissa was saying. 'We've been out putting posters on lamp posts. It's hard to know if it helps but' – her voice faltered, cracked, and fell to a whisper – 'we have to do something.' Her finger was on her chin again, and she sounded so utterly broken, Jenny could feel more tears welling up.

'I could help with that,' she said. 'Do you have posters I can take with me?'

Marissa cleared her throat, composing herself. 'That would be great. We're getting more, Peter's brother Brian is down in the print shop now. Thank you.'

Jenny nodded, just as Marissa's husband walked into the room. Jenny had seen him at the social but only in the distance. Like his wife, his eyes were red-rimmed and there were dark circles beneath them, but Jenny could tell he was a good-looking man, maybe a few years older than Marissa. Short curly grey hair and confident, strong features – she could picture him at the head of a boardroom table.

'Peter, this is Jenny, a friend from the school.' Peter came towards her, holding out his hand to shake hers. 'Carrie is her nanny,' Marissa continued. Peter stopped and dropped his hand.

'Jesus Christ.'

'I'm so sorry, I feel terrible. I had no idea . . .' Jenny was babbling again, but she couldn't stop. 'If there's something I can do . . . I've talked to the police and told them everything I know, and I've searched her room, there was this photo . . .'

'Didn't you do background checks?' Peter asked, in a tight voice.

Oh God, she should never have come. She swallowed.

'We did – she had been minding a family in Galway, and I phoned them to ask for references. The father of the kids she

71

minded chatted to me for ages. Of course, I know now that just because she was a perfect employee for them doesn't mean she was never going to be any trouble . . .'

'Any *trouble*? Talk about an understatement. Why has she taken Milo? Can you tell me that? Why *my* son? I mean, your son was right there – what made her look past him and take Milo?'

He stared, wide-eyed, as though waiting for an answer. What could she say? Of course it made no sense. But agreeing that Carrie could more easily have taken Jacob made her feel sick. Is that what he wished? Would she wish that on someone else if she was in his place? God. Maybe.

'I'm so sorry. I don't know. If it helps, Carrie was always gentle with our son. I can't imagine her ever hurting a child.'

Marissa started to cry then, and Jenny wished she hadn't said it.

'I think you should go,' Peter said.

But Marissa spoke up, between sobs.

'No, please stay, Jenny. You're the only person who's come to check on us. People are texting and sharing the posters on social media but nobody has phoned or come in person – they don't know what to say and they're all staying away. It's good to have you here.'

Peter looked like he was going to say something else but instead he walked out of the room, muttering about phoning Brian.

'I'm sorry about that,' Marissa said.

'Oh no, please don't apologize.' Jenny could feel her hands flapping. 'What you're both going through, I can't even imagine. If there's anything I can do . . .' It sounded so useless.

'There is. Sit and have a cup of tea and tell me everything you know about Carrie. Even if you've already told the police, there might be something that makes sense to me, as Milo's mother. Can we do that?'

Jenny looked at the woman she'd met at the school social, the woman who'd seemed so poised and together, with her perfect make-up and glossy hair and easy smile. There was no sign of that woman now. Jenny nodded. Of course she'd stay. She'd do anything she could to help.

An hour and two cups of tea later, she'd told Marissa everything she knew about Carrie – her childhood in Wicklow, her love of animals, how good she was with Jacob. She'd told her about Kyle Byrde, a diluted version so as not to scare Marissa, and the bedroom that seemed to contain most of Carrie's belongings. If she'd left without packing, surely that was a sign that she didn't mean to disappear for good, they agreed, reassuring one another. Then the doorbell rang, and Peter came in to say Colin Dobson was there.

'My partner at Irvine and Dobson Associates,' Marissa explained. 'Well, a college pal first, and then we started our solicitors' firm when we both moved back here. He's an absolute rock.'

'I should go,' Jenny said, her head beginning to ache from the intensity.

'Thank you for calling, and please come again. We could do with all the help we can get. And the company,' Marissa said, looking so lost Jenny thought she might bawl. Instead she hugged her and left, nodding hello to a tall man with an anxious frown on what was an otherwise attractive face as she passed him in the hall.

15

Marissa
Saturday – one day missing

IT WAS A BLUR. People coming and going – the police, some technical person who wanted to look at Milo's room, two reporters – and then, Jenny. When Marissa saw Jenny waiting on the doorstep, nervous as hell but standing her ground, she stopped thinking about what was going on for just a tiny fraction of a second. Jenny had looked so surprised when Marissa invited her in, and so miserable when Peter started his interrogation, yet she stayed and she talked and she listened. The first person since Esther left to offer any human comfort. Jenny and Esther. Two relative strangers, two women Marissa didn't know at all until this brought them crashing together. *This.* Twenty-four hours in – twenty-four agonizing, sleepless hours since she'd stood on Esther's doorstep – and still, she couldn't give it its proper name. But there was no way around it any more, it was a kidnap.

When Colin arrived and Jenny got up to leave, Marissa had the oddest instinct to grab her hand and beg her to stay. Somehow talking to her was a million times easier than talking to Peter. Maybe because Jenny was an outsider, or because she wasn't suffering like Peter was. Marissa couldn't take care of

74

Peter and take care of herself at the same time – they were two broken people with no idea what to say to each other.

Colin walked in, ducking his head as he came through the kitchen doorway, and reached to embrace her.

'Mar, I'm so, so sorry – can I help in any way?'

She let herself be hugged, closing her eyes and wishing it brought the comfort he intended, but inside she was cold and sick and hollow, her mind in overdrive again, brimming with images of dark cellars and damp walls and threatening words. The sound of a throat being cleared brought her back to her kitchen. Peter, standing in the doorway, with the mildly irritated expression he found hard to hide whenever Colin was around. In the oddest way, it was reassuringly normal. She pulled out of the hug.

'Guys, I saw the photo online of that woman Carrie. Who is she? What the hell was she doing, like?' Colin looked over and back between Marissa and Peter.

'She looks after another child in the class,' Peter said, 'but other than that we have no idea who she is or why she did this.'

'So you guys don't know her at all?'

Peter shook his head. 'We were hoping it would be someone familiar and it would all make sense, but no. I've never seen her in my life.'

'Well, someone will come forward soon, no doubt. The photo is all over the internet – her parents or family will surely recognize her,' Colin promised, looking from one to the other, as though he actually knew what he was talking about. 'And Milo's photo is everywhere – his little blond head, it's so distinctive. She won't get far. Don't worry, guys.'

Marissa nodded on autopilot, but Peter's face crumpled. He was past platitudes.

Marissa took the helm and moved things back to the practical. 'We're going out soon to do leafleting, as soon as more posters and leaflets arrive,' she said to Colin, then turned to Peter. 'Is Brian on his way?'

'Yeah, I was just on to him.' His voice was wobbly. He cleared his throat. 'He'll be here in twenty minutes. We might take two cars this time, Marissa, if you're OK to go on your own? It means we can cover more ground?'

'OK.' She nodded, though she wasn't sure. Being with Peter, not knowing what to say or how to mind each other was hard, but being without him was even worse. Colin must have read something on her face.

'I can go with you, Mar, if you like?'

'Thanks, Col, that'd be good.'

'So do they think it's a kidnap? Some kind of criminal gang? Has there been a ransom note?'

Marissa bit her lip. Colin never changed – no rugby-school education could knock the clumsy bluster out of him.

'No, there hasn't been any kind of note or contact, the police still don't know what's going on,' Peter said tightly. 'They're trying to trace this woman Carrie's family and find out as much as they can about her. They're talking to all the teachers, and all the parents and minders who did pick-up yesterday, and going door-to-door at the houses near the school.'

'Ah, that's good so, sounds like they're on top of things,' Colin said, nodding like one of those dogs you see on car dashboards sometimes. 'Great stuff. They'll have him back in no time. No time.'

And perhaps because it was all so utterly meaningless, or because she'd held it together for over an hour, Marissa began to cry again. Heaving sobs that choked her throat, her chest so tight she thought she might just die, there and then.

Colin moved towards her.

'Ah Mar, I'm sorry, I didn't mean to upset you.' He led her to a kitchen chair and sat opposite. With her hands on her eyes, she rocked back and forth, aware that it would take every ounce of energy to stop the tears and she didn't have it in her. Somewhere in the background, she heard a knock at the front door and heard Peter go to answer.

'Mar, look, don't worry about a thing while this is going on. I'll take care of the office, you know that, right? Shauna will have all the admin under control, and I'll have everything else. You're not to even think about it.'

The office was the last thing on her mind – did Colin really think that was worrying her? Then again, she was learning fast that people don't know what to say in this situation, and in fairness, he was one of the few who had shown up in person. She took one hand away from her eyes and reached out to put it on his.

'Thanks, Col. Jesus, I can't bear the thought that this could still be going on next week. But either way, I guess I won't be in on Monday.'

'Remind me to take the keys to your office and filing cabinet before I go, and I'll take over whatever you're working on, OK? Anything urgent?'

She tried to think. It felt like a million years since she'd been at work, though it was just over twenty-four hours.

'I was mostly looking at those two files I mentioned – the Fenelon and Downey estates. I wanted to work out the figures and see where I'm going wrong before the audit. But now, this . . .'

'Don't worry about a thing, I'll take care of all of it.'

She nodded, though she wasn't really listening any more. Her mind had gone there again – to Milo, to a dark room, to whispering voices and rough hands and unimaginable horrors that were in fact all too easy to imagine.

16

Irene
Saturday – one day missing

'IRENE, IT'S ON THE news again – come in!' Frank called from the sitting room, where he was sitting with his slippered feet up on the coffee table. She hated those slippers. The man was sixty, not eighty, yet as soon as he came into the house, he was straight into his slippers. Not when they first met of course – back then he was all champagne and flowers and surprise dinners in that posh restaurant on St Stephen's Green with the fifty-euro steaks. Newly separated and pretending he loved the freedom, but desperate to find a replacement wife all the same – Irene could tell, from the self-conscious way he touched the unoccupied space on his ring finger and how vehemently he claimed to like the bachelor apartment he planned to buy. That's how they'd met. Irene had been down at the shop to pick up a few bits; Frank had been due to view a show apartment in a glossy new city centre development. He'd taken a wrong turn and ended up in the shop, asking Irene for directions. She took it all in – the tan line on his ring finger, the manicured nails, the nice car, the lost look in his eyes. She'd walk with him to find the show apartment, she said, in case he took another wrong turn. They chatted on the walk, Irene filling him in on local knowledge and complimenting his taste in property, and with no reason to leave, she ended up viewing the apartment with him too. Back then, Irene still showed a glimmer of her younger self – shades of a face that had started out pretty, skin that was soft before the sun took its toll. Frank was relieved to have a wingman, it seemed, and was charmed by her patter. In the end, Frank didn't buy the apartment. He wined her and dined her and bought her a three-bedroom family home in Dún Laoghaire. And now, here they were, fourteen years later, and all he wanted was a quiet life. And his slippers.

'What are they saying this time?' she asked, sitting beside him to look at the TV news.

'There's a nationwide search for the child and for Caroline, and they don't seem to be saying she *took* him – keeping it open as though they were both taken. That's not what the papers are saying though. One of them called her an "Evil Kidnapper" in the headline.'

'Call it what it is, don't be pussyfooting around, that's what I say,' Irene said, reaching for the remote.

'That's your daughter they're talking about – aren't you worried about her?' He looked genuinely puzzled, and she studied his face, marvelling at how little he understood her. *Always keep a little of yourself back*, her mother used to say.

'Frank, it's nine years since I last saw her, and she was nothing but trouble when she was here – stealing, lying, shouting – she even hit me once, slapped me right across the face. I was frightened of her in the end, you know. So don't be making me feel guilty now for not wringing my hands over this mess she's got herself into.'

He reached over and patted her knee.

'Sorry, love, I wasn't trying to make you feel guilty. I suppose I just mean if it was one of mine, no matter what they did . . .'

The idea of one of Frank's perfect children getting involved in anything more serious than a parking ticket made her want to laugh. A banker, a solicitor and a GP, all with their own beautiful homes and well-behaved children. And of course, no animosity whatsoever towards Frank and his ex-wife for the divorce. Perfectly well-adjusted adult children, and three of the most boring people she'd ever met in her life.

'And the police haven't been in touch?' Frank continued.

'No. She seems to be going under the name Carrie Finch, so it'll take them a while to find us.'

'But wouldn't it be helpful to the search if we speak to them? The little fella who's missing – he's only four. Surely anything we can do to help, we should?'

She shrugged. 'What can we tell them that's of any use?'

'I don't know. Something about her childhood that might be a help? They could go through her stuff?'

'You've been watching too much TV, Frank. In real life, what someone was like when they were ten doesn't tell a thing about what they're like at twenty-five. And it's not like we have any of her stuff here.'

'I thought we still had boxes with her things?'

'One box. I gave all her clothes to charity and threw out her books.'

Frank's eyebrows went up but he said nothing.

She heaved herself off the couch. 'Fine, I'll go up and see what's in that box. I'm still not calling the guards though – it's up to them to come to us if they need us.'

Rule number one: the guards are the enemy and you never give them anything. Her mother taught her that.

The box was inside the wardrobe, under a bag of old coats. This Side Up, it said, upside down. Not that it mattered. The original contents, whatever they were, were long gone, and Caroline's stuff wasn't fragile. Irene pulled out the box and opened it, kneeling to examine her daughter's belongings. Two diaries. An old watch. Some cheap jewellery. A scarf that looked expensive – probably nicked, she thought, examining the label. She might keep that. At the bottom of the box lay a scrapbook. She remembered the cover – Caroline had written her name in glue and stuck glitter on it – but until now, Irene had never looked inside.

On the first page, Caroline had glued in a poem that had been ripped from a book – her English poetry book for Junior Cert maybe. Little vandal. The poem was about a horse coming down a road near Enniskerry, wreaking havoc – or not, Irene wasn't sure. She turned to the next page. An A4 sheet of paper with Caroline's name on it, over and over in squiggly writing. First name constant, surname varied. *Caroline Murphy.* The name on her birth cert but never used. *Caroline Holohan.* The name the neighbours in their old estate called her. *Caroline Turner.* The name she tried out after Irene got married, until the novelty wore off. *Caroline Byrde.* That bloody Byrde fella, she was always mooning over him back then. Below the various signatures were band names – The Cure, New Order, The Smiths. Irene couldn't remember much about Caroline's music tastes, now that she thought about it. Maybe they'd never talked about music. The page opposite had days of the week, written in bubble writing, like a homemade diary, but with no entries. That triggered a memory – a rhyme Caroline used to recite, something about being blue on Mondays. Little weirdo was so full of it, fancied herself as a poet. Irene pushed away any belated questions about why Caroline might have been feeling blue on Mondays or any other days. The next page had what looked like a sheet of her homework journal pulled out and glued in. On it was a list of names, with deep red lines through them. Irene could hardly make out the names beneath. Sarah something? Nadine? She couldn't remember any friends called Sarah or Nadine, but then these girls were probably not friends if the anger behind the red lines was anything to go by. Jesus, who'd be a teenager? An unfamiliar pang of something like sympathy hit her. Caroline had never said she was having any trouble with friends.

The next page surprised her. A photo of Caroline as a baby in Irene's arms. Where had that come from and who had taken it? A neighbour maybe? That Caroline had kept it and taken the time to put it in her scrapbook . . . well, it wasn't what she was expecting. She shook her head. She was getting sappy in her middle age.

It was the following page that stopped her cold. A print-out of a newspaper article from the internet. A feature on Dublin career criminal Rob Murphy, and his new life in London after doing time and going straight. Irene sat back on her heels. Jesus. Caroline knew about Rob? Well. That changed everything.

17

Four months earlier

CARRIE WATCHED AS JENNY'S eyes flitted to the wine rack and back to her. She imagined the inner monologue. Jenny wanted a glass of wine, but Richie was out. It would be weird if she opened a bottle and didn't offer Carrie a glass. But Carrie Finch wasn't really a bonding-over-Beaujolais kind of girl, and Jenny clearly wasn't sure she wanted to muddle her way into an awkward evening of short answers and long silences. Maybe it was time Carrie Finch opened up a bit, gave her something that might slow things down later. When they came looking. So she did something she almost never did in the Kennedys' house – she smiled. Then she sat at the breakfast bar and let out a 'whew' sound. A *that was a long day* kind of sound. It was enough. Jenny smiled back.

'I'm wrecked too. Actually, I was thinking of opening a bottle of wine – would you have a glass?'

So predictable. It made Carrie happy when Jenny did exactly what she expected her to do.

'I don't usually drink wine . . . but yes please, I'd love a glass.'

Jenny beamed, and Carrie knew she'd decided this was the night she'd crack the exterior of her quiet, mousy nanny.

'What do you normally drink – when you go out, I mean?' she asked, pouring the red liquid into an oversized glass.

'I don't really go out,' Carrie said. 'I'm not into drinking anyway, but when I was away, I lost touch with a lot of my friends so . . .'

Jenny's face fell.

'Oh. That's hard, Carrie. Is there any way to get back in touch?' Jenny asked in that sing-song Cork accent that always got stronger when she relaxed. 'I imagine some of them are on Facebook – you could find them there?'

'I'm not on Facebook either.' Carrie took a sip of her drink. 'Maybe I'll join though,' she said, throwing her a bone.

Jenny's phone beeped and she picked it up, frowning.

'Is everything OK?' Carrie asked, creasing her face with concern.

'Yeah.' Jenny sighed. 'Just someone at work who . . . anyway, back to you – what about family, you mentioned you have brothers?'

'Yes, three brothers.'

'That's nice. And are they living nearby?'

Nice. Such a Jenny word. 'No. One in Alabama, one in Boston, one in California.' Easy as ABC. Carrie hid her smile with another sip of wine.

'Ah, so far away. That's hard. Are you close? What are their names?'

'They're Caleb, Scott and Cole,' Carrie told her, immediately wondering if she'd pushed it too far. But Jenny didn't blink.

'And are they all older than you?'

'Yes, I'm the baby. I miss them sometimes,' Carrie said, in the kind of wistful tone someone like Jenny would expect to hear.

'I can imagine. I've no siblings but Richie is one of six. Mind you, they're not that close – sometimes I reckon he wishes they lived further away.' She grinned and leaned in, her eyes wide behind her glasses. 'And sometimes I wish his mother lived further away.'

So this was her trump card in her effort to bond – show a chink in the armour, make a disparaging comment, see where it lands. Carrie decided to bite.

'Ha! I was wondering about that. I could tell when she called in that she's hard work.'

Jenny relaxed. Happy her card had paid dividends. Happy to have an ally. Her husband was no ally. There were many chinks there, chinks they were both hiding from the rest of the world. But nothing gets past the person who lives in your house, the person you entrust with your child. The person who spends hours in your home when you're not there. The person who has access to every room, every drawer, every letter, every inch. Every hair on his head. Carrie sipped her wine and made her plans.

18

Jenny
Monday – three days missing

Concentrate, Jenny, she told herself as the Monday morning video conference droned on. But she didn't have it in her today. She could think of nothing but little Milo Irvine, now missing sixty-five hours. His photograph was all over the front pages of the papers, his shoulder-length blond hair surely making it easy to spot him if he was in any kind of public place, and it was the first story on every news show. The country was on edge, waiting for updates. Children went missing from time to time but were usually found within hours – lost in parks or staying with estranged parents. Nobody could remember the last time a child had been kidnapped. That word – kidnapped – was being tossed around in the tabloids and on social media, but the TV news and broadsheet papers were still referring to it as the 'disappearance of Carrie Finch (25) and Milo Irvine (4)'. Presumably so she wouldn't be afraid to turn herself in, Jenny reckoned. There was also a theory gaining traction in various comments sections that Carrie was rescuing Milo from something or someone – hints at a less-than-perfect home life.

'Ah, that's awful! Pure jealousy from people who like to believe the worst about everyone,' Jenny had said to Richie when he showed her the comments under one news article. 'They're just bitter because Marissa and Peter are wealthy.' Of course, the other reason for that theory was self-preservation – people needed to believe there weren't kidnappers plucking children from the school gate. It couldn't be random, because then it could happen to anyone. There had to be someone to blame. So why not the beautiful couple with more money than anyone else?

Gossip emerged from 'friends of friends' – stories of relationships both Peter and Marissa had had when they were younger and living a party lifestyle. Stories of friends in high places and speeding tickets that went away. A rumour of a dangerous driving incident. And the suggestion that Peter's family had contributed a huge chunk of money to the purchase of Maple Lodge.

What kind of people have that much cash lying around? wrote one anonymous commenter on TheDailyByte.ie. *Something dodge there.*

No smoke without a fire, said someone else.

Jenny winced. People were so quick to judge, even in horrible circumstances like these.

As the video conference trundled on, Jenny clicked into news headlines on her phone, holding it under the table. Police were now looking to speak to Kyle Byrde, described as an acquaintance of Carrie's. Anyone who knew his whereabouts was asked to get in touch with the gardaí. Jenny clung to this – it was easier to believe that the hard-faced man in the photo might have somehow forced Carrie to kidnap Milo than that she and Richie had let a monster mind their child.

As the meeting ended and the group dispersed around the building, Mark fell into step with her.

'Hey, how was your weekend?' he asked, following her through to her office and taking a seat. She sat behind her desk and stared at him.

'You don't know?'

'Know what?'

'That story that's all over the news – the little boy Milo who's missing along with the childminder – that's *our* childminder.'

'Jesus, I heard it on the news but didn't catch the details,' Mark said, eyes wide. 'What happened?'

And maybe because she desperately needed someone to confide in, or because Richie was being so distant, or just because Mark was so easy to talk to, she told him everything – the fake playdate, the police questions, the visit to Marissa, Richie's warnings about getting involved, and most of all, the guilt.

'I hired her, Mark, and I didn't spot any of it. I let her look after my child. What if she'd taken Jacob? I keep thinking that, then I feel terrible because she didn't, he's fine, but she took that poor little boy. And it's all my fault.'

She waited for him to tell her to steer clear of taking blame, to distance herself – as Richie had done, as Adeline had done. But he didn't.

'I get it. I'd feel the same. Of course you can't help thinking about the fact that she could have taken Jacob. It's not selfish, it's because like any mother, you'd protect your child at all costs. It doesn't mean you don't care about what happened to the little boy.' He leaned forward, his brown eyes full of compassion. 'You're a good person, Jenny, and it's normal to react like this.'

'When did you become a therapist?' She laughed, as tears sprang to her eyes.

'Ah, a man of many talents. It's good to talk and all that.' He leaned back again. 'What are the police thinking – is there a ransom note?'

'Nothing so far, but it doesn't mean it won't happen, apparently.'

'And why *this* little kid – why was he targeted?'

'Because they're rich, I suppose. They live in this stunning house just off Northland Road, and judging by what they're saying in the newspapers, they're millionaires.'

'Wow. Maybe I won't be so down next time I don't get a raise. Not sure I'd like to be a kidnap target.'

'Me neither.' Silence then, as Jenny thought about what she'd just said. It was all very well not being a target, but she'd actually let a criminal live in her house and mind her child.

'Where'd they get all the money?' Mark asked, crossing an ankle over his knee. His socks were black with little footballs on each side, and in the midst of everything, it made her smile.

'According to the papers, he's an investment broker, along with his brother. They managed to keep everything together during the downturn, when every second business was going bust. And she's a solicitor, partner in a local firm. There's family money too, I reckon. Not just because that's what the online rumours say, but no matter how much money they make from their jobs, they must have had help to buy that house.' She pushed her glasses up her nose and gave a watery smile. 'That's what Richie and I tell each other every time we meet someone with a huge house. "Family money. Must be." It makes us feel less inadequate.' The smile slipped away as she remembered why they were talking about the Irvines. 'Anyway, I better get some work done, I've to leave at lunchtime to collect Jacob.'

'I better do some work as well,' he said, standing up. 'I hope there's good news soon – I'll message you later to check in?'

She opened her mouth to tell him not to, but closed it again. He was just being kind. And right now, that's what she needed – someone to look out for her.

19

Marissa
Monday – three days missing

THIS WAS WHY SHE didn't want to sleep – this awful moment, this waking up, forgetting for just a fraction of a second. Then the crash, the crushing realization that it wasn't a dream, that Milo really was missing. The images again – dark rooms and strange hands and hissed threats. The surge of desperate fear. How scared he must be. She couldn't think about it and she couldn't not think about it.

She sat up on the couch, pushing off the throw. What time was it? The clock on the mantelpiece showed ten past ten – she'd been asleep for six hours. Immediately, guilt swamped her – how could she sleep when Milo was out there somewhere, terrified? She swung her legs to the ground and stood, swaying slightly, dizzy from sleeping tablets and lack of food, though she couldn't remember feeling hungry since all of this started. Peter came in, carrying two mugs of tea. Her eyes met his and he shook his head. No news. She reached out to take a tea.

'McConville called by this morning with a photo of this guy Kyle Byrde, but I couldn't help – I've never seen him in my life. He looks like a scumbag drug dealer or . . .' He stopped, maybe seeing the look on her face. She didn't want to think of Milo with someone like that. If he was with Carrie, it was easier. Not because she knew Carrie or trusted her – God, she didn't trust her – but women didn't hurt children, did they?

'Didn't she need me to look at the photo? Is it different to the picture we saw online?'

'No, same photo, but she said no harm having a look again, so she left it here. It's in the kitchen. Brian's on his way back, he's going to drive you around to do posters if you're up to it – I'll take the other car, and a bunch of guys from work are out there already. They've been fantastic. The search centre at the church is packed again today, Brian said, loads of volunteers. People are brilliant.' His voice choked on the last words.

She squeezed his hand and felt like she was going to throw up. Again. But they had to stay focused. Falling apart wouldn't get Milo back. 'I'll go out with Brian, that's fine. Colin said he'd shut the office at lunchtime so himself and Shauna could go out too.'

'Shauna?' Peter looked confused, though Shauna had been with them a few months now.

'Our legal secretary,' she reminded him. 'Peter, did McConville say anything about why there's no note – how long does it usually take before people look for a ransom?'

'She was cagey, I think she didn't want to say anything that would worry me. But Brian spoke to a guy he knows who works as a private investigator, and he said normally you'd expect something in the first twenty-four hours.'

Marissa could barely believe what they were talking about. 'Oh God, it's all so insane. She'll be looking after him, won't she, Peter? Carrie is there to make sure Milo is OK, to keep him calm and safe?'

'Definitely. She's not going to let anything happen to him. He probably thinks he's on a holiday.'

He squeezed her hand and they sat in silence. She pushed away the dark voice that jeered at Peter's words – the one that told her Milo was cold and scared and definitely not thinking he was on holidays. She had to believe he was OK because the alternative would crush her to dust.

By accident or unconscious design, Marissa found herself near the school just as classes came to an end. With a coil of deepening anxiety in the pit of her stomach, she touched Brian's arm and nodded in an unspoken request to pull over. She stepped out, suddenly unsteady on her legs. The cluster of Junior Infant parents were huddled more closely than usual and when they saw her, a collective jaw dropped.

'Marissa, my God, any news?' That was Sarah Rayburn, the woman whose house Jacob Kennedy was in on Friday. She'd gushed on the phone about bringing over a casserole, but Marissa hadn't heard from her since. Anyway, they didn't need casseroles. They needed volunteers.

'Most children in this kind of situation turn up unharmed – usually it's a family member or someone the child knows,' said Victor Waddock, the dad who knew everything. Marissa ignored him.

'I don't know what to say – is there anything we can do?' Grace Loftus asked, looking sincere.

'If anyone could take some posters and put them up, that would be great?' Hesitation from all three. 'It just means going into shops and businesses and asking if they'll put them up, or putting them on poles and lamp posts – it's really straightforward.'

'Of course, I'll take some,' said Grace, reaching for posters.

Victor and Sarah followed suit, but with less enthusiasm. Maybe they meant they'd help in any way they could, as long as it only involved sending thoughts and prayers.

'How are *you* doing?' Sarah asked with a head tilt. There was something hungry in her expression.

Marissa held out her hands to say *oh, you know* but her throat was too tight. It was easier to focus on the practical things – posters, police questions, media interviews. She closed her eyes for a second and swallowed.

'It must be horrendous,' Sarah continued, in what seemed like a kindness; filling the gap so Marissa didn't have to speak. 'And look, I know you're thinking if only you'd double-checked everything when she set up the playdate, none of this would have happened, but there's no point dwelling on that.'

Marissa grimaced. Not a kindness, then. She decided to ignore the barb and move on to something more practical.

'Did any of you know Carrie – maybe you talked to her at pick-up?'

Three heads shook slowly.

'I spotted her once or twice – I recognized her when I saw the photo on TV,' Grace said, tucking a stray hair behind her ear. 'But I never spoke to her. I didn't realize she was a minder for anyone in our class.'

'I didn't recognize her at all!' Sarah said. 'Wouldn't know her from Adam. But I don't know any of the minders or au pairs.'

Marissa didn't either. There was a code at the school gate – parents talked to parents, nannies to nannies, and mostly, they didn't mix. Maybe Ana would have chatted to Carrie. She made a mental note to ask McConville if they'd checked that with her.

'Hard to believe though, isn't it,' Sarah said, looking around with exaggerated care, and lowering her voice, 'that Jenny would hire someone like that.'

'I know,' Victor stage-whispered, shaking his head, 'I'd be absolutely morto. I feel sorry for her, but she should have been more careful.'

'That's why I gave up my job,' Sarah said. 'My boss begged me to stay, but I just couldn't trust someone else to mind my children.'

Grace pursed her lips but said nothing. She was at the school gate once a week as far as Marissa knew, with an after-school bus collecting her children the rest of the time.

'Well, I wouldn't go as far as saying I wouldn't trust someone to mind my kids, but it's about doing good background checks,' Victor said authoritatively. 'Our childminder Claudia was a godsend when we were both working – she was like a second mother to the kids. But Jenny Kennedy clearly didn't do the kind of checks she should have done.' He looked over Marissa's shoulder and his face changed. 'She's coming.'

Marissa turned to see Jenny coming towards them, a lamb approaching a pack of wolves. Her strawberry blonde hair was tied back in a neat bun and her make-up was perfectly applied, but underneath the mask, she looked pale and worn.

'Marissa,' Jenny said as she drew near, 'can I take some more posters for you?'

Marissa passed a bundle to her. 'Thank you, that would be great.'

'Richie and I went around Stillorgan with them yesterday, I could do Dundrum tonight – or is that already done?'

'I'm not sure . . .'

'Don't worry, I'll head up there anyway and if there are already posters up, I'll go on to Ballinteer.'

Marissa nodded gratefully.

'So, you're picking up Jacob for the next while I guess,' Sarah said, looking at Jenny, 'or do you have a new nanny on the way?'

Jenny's face coloured. 'No, I'll be picking him up.'

'You know, there's this agency I heard of,' Sarah continued.

'They do all the vetting for you. Costs a bit more than just hiring a randomer, but worth it. If you go down the nanny route again, I mean.' The challenge was clear.

'Thanks, we might do that,' Jenny said quietly.

But Sarah was on a roll. 'Could you, though? Go down that route again? God, I don't know. I'd be scarred for life if I hired a kidnapper to look after my child.' She laughed. 'Maybe that's just me!'

Silence. Jenny looked at the ground.

'I use Little Monkeys,' Grace said. 'It's an after-school attached to a crèche and they're brilliant. Might be safer than hiring a nanny, you never know what they're up to when you're not there . . .'

Victor bristled visibly. 'Unless you know the nanny really well – we had Claudia years and she was genuinely part of the family. She even stayed here one Christmas instead of going home to Brazil.'

'Wasn't that because you were only giving her four days off and it wasn't worth the cost of the flights for such a short visit?' Sarah asked with a smile.

Victor sniffed. 'Not at all, she said she'd always wanted to have Christmas in Ireland and she was more than happy to stay.'

'What a find, happy to forfeit seeing her own family at Christmas,' Sarah said, still smiling, shark teeth bared. 'Good nannies are worth a king's ransom! Oops, sorry, bad choice of words.' Innocent eyes wide, she looked over at Jenny, then turned ever so slightly, closing the circle and locking Jenny out.

'Jenny,' Marissa said, stepping away from the other three, 'thank you for helping with the posters. If you have time one of the nights, would you call over for some more?'

'Absolutely,' Jenny said. 'I'll come over tomorrow night. Anything I can do, Marissa, I mean it.'

Marissa nodded. 'Thank you.'

And five heads turned as Mr Williams led a class of Junior Infants across the yard, and four parents rushed to greet their children, while one walked away, her heart smashed to pieces all over again.

20

Two months earlier

THE COVEN. IT WAS the perfect name for them, Jenny thought, as she stood at the school social, smiling and gripping the stem of her white wine glass. The one with the extraordinarily white teeth was called Sarah Rayburn – Jenny couldn't help thinking of a shark every time she smiled. Which was a lot; each time she commented on someone else, she did so with a huge smile, to take the bite out of it. She'd already pointed out one woman whose husband had left her, another who'd lost her job but was keeping it to herself (unsuccessfully, clearly), and a man who – Sarah lowered her voice for this bit – had a gambling problem. 'He thinks no one knows but our business is next door to Shamrock Sports . . . The poor wife.' She shook her head, and the other two followed suit. The other two were Grace and Victor, Jenny had discovered an hour earlier when she'd inadvertently joined their circle.

Beside her stood Victor, a short man with dark, thinning hair, and a complexion like raw ham. He was a stay-at-home dad, a status he liked to bring up at every opportunity as though waiting for a pat on the head. 'It's the twenty-first century, for God's sake, why wouldn't I stay home with my kids? I'm not one of these guys who feels emasculated by having a super successful wife. And people never believe me, you know, they assume just because I'm well educated and look successful that I'm making it up.'

Jenny snorted her wine at that point and turned it into a cough.

Grace, the third member of the Coven, had a whiff of normal about her – Jenny couldn't help thinking she might be all right if she got her on her own. But the three of them together – in the short space of time Jenny had been speaking to them – were lethal. And Jenny desperately wanted to escape, even if it meant her ears would be burning.

'Sorry, would any of you know where the bathrooms are?' she asked, knocking back the last swallow of wine in case one of them offered to mind her drink.

'Go around the bar, towards reception,' Grace said. 'I've two older girls in the school as well as my new starter, and every single Kerryglen School event is in the Eliot hotel. You'll be sick of it in a few years!'

'The hotel's owned by Dermot Downey – you know, the builder?' said Sarah, with a slight curl to her lip. 'He has kids in the school. So the school gets a discount.'

They'd want to be getting a discount, Jenny thought, looking around at the trays of wine and prosecco, the canapés that definitely didn't come from a supermarket, and the smartly dressed waiters making sure the new Junior Infant parents were well fed and watered.

'Right, well, I'll go check out the bathrooms to see if they're as fabulous as everything else!' Jenny said brightly, and slipped away, wondering if she'd manage to avoid the Coven when she came out. Or she could just hide in the bathroom for the next two hours. If only Richie had come, but he was (officially) correcting essays and (unofficially) not remotely interested in getting to know other parents at the school. *What's the point in having a live-in childminder if we never go out at night*, she'd said, but Richie just shrugged and pointed to the stack of essays. In fact, in the three months since Carrie had been living with them, they hadn't had a single night out, Jenny realized. She'd have to fix that – they could do with some conversation and connection.

She pushed the door to the Ladies – a wide, spotlessly clean bathroom with baskets of pristine white towels and Molton Brown hand soap at every basin. Maybe she *could* spend the next two hours here, she thought, eyeing up a cushioned mahogany chair at the far end of the bathroom.

She stood in front of the mirror, smoothing down her hair. What would the Coven be saying about her now – how would they sum her up? She tilted her head to one side, eyeing herself in the mirror. No spring chicken, they might say, but then again, none of them were. Could do with a bit of Botox, she thought, wrinkling her brow behind her glasses, but maybe not yet. Designer dress, they would decide, and they'd be right, though they probably wouldn't know she'd bought it for half-nothing in a sale. It was a treat she'd promised herself if she got the promotion – her first and only Diane von Furstenberg wrap dress. The black-and-white print contrasted with her red hair and the wrap shape was forgiving, complementing her narrow waist while skimming her less-narrow hips. She pulled her lip-stick out of her bag and reapplied it, not because it really needed doing, but because it felt like a bathroom that demanded some kind of pampering.

Then, reluctant to face more small talk, she walked to the chair at the far end of the bathroom and sat, taking out her phone to see what was going on in the world outside the ivory tower of the Eliot.

As she browsed, the door to the bathroom was pushed open, and in walked a petite woman with beautiful, long glossy dark hair tumbling down her back – the kind of slightly tousled look that took hours to perfect. Her colouring was olive, almost Mediterranean, but her wide-set eyes were deep blue. She looked like a model or a celebrity of some kind, yet here she was, standing in the bathroom of the Eliot. Wearing Jenny's dress.

'Oh! That's hilarious!' the woman said, pointing at Jenny. 'What are the chances – I've had this about two years and haven't worn it in ages!'

Jenny smiled, groaning inwardly.

'I guess we can just stay at opposite ends of the room for the night,' she said. 'Or I can keep hiding in here.' She was only half joking.

'Gosh, no,' the woman said. 'This will be immense fun – we'll take a selfie, then go out together, arm in arm. Are you at the Kerryglen Junior Infants Social?'

'Yep, not doing a great job of being social,' Jenny said, standing up.

'Oh look, you can't hide in here all night – come out with me and I'll look after you. I'm Marissa, my son's Milo.'

'I'm Jenny, I have one of the Jacobs – Jacob K.'

'Fabulous! Now, let me put on my lipstick, then we'll get the selfie, and we'll march out together for the laugh. Deal?'

Jenny found herself nodding as she watched Marissa apply lipstick to her already perfectly pink lips, and fluff her hair. She dabbed concealer under her eyes and on a small scar on her chin, then she pulled a rose-gold phone out of her clutch and beckoned Jenny over. Putting one arm around Jenny's shoulder, she stretched the other to take the selfie. At the very last minute, Jenny removed her glasses and remembered to smile.

'That's gorge!' Marissa said, looking at the photo. 'I'll put it up online. I'm @MarissaNotMelissa on Instagram – what's yours?'

'My . . . oh, I'm not on Instagram.'

'Are you not! Well, if you ever set up an account, that's where you'll find our photo.' She typed something and held up the phone for Jenny to see. She'd added a filter to the picture and cropped it, though just a little so the matching dresses were still visible. Jenny had to admit, it was a good photo. Marissa looked incredible, but even Jenny looked nice.

'Now, are we ready to make our entrance?'

Jenny nodded, not entirely sure what was going on. They walked together back towards the function room, and as they were about to go through the doors, Marissa linked her arm through Jenny's. When they walked in, every head in the room seemed to turn, though Jenny knew that was probably her imagination. Marissa took a small bow, smiling widely, and turned to clap Jenny. Jenny could feel her cheeks going red as she realized people were cheering and laughing and applauding.

'See, it's the only way to do it,' Marissa whispered, her eyes shining. 'No point in hiding at opposite ends of the room!'

She loves this, Jenny realized, watching Marissa's face light up. The attention – the room turned towards her. Jenny was way out of her comfort zone, but somehow with Marissa in charge, it wasn't so bad.

'Let's get some bubbly,' Marissa said, linking arms again and leading Jenny towards a man with a tray of drinks. She passed one to Jenny and took one herself, then stood to survey the room.

'Right, who do you know? Who would you like to meet?'

'We're new to Kerryglen,' Jenny said. 'So I don't know anyone really . . .'

'From Cork? I can hear the accent?'

'Yeah, but I've been in Dublin fifteen years. We used to live in Rathmines and it was great, but my mother-in-law wanted us closer to her, out here in Kerryglen.'

'Well, Kerryglen is lovely, I promise. We don't bite. Where exactly are you living?'

'A new development called Belton Heights?'

'Oh yes, I know it. They're still building there, yes? Downey Homes? Dermot Downey is one of Peter's clients and his sister Sinéad is a GP, they both have kids here in the school.'

'That's the one. We live next door to Sinéad actually. It's lovely and all, but we're still so new – I haven't really met people yet, and I don't know the school parents at all.'

'Well then, stick with me. I know everyone,' Marissa said with a wink.

'Everyone?' Jenny asked. The social had only started an hour ago; how had this woman made her way around the room so quickly?

'Yep. Between Milo's Montessori and tennis and the gym, I'd met a good few of the parents already. The mums anyway, though a few of the dads too, through work.'

'Oh, do you work here in Kerryglen?'

'I'm the local solicitor, so I hear all the secrets.' She winked again. 'It's like *Midsomer Murders*.' She took a sip of her drink and grinned. 'I'm kidding. Sort of.'

'I see!' Jenny said, trying to picture this exotic butterfly behind a desk in a local solicitor's firm.

Marissa pointed to a man at the other side of the room. 'That's Peter, my husband, and I can tell from the look of intense interest on his face that he's buttering up a future client.'

Jenny looked over, curious to see what kind of man had talked Marissa into marriage. Even from a distance, Peter was attractive – an open, expressive face, dark, greying hair, but it went beyond physical features. Somehow his stance said he was sure of himself and had all the power in the room. A golden couple then, these two.

'I know some of the parents through Peter's work, they're clients of his. He manages investments. If you need financial advice, he's your man!'

A waiter was gliding towards them with a tray of canapés. Marissa took a look, wrinkling her nose just a little.

'I'm thinking of going vegan, but maybe not today,' she said, taking a smoked salmon blini off the tray. 'What about you?'

'Sorry?'

'Veganism? I did Veganuary at the start of the year but I did Dry January at the same time, and to be honest, it was too much. No steak, no wine, no sushi, at the drabbest time of year. Big mistake.'

'Uh, no, I'm not vegan.'

'Great, have a blini! And I'll nab us some more bubbly.'

She didn't need to go far. A waiter was over within seconds, somehow reading her signals. Marissa seemed like the kind of person who didn't have to wait long to be served anywhere.

Now Jenny had one and a half glasses of prosecco in one hand and a blini in the other. She shoved the food into her mouth to free up a hand, hoping nobody would ask her a question while she chewed. But Marissa was doing all the talking.

'See over there? That's the principal's husband. He's a client of Peter's. There's a lot more money in that household than you'd think, for a couple working in education. I'm probably not meant to say that, but I know you won't repeat it.'

Jenny nodded, her mouth still full of blini.

'And that guy?' Marissa pointed across the room at a small, round man. 'He's got a son in our class but it's his third marriage. Kerryglen's answer to Zsa Zsa Gabor. Fair play to him – why wouldn't you, if you can get away with it. Let's see, who else . . .' She scanned the room. 'Did you meet the three witches?'

'Who?' Jenny said with a splutter, though she guessed who Marissa meant.

'Sarah, Victor and Grace. The self-appointed queens of this year's Junior Infants class. Watch now, as soon as there's anything up for debate – class nights out or teacher gifts or birthday parties – they'll be telling us all what we have to do. Sarah already commented on Milo's hair one morning – he has shoulder-length hair and I can't bear to cut it yet – she smiled the sweetest smile and said, "It's great he's too young to be self-conscious about how much it stands out."'

'Oh God!'

'I know. Wagon. I mean, what's wrong with standing out anyway – we all spend too much time trying to fit in.'

Jenny nodded, strongly suspecting Marissa didn't waste a second trying to fit in. Maybe it was the two glasses of bubbly, but there was something infectious about Marissa's view of the world.

'I told her it was up to Milo – as soon as he wants to get it cut, we'll get it cut. Sarah is one of those people who's always look-ing for a little wound to niggle. You know?'

'Oh, I know. I have a mother-in-law like that. Carrie – our childminder – has red hair, and my mother-in-law once asked my husband if I deliberately hired a nanny with the same col-our hair as mine so that Jacob would think it was me and feel less upset that I'm never there.'

Marissa threw her head back and cackled, and Jenny felt an unexpected surge of pleasure at having made her laugh.

'Mothers-in-law.' Marissa rolled her eyes. 'Actually, that's a bit mean – my mother-in-law has been in a nursing home for years, the poor pet hasn't done a thing to earn that eye-roll. I donate it to *your* mother-in-law.'

'My mother-in-law thanks you,' Jenny said with a grin.

'Oh crap,' Marissa said, glancing at an expensive-looking copper-coloured watch, 'speaking of childminders, I need to phone Ana – Milo had a bit of a temperature when we were leaving and I meant to call sooner. He sometimes has a funny reaction to medicine so I told her to wait it out. I'll catch up with you later?'

Jenny nodded and smiled, feeling suddenly lost in the crowded room as Marissa whirled away.

21

Irene
Monday – three days missing

IRENE GLANCED ACROSS AT Frank on the other couch as he flicked through the channels on Monday night. Nothing, nothing, and more nothing. It didn't bother him though, he liked flicking. He never seemed to mind if he started up the stairs for bed having done nothing more than hop from one show to another without actually watching anything. His brow was furrowed, as though whatever he was seeking was meaningful and important. She examined his white hair, receding now, making him look older than his sixty years, and his glasses that gave him a serious air, the kind of look that fitted perfectly with his job at the bank, she always thought. What was going on in his mind? Nothing much at all, she figured, as he settled on a show about retirement properties in Spain. She had him fairly well sewn up, but he rarely knew what was going on in her head – in fact, he'd probably be shocked if he did. *Always keep a little of yourself back*, repeated her mother's voice inside her head. *Yes*, Irene thought, *but Frank has his uses too*. And to her surprise over the years, he could be a pretty good sounding board – especially if flattered into the role of the expert.

'Frank?'

'Yes, love?' He didn't look away from the property show.

'I discovered something recently about Caroline, and I'd love to get your advice on it.'

He muted the TV and sat up straight, turning to face her. Expert mode.

'Of course. What is it?' He was only short of taking out a notebook and pen.

'You know how I told Caroline her father was a sailor called Murphy? Well, I found a scrapbook in her old room the other day, and there was stuff about Rob Murphy in it. The actual Rob Murphy, not the made-up sailor. The only reason she'd have anything on him is if she knew he was her father.'

'Oh. How would she have found out?'

'Probably not that hard if she went looking – the neighbours round our place would've all known he was her father. Though you'd think they'd have known better than to say.'

Frank nodded slowly, his eyes unblinking. He put the remote control carefully on the side table.

'Do you think they were in touch – Caroline and Rob?'

'God no, I'd surely have known about it if they were.'

'But you haven't seen her in nine years – maybe they're in touch now?'

'I suppose . . .' She turned it over in her mind. Did it matter if they were? Somehow the idea rankled. She was the bridge between them, they couldn't – they shouldn't – bypass her. Surely.

'Why don't you ask Kathy? That's the quickest way to find out if Caroline has ever made contact with Rob, isn't it?'

Irene nodded. The quickest way was actually to contact Rob directly, but Frank wasn't going to suggest that. Anyway, he was right, Kathy would know – she and Rob were close. Irene picked up her phone and dialled the number she hadn't used in years, walking through to the kitchen as she waited for Kathy to pick up.

The bright red cupboards glared at her, and she winced, wishing for the hundredth time she'd gone for something more muted, like Frank suggested. She'd always wanted a red kitchen; ever since she'd seen one in a magazine, and when she met Frank she got it. Once it was in, it was clear it was too much, but she never admitted it. And Frank, to his credit, never once said *I told you so.* Give it another year, she figured, and it would be reasonable to suggest a change. She plopped into a kitchen chair – white Formica to contrast with the red cupboards, very 1960s chic, or so she had thought in her mind's eye – and crossed her legs, turning her foot from one side to the other to examine her fire-truck-red polish. Kathy must be out; she'd try the mobile.

This time, Kathy picked up after two rings.

'Irene! It's been a while – how're you doing?'

'Grand, Kathy, how're you? Any news?' Irene bit her lip and waited.

'Nothing at all – God, it must be three or four years since we were last speaking – is everything all right?'

So, Kathy hadn't made the connection – she hadn't copped that the Carrie Finch all over the news was her niece, Caroline Holohan. And why would she – Caroline was a newborn baby the first and last time Kathy had seen her, looking exactly the same as every other newborn.

'I was wondering about something – was my Caroline ever in touch with Rob?'

'What? Sure, Jesus, wouldn't you know if she was?'

'Well, I haven't seen her in a bit – I think I said that to you the last time we were on the phone.'

'Ah Irene, I'm sorry – you still don't see her then?'

'No,' Irene said, glancing through to the sitting room, where her daughter's face was again splashed all over the TV news. 'Never.'

'That's sad. I hope you two find a way to make up – teenage hormones probably behind all of it. I remember it myself growing up. I used to drive Rob mad, slamming doors and picking fights.'

'Speaking of Rob . . . in your note in my birthday card, thanks for that by the way, you said that he's moving home with his new girlfriend, Sienna or something – or did you say they're married?'

'Oh Irene, you haven't changed a bit.' Kathy laughed. 'You're still holding a candle for him after all these years, aren't you?'

'God no,' Irene said, lowering her voice and getting up to nudge the door to the sitting room closed. 'Just curious. He's the father of my child and it's no harm to keep up to date with what he's doing.'

'*Right* . . . Of *course* . . .' Kathy said with exaggerated emphasis. 'I believe you, thousands wouldn't. But yeah, he's moving down here to West Cork. Though what he'll find to do in Schull after the bright lights of London, I really don't know.'

Irene said nothing, and Kathy went on to answer her other question without making her repeat it.

'And yes, the new girlfriend is coming – she's a barmaid from his local, blonde, half his age – the usual.'

Still Irene said nothing.

'Ah, Irene, I was only joking earlier about holding a candle – you're not still hankering after him, are you? He's my brother and I'll love him to my grave but he's . . . Well, look what he did, running off on you. And the rest of it.'

And the rest of it. That was about as close as Kathy ever got to referring to Rob's record and time in prison. She was absolutely certain he had been set up and wrongly imprisoned for every one of his sixteen convictions, and Irene knew from experience she'd bite the head off anyone who implied differently.

111

'Jesus, not at all, I'm only curious. And wanted to be sure he wasn't going to turn up at my door, bothering me.'

'No,' Kathy said, gently now, 'he'll be down here in Schull, not bothering you at all.'

Back in the sitting room, Frank was still watching the news.

'Did you get her?' he asked, muting again.

'Yeah, and she doesn't think they've ever been in touch. So that's that, I suppose. I don't even know why I wanted to know.'

Frank stared at her. 'You can hardly say "that's that" – the scrapbook you found is a sideshow, Irene. The real story is here.' He jerked a thumb at the television. 'Caroline is all over the news for kidnapping a child who is still missing, and I'm increasingly uncomfortable with the fact that we haven't spoken to the police. This isn't going to look good for me in the bank if my name is attached to it, but it'll be even worse if they realize we delayed.'

Oh, Frank. Always obsessing over doing the right thing. She shook her head. 'It's not up to us to call the guards – if they want us, it's their job to find us. And like I keep telling you, we've nothing to say that'll help find that child.'

And that's when the knock came at the door.

22

Three months earlier

CARRIE WATCHED AS JENNY kissed Jacob's head and sent him to brush his teeth, staring after him as he ran up the stairs, a look of wonder on her face. What was there to be so astonished about? He was a kid, like any kid. Not a bad kid, admittedly. But the way she mooned over him. Like she was the first mother, and he was the first son. Carrie didn't hate Jenny, but sometimes she wanted to punch her.

Jenny turned unexpectedly, and Carrie rearranged her face into a smile. Looking sheepish, Jenny dropped her gaze.

'I know I dote over him,' she said, not quite but almost reading her nanny's mind.

'He's a great kid,' Carrie said, the words coming automatically. She'd learned this language well in the time she'd been picking Jacob up from preschool. The inane mommy talk. The way they all exalted their own children as though they were somehow unique. Standing outside the preschool, swapping stories of baby nap-times and toddler sleep-times. They had no idea how boring they were.

'Listen, Richie's still away in Scotland,' Jenny was saying, 'will we grab a glass of wine?'

Bonding time, to make up for yesterday's fly-swatting incident, no doubt.

'Sure,' Carrie said, ducking her head shyly, the way Carrie Finch would. Carrie Holohan would have preferred a vodka, but she knew better than to ask.

'Great! I'll do Jacob's story, you go ahead and open a bottle.'

Jenny paused, perhaps wondering if Carrie Finch could operate a wine opener. Carrie watched her face as she wrestled with the question – would it be rude to ask if she could use a cork-screw? Jenny obviously decided it would. A brief smile and she was gone, after her precious son.

An hour and a half later, the first bottle was empty and Jenny was opening a second.

'I never do this on a work night!' she said. 'But it feels good to let loose every now and then. Especially with this new job . . . I still think they're going to turn around any day and tell me the promotion was a mistake.' A splash of wine went over the side of Carrie's glass as Jenny poured. 'God, sorry! I'm half cut already.'

Carrie smiled. 'Don't worry. Your job sounds stressful.' And extremely boring, she wanted to add, as she grabbed kitchen roll to mop up the spill.

'I shouldn't complain, it's what I wanted. Everyone thought my colleague Mark was going to get the promotion – even I thought that!' Jenny laughed. 'He's been a pet about it. Like, *lovely*.'

'Sounds like a good guy.'

'He's fab,' she said, slurring slightly. 'A bit too fab sometimes.'

'Oh?'

Jenny waved it away, like she was swatting a fly. Ironic.

'Don't mind me. It's just that he's a very kind man, and sometimes he's nicer to me than my own husband is. Lots of times.' She paused. 'There was this one night on a work trip when he was maybe a bit *too* nice. But I resisted. Just about.' She grinned sloppily, then seemed to remember who she was talking to. 'Anyway, enough about me, how're things with you? All OK at pick-up today?'

'All good,' Carrie said.

'Do you get the chance to chat to any of the other minders or mothers?'

'Not really. The parents talk to the other parents, and most of the childminders know each other – the Brazilian ones seem to anyway.'

Jenny's face fell.

'Ah, I'm sorry. It must be lonely for you? You'd think they'd make an effort!'

Carrie shrugged and did the shy smile thing again.

'I don't mind. The mothers all seem really nice, there's no badness in it.'

Jenny's face changed again.

'You must miss your own mother – you were young when she passed away?' she asked, slurring softly.

'Yes,' Carrie said, giving her what she came for. 'I think about her a lot.'

'What was she like?' she asked, in therapist mode now. *Oh Jenny, you do try*, Carrie thought, *I have to give you that.*

'She was beautiful,' she said out loud, picturing Irene's hard, sun-damaged face. 'She had gorgeous long red hair, much nicer than mine, a darker shade. She was small, softly spoken.'

Carrie thought back to the last time she saw Irene. Roaring at her. *I never should have had you. I should have gotten rid of you. He'd have stayed with me, and I'd never have gone through sixteen years of hell, trying to raise you right.*

'She was soft and kind, so gentle,' Carrie went on, as Jenny's eyes started to glisten.

115

'Ah, you must miss her terribly. Have you any photos?'

'Yes, one of both my parents on my bedside locker here,' Carrie told her, wondering if Jenny had ever snooped in her room and seen the framed photo she'd nicked from the hostel. She didn't think so. Snooping would be beneath Jenny. Kyle had seen it once and asked her what it was about – why she had a framed photo of two complete strangers in her bedroom. She told him they were Carrie Finch's parents, and he looked at her like she was taking all of this a bit too seriously. But she wasn't. She knew what she was doing. She took another sip of wine and smiled a sad smile at Jenny, whose eyes were still glistening. She knew exactly what she was doing.

23

Irene
Monday – three days missing

IRENE SURVEYED THE TWO gardaí. The one called McConville –
Detective Sergeant McConville apparently – was fairly fond of
herself. Peachy skin and highlighted hair and a bossy voice that
didn't quite hide her posh accent. The Breen fella was like a
long drink of water. Did he mind having a woman as a boss?
Irene scrutinized him as he stood by the fireplace, notebook in
hand. Light hair, pale skin, red cheeks, watery blue eyes. A
nothing-y kind of fella who looked like he joined the guards
because his mammy told him to.

Frank had moved and McConville was now sitting on the
two-seater couch in his place.

'Mrs Holohan, we're looking for a missing twenty-five-year-
old woman called Carrie Finch, and we believe she may be
your daughter?'

Irene tilted her head and gazed across at McConville.

'That's not correct,' she said.

Frank stiffened beside her. Poor old Frank, the only time he
ever saw the guards was getting his passport form signed.

'You're claiming you're not Carrie Finch's mother?' McConville sounded unconvinced.

'You're wrong about my *name*. It's Mrs Turner. Not Holohan.'

McConville's mouth twitched and her eyes narrowed. This might turn out to be fun.

'Apologies, Mrs Turner.' No trace of impatience. 'Is Carrie Finch your daughter?'

'I don't have a daughter called Carrie Finch, no.'

Frank turned to look at her, a worried frown on his face. But McConville was having none of it.

'I see. But you do have a daughter called Carrie?' she asked, with a hint of a smile.

'Maybe I do.'

Irene sensed rather than saw the eye-roll from Breen as he shifted from one foot to the other.

'Mrs Turner, this is a serious matter. As I'm sure you're aware, a four-year-old boy is missing, along with your daughter Carrie. Has she been in touch with you?'

Irene relented. 'Yes, I have a daughter. Caroline. No, she hasn't been in touch.'

'When is the last time you saw your daughter?'

'Nine years ago. She moved out when she was sixteen and I haven't heard from her since.'

'Right.' McConville sat back on the couch, visibly relaxing at what she must have seen as a breakthrough in the interview. 'And do you know where she is now – do you have any mutual contacts?'

'No.'

McConville sat forward again.

'Mrs Turner, any help you can give us could be instrumental in getting this little boy safely home. Do you understand that?'

Irene shrugged. 'What do you want me to say? We're not in touch, haven't been for years, and we have no "mutual contacts".'

'What about her father?'

Frank shifted again, this was way out of his comfort zone –
cops and Rob all in one evening.

'What about him?'

Irene was sure she heard a mutter from under Breen's breath –
McConville shot him a look. This was a lot more fun than the
usual Monday evening soaps.

'Is he in touch with Carrie?' McConville said, enunciating
every word slowly and carefully, as if she was speaking to a
naughty child. Irene had a sudden flashback to the time she was
caught nicking penny-sweets from the shop on the corner. Her
mam had told those coppers where to go, while Irene hid behind
her skirt, smirking. Then her mam had beaten Irene with the
wooden spoon for being stupid enough to get caught.

'No, Caroline doesn't know who her dad is, he ran off as
soon as he found out I was pregnant.'

Frank looked at her again, clearly worried about the part of
that sentence that wasn't true. Well, it would have been true if
they'd asked her two days ago, at least as far as she knew, so
that was enough.

'Can you give me his full name, please?' That was Breen, self-
important with his notebook.

'Robert Murphy.' She smirked at him. Good luck trawling
through all the Robert Murphys in the world, her smirk said,
and she knew he caught it.

'And where is Robert Murphy now – where does he live, and
what does he do for a living?'

'London, and no idea what he does for a living. How would
I know?'

Breen let out an audible stream of air through his teeth.

'OK, back to your daughter. Could you tell me about Carrie
as a child?'

Irene looked at McConville's grey eyes and creamy skin and

wisps of blonde hair falling out of her ponytail. A woman who'd never had a second of hardship in her life. What would she know about how real people lived and why they did the things they did? And here she was, expecting that her badge could make Irene talk, cough up a lifetime of stories to make her job easier. Well, she had another think coming.

'A normal child, like any other.'

Frank gave her a sideways look. Jesus, he hardly thought she was going to start telling the guards about Caroline robbing from her purse and taking drugs, did he?

'What kind of childhood did she have?'

'Normal.'

Irene could feel the *for fuck's sake* vibes from Breen now and she wanted to smile but held it in.

'Did you ever live in a big house in the country – between Bray and Enniskerry?'

Where was this coming from? Had they mixed Caroline up with someone else after all? Irene shook her head. 'No, we never lived anywhere but St Colman's, and then here. Where did you get that from?'

McConville ignored that question and went on to the next one. 'Any trouble at school? Any behavioural or mental health issues? Come on, Mrs Turner, anything you can tell us will be a huge help.' A pause. She pulled something from a file on her knee. 'Have you seen the photos of Milo on the news? Look at him, four years old. His parents are frantic. Please, help us.'

She held out the photo and Irene hesitated, then stretched across to take it. A different photo to the one that'd been on the news, but the same bright blond hair, down to his shoulders, bright blue eyes and a cheeky smile. He was a cute kid all right, no denying it. What the hell was Caroline doing kidnapping him?

'Mrs Turner.'

'Yes.'

'Any behavioural or mental health issues?'

'No.' Irene sighed, still looking at the photo. The game was getting old now. 'No mental health issues as you call them, not that we'd have got any help if there were.'

Frank patted her hand.

'And what about trouble – any friends or acquaintances who had run-ins with the law?'

An image of Kyle Byrde flashed into Irene's mind. The boy next door, only nothing sweet about him. Throwing stones when he was five, empty beer bottles a few years later. Nicking stuff from wherever he could, guards on the doorstep every other night by the time she and Caroline were packing up to leave, Mrs Byrde adamant her son had done nothing wrong. A scapegoat, because the guards were too lazy to do proper investigations, she always used to say. Irene had little faith in the guards but when it came to Kyle Byrde, they'd been spot on.

'No,' she said to McConville, 'no one I can think of at all.'

Frank waited until McConville and Breen were back inside their car before he spoke, and even then, it was in a whisper.

'Irene, why didn't you help them?'

'I did help them. I answered all their questions.'

She curled her legs up on the sofa and tucked her feet under her, checking the time. Had she missed the soaps?

'But you were . . .' He was struggling to put a word on it. 'Holding back.'

'I answered what they asked. You don't give anything to the guards unless you have to.'

'Irene!' He took the remote out of her hand. This wasn't the mild-mannered Frank she was used to. 'I don't understand why

121

you were so . . . obtuse. Surely any right-minded citizen would be doing anything and everything to help?'

She stood up. 'I'll give you *obtuse*, Frank Turner, I'll give you *right-minded citizen*,' she hissed. 'You can't trust them, Frank. Only people who grow up in fancy houses like you did think you can.' To her great surprise, her eyes were wet.

Frank ran a hand over his head. He wasn't used to this, they never fought. She told him what to do and he did it. It was why she'd married him in the first place.

But it was time he had his eyes opened to reality. There was no right or wrong, no good or bad, just people who were born on one side of the tracks, and people born on the other.

24

Jenny
Tuesday – four days missing

NOBODY IS LOOKING AT *you, you're just being paranoid, they're all too busy with their own lives.* Jenny repeated it silently, over and over, as she and Jacob walked into Esther's Tea Garden on Tuesday afternoon. But who was she kidding. The sea of faces were all turned one way and one way only, eyeing up the woman who'd hired the kidnapper.

Cheeks flaming, eyes down, she slid into a seat at the only free table and helped Jacob with his jacket.

'Can I have a babyccino with my brownie?' he asked, blissfully oblivious to the stares. 'And extra marshmallows for Jem?' he added, nodding towards the teddy under his arm.

'Yes to the babyccino, no to extra marshmallows, but nice try.'

He nodded and clambered on to the wooden chair, perching Jem on his lap. She pulled crayons and a colouring book from her bag and watched as he started to colour.

'Any news at school today?' she asked quietly, scrutinizing his face. He didn't look up from his colouring as he shook his head.

The school had called an assembly that morning to tell the children Milo was missing – texts had been sent to all the

123

parents on Monday afternoon to let them know it was coming. The principal said she knew it might be upsetting for the children, but was also worried they'd hear it anyway and feel even more anxious. Some of the parents had been complaining about it at drop-off – not appropriate, they said, the kids were too young. But then what could the school do, Jenny wondered; it was all over the news and there were posters on every lamp post. Better to hear it from the principal or a parent than to see it on the TV.

She and Richie had decided to tell Jacob themselves after they saw the text. He'd had surprisingly few questions, but then kids that age tended to take things in their stride. Jenny had gone on to warn him about going off with strangers.

Did Milo go with a stranger? he'd asked.

She and Richie had looked at one another. They weren't ready to tell him who took Milo. So they told him they weren't sure what happened but they knew he'd turn up safe, and that Carrie was on holidays. Jenny waited for him to put two and two together, but he didn't. *Long may that innocence last*, she thought, watching him colour.

'What can I get you,' came a voice, 'and for this little man here?'

Jenny looked up to see an older woman with a mass of curly hair and a twinkly smile.

'A brownie for Jacob, and I'll take a cappuccino, please.'

'Anything to eat? We've just two scones left, but lots of cakes and muffins?'

'Oh, no thanks.'

'Mummy!' Jacob looked up, eyes wide.

'What is it?'

'My babyccino!' Then he was back to colouring.

She laughed. 'Sorry, yes, a babyccino. God, I'm on edge. I didn't know what he was going to say there.'

'We all are, don't worry. I'll get those for you now.' The lady headed back behind the counter.

'Jacob, did they say anything about Milo at school?'

'They said he's gone away but the police are going to find him and bring him home.'

'And . . . did anyone say who he went away with?'

A woman at the next table glanced over and whispered something to her friend. Jenny focused on Jacob.

'A boy in yard told me he went with Carrie.'

Her stomach clenched. 'And what did you say?'

Jacob looked up, pulling Jem closer to him.

'I said Carrie is *my* minder, not Milo's. If she goed on a holiday she would bring me, not him.' His lower lip stuck out as he looked up at her, waiting for her to tell him otherwise. She stared, with no idea what to say next. Then the curly-haired lady swooped in, putting a tiny cup of foamed milk in front of Jacob.

'Now, young man, this coffee is for you, and here's one for your mammy. I have a brownie here, anyone waiting for it?' She pretended to look around. Jacob raised his hand.

'Me!'

She put it down and put a giant scone in front of Jenny.

'It'll only go to waste if someone doesn't take it. On the house.' She smiled and walked to the door to sign for a delivery. Jenny started to call after her, to tell her there was no need, but suddenly she was ravenous. Jacob ate his brownie without ever putting down his crayon, and Jenny checked her emails. Nothing that couldn't wait until morning. She watched as the lady sent a younger girl out to the bank to get change. Maybe she was the manager, or the owner. The eponymous Esther, presumably. And suddenly she remembered the voice on the phone Friday night – the woman who'd called her when Marissa first discovered Milo wasn't where he was supposed to be.

'Excuse me,' she called, raising her hand. The woman came over, still smiling. 'This is going to sound weird, but are you Esther who was with Marissa Irvine the other night?'

The woman nodded. 'I am, and you're Jenny Kennedy? I recognized you from a photo on the internet.'

'Yeah, the papers took my Facebook profile picture, they didn't even ask.'

'You know how it is – the papers look for anything they can publish with something like this.'

Jenny shook herself. 'Listen to me, complaining about a silly picture, it's hardly a big deal in the middle of what's going on.'

'Well, the whole thing is strange for everyone. I think I'd be the same if someone put a photo of me on the internet.'

'And they didn't?' Jenny asked. 'Even though it was your address Carrie put in the message?'

'No, but I'm not that interesting, and I've no Facebook for them to borrow photos from.' The woman's eyes twinkled, and suddenly Jenny had the most overwhelming sense of gladness that this was the person to catch Marissa when her world came crashing down on Friday night.

'I wonder why Carrie picked your address – do you think it was deliberate?'

'Just a random address, I'd imagine,' Esther said after a pause. 'I've never met her anyway, so I can't imagine why she'd pick me. But how are *you* doing?'

Jenny stirred her almost-gone coffee. 'Oh, you know, just busy being that woman who hired the kidnapper.' She laughed but it came out high and stretched.

'When mine were small,' Esther said, 'I used to leave them outside the shop in the pram while I went in. Nothing ever happened. But nobody would do it today, even though life isn't any more dangerous now than it was back then. We just *hear* all about the danger more than we did before – TV, internet. But the thing is, we all get on with life as best we can, following the rules and the norms of our time. It's perfectly normal to hire a childminder to look after your children, and that's all you did.'

'But if I had just taken more care . . .'

'Did you cut corners? Did you have a bad feeling but hire her anyway? Did you forget to check her references?'

'Oh, God no! I checked everything, spoke to her previous employers, I was so careful – I wouldn't let any old person mind Jacob.'

'Well, there you go. You did everything correctly and you couldn't have known any better. There is only one person at fault for the disappearance of that little boy, and it's not you, pet.' She put her hand on Jenny's, nodded emphatically, then turned to clear plates from the two gawping ladies at the next table. 'If everyone spent more time helping and less time gossiping, wouldn't we all be better off,' Esther added in a slightly louder voice, to no one in particular.

Jenny swallowed and stared down at her half-eaten scone, her eyes blurred with unexpected tears.

25

Jenny
Tuesday – four days missing

RICHIE'S VOICE WAS STILL ringing in Jenny's ears when she pulled up outside Maple Lodge on Tuesday night: *Stop feeling guilty, it's not your fault, but if you keep turning up at their house they're going to think you're in some way to blame.* And she could see his point – the police seemed satisfied that neither Jenny nor Richie had any idea what Carrie was planning and Richie couldn't understand why she wouldn't take herself out of the situation. But Marissa's tear-streaked face was on her mind constantly, and every time she looked at Jacob, her stomach churned. It could so easily have been him. If the Irvines were going to read something into it, so be it. That's what she'd told Richie, resolute in her plan, though as she got out of the car and pressed the doorbell, she wasn't feeling quite so confident. Especially if Peter was there.

But it was someone else entirely who answered the door – a very tall, thin man with a shock of dark hair and pale, waxy features. He had a phone in one hand and just about looked up from it as she started to explain who she was.

'Hi, I'm Jenny, a . . . friend of Marissa's. She said to call in for more posters?'

'Right. Come through,' he said, turning to walk back into the house.

She followed him to the kitchen, where Marissa and a man she recognized as her business partner were separating bundles of posters and flyers into piles.

'Jenny!' Marissa stood and hugged her. She turned to the tall man who had answered the door. 'Brian, this is my friend Jenny, she's been a terrific help. Jenny, this is Peter's brother Brian – also a terrific help, the third in our trio of Irvine Musketeers. He lives in the other house on the grounds, but luckily for us, he spends most of his time here.' She smiled, the easy smile of a natural hostess, then stopped and shook her head as if remembering again there was nothing to smile about.

Brian gazed at her for a moment, then walked through to the sitting room, looking at his phone.

'Brian is coordinating the printing, and though his people skills can be, um, quirky, he is an absolute trooper,' Marissa said quietly. 'And this is Colin.' She gestured to her business partner. He stood, his pink cheeks pinkening further as he held out his hand.

'Colin Dobson, solicitor, college friend, all round dogsbody, at your service.'

Jenny took his hand. He reminded her of an overgrown schoolboy – ruddy cheeks and wide-set, puppy eyes – in a suit that looked like he'd borrowed it from his dad. Only he was probably in his mid-thirties and way past borrowing suits from anyone.

'Hiya, I'm Jenny.' She turned back to Marissa. 'I thought I could take some more posters?'

'Thanks, Jenny, that would be great. Have you time for a cup of tea?' Marissa asked, and she looked so imploring, Jenny couldn't say anything but yes.

'Where's that woman who was here making tea yesterday?'

Colin asked, looking around, as though he expected a tea lady or housekeeper of some kind to materialize out of the woodwork.

'Esther?' Marissa asked.

'Yeah – the lady with the curly hair, looks like she belongs in a kids' fairy-tale book – is she not working today?'

'Colin, Esther doesn't work here – she's been helping us with the search.'

He scratched his head. 'Oh, right.' He looked at Jenny, then over at the kettle, and back to Jenny.

'Col, would you mind sticking on the kettle,' Marissa said patiently. 'I need to talk to Jenny.'

Colin lumbered over to the counter, still scratching his head, and Jenny sat.

'My partner in the solicitor's,' Marissa whispered. 'Better at his job than he looks, I promise.'

Jenny would have to take her word for it. She pointed at a pile of posters. 'Is there anywhere in particular you'd like me to go next?'

'We had a huge number of volunteers out today so we've actually covered most of south Dublin now. People have been amazing.' Her voice started to break. She cleared her throat. 'We're going north-side tomorrow, but the big thing is social media, we can reach far more people that way.'

'I've seen the photos online, you're getting huge coverage.'

'We are, but it'll wane – from what I hear, these things always do. The next shiny thing comes along and people move on.' She sounded cynical and panicky all at once.

'Maybe I can help? I'm in business development now but my background is marketing. Though you probably have experts who'd be way better than me . . .'

'Well, Brian found this guy Michael who actually does it for a living – can you imagine? Running high-profile missing persons campaigns as your job. It must be soul-destroying . . .' She trailed off, lost for a moment, maybe remembering that's what they were actually talking about – her missing child. Jenny glanced over at Colin who was waiting by the kettle, frowning at something on his phone.

Marissa shook herself. 'Anyway, Michael is great but kind of . . . cold? I suppose you have to be. So yes, if you have any advice on the online side of things, I'd be grateful.'

Jenny looked at Marissa – the dark circles, the sunken cheeks – she looked like she'd aged a decade since Friday. How was she even still able to speak? Jenny wasn't sure she'd function at all if anything happened to Jacob. But then falling apart wouldn't get him back.

'Anything I can do, I will. Do you want me to take a look at what you're doing now and throw out suggestions?'

Marissa nodded and slid an iPad across the table.

Jenny had seen the photos and read the description a hundred times since Friday, but she read it again now:

> *Milo Irvine, age 4, blond, shoulder-length hair, blue eyes, 1m tall. Small for his age, may look younger. Last seen wearing Kerryglen National School tracksuit: navy crested sweatshirt and navy tracksuit bottoms. Navy and bright green Skechers trainers, lime-green rain jacket with silver dinosaur print.*

'That's from the *Find Milo Irvine* Facebook page,' Marissa said. 'People have been sharing it all over the place.'

'What about a video?' Jenny said. 'Video is huge now and gets greater reach online. Do you have some clips of Milo?'

Marissa picked up her phone and put in her ear buds without saying anything. Jenny watched as Marissa scrolled. The kettle came to a stop and Colin started his search for mugs. *Why wouldn't you do that while the kettle is boiling*, Jenny wondered. Marissa was still scrolling, eyes down, chin buried. As Jenny watched, she realized Marissa's shoulders had started to shake. Her finger had stopped moving on the screen. With a tiny splash, a tear hit the phone, then another. Jenny said nothing, she just sat and waited while Marissa watched her son on her phone but not in real life.

It was Colin who jolted them back when he put a mug of tea in front of each of them.

'Will I get milk?' he asked Marissa.

She looked up, as though she had no idea who he was.

'Thanks, Colin, there's probably some in the fridge,' Jenny said. He ambled over to the huge American-style fridge and began scanning the shelves. Jenny put her hand on Marissa's knee. Marissa took out the ear buds.

'Is that the first time you've watched a video since Friday?' Jenny asked.

Marissa nodded, and inwardly, Jenny flinched from the pain in her eyes.

'Is it one you could share online?'

Marissa nodded again and took a sip of black tea that was surely still too hot.

'Do you need to check with Peter or with the guy who's advising you?'

Marissa looked unsure. Who knew the rules of these things, if indeed there were any.

On cue, the kitchen door opened and Peter arrived. He stopped and a look crossed his face when he saw Jenny, but whatever he was about to say, a glance from Marissa stopped him.

'Jenny's helping with social media, she has a background in marketing.' She said it in a way that made it clear there was no room for debate. 'And we're going to put a video online, because it will get more attention than photos.'

Again, Peter looked like he wanted to say something, but he just nodded.

'Can you or Brian let Michael know?'

He nodded again and leaned against the breakfast bar. He looked grey and exhausted. 'Is Brian here?'

Marissa pointed to the sitting room. 'In there, on the phone.'

As she spoke, Brian came back into the kitchen, still clutching his phone. He nodded at his brother.

'Did you get those posters I told you to get?' Peter asked him.

Brian nodded. 'I dropped them at the search centre.'

'And leaflets? The right size this time?'

Jenny cringed at Peter's tone but Brian didn't seem fazed. Maybe work and home lines were blurred for the Irvines.

'Yes, right size.'

Marissa looked at the two men. 'Thanks, Brian, you've been brilliant. The leaflets are perfect.'

Brian nodded at Marissa, his eyes unreadable. Then he cleared his throat and held up his phone. 'Lia is coming home. Flying in on Saturday from JFK.'

Peter looked surprised. 'Really?'

'Their younger sister,' Marissa mouthed to Jenny. 'Black sheep.'

'Yes. She just texted. Said she wants to help.'

Peter shook his head, clearly not convinced his sister could be much help. Jenny thought she might like to meet the person who was a black sheep in this family of over-achievers.

Brian shrugged. 'The more people we have on the ground, the better.'

'Yes, but Lia won't be helping, she'll have some madcap idea that makes no sense to anyone else. She'll be a distraction.'

Marissa stood and walked over to put her hand on Peter's arm.

'It'll be OK, she's just worried. Family rally around in times like this, it's normal.'

Peter hugged Marissa to him and kissed the top of her head. 'You're right, I'm just stressed and not being fair.'

She hugged him back, burying her head in his chest, and then they were both sobbing, wrapped together, shaking, oblivious to the onlookers. Colin took out his phone and ambled into the sitting room. Brian watched Marissa and Peter for a moment, an odd look on his face, then followed Colin. And Jenny, feeling like a voyeur to their grief, stuffed some posters in her bag and slipped quietly out the door.

26

Marissa

Tuesday – four days missing

LOST. THAT'S HOW MARISSA felt when she looked up and realized Jenny was gone. Lost, again. Her *actual* best friends had been over on Sunday – arriving in a pack, safety in numbers – but it was odd and somehow not as comforting as it should have been. Maybe because they were too close; friends since college, women who knew everything about one another, and about each other's children. Somehow it made it hard to be around them. They'd shared their own traumatic birth stories after Milo's traumatic birth (not *before*, of course, because who does that) and they were great at reading the signs – knowing not to ask about the horrific aftermath, the time she never wanted to talk about. They spent hours visiting with their babies, swapping sagas of sleepless nights, when she finally came home from hospital. They'd always been there for her. And it made no sense at all, but she almost couldn't bear to be around them now. Even Tara, who was a psychologist and could potentially help. But they reminded her too much of life before *this*. Jenny was new. Jenny came *after* this. She was a stranger. And that made it easier to be around her.

'She'll be back,' Peter said, reading her mind. 'Though how she could have hired that—'

135

She put a finger against his lips. 'Please don't. There's no point raking over it, and she's doing everything she can to help. The video idea was—'

She stopped as the doorbell rang. Who was calling at this time of night?

'I'll get it,' came Brian's voice, and they stood still, listening.

Then the kitchen door opened, and Brian, even paler than usual, led Detective Sergeant McConville through. In her hand, a clear plastic bag.

And in the bag, a lime-green raincoat with silver dinosaurs.

Marissa stared at it, then ran to the kitchen sink and threw up. Peter was straight over, rubbing her back, and she could feel the sobs running from his body into hers. She didn't want to look up, she didn't want to hear whatever it was McConville was going to say. She didn't want to see the jacket ever again but she did, she wanted to take it and hold it and smell him.

Oh God, Milo.

She collapsed against the counter and slid to the floor. Peter dropped beside her, his arm around her now, working to choke back sobs. McConville was saying something but Marissa couldn't make it out, the white noise inside her head was too loud. Brian was over to them then, stooping down, his hand on Peter's shoulder.

'Listen,' he was saying, 'you have to listen.'

Wiping their faces, they both looked towards McConville as she stepped closer, still holding the bag.

'I need you to tell me if this is Milo's jacket,' McConville was saying. 'The one he was wearing on Friday?'

Peter looked to Marissa for confirmation even though he surely knew as well as she did. Of course it was Milo's.

'Where?' was all Marissa could say.

Oh God, oh God, oh God, please let him be OK.

'It was found on Killiney Hill.'

'Killiney Hill?'

It was a favourite spot for crisp sunny winter walks and warm summer picnics. Milo loved the hot chocolate in the cafe half-way up the hill, and running on the rocks at the top, looking out over Dublin and the sea below.

'Where on Killiney Hill?' Marissa asked, bile in her throat.

McConville hesitated, the first time she'd done so since Friday.

'We found it on the rocks on the south side of the hill.'

'The rocks that lead down to the sea?' Peter asked in a whisper.

McConville nodded and hunkered down. When she spoke again, her voice was softer.

'The coastguard has been alerted and the Water Unit is on the way.'

No, no, no, no, no! Marissa was screaming but she couldn't tell if it was out loud or in her head. McConville's hand was on hers, and Brian was saying something about a doctor. She was aware of Peter still sitting beside her, his arm around her, shaking and sobbing. She stared at the plastic bag and the little green jacket with the familiar beloved dinosaurs, and felt something inside her shatter.

27

Jenny
Tuesday – four days missing

JENNY'S HANDS WERE STILL shaking when she put her key in the door, and she was so preoccupied with what she'd seen when she was driving away from the Irvines' – the little raincoat, the plastic bag – she didn't notice at first that Adeline's coat was on the end of the bannister. In the sitting room, her mother-in-law was perched on the edge of the couch, deep in conversation with Richie. Jenny coughed, and they both looked up.

'Jenny! Richie tells me you were over with those poor Irvine people again – are you sure it's wise? Maybe they don't need hordes of rubberneckers descending on them.'

Rubberneckers. Jenny sighed inwardly.

'I suppose the more people they have helping with the search, the sooner they'll find Milo.'

'But you weren't searching, were you, dear, you were in their house. That's hardly the same thing?'

'Oh – I was collecting flyers,' Jenny said, adding, 'I can give you some to hand out when you're leaving?'

'Goodness, not with my arthritis.'

This was the first Jenny had heard of any arthritis, Richie too by the look on his face.

'How's Jacob?' she asked her husband.

'All good, full of chat about his trip to the cafe earlier. He seemed to enjoy spending time with you.'

Was he making a point? She shook herself. *Come on, Jenny, stop overthinking, he's just being nice.*

'I loved it too. Actually, the owner of the coffee shop is Esther – the person who lives in Tudor Grove, where Carrie sent Marissa.'

'Bit strange her address was used, does she know why?' Richie asked.

'No idea. She seems lovely though. There were some women in the coffee shop giving me the evil eye and she was having none of it.'

'Can't be helped,' Adeline said brusquely, before Richie had a chance to reply.

'What do you mean?'

'The "evil eye", as you call it. You did hire the woman after all, you have to take your share of the blame.'

'Mum!' Richie hissed.

'I've always been a straight-talker, Richard, you know that. Jenny hired that woman and she kidnapped a child. There's no other way to look at it.'

Jenny stared at her mother-in-law, her perfectly set hair, her overdone make-up, the red talons at the end of bony, heavily ringed fingers, and at that moment, she hated her. But as always, she bit back what she wanted to say.

'Sorry, I'm wrecked, maybe we can chat about this another time. And you don't want to be driving too late at night,' she said quietly.

Adeline's brow crinkled, her dark red lips set in a thin line.

'I'll go when Richie wants me to go, and not before.'

'Adeline, I just meant—' Jenny started, but Richie interrupted.

'Mum, I'm sorry but Jenny is right, it's time to go. You might call it straight-talking but to the rest of us, it sounds rude. Jenny and I hired Carrie together, and if it's on her, it's on me. You're welcome here, but not if you speak to Jenny like that.'

Without a word, Adeline got up from the sofa, and with great agility for a woman who had just developed arthritis, she stalked across the room, grabbed her coat, and stormed out the front door. Richie and Jenny looked at one another and burst into laughter.

'Oh God, Richie, you've done it now – you'll be out of the will!'

Later, over an uncharacteristic Tuesday-night bottle of wine, she told him about her visit to Maple Lodge and the encounters with Colin and Brian. And about what she saw as she left – the police car pulling up, the guard who got out and rang the bell. About the transparent bag holding the little green raincoat mentioned in every description of Milo Irvine since he disappeared. It wasn't looking good, she told Richie. They were on the same sofa for the first time in a while, she realized, curled up facing one another from opposite ends. Phones aside, TV on mute, wine in hand, actually talking.

Then her phone beeped and broke the spell. She glanced at it but didn't pick it up. It beeped again. Still she didn't react.

'Work, I suppose.' Richie sighed, standing up. 'I'm going to bed anyway. I'm taking the Fourth Years to the Natural History Museum tomorrow so I'm going to need all my energy. Not as big a deal as *your* work,' he continued, nodding towards her phone, 'but still.'

As he walked through to rinse his glass in the kitchen, Jenny picked up her phone. Two messages, both from Mark. Instinctively, she tilted her body so she and the screen were facing away from the doorway. As the sound of running water drifted in from the kitchen, she clicked into the first message.

How're you doing – you looked very shook at work this morning again, just thought I'd see if you're ok?

And the second one:

That came out wrong. By shook I don't mean bad! You looked great as ever, but I can see this is hitting you hard. I'm here if you ever need to talk xx

Her fingers hovered over her phone, but she didn't know what to reply. Was he crossing a work colleague line, or was she overthinking again? If he were a female colleague, it wouldn't matter at all. But then maybe that was the point: he wasn't. She started typing.

We should probably stick to email, think it's a work policy or something . . .

Too much. Mark would be baffled – he was only being friendly. So why was she hiding the phone screen from her husband? And why – she put her hand to her face – were her cheeks suddenly flaming?

Richie stuck his head around the door and she put the phone on her knee, screen down.

'I'm going up, goodnight,' he said curtly. Adeline's unintended bubble of bonding had well and truly burst.

Sighing, Jenny picked up the remote and unmuted the TV. On screen, Pacey from *Dawson's Creek* was arguing with another man. Only he wasn't Pacey any more, of course, and it wasn't *Dawson's*

Creek – those days were long gone. Jenny's one-time crush now had stubble and fine lines, and was called Cole, it seemed.

Suddenly, she sat up straighter. The on-screen argument was escalating, and 'Cole' had just called the other man Caleb. Cole and Caleb. Jenny pressed the Info button on the remote to find out the name of the show. She typed it into her phone and began to read.

Minutes later, she put down her phone. Carrie's 'brothers' were straight from an American TV series called *The Affair*. Caleb, Cole and Scotty Lockhart. Jenny shook her head. Carrie had been laughing up her sleeve at all of them. And they still had no idea why.

28

Two months earlier

JENNY STARED AT THE crowd through which Marissa had disappeared to make her call, suddenly self-conscious as she stood on her own in the hotel function room. She took a big swallow of prosecco, plucked her phone from her bag, and pretended to check her messages.

Within seconds, the Coven had swooped in and surrounded her.

'So, you met the lovely Marissa,' Sarah said, her fake smile even wider than before. 'She's *so* nice, isn't she? And so *confident*. It's great to see someone so sure of themselves, isn't it?'

Ouch.

'She seems great, yes,' Jenny said, wondering already how to extricate herself. But other than Marissa, who was still outside on the phone, she knew nobody in the room. And it was a bit soon for the bathroom excuse again, even if now she actually did need to go.

'She knows *everyone*,' Grace said with naked yearning. 'I have three kids in the school and I don't know half as many people.'

'Yes, well, it's not the be all and end all,' Victor said. 'You can *know* people, but that's not the same as having friends, is it?'

Ouch again.

'That's her husband over there, he looks nice,' Jenny tried.

'Oh yes, the golden couple, Peter and Marissa Irvine, and their so-called gifted son. There's a lot to be said for living in the real world though,' Sarah said. 'I don't know if it's good for kids to be brought up in huge houses with nannies and servants and no attention from their actual parents.'

'They have *servants*?' Victor said, spluttering into his wine.

'Well, not literally, but you know what I mean.'

'Marissa's stunning, isn't she?' Grace said, raw envy in her voice.

'She looks good,' Sarah conceded, 'but it's all surgical. I mean, we could all do that if we were so inclined.'

'But wasn't it a medical thing – some kind of accident a few years ago, back before they moved here? She needed skin grafts or something?' Grace said. 'It's not like she went under the knife deliberately. Not that there would be anything wrong with that,' she added hurriedly, perhaps unsure of her audience.

'That's the story. Handy that she *needed* it though, wasn't it?' Sarah said, tapping the side of her nose. 'Like a great excuse for suddenly looking way better than before without having to admit going for cosmetic surgery. "Oh, it was *medical*."'

'Wow, are you serious?' Grace's eyes were wide at the gossip.

'I heard it from a girl at tennis whose sister knows them quite well. She said Marissa came out of hospital after having Milo looking a hell of a lot better than she did when she went in. Like, barely recognizable when you compare before-and-after photos. Little nip-tuck, little bit of facial work, while you're in having a baby anyway. Just like that.'

'Lucky cow. I wish I had the money for it,' Grace said mournfully.

Jenny could think of nothing to say – it was time to change the subject, or escape. She looked around and spotted Marissa with Peter on the other side of the room, deep in animated conversation with another couple. And suddenly she felt inexplicably sad, as though her short-lived friendship was over. She shook her head. *Get a grip*, she told herself, *you hardly know the woman.*

'Oh look, our teacher's brought his trophy fiancée,' Victor said, nodding to the entrance doors, through which Mr Williams had just walked with a willowy woman on his arm.

'Ah, the lovely May,' Sarah murmured as the couple drew closer. 'He's punching above his weight there, isn't he?'

Jenny watched as the couple passed, smiling in unison then moving on.

'She's beautiful,' Jenny agreed.

'She works for my husband, you know,' Sarah said, in a way that suggested everyone knew what that meant. Jenny looked blank.

'Rayburn Estate Agents,' Sarah clarified. 'We own it, Mr Williams's fiancée works there. So I have to be careful of conflicts of interest. *No need to fudge the spelling test results just because I pay your fiancée's wages, Mr Williams!*' She gave a tinkly laugh.

'She left her husband for Mr Williams,' Grace said in a whisper. 'Pretty scandalous for them to shack up before the ink on her divorce papers is dry.'

'I suppose teachers have to have lives like everyone else,' Jenny said, without thinking. There was a pause then, while three pairs of eyes assessed her, deciding perhaps she wasn't in the gang.

'Do any of your kids play tennis?' Jenny asked to fill the gap, grasping at the first thing that came into her head. 'Jacob is looking to play but he definitely needs lessons.'

'Yes!' Sarah said. 'We're in Castle Tennis Club – it's *amazing*.

You should come down with Jacob – I'll give you my number and I can show you around.'

Jenny smiled. She was back to speaking their language.

It wasn't until Jenny was putting on her coat to go home that she saw Marissa again.

'Sorry, I never got a *second* to come over to you after that,' Marissa said, coming towards her in a cloud of perfume and gin cocktails. 'But we *must* do a playdate for the boys some time. And drinks – introduce the husbands? Wouldn't it be enormous fun?'

Jenny smiled and said yes as she pulled the belt of her coat. Marissa hugged her goodbye and disappeared into the thinning crowd as Jenny left the hotel, light as a glass of champagne.

29

Irene
Wednesday – five days missing

IRENE WAITED UNTIL FRANK had gone to work Wednesday morning to start her research. She'd been thinking about it ever since the police had asked the question on Monday night – she knew very little about what Rob had been doing since he walked out. The official line from Kathy was that he'd gone to London and made good. But doing what? What did he look like now? And this Sienna one – what did she look like?

She lifted her cup from the bedside locker to take a first sip of tea. Just the right temperature – Frank was good at getting her tea just right – and she opened the iPad.

Rob had privacy settings on his Facebook but she could still access some photos. His cover photo showed a group at a barbecue, outside what looked like a huge, mock-Tudor house, the kind footballers lived in. She clicked into it for a better look. A group of about fourteen or fifteen people, and Rob in the middle, beer bottle in hand. The woman to his left had her arm around his waist, the way people do in group photos. Or something more? Was this Sienna? Irene peered down at the iPad screen. Blonde hair but hard to tell her age, because of the sunglasses. Tarty pink top showing a fair bit of cleavage, that'd be

Rob's type all right. A kid of four or five beside her. Something grabbed at her insides. How could Rob take on a kid that wasn't his, when he had absolutely no interest in sticking around to see his own? What did Sienna have that Irene didn't?

She scrolled through his profile pictures and cover photos as they changed – Rob on a boat, Rob on a beach, Rob getting into a fancy car. He had money, that was clear, and not the kind of money that comes from going straight. On top of that, he was looking good. Very bloody good.

She looked at the little Add Friend button. Tempting. But too many worms in that can. She was 100 per cent happy with Frank, and better off steering well clear of Rob Murphy. *Give me a man you can rely on any day*, she thought, closing Rob's Facebook page and stretching, catching sight of Frank's slippers as she did.

She stared at them for a beat, then went back to Rob's Facebook page to scroll through more profile pictures. More holidays, more fancy restaurants. She stopped reading and sat back against the cushioned headboard for a moment. Odd to think he'd gone on to do so well for himself. Maybe she should have tried harder to hold on to him. She stared across at herself in the mirrored Sliderobes, at her bright blonde hair, at the roots that'd need doing next week, at the skin on her face that was looking worryingly doughy. She worked her hair into a bun, which pulled back the skin at her temples. That was better, but only just.

Sighing, she looked around her spacious bedroom; at the deep pile carpet, at the expensive wardrobes, at the custom-made curtains, and she wondered where it all went wrong.

30

Marissa
Wednesday – five days missing

MARISSA GRIPPED THE CUP, staring at the cooling tea inside. Peter had just said something, but she had no idea what.

'Marissa, don't go out this morning. You're not up to it, neither of us are. We should wait here – McConville will call if there's any news . . .'

He trailed off. He didn't need to say it. She hadn't thought of anything but that little green raincoat since the night before, and she knew Peter hadn't either. Dear God, let Milo be OK. She'd give up everything to have him back, give all their money away, give their house away. Anything.

'Why don't you take another one of the tablets Dr Downey left – you heard what she said, your body needs sleep even if you don't feel like sleeping.'

'No, I need to be awake. In case.' She didn't need to finish the sentence.

He walked to her and put his arms around her, and she let him because he needed to comfort her, because it helped him to do that, but in that moment it was all she could do to stop herself from pushing him away and screaming and screaming and screaming.

When the doorbell rang, they sprang apart. The colour disappeared from Peter's face and for a moment, neither of them could move. Then he took her by the hand. They'd face it together. Whatever it might be.

But it wasn't McConville at the door, it was Ana.

Her eyes were red from crying, her normally sunny face pinched and pale. Marissa wasn't sure she had the energy to comfort anyone right now, but politeness kicked in and despite a look from Peter, she invited Ana in.

At the kitchen table, she gestured for Ana to sit. Her hand went instinctively to her phone for the hundredth time that morning. Nothing, no word from McConville. She looked over at Peter – he was checking his phone too. She closed her eyes for a moment and said another small prayer. *Anything.*

'I'm so sorry,' Ana said, and Marissa opened her eyes.

'That's OK, it's not your fault.'

'It is, it is all my fault,' Ana said, and burst into loud, ugly sobs.

'Of course it's not, you weren't due to pick him up Friday.'

Peter walked through to the sitting room, unable, Marissa guessed, to cope with soothing an emotional au pair on top of everything else.

'But I am the reason she knew Milo.'

Marissa's skin went cold.

'What do you mean?'

Ana must have heard something in her voice. She looked at Marissa through tear-filled eyes, perhaps regretting her words.

'Ana. What are you talking about?' Marissa asked again.

'We went to playground together. Some days after school, instead of coming home with Milo, Carrie and me take Milo and Jacob to playground.'

Marissa sat back.

'Why didn't you tell us this on Friday night? Or any time since? The guards are interviewing everyone who could possibly help – didn't it dawn on you that you should speak up?' She was shouting now, and Peter was back in the room.

'I am so sorry.' Ana convulsed in tears again. 'I am afraid the police think I am good friend of hers and I did it with her maybe. You know?'

Marissa shook her head at the stupidity.

'Ana, why the hell would the police think you were involved, just because you went to a bloody playground with her? You should have come forward.' She turned to Peter. 'She says she used to go to the playground with Carrie after school – that that's how Carrie got to know Milo. Can you call McConville?'

Peter nodded and moved to the hall to make the call. Ana looked petrified.

'The police lady who was here Friday?'

'Yes, Ana, she'll need to send someone to interview you. This is serious! My God, why would you keep something like this to yourself?'

'But it does not help to find him, I think? I feel bad it's my fault she came to know Milo, but there is nothing I can tell to police to help search, you know?'

'That's not for you to decide, Ana. There could be something that will help. Nobody seems to know her very well – Jenny Kennedy told the guards all about Carrie's childhood and family, but it turned out to be a lie. Her own mother hasn't seen her in nine years. She has no friends they can trace, and they can't even get the Drake family she worked with before. It seems they were made up and the phone reference was someone pretending to be her ex-employer. You're the first person who's said they actually know her. So of course it's bloody important.' Ana stared across the table like a frightened lamb, and

151

Marissa wanted to shake her. How had she not thought to come sooner?

'I sorry,' she whimpered, and on some level Marissa felt that the *old* her – the person who existed before five o'clock last Friday – would have felt sympathy for Ana, but not now. Now only one thing mattered.

Peter arrived back into the kitchen and sat beside Marissa.

'McConville was on her way here when I rang.'

Marissa's stomach plummeted. She opened her mouth to ask the question but it was impossible. Peter was shaking his head.

'No, they haven't found anything, she wants to update us but there's no news of any . . .' He didn't finish the sentence.

Marissa let out a breath and put her hands on the table in front of her.

'Right.' She looked at Ana. 'Tell me all of it – what you talked about, what she's like, if she spoke to Milo – everything.'

'Shouldn't we wait for the guards?' Peter asked.

'She can say it again when they get here,' Marissa said, never taking her eyes off Ana, 'but I want to know now. I need to understand this woman Carrie and what she's doing with my child. Now please, *talk.*'

And haltingly at first, bit by bit, Ana did. She told them about the early days at the school gate, standing on her own. About the mothers who clustered together, and the other minders who stayed apart. It was lonely, she said. Some of the nannies seemed to know one another already, chattering in English or Portuguese. Maybe their charges had gone to preschool together, she thought, or maybe they were just better at socializing. Then one day in mid-September, an Irish girl stood beside her and struck up a conversation. Grateful for any company at all, Ana had turned and smiled, and they got chatting. Just like that, no big deal, two nannies at the school gate.

Ana reckoned it was a few days later when Carrie first suggested going to the playground near the school. They soon got into the habit of going there two or three times a week – sometimes it was raining, but mostly, when the weather was nice, the four of them walked together to the playground. Milo and Jacob played on the swings, while Ana and Carrie sat on the bench and talked.

'What did you talk about?' Marissa asked, never taking her eyes off Ana.

'Anything. The weather. It is so cold here, not like Peru. We talk about our family – I mean, family we work for.' Ana looked down at the table. 'I say you are good family to work for, and I am lucky to mind just one child. Carrie ask why Milo have no brother or sister.' She looked up at Marissa from under wet lashes. 'I say not my business but you seem like very happy family with one child.'

'OK, go on.'

'She asks if you have a big house and I say yes. She says the Kennedys have a nice house too and I say, not like this one – this is *amazing* house.' She stopped.

'It's fine, keep going,' Marissa said, though of course it wasn't really fine – how much had Ana told Carrie about their house?

'I . . . I tell her to google it.' She looked like she was going to start crying again. 'I tell her that it was in newspaper before you buy it, and she can see how big it is on internet.'

'So you gave her our address?' Peter asked, his voice tight. Marissa shushed him with a look. They needed her to keep talking.

'Yes.' So quietly they could hardly hear her.

'What else did you talk about?'

'She asks if you have nice cars too – she says Kennedys have boring, sensible cars but she thinks you have more fun cars. I tell her about the new Lexus you get.'

Peter winced. 'Jesus, Ana, why didn't you just go ahead and give her our bank details while you were at it?'

Marissa nudged him under the table. That wasn't helping.

'Ana,' Marissa said softly, 'don't worry about that now. Keep going, tell us everything you can.'

'OK.' A gulp. 'I tell her how smart Milo is, the way he is with numbers and colours. She asks me for idea for books to buy for Jacob – what kind of story Milo like at bedtime. I tell her is normally you and you,' she nodded at both of them, 'who do story-time, but I check what books he has. She asks him if he likes those stories when we are walking back from playground, they have many chats about his favourite books.'

Peter and Marissa exchanged a look.

'She spoke to Milo too?' Marissa asked.

'Yes, she good with him, always asking what he like, what he watch on TV. I am not so good with Jacob but maybe my English . . .'

'Milo chatted back to her? He was relaxed with her?'

'Oh yes, he like to chat with her.'

Marissa turned to Peter. 'Was she grooming him? Making him feel comfortable with her?' It came out strangled.

Peter's face was grey. 'Jesus. It sounds like it.'

'He didn't just go with her on Friday because he thought he was going on a playdate,' Marissa whispered – the thought of him going on a fake playdate she had arranged, crushing her for the millionth time. 'He was happy to go with her. He *knew* her.'

31

Marissa
Wednesday – five days missing

WHEN DS MCCONVILLE ARRIVED, Marissa looked at Peter, willing him to ask the question she couldn't ask. He nodded.

'Has there been anything new about the . . . the raincoat?'

McConville shook her head. 'The search at Killiney Hill hasn't yielded anything. We're still following every angle; we'll go back to Carrie's mother, and we're trying to trace Rob Murphy – Carrie's father – and Kyle Byrde, her ex.' She turned to Ana. 'Mr Irvine tells me you knew Carrie?'

Ana nodded, looking like she dreaded going through all of it again, but she did – repeating everything she'd just told Marissa and Peter.

'And when you told her to google the house, did she come back to say she'd done it?' McConville asked.

'Yes. She say it look like a palace.'

'Did she ask you anything else about the house, or Mr and Mrs Irvine?'

Ana thought for a moment. 'She wonder where they get so much money and she ask about their jobs.' She looked uncomfortable but kept going. 'I tell her Mrs Irvine is lawyer, in charge of own business, and Mr Irvine do something with rich people money.'

Jesus, she may as well have put a bullseye on their backs, Marissa thought. Ana read her mind.

'I so sorry, Mrs Irvine.'

McConville didn't have time for emotions or apologies. 'Did she ask more questions when you told her about their jobs?'

Ana considered. 'Yes, she did. She curious about Mrs Irvine lawyer job and being the boss. I tell her about Mr Dobson, the other lawyer who in charge too. She ask me about him.'

Peter cut in. 'Sorry, but did you not for one second think it was odd that she was asking about our businesses, and about Marissa's partner?'

Ana shrugged helplessly. McConville opened her mouth to say something, but Marissa got there first. The last thing they needed was Ana clamming up.

'Peter,' Marissa said, putting a hand on his knee. 'I've been there. It can be lonely looking after kids. If you find someone to talk to, you end up talking about all sorts of things.'

'What did you tell her about Mr Dobson?' McConville asked, steering things back on track.

'That he is here in the house many times, that he a bit . . .' She looked at the three waiting faces. 'Goofy? And I am surprised he can be a smart thing like a lawyer, but that he and Mrs Irvine know each other since a long time, and maybe that's why they work together.'

McConville flipped some pages back in her notebook.

'We haven't interviewed Mr Dobson yet, could you give me his contact details?'

'Of course. He wasn't around on Friday though when all of this happened, and he doesn't know Carrie, so I'm not sure he'll be able to help.'

'We'll talk to everyone, it helps build a picture.' She turned back to Ana. 'What else did Carrie ask about?'

'She say she sometimes get visits from Mr Kennedy's mother but she doesn't like that woman. She asks if I see Milo's grandparents. I tell her this sad story of Mrs Irvine's parents who die six months apart when she young, and I don't know Mr Irvine parents.'

McConville looked over at Peter, an unspoken question.

'My dad's long gone, and my mother's in a nursing home.' He looked at Ana then back to McConville. 'That's beside the point though – the question is what the hell Carrie was doing asking all these questions?'

'She may have been trying to get a picture of your finances, or Milo's typical routine,' McConville said, 'or both.'

'Yes, she ask about routine,' Ana says, her voice a whisper. 'She say she is having trouble with Jacob's routine. Jenny – the mommy – she works a lot of hours, and it is difficult for the husband. Carrie tells me Mr Kennedy is angry in a quiet way where he says nothing but everybody knows he is unhappy. Including Jacob.'

'And what did you tell her about Milo's routine?' McConville asked.

Ana's shoulders dropped. 'Everything. I tell her what time he get up, his favourite breakfast, that I drive him to school in the spare car.'

'The spare car?' McConville looked at all three of them.

'We bought a little runaround so Ana could drive Milo to school if Marissa had to go into the office early,' Peter explained, 'and to take him to activities.'

Marissa watched McConville as she took that in, imagining how it must sound. The people who have so much money, they can buy an extra car for their childminder to use. But it just made sense at the time – they both needed their own cars to get to work, and it was hardly fair to expect Ana and Milo to walk

157

everywhere. The car was a little Micra that had cost next to nothing in the bigger scheme of things.

'Go on, Ana, what else did Carrie ask?'

'She says Jacob won't eat lunch she makes so I give her ideas of healthy snacks Milo like. Never any dairy or shellfish, because he allergic.' Ana nodded almost proudly. 'Is good she knows that, yes? She won't give him food that makes him sick.'

Peter looked ready to explode.

Marissa replied before he could say anything. 'It's good that she's aware of his dairy intolerance, yes. He's possibly not actually allergic to shellfish – Peter is – but that's good too.' It felt like humouring a child. But it was true, it *was* good. The more Carrie knew about Milo, the better she could take care of him. Marissa had to believe she was taking care of him. She ignored the little voice that said all of this had been a means to get Ana talking, to give Carrie as much information as possible about their home, their businesses, their finances – and their vulnerabilities. Jesus, Ana had access to every part of their lives, every element of their routines – how easy it had been for Carrie to mine her for information and find out everything she needed to know.

McConville's phone buzzed to life. Marissa went cold and hot all at once, as she did every time anyone's phone rang now.

'Just something I asked Breen to check,' McConville said, moving to the hall to take the call, closing the door behind her.

Silence, as Peter and Marissa stared at Ana, and she looked down at her hands. Marissa could feel the questions building up in Peter again, about to burst out of his mouth like a hailstorm of what-the-hells and are-you-stupids. It wouldn't help though. She put her hand on his, soothing him.

'Ana,' she said, suddenly remembering something, 'you know the way you send me photos of you and Milo when you're out? Did you ever take any with Carrie?'

'Carrie not like photos, she says I take too many.'

'Ah.'

'But I take really nice picture of her with Jacob one time when she did not see me do it. Pushing him on swing.'

'Really? Can you show me?'

Ana pulled out her phone and scrolled for a moment, then turned the screen to Marissa and Peter. The photo was taken from a slight distance, but zooming in, Marissa could see Carrie's face clearly, much more clearly than the photo Jenny had sent the police. Her hair was tied back in a low ponytail, and for the first time, Marissa could clearly see her face. The milk-white freckled skin, the fox-like colouring. The tightly set mouth, as though she was focused on a very serious task, not just pushing a child on a swing.

'This is great, Ana, we'll show it to McConville as soon as she comes back in.'

'Will . . . will she arrest me now?' Ana said, tears in her voice.

'What? Why would she arrest you?' Marissa said, her tone sharper than she intended.

'Carrie say police arrest people like me all the time. That you cannot trust Irish police.'

'For fuck's sake, Ana, are you for real?' Bits of spit flew out of Peter's mouth. 'Why are you quoting Carrie's words of wisdom back to us? She's a kidnapper, for Jesus' sake. Of course she doesn't trust the bloody police.' He stood, running his hand through his hair. 'I can't deal with this shit any more.' He stepped around the other side of the table and stood over Ana, glaring down at her. 'You basically wrote a how-to guide for her, to help her kidnap our son. Excuse me if I can't find it in me to hold your hand now and reassure you that you're not in trouble with the police. Fuck's sake.' He walked over to the other side of the kitchen, staring out the big picture window at the garden beyond. His shoulders were shaking. Marissa couldn't remember a time when he'd cried, not before this week. She got up to go to him, but the noise of an incoming text pulled her back to the table. Jenny, offering more help. It brought her back to centre. That's what they needed to do – stay practical, stay focused. She cleared her throat.

'Peter, Jenny has messaged me to see if she can do anything – I'm thinking we might go door-to-door in Pine Valley tonight, talking to neighbours who live near the school. I know the police have done it, but' – she glanced over at Ana – 'people are funny with the guards sometimes. Nervous. They might remember something or say more if it's me on the doorstep. And I could bring Jenny so I'm not on my own.'

His shoulders had stopped shaking.

'OK,' he said quietly, 'I'll go out too, with Brian.'

Ana looked like she was going to speak up, to offer to help too maybe, but she didn't. That's what it came down to, Marissa thought; those who hovered on sidelines, making half-offers, and those who arrived unannounced and insisted on helping. She'd remember all this afterwards, after they'd found him. *If they found him.*

Peter walked back to the table and sat again, his eyes red and damp.

'Ana, I'm sorry for how I spoke just now. Please carry on. What else did Carrie ask? Anything else about money or the house or the business?'

Ana looked towards the door, as if wondering whether or not they should wait for McConville. They could hear low murmuring from the hall; the call was ongoing.

'She ask where Mrs Irvine office is – the one she share with Mr Dobson. And she ask where your office is, Mr Irvine, and about your brother. How you make the money. But I don't really know these answers.'

McConville arrived back then, and there was something in her expression.

'What is it?' Marissa whispered, her breath stuck inside her.

'We have a witness who was on Killiney Hill on Monday evening at dusk. He was in the Obelisk – the stone tower on the top of the hill?'

Marissa nodded, she knew it well.

'He says he had permission to go inside it to take photos through the window for some art project, and that he saw a man walk up the hill and over to the edge. The area that looks down over the sea and the rocks.'

Marissa thought she might throw up.

'The man had a bag with him – one of the long-life supermarket ones. He saw the man look around, then take something out and throw it over the side. He couldn't make out what it was. The man went back down the hill, and our witness thought no more of it until he saw the appeal we put out for people on Killiney Hill in recent days.'

The world had turned to quicksand and Marissa couldn't make sense of anything McConville was saying.

'What does it mean?' she managed.

'It's by no means conclusive, but we think this man may have thrown Milo's raincoat over the side.'

'Why would someone do that?' Marissa asked.

Peter answered her, though his eyes were still on McConville. 'To make it look as though Milo had gone over the edge. That's it, isn't it? To make us think he was . . . gone?'

McConville looked from Marissa to Peter.

'We can't say anything for certain. But yes,' she conceded, 'that's one possibility.'

'Why would someone want us to think that?' Peter asked.

'I don't know, but I think it means we won't get a ransom note,'

Marissa said quietly. 'It's not a kidnap for money. And if it was definitely a man, then Carrie is not working alone. She hasn't just lost the plot. She's working with someone.' She looked to McConville for confirmation. The detective sergeant didn't confirm, but she didn't say anything to contradict Marissa either.

'So,' Marissa went on, her voice so low she could hardly hear it herself, 'what does that leave?'

She knew what it left, she'd read stories online about children being trafficked and sold and abused, but she couldn't say it, and neither, it seemed, could anyone else.

32

Irene
Wednesday – five days missing

IRENE STOPPED AT A rail of leggings and tank tops as she made her way through Leisurewear. She could do with a few new bits, she thought, checking a price tag. *Ah, stop!* €49 for a pair of leggings! Daylight robbery. These fancy department stores were all just gougers. She should shop somewhere else, show them she wasn't paying their ridiculous prices. Then again, the leggings were very nice ... She draped a pair over her arm and made her way upstairs to homewares. They needed a new towel rail in the downstairs loo, and maybe she'd get some towels too. You could never have enough towels.

Forty minutes later, as the girl behind the till scanned her items, she rooted through her bag for her debit card. Lip gloss, plasters, tissues, two magazines, make-up bag, hairbrush – where was her card? She found it just as the girl announced the grand total – €126.75. Shit, she didn't expect it to be quite that much. She inserted her card and typed in her PIN.

'Oh, I'm sorry, that didn't go through, let's try again,' the girl said. But Irene knew the drill. It wasn't going to work the next time either. She went through the motions anyway.

'Sorry, that's still not going through, would you have another card?' asked the girl.

'Stupid machine,' Irene said loudly. 'I'll shop somewhere else next time.' She stalked off, leaving her would-be purchases behind.

She didn't stop until she reached the ATM near the exit of the department store. She'd try for twenty – surely there'd be twenty left. The machine made a reassuring whirring sound, and moments later, a pristine twenty-euro note slid out of the drawer. She'd try for another, she figured, but this time she was out of luck. *Insufficient funds.* Bloody Frank and his stingy allowance. He couldn't understand why she needed so much, no matter how many times she explained the cost of things. And it's not like it was all for her – the household stuff was for him as well. If she didn't buy it, he'd be coming home to the same depressing empty house every day, probably complaining about *that*.

Anyway, she had enough for a cuppa, she may as well have one. She slipped into a seat in the cafe and ordered a latte and a doughnut – one of the ones with cream and jam down the middle. Caroline used to love those. She shook her head. Where had that memory come from?

Stirring two sugars into her latte, she pulled out her magazine and scanned the cover.

Kept in a Torture Chamber – What Would her Date do Next?

God, people were so stupid. Meeting men on the internet, then acting all surprised when they turned out to be psychos.

He Tried to Kill his Wife with Pizza!

That one sounded kind of interesting actually, she thought, turning the pages to have a look.

But it was a story opposite the pizza-murder that caught her attention – an interview with a man whose son had been convicted for a rake of murders. A big article on the son's childhood –

the interviewer asking whether or not he'd pulled wings off flies or tortured cats (he hadn't, according to his father, but then he *would* say that). Irene read it through and stopped to think. She looked for the journalist's name and Google told her he was a UK-based freelance writer, but that was hardly surprising, the magazine was published in the UK. Still. Interesting. She popped the last piece of doughnut into her mouth, deep in thought.

Passing the newsstand at the department-store exit, Irene stopped. There, on the front of every single paper, were photos of her daughter and Milo Irvine. She didn't need to contact any journalist in the UK – she'd get what she wanted right here, wouldn't she? Scanning the papers, she made mental notes. The broadsheets probably didn't pay for tell-all stories, but the tabloids surely would. On impulse, she pulled out her phone and photographed the front pages of three red-tops, including the names of the reporters writing about Carrie and Milo. A man in a suit was watching her – a store manager maybe. What the hell did he want – there was no law against taking photos of newspapers, was there? As he approached, she decided it was time to go. Hiking her bag on to her shoulder, she stood up straight, and marched out of the store.

At home at her kitchen table, she pulled out her phone and opened her Camera Roll, zooming in on the three photos of the tabloids and the three journalist names. Robert Melville. Sounded too poncy. Sorcha Ní Ríada. Too Irishy. Faye Foster. She might be all right. Irene googled Faye Foster and found her email address on her Twitter account. What happened to keeping things private? Then again, journalists probably needed people to be able to reach them. People like Irene, with a story to tell.

*

Upstairs, she picked the iPad off her bedside locker and sat on her bed to type an email to Faye Foster. Halfway through, she stopped to think about it. If she did a tell-all story, her neighbours would know. Fuck it, she didn't really like her neighbours anyway. Frank's three kids and ex-wife would be horrified. She grinned, imagining their reaction. Kathy would find out of course. She turned that over in her head. That would be OK. Kathy was well used to seeing both sides of the story, she knew what the system was like – she wouldn't automatically assume Carrie was in the wrong. And Rob? Rob would find out too. She licked her lips and got back to typing.

33

Jenny
Wednesday – five days missing

JENNY LOCKED HER CAR and moved towards the muffled-up figure. Marissa was wearing a long, padded coat and a scarf that
covered her nose and mouth. She looked tiny inside all that
wrapping – like she'd shrunk a little more each day since
Friday.

What to say to her? *How are you doing* seemed ridiculous. On
impulse, Jenny hugged her, and in the end, Marissa spoke first.

'Peter and Brian went off already – they're doing Pine Valley
Drive. We'll do the Avenue, starting this side with the odd
numbers. Is that OK?'

'Of course, absolutely.'

Together they turned into the first house beside the school,
1 Pine Valley Avenue. A 1950s semi-detached house with a
garage conversion; a scooter and a bicycle visible through the
glass porch. A harried-looking woman with a baby in her arms
and a toddler clinging to her leg answered.

'I don't need any gas or electricity or whatever it is,' she said,
starting to close the door.

'We're not selling anything – my son is missing and we're going
door-to-door to see if anyone remembers anything,' Marissa said,

in a voice that was a lot stronger than Jenny expected. God, how did she do it.

The woman's eyes widened.

'Oh my God, I'm so sorry. You poor thing.' Her voice broke on the last words.

'Can you think of anything you might have seen on Friday?' Marissa asked, her question ringing out clearly in the night air. 'The woman who took him more than likely walked down this way after picking him up.'

Jenny knew that wasn't strictly true – there was no CCTV anywhere in Pine Valley so the guards didn't know which route Carrie and Milo had taken, but the fib made sense – it might focus the woman's mind.

'I didn't see a thing, I'm sorry. We were down in the play-ground in Dún Laoghaire on Friday afternoon.' She nuzzled the baby. 'Mine aren't in school yet.'

Marissa handed her a flyer, one with pictures of both Carrie and Milo.

'Have you ever seen her around?' she asked, pointing at Carrie.

The woman took the flyer and shifted the baby to her other hip. The baby stuck his finger in his mouth and surveyed them, a slip of drool sliding down his chin. The toddler, clearly bored with the callers, had gone back into the kitchen.

To her credit, the woman really did look at the photo, screw-ing up her eyes, almost willing herself, it seemed, to remember something. But eventually, reluctantly, she shook her head and handed back the flyer.

'Keep it – in case you think of something later?'

The woman nodded. 'I hope you find him safe and sound, poor little mite.' Tears filled her eyes, and from the back of the house somewhere, the toddler began to wail.

ALL HER FAULT

'Thank you, now you go on in,' Marissa said, and to Jenny, it felt for a moment like the world was skewed and she was comforting the woman instead of the other way around. But that was the way it was, she supposed. A bit like when someone dies, and you end up hugging the crying masses. She shook herself. Nobody had died. They weren't going there.

At the next house, an older man answered; tall, white hair, and a pompous air about him, like he was waiting for them to try to sell him something, Jenny thought, so he could give them all the reasons why he wouldn't buy. When Marissa explained who she was, his expression didn't change – no sympathetic tears here, and no useful information either. They passed him flyers and moved on.

At the next house there was nobody home. Or someone in the back who didn't want to answer the door after dark. They stood side by side, trying the bell a second time, waiting. The silence felt heavy now, and Jenny searched for something to say.

'Did the guards have any news today?' she tried.

'They think someone left his raincoat on the rocks at Killiney Hill on purpose, to make us think . . .'

Jenny nodded vigorously in the dark. There was no need to say it.

'It was a man, so we know now Carrie's not working on her own. It might be her ex, Kyle Byrde. The police still can't track him down,' Marissa continued. 'Let's try the next house.'

Did she want to move away from talking about the investigation? Jenny wasn't sure. She tried to imagine what she'd want to talk about in similar circumstances, but she couldn't. She watched as Marissa marched down the driveway. She was a lot stronger than she seemed. Jenny remembered summing her up at the school social the first time they met: friendly, confident, privileged. Someone who'd grown up in a world where nothing

169

ever went wrong. Probably blinkered, a bit flaky, but sociable and fun – that's how Jenny had assessed her that night, when they both turned up in the same dress. How quickly she'd put the picture together, and how wrong she'd been. Marissa had something steely at her core, something keeping her going when most people would surely fall apart.

Jenny followed her into the next driveway.

Number 7 was opened by a blonde woman in her twenties whose beautifully defined brows went up as far as her hairline when she understood why they were calling. She wasn't there on Friday, but she'd pass out flyers, she said, taking a bundle.

As they approached the door of number 9, Marissa slowed.

'Are you OK?' Jenny asked.

'Yes,' Marissa said, stepping forward to ring the bell. 'I've just remembered who lives here.'

The door flew open and Jenny looked up at a very tall man with jet-black hair swept to one side and kept in place with far too much gel. His pointed nose was in perfect symmetry with his pointed chin, and his inquisitive eyes reminded her of a nocturnal animal.

'Yes?' he said, looking at Marissa and then at Jenny.

Marissa stepped under the porch light.

'Alex, it's Marissa Irvine.'

'Marissa!' He smiled, then stopped. 'God, I'm so sorry. I saw it on the news. If there's anything I can do to help, just let me know.'

'Thank you. We could do with more volunteers to hand out flyers?'

'Yes ... absolutely. It's so busy with the business at the moment, but next week is looking better. I'll be in touch?'

'Next week. Fantastic,' Marissa said, and Jenny couldn't tell if the man could hear the sarcasm. 'Anyway, we're going door-to-door to see if people remember anything from Friday,' Marissa continued. 'I forgot you live near the school – Milo was only a baby back when we handled your father's estate, so it didn't register with me.'

'Yeah, that was what – three or four years ago? You were still recovering from your *surgery*?'

The inflection on 'surgery' was subtle but Jenny caught it. Marissa's face remained impassive.

'Hard to believe it's that long since the old man popped his clogs,' Alex continued, glancing over at Jenny. 'Sorry, that sounds a bit off, doesn't it.' He barked a laugh.

Jenny worked hard to keep her face neutral. *Popped his clogs?* What a charmer.

'This is Jenny,' Marissa was saying. 'She's been helping out.'

'Oh!' Alex said. 'You're the one who hired the nanny! No wonder you're helping out – hard to make up for that one. I mean, it's not like an "I spilt tea down your top, give me the dry-cleaning bill" kind of thing, is it.'

Jenny's mouth dropped open.

'The great thing is,' Marissa cut in, as Jenny scrambled for something to say, 'Jenny puts her money where her mouth is – she doesn't just offer to help, she gets out there and does it. You wouldn't *believe* the number of people who've offered to help but then done nothing at all, Alex, it's incredible.' She smiled sweetly at him. 'Really tells you something about a person. But anyway, back to Friday.' Her smile vanished. 'Did you see anything?'

'No. I was out in our Blanchardstown branch on Friday.'

'What about May? Was she here?'

'May's gone. Left last year. She waited and waited for the old man to kick the bucket, and then the will didn't quite live up to her expectations. Not enough to make it worth her while staying. Shacked up with a teacher now, can you believe.'

171

'I'm sorry to hear that,' Marissa said, not sounding very sorry at all.

'Better off without her, she had bloody expensive tastes!' Alex said, laughing like an injured hyena.

Jenny looked from one to the other, trying to keep up with the story as fragments of another similar story filtered back.

'Anyway, we should go. Huge amount of ground to cover, and there's just the two of us,' Marissa said.

Jenny watched Alex's face, but if he picked up on the dig, he didn't show it.

'Bye then, good luck with it all,' he said, as though they were collecting for a sponsored run. He shut the door.

'C'mere,' Jenny said, as they walked down the driveway. 'I might be wrong, but did you see the woman with Mr Williams at the school social? Isn't she called May? I think she works for Rayburn Estate Agents.'

'No, I didn't see her,' Marissa muttered. 'Christ, he's such an asshole. Always was. Used to make snarky comments about my recovery, commenting on my scar. Practically giving a week-by-week account of how it was doing.' Her finger went to the small mark on her chin.

Jenny couldn't help thinking of Sarah Rayburn's gossipy reference to cosmetic surgery. Was it true, then? She opened her mouth to ask but couldn't find a polite way to do so. Marissa carried on ranting about Alex.

'That cretin is the reason I wonder why I do the job I do sometimes. Then again, I guess you get idiots in every walk of life – it'd be no different if I was a dentist or doctor. At least if I was a dentist, I could stick needles in him – whereas all I did was help make him rich.'

'How did you make him rich?'

Marissa hesitated for a moment. 'Oh look, it's all public

record anyway – his dad owned a chain of bookies. Shamrock Sports?'

Jenny nodded; everyone knew Shamrock Sports and their ubiquitous branches dotted all over the country.

'When the dad died, Alex got the business plus all his dad's personal wealth. And it's, well, let's say, a lot. I'm surprised to hear him say May left because there wasn't enough in the will – I suspect it had little to do with money and everything to do with Alex.'

'You must have all sorts of stories from your job,' Jenny said. 'The secrets of Kerryglen, all held in the four walls of your office.'

'Oh goodness, it's a lot more boring than you'd imagine, but yes, we do tend to see the quirkier side of village residents. And when it comes to wills, you quickly find out who really likes their spouse and who's got a special "friend".'

Marissa stopped abruptly and reached out to touch a garden wall, as though to steady herself.

'Are you OK?' Jenny asked.

'No,' Marissa whispered. 'What am I doing gossiping about Alex Fenelon when . . .' She took a deep breath in and let it out slowly, still touching the wall. She looked at Jenny, resolute again. 'Let's keep going to number 11. I'll be OK.'

But she wouldn't be OK, she couldn't. Jenny knew that. Not until they found Milo, one way or another.

34

Jenny
Wednesday – five days missing

AT NUMBER 11, ANOTHER older man answered the door. Much older this time, Jenny realized, stooped and small, with watery eyes and bristles on his chin. He was wearing a buttoned-up white shirt and dark trousers, with slippers on his feet. Jenny could see that he looked apprehensive, and Marissa was quick to explain who she was and why they were there.

'Have you ever seen the girl with the red hair?' she asked, handing him a flyer.

He held it up to the porch light to get a better look.

'I've seen her,' he said in a quivery voice, like stones in syrup. 'I see them all when they walk past. She normally walks with a little red-haired fella.'

Jacob. Jenny shivered.

'Did you ever see her with any other child – on Friday maybe?' Marissa sounded breathless.

'I see her with a black-haired girl and a little blond fella every now and then. The four of them walking together.'

Ana and Milo. Jacob and Carrie. Jenny glanced over at Marissa, but her eyes were firmly on the man.

'Did you see her on Friday?'

He looked down at the flyer.

'I think so. Friday was sunny, and the binmen had been but I hadn't brought back in my bins. I remember sitting on my chair in the sunny spot in the sitting room, watching as they all went past. The bins were there, so it was Friday.' Triumphant.

'You saw Carrie on Friday?'

He nodded.

'And who was with her?' Marissa asked.

The man pointed a yellow-stained finger at the other picture. At Milo.

'You saw Carrie and Milo together?' Marissa's voice went up a notch. 'Did you tell the guards?'

'I haven't seen the guards.'

'But they called at all the houses – didn't they call here?'

'Maybe they did,' he said, his watery blue eyes going from Marissa to Jenny and back again. 'But I was in my daughter's until last night. Nobody here.' He smacked his thin lips together.

'OK, can you tell your story to the guards?'

'I can of course, but what good it'll do, I don't know. I just saw them walking past, nothing strange about it.'

'Did he look—' Marissa's voice shook and she cleared her throat to start again. 'Did he look upset?'

The man gazed at Marissa, and Jenny had the strongest sense he was searching for the right words to make it better.

'He didn't look upset, no,' he said gently. 'He was holding her hand, walking along like any child might.'

Jenny put her arm around Marissa as they walked down the driveway. Out on the street, they leaned against the wall, Jenny rubbing Marissa's shoulder. She couldn't shake the image from her head – Carrie leading Milo by the hand, and Milo going willingly.

'It doesn't mean anything, the fact that he wasn't upset,' she tried, though she didn't really know what she meant or how it could help.

'Of course he wasn't upset,' Marissa said, looking up at the tarry, starless sky. 'He knew her from the playground. The four of them used to go together – Ana and Milo, Carrie and Jacob. Did you know that?'

Jenny shook her head. Jesus, it could so easily have been Jacob. And again came the relief; the *there but for the grace of God*, followed by the crushing guilt.

'Carrie used to quiz Ana about our lives – our house, our jobs, Milo's routine. Ana came this morning to tell us all this. I could have throttled her for leaving it so long. Good God, the girl has time off because obviously there's no reason for her to—' Marissa's voice cracked. Jenny nodded. There was no need to explain why Ana had time off. 'Anyway, she has all this free time, and we're still paying her of course, but it didn't dawn on her to come sooner and let us know that Milo had met Carrie.'

'So, he trusted Carrie,' Jenny said, thinking out loud. 'If Milo was wondering why Jacob wasn't with Carrie on Friday, and why they weren't coming to our house, she could have told him whatever she wanted, and he'd have believed it.'

Marissa put her face in her hands. Jenny rubbed her arm, then pulled her into a hug.

'He's only four,' Marissa said, her voice swollen with tears, 'of course he believed her.' Her body shuddered in Jenny's arms. Jenny felt her own throat tighten.

'I know, I know,' she whispered, because there was nothing else to say.

'Jesus Christ, what kind of woman does this?' Marissa sobbed, and there was anger there too. 'Grooms a little boy into taking her hand and walking off – stepping off the edge of the world?'

Jenny hugged her tighter, thinking that's exactly what it was like – as though Carrie and Milo had stepped off the edge of the world.

35

Jenny
Wednesday – five days missing

JENNY WATCHED HELPLESSLY AS Marissa pulled out of the hug and sank to the ice-cold pavement, sitting with her head in her hands. God, she was in no fit state to be going house-to-house – what had they been thinking?

'Marissa, do you want to pass me your phone and I'll call Peter?'

No answer.

'I think you need a break. You'd be in much better shape to go out tomorrow after some sleep?' It sounded so trite.

Marissa shook her head, without lifting it from her hands.

'It's just, the police have already gone door-to-door, and I'm sure they will again. I don't think you're up to this tonight, and it won't help Milo if you make yourself sick.' Did that sound harsh? She crouched down and rubbed Marissa's back. 'He needs you strong for when he comes home.'

Marissa turned her head sideways to look at Jenny. Her face was pale, eerie in the light of the streetlamp. Ghostly. Tear-tracks stained her cheeks, but her eyes were dry now, and somehow empty. Was she losing hope?

'Marissa, let me have your phone so I can call Peter.'

Without saying anything, Marissa shifted on the pavement and slid her phone out of her back pocket. She unlocked it and searched for the number, then passed it over. Jenny stood to make the call.

'Are you OK?' was how Peter answered, and the raw need in his voice made Jenny's eyes prick with tears.

'Sorry, it's Jenny here on Marissa's phone.' She took a few steps away. 'She's sitting here on the ground and she doesn't look well. If you like, I can drive her back to your house and stay with her?'

'No, that's fine – we'll come and get her.'

She could hear him speaking to someone else, as though he had his hand over the phone.

'Where exactly are you?' he said after a moment.

She gave him the address and sat down beside Marissa.

Five minutes later, a silver Lexus pulled up and Peter jumped out of the driver's seat. He hunkered down to pull Marissa into his arms, and Jenny stepped away to give them space.

'Come on, we'll get you home. I don't know what we were thinking – neither of us is up to it.'

Marissa allowed herself to be pulled to standing. Like a sleepwalker, she got into the back of the car, and Peter clipped her seatbelt closed.

Jenny watched as Brian got out of the passenger's side and circled round to the back of the car to join Peter. He raised a hand in a small salute to Jenny, and she took it as a cue to join them.

'Is she OK?'

Peter shook his head. 'We need to get her home. Brian, will I drop you back to your car, or do you want to come home with us now and we'll pick your car up tomorrow?'

Brian, his bony features neutral, stood with his hands in his trouser pockets, saying nothing for a moment.

'Brian.' It was not quite, but almost a bark.

Jenny watched the exchange, curious about the dynamic between these two.

Brian looked like he hadn't heard the question, or was he searching for a reply?

'Brian!' Jenny jumped. Definitely a bark this time, like an exasperated parent speaking to a naughty child.

Brian looked at his watch, oblivious to his brother's tone, outwardly at least. 'I have to meet the social media campaign manager in the Swan at eight. I'll walk back to get my car, it's not far.' He was like a wax doll on the outside and a robot on the inside, Jenny thought, as she watched him turn and walk up the street. That left just her and Peter, standing looking at one another.

'Can I drop you to your car?' Peter asked, and if he was still angry about her part in all this, he did a good job of hiding it.

'No, not at all – it's literally there.' She pointed. 'A few houses back. I'll head off.' She paused. 'I'm here though, whenever you guys need me – social media stuff, door-to-door, posters – anything I can do.'

'Thank you,' Peter said, his voice hoarse with threatening tears, 'we appreciate that.'

Biting back tears herself, she turned and walked towards her car.

The narrow backroads around Kerryglen were dark and almost eerie as she made her way towards Belton Heights. Was it her imagination, or were there fewer cars than usual on the roads? Maybe what happened to Milo was making people nervous. Or making her imagination run wild. Turning into the far side of Belton Heights, she drove slowly through the unfinished part of the development, wary of loose rocks and iron bars. There was nothing to hear but the purr of her car engine as she passed half-built houses, dark windows and fluttering plastic sheets. By day, it was a hive of activity, and a source of constant fascination for local kids. At night, it was a ghost town. She shivered. Ahead, the welcome lights of her own street beckoned and she tapped the accelerator, eager to get home.

Then she saw him.

At the last empty house, the show house, a man was letting himself in with a key. Surely nobody was living in the show house when the rest of the development was only half built? As she approached, the man turned slightly to look in her direction, and her headlights lit him up. Just for a second, as she rolled past and on to the occupied part of the road. But for that brief moment she saw his face, and she was almost certain it was Brian Irvine.

She looked at the clock on the dashboard – two minutes to eight. Why would he be here, when he was meeting the social media manager in the Swan at eight? The Swan was on Castle Street, a good ten-minute drive from Belton Heights – maybe they were meeting here instead? But that made no sense – people don't have meetings on building sites. She passed the sign, the big *Another Graceful Development Brought to You by Downey Homes* plastered over an image of a woman in a hot tub. Because yeah, they all had hot tubs in Belton Heights, and they all got into them with immaculate make-up and just-done hair. She rolled her eyes. A more realistic ad would show someone like Jenny, flaked out in tracksuit bottoms after a long day at work.

She pulled into the driveway but didn't feel ready to go inside. Sitting in the car, she took out her phone and clicked into the *Find Milo Irvine* Facebook page. Two new videos had been added, one showing Milo playing on a beach, and one of him sounding out words while doing his homework. Just like Jacob did. She swallowed and clicked into a story on TheDaily-Byte.ie about Marissa and Peter's wedding in the Caribbean. One of two weddings – they had a party in Ireland for four hundred guests after the smaller wedding on a beach in Antigua. The story had nothing at all to do with the disappearance, but then anything in the media would help focus people on watching out for Milo. She scrolled through the comments.

Self-absorbed narcissists showing off about their wedding while their son is missing.

Did people think Peter and Marissa had written the story themselves?

Nobody with that much money gets it legally. And even if it's not technically illegal, they made money out of poor schmucks during the boom and left them for dust when the economy collapsed.

I've heard she's had a ton of surgery, looks nothing like what she used to look like before. You can totally tell when you zoom in on recent photos, esp around the eyes.

Jenny looked at the wedding photo in the article, but it had been taken at a distance and Marissa's face was a blur; it was impossible to say if she looked different today. And – Jenny shook herself – why did it even matter? She carried on reading.

Luv her dress – anyone know where it's from?

Anyone with a wedding as fancy as that is asking for trouble, and sorry, but they look like they're so up themselves in those photos.

Peter and Marissa breaking that great unwritten Irish rule: No Showing Off. Jenny rolled her eyes and read on.

> If people looked after their own kids instead of farming them out to 'nannies' FFS, this kind of thing wouldn't happen.

> Someting stinks about dis – whats the bets the kid turns up safe + we suddenly here the mother has a book deal or the dad has a new job.

What the hell was wrong with people? Jenny switched off her phone.

36

Irene
Thursday – six days missing

IRENE YAWNED AND BLINKED, looking around the cafe – she hadn't been up and out this early in a long time. Frank had looked surprised to see her dressed before he even got out of bed, and asked where she was going so early. She said she was meeting a friend for coffee, which was sort of true. The coffee bit anyway.

She read the menu a second time and shook her head. *Smashed avocado* this and *compote* that – what was wrong with a plain scone and a cup of tea? Places like this wanted to put goat's cheese and beetroot in everything and thought writing 'hand-cut chips' made them special. If someone was too stupid to buy their chips already cut and frozen, charging the customers extra was a bit rich. She put down the menu and looked towards the door, wondering if she'd recognize the journalist. Faye Foster had written loads of articles – Irene had done her research – but didn't seem to have any photos of herself on the internet. Maybe journalists were too smart to be sticking their photos all over the web, unlike the rest of the world. Well, the rest of the world except Rob and his bloody privacy settings.

'Irene Turner?'

Irene looked up. The owner of the voice looked like she was barely out of a school uniform. Her dark hair was tied up in one of those messy buns everyone was into, and her coloured-in eyebrows were like something out of a fashion magazine. She wore a grey sweatshirt and skinny jeans, and a laptop poked out of her giant handbag.

'Yes. Are you Faye Foster?'

The girl sat at the table and stuck out an undersized, ringless hand. Irene hesitated, then shook it, comparing her own salon manicure with this girl's bitten-down nails. None of this screamed money so far. Hmmm.

'So,' Faye said brightly, 'you're Carrie Finch's mother?'

Irene nodded.

'I'm sure you'll understand if I ask to see some ID – we've had calls before that turned out to be cranks looking for attention.' She smiled, her extraordinarily white teeth gleaming in the sunlight that streamed through the window. How did this generation have such white teeth? And such confidence? Irene hadn't been asked for ID by anyone for as long as she could remember, yet here was this young one treating her like she was a schoolkid trying to buy drink.

'ID? To prove I'm her mother? What kind of ID would show that?' Irene shook her head.

'I've done the research; I know Carrie's mother is Irene Holohan, now Turner, so I just need ID to prove that's you.' Faye tilted her head to one side. 'Listen, I can tell from looking at you you've an honest face, I don't doubt for a second you're Irene Holohan – but my editor will go nuts if I don't confirm I checked.'

Irene nodded and rummaged in her handbag.

'Driver's licence,' Faye said, 'that'd cover it.'

'Don't drive,' Irene mumbled, her face inside her handbag. She pulled out her purse and dug her Public Services Card from its spot beside her defunct debit card. 'My PPS number's on that, and my name and photo, that good enough?'

'That's perfect,' Faye said brightly, taking a photo of the card. She put her phone down on the table and clicked a button. 'I'm going to record this, for accuracy, OK?'

Irene frowned. This was all getting a bit too formal.

'I don't know if I want to be recorded. You could doctor it some way and make out I said something I didn't.'

'It's actually precisely to prevent any inaccurate representations,' Faye said. 'It's to protect you. If you see something I've written and you don't agree you said it, we can go back to check the tape.'

Irene nodded, still eyeing the phone with distrust.

'We need photos too, will that be OK?'

'Of Caroline?'

'Yes, childhood snaps would be brilliant, but I meant photos of you – we'd send a photographer to your house. Is this afternoon OK? We kinda want to rush this out.'

Now wouldn't that be something. A photographer coming to the house. She could wear the royal-blue dress she got for Frank's daughter's wedding, may as well get another wear out of it. Would there be time to get her hair done? Only if they came later in the evening. But by then, Frank would be on his way home.

'Just me in the photos though, my husband is . . . quite a private man and he works in a bank. You understand.'

Faye nodded.

'That's fine – he's not Carrie's dad anyway, right?'

'That's right.'

'So, who is Carrie's dad – will we start there?'

It always came back to Rob. Irene took a deep breath.

'His name is Rob Murphy. I met him when I was sixteen.

Mad about him, I was. Then he had to go away for a few years, so we broke up, but we stayed in touch.'

'Oh, where did he go?' Faye asked pleasantly, and something told Irene she knew exactly where he went.

'Mountjoy jail. For a crime he didn't commit, mind, he was stitched up by the guards. But he did his time and didn't snitch.'

A waiter came to take their order, apologizing for the delay. Faye ordered a coffee, and Irene did the same, suddenly sorry she didn't seem to be getting a smashed-avocado-anything on the newspaper budget after all.

'So, you got back together when he came out?' Faye asked, pushing up her sweatshirt sleeves. Irene could see what looked like a tiny Chinese symbol tattooed on her inner forearm.

'Yeah, and it was all good till I told him I was up the duff. Next day,' she clicked her fingers, 'he was gone. Never heard from him again.'

'You brought Carrie up alone?'

'Too right. Not a bit of help from anyone.'

'And can you tell me what Carrie was like as a child?'

Irene hesitated. Fuck it, in for a penny, in for a pound. Or lots of pounds, if she got paid. *If.* Faye had said on the phone that it would depend on the legal team, because apparently relatives of criminals weren't supposed to profit from selling their stories. But Caroline hadn't been convicted of anything, had she, Irene told herself, as she spent the money in her head. And why should Irene be done out of her payoff by some legal mumbo jumbo – it wasn't like *she'd* done any kidnapping.

'She was trouble, right from the start. Her dad's genes, of course. Trouble at school, nicking things from the local shop, no matter how much I tried to teach her right from wrong. And always moaning, writing poems about "feeling blue". As if that made her different from every other kid in the country. She thought she was better than everyone, though, something special.' Irene shook her head. 'And all the while, getting in trouble left, right and centre. By the time she was a teen, I was at my wits' end. And Frank – maybe don't print his name – he didn't know what to make of her. She slapped me once, you know.' She nodded for emphasis and Faye made an appropriately shocked face.

'Sounds difficult for you. Any behaviour that might have indicated she'd resort to kidnapping?'

The coffees arrived just then, giving Irene a moment to think about her answer. The last thing she wanted was for people to think she should have seen the signs. But then again, papers wanted juicy stories, not wishy-washy stuff.

'I did catch her pulling wings off a fly once.'

Faye's eyebrow went up.

'Anything else?'

'She was kind of creepy, you know? Always skulking around, spying on people. Listening at doors.'

'How about friends – who were her friends in school?'

'That's just it,' Irene said, shaking her head sadly. 'She didn't have any friends. Too creepy. Too – what's the word – unpredictable.'

'Right. But it's a big leap to go from "creepy and unpredictable" to kidnapping and potential extortion. How do you think she ended up at this point? I mean, plenty of kids have tough upbringings and don't end up kidnapping anyone.' Faye sat back in her chair and waited.

Irene pursed her lips. Who did this one think she was?

'Are you trying to say it's my fault – that I didn't do a good enough job raising her?'

'No, not at all,' Faye said, stirring her coffee without breaking eye contact. 'But our readers will be trying to figure it out – what makes someone go to this extreme?'

Irene bit her lip and looked down. An outward show of reluctance belying an inner search for ideas.

'I remember . . . we were watching a film once about a missing child, and the ransom was like, a million dollars. And Caroline was glued to it. Couldn't take her eyes off it. I remember thinking there was something unnatural about it.' She paused. 'Like she was taking notes in her head, you know?'

'Really? Can you remember the name of the film? The more details we have the better.'

'I'm terrible with film names, what was it . . .'

'It's fine, don't worry about the film.'

Something in Foster's tone suggested she wasn't taking Irene seriously at this point. No matter.

'When is it going to be published?' Irene asked.

'As soon as possible. There's obviously huge interest in the story, and we're hoping it'll jog someone's memory – maybe someone who's seen Carrie in the last week and can help find the little boy.'

Irene gazed at her. But there was no hidden meaning, no falseness. This one seemed to really think her story could help. And actually, wouldn't that be something? *Kidnapper's Mother Saves the Day.* Irene smiled and sipped her coffee.

37

Jenny
Thursday – six days missing

THAT SAME THURSDAY MORNING, in what felt like the longest week of her life, Jenny was sitting at her desk, about to read the latest articles on Carrie and Milo. She went first to TheDaily-Byte.ie for headlines, and her stomach turned when she saw the top story.

Body Found in Bedroom in Dublin North Inner City.

She pushed her glasses up her nose and clicked in, but the harder she tried to skim-read the details, the more difficult it was to take in what it said. She felt sick. It couldn't be Milo, could it? Would they say? Slowing her breathing, she tried again.

Gardaí are awaiting the formal identification of a body found in Dublin today.

They have said it will not be formally identified until a post mortem has been carried out by the State Pathologist. This is expected to take place tomorrow.

The body was found in a house in the north inner city in Dublin early this morning.

It didn't say if it was a man or a woman or a child. Jenny clicked into Google and searched for 'body found Dublin' in the News tab. The story was in all the main newspapers. She tried the first link.

Gardaí are awaiting the formal identification of a man's body found in Dublin house this morning.

A man's body. It wasn't him. Jesus. Still shaky, she clicked out and resumed scrolling through dozens of articles about the Irvine family.

A knock on her open office door jolted her out of a story about an ex-boyfriend of Marissa's. She looked up to see Mark.

'How're things?' he asked, stepping in. 'Any news on the little boy?'

She motioned him to sit. It still felt a bit odd doing that – she and Mark had gone for the same job and she'd got it. Not only did she get the promotion and the salary increase, but she also got the move from the open-plan area into her own office. She wondered sometimes if he resented it. But Mark didn't seem like that kind of guy.

'No.' She sighed. 'Hard to believe this time last week none of this had happened – I was heading off to Paris leaving a perfectly happy Jacob with a perfectly normal childminder, or so I thought. And poor Marissa was kissing Milo goodbye, with no idea . . .' She felt her throat constrict. God, she didn't want to cry in front of Mark.

As though sensing it, he launched into a long story he'd read about a kidnapped child and a ransom request the police had publicly said wouldn't be paid, but privately the parents did pay, and they got their child back. 'Maybe that's what's happening here,' he suggested.

'No,' she shook her head, 'there's been no ransom request. They know there's more than one person involved so it seems like some kind of gang, and they still haven't found her ex, Kyle, so it's possible he's in on it. But no request for money.'

'Ah,' Mark said, his brown eyes sad. 'So, they're thinking child trafficking?'

She nodded. 'No one's said it out loud, but it's what everyone's worrying about now. The poor little guy.' Her eyes filled.

'Well.' Mark looked like he was scrambling for something, anything he could say to comfort her. 'If it's for trafficking . . . it sounds like an awful thing to say, but if that's what it is, they won't hurt him.'

The reality of that truth and what it meant hit her in the stomach like a punch. She cleared her throat, desperate to change the subject.

'I went out with Marissa last night, door-to-door. We spoke to an elderly man who thinks he saw Carrie and Milo on Friday, but then you don't know if it was power of suggestion. There was this other guy too, making jokes about his dead dad and about me hiring Carrie.'

'Wow, sounds like a top bloke.'

'Yeah. He owns that bookmaker's, Shamrock Sports, inherited from his dad apparently. And seems like he's *all* about the money, or else he's one of those guys who hides how he really feels by acting like a dick.'

Mark laughed. Jenny couldn't help but smile. Dick was one of her favourite aspersions, perfect in its simplicity, but not one she used at work.

'I read something about him,' Mark said. 'Alex Fenelon, right?'

'That's him.'

'Hmmm, Shamrock Sports is in trouble I believe – article in

192

the paper last week about falling profits. Reading between the lines, it sounds like bad management practices since Mr Fenelon Senior died. Mr Fenelon Junior, also now known as *Dick*,' he grinned at her, 'doesn't seem to be up to the task.'

'Oh, really? I'm starting to feel sorry for him now. His wife left him too.'

'Maybe when Fenelon started to run the place into the ground, she got sense and scarpered.'

'That doesn't sound like a good reason to leave someone!'

'What's a good reason to leave someone then?' he asked, head tilted, voice soft.

She swallowed and clicked her mouse to bring her screen to life.

'Damn, I've a meeting in a few minutes and I've to get out of here at lunchtime to pick up Jacob.'

He got the message and stood, departing with an offer of help if she needed it. People were offering help all over the place, it seemed, but what did it really mean – it was starting to sound like a thing people say when they don't know how else to fill a silence.

Pulling into her driveway that afternoon, Jenny spotted Joe Downey standing on the porch next door. Blue smoke spiralled above his head as he cupped a cigarette in his hand in a futile bid to hide it.

'Don't worry, Joe, your secret is safe with me,' she said as she locked the car. 'Sinéad will go mad if she sees you though!'

Joe nodded. 'We were so proud to have a doctor in the family until we realized she wouldn't let us do anything fun. Her mother, God rest her, was stashing chocolate all over the house, right up until the end.' He took a drag of his cigarette and a careful step down from the porch, leaving his walking stick where it was, propped against the doorjamb. 'How are you doing, Jenny, with all this stuff going on?'

Jenny didn't need to ask what stuff he meant. It was the only story in town.

'Oh, you know . . .' She tried to smile. 'Not brilliant.'

'You couldn't have known, though. It's not your fault. She seemed like a perfectly fine girl any time I met her.'

'You met Carrie?'

'I meet everyone, out on my walks. See everything too, from up there.' He pointed above him. 'Strange to think I built all these houses, and now here I am in the box room of one of them.' He took another drag of his cigarette. 'But once Sinéad decides something, there's no talking her out of it, and if she says I can't live on my own any more, then I can't live on my own any more.' He shook his head in resignation, but there was affection there too.

'You must miss your old house,' Jenny said. She'd only ever driven past it, a sprawling mansion on Northland Road. Rumour had it the house was gifted to Joe's wife when they got married. Imagine having in-laws who could give you a house like that, Jenny thought. As opposed to in-laws like Adeline who insist you move closer to them, even when you can hardly afford it.

'I do miss it, but it's nice to have company here and neighbours to talk to. Even the ones who turn out to be kidnappers.' Joe smiled wryly at Jenny. 'She really did seem perfectly fine. Not so much the fella who used to call in though.'

Jenny looked at him in surprise. 'What fella?'

'The boyfriend. Dark-haired. Tall. Skinny. You know those ones that are so skinny, you can tell they're trouble.'

'And you saw him calling in to our house?'

'I did, indeed. I told you, I see everything.'

'Did you tell the police?'

'Tell the police that some fella was calling in to her? God no, not my business.' He paused. 'What, do you think I should have?'

'Well, it might help them in the investigation . . .'

'Ah, not a fan of the guards, Jenny. Bit of a run-in with them years ago over security on one of the construction sites.'

'Look, I can mention it to the guard who's dealing with the case, and she can decide what to do about it. Does that sound OK?'

Joe nodded, extinguished his cigarette in a planter on the porch, and carefully placed the butt inside a cigarette packet.

'That sounds OK. Just don't tell Sinéad about this.' He winked, waved the cigarette packet, and stepped back inside his daughter's house.

38

Two months earlier

WAY TOO MUCH PROSECCO for a work night, *way* too much. Jenny shook her head at her reflection in the bathroom mirror, and immediately regretted the movement. She grabbed the paracetamol and padded through to her bedroom to get the water from her bedside table. One pint glass, full to the brim, untouched. Someday, she'd remember to drink the water.

She gripped the bannister as she came down the stairs, feeling slightly unsteady, and at first she didn't notice Richie standing by the front door. He had his back to her, but it looked like he was staring down at something in his hands.

'What have you got there?' she asked, as she got to the bottom step.

He whirled around, sliding whatever it was into his back pocket.

She looked at him, puzzled, but his expression was hard to read. Guilt? Anger?

'Richie, is everything OK?'

'Sure. Everything is fine.' He eyed her pyjamas. 'Aren't you going to be late for work?'

'I'm going to work from home, I'm a bit tired from last night. I can do Jacob's homework with him as well, which is nice.'

'Good idea, you should do it more often. It'd be good for Jacob!' he said, with deliberate brightness.

Here we go, she thought.

'Yeah, every now and then is fine, but mostly I need to be in the office, you know that. To see clients and the team.'

'Of course. Right, see you later,' he said, and with that he was gone out the front door, along with whatever was in his pocket.

In the kitchen, Carrie was pouring milk over Jacob's Weetabix. She looked surprised to see Jenny.

'Morning, Carrie, how are you? I'm working from home today by the way.' She walked over to the table and kissed Jacob's head. 'I'll be in the den at my desk, so I won't be in your way,' Jenny said, as she made herself a coffee. 'Would you like one?'

Carrie shook her head. 'No, thank you.'

'So, the school social was grand in the end,' Jenny said, in an effort to make conversation, as she sat at the breakfast bar, nursing her coffee and her sore head. 'I met some interesting people – it was a bit "how the other half live". One group in particular who seemed to thrive on ripping people apart.' She rolled her eyes. 'And of course, that's exactly what I'm doing now, bitching about them. But they deserve it.' She grinned at Carrie and got a small smile in return.

'Then there was this woman called Marissa. Utterly stunning. Like if you imagine the most gorgeous woman you can, then multiply that by another fifty per cent, you've got Marissa Irvine. Some of the others were saying she'd had surgery done but I think that's jealousy talking.'

'Oh yes? And she's one of the parents in the class?' Carrie asked, filling Jacob's water bottle.

'Yeah, her little boy is Milo. She's not at the school much, so you probably haven't seen her there. They have a childminder too; Ana I think her name is. But yeah, gorgeous woman, the kind of person you nearly want to hate because she's so perfect, except for the fact that she's really good fun and kind of addictive, if that makes sense? Infectious? Anyway, I really liked her.'

Carrie nodded.

God, it was a one-way street. 'We were saying we should do a playdate, for Jacob and Milo.'

'Oh, that will be lovely for Jacob,' Carrie said, as she put his water bottle in his schoolbag and glanced at the clock.

'What time do you usually go?' Jenny asked, then wondered if it sounded like she was trying to get rid of her. Which she was – small talk was hard at the best of times, but even more so with a hangover.

'Five more minutes,' Carrie said. 'Jacob, are you ready to do your teeth?'

Jacob jumped off his seat and ran upstairs.

'The way we met was funny actually,' Jenny said, searching on her phone. 'We were wearing the same dress. Marissa took a photo of us and put it on her Instagram. I wonder if I can see it, even though I don't have an account. Do you have Instagram?'

Carrie shook her head.

'Oh good, then I'm not the last person on the planet who doesn't. She said her account is @MarissaNotMelissa, but maybe I need to set up an account to see it.' Suddenly, she really wanted a copy of the photo – she was the cliché, the mother behind the camera, and she didn't see herself as photogenic. But that picture last night was different. Maybe some of Marissa's magic had rubbed off on her.

'Oh, there it is!' She held up the photo to show Carrie. 'Now, clearly the dress looks better on her, but it's a good photo, isn't it?'

Carrie took the phone and examined the screen.

'Yes, very nice,' she agreed, and handed back the phone.

And that, it seemed, was as far as Carrie was to be drawn on a chat about the night out. Jenny got up to make another coffee, a feat that led to an awkward dance when Carrie stood in front of the cutlery drawer just as Jenny pulled it out to get a spoon. Maybe this was why she didn't work from home more often, Jenny thought, as she headed for her desk in the den.

Two kilometres away, in a bigger, shinier kitchen, Marissa was glugging back a second cup of coffee and checking work emails on her phone. She didn't have a hangover – she never got hangovers. It had annoyed her friends immensely when they were experimenting with peach schnapps and Malibu in their teens and it annoyed them just as much today, now that they were fielding 5 a.m. wake-up calls from babies who didn't understand that their parents had only just gone to sleep. This morning, Marissa sat opposite her husband, in perfectly applied barely-there make-up and a green shift dress, looking for all the world like she'd been in bed at ten o'clock.

Peter, on the other hand, was a little bleary-eyed.

'It's because you're so much older than me,' she said, smirking at him, as he swallowed two painkillers. 'You can't hack the nights out any more.'

'Hmm. Or maybe it's because you were out for the count when Milo came in for a glass of water at three, and again an hour later because he had a nightmare,' he said. 'Snoring your head off.'

'I don't snore!'

'I'll record you next time,' he muttered, finishing his coffee. 'Jesus, I am getting a bit old for weeknight drinking though.'

'Yes, but it was terrifically good fun, and nice to meet parents we hadn't already met. I got chatting to a lovely woman called Jenny, I think her son and Milo would make great friends.'

Peter grinned at her. 'So, eh, was her son at the social? Is that how you sized up his suitability?'

'Of course not. But if the parents are nice, the kids are nice – that's a rule of thumb.'

'Oh Jesus, you're going to be one of those mothers who chooses her favourite parents and makes her child be friends with their kids, aren't you.'

'I'm not! Who on earth would do that?'

He gave her a sidelong glance. 'Milo will make friends in his own time – he's only been there a couple of weeks. Let's not be those parents who dictate everything in their children's lives, eh? What's it called, helicoptering? Hothousing?'

'Hothousing is about pushing them too intensely educationally, which I would never do.' She paused. 'Though I was thinking about having him tested to see if he's in the gifted range. No harm, right?'

'Marissa, give him time to find his own way – I don't think we need to pressure him or have him doing tests.'

'It's not pressuring, it's just reaching his potential. He sees the world differently – we should explore it.'

'Maybe, when he's old enough to decide for himself. For now, let him be a kid, and let him pick his own friends. Don't turn into one of those pushy mothers!'

With that, he kissed her and left for work. Marissa poured a third cup of coffee. She wasn't going to be one of those mothers – she just wanted the best for her child. And if he needed a little nudge along the way, was there anything wrong with that?

Back in Belton Heights, just before three o'clock, Jenny heard the key turn in the front door as Carrie and Jacob arrived back from school. The time Carrie had been gone had been a welcome break – there was something not quite relaxing about skirting around someone in the house all day. And although Carrie was quiet and shy, Jenny found herself feeling self-conscious and awkward around her.

'How was his day – all good?' Jenny asked, after hugging Jacob and helping him off with his coat.

'Yes, fine. Oh, I met the girl Ana you mentioned, Milo's minder?'

'Ah great!'

'I hope you don't mind, but she asked for your number so Milo's mother could set up a playdate – I passed it on to her. Is that all right? Maybe I should have asked you first . . .'

'No, that's perfect!' Jenny said, fizzing a little as she realized she hadn't been sure she'd hear from her new friend again. 'Marissa said she wanted to set something up. I'd say their house is going to make ours look like a hovel if Milo comes here, but hey, we knew that when we moved to Kerryglen.'

'Oh, are they wealthy or something?'

Jenny shrugged. 'I don't know really, but they look very glamorous. He's something big in finance and she's a solicitor, and she just looks really groomed – like she gets her hair and her nails done every week? But sure look, what do I know?'

Carrie nodded, but said nothing else. Dear God, it was like talking to a rock. But then, that's not why they hired her. As long as Jacob was happy and safe in her care, that's all that really mattered.

39

Jenny
Thursday – six days missing

JENNY PULLED INTO SCHOOL pick-up traffic and drove slowly out of Pine Valley. Jacob was quiet, not even giving his usual mono-syllabic response to her 'how was your day' question. Had he heard something else about Carrie?

'Jacob, did anyone in school talk about Milo today?' she asked, glancing in the rearview mirror. His face fell. 'What was it, love, you can tell me.'

'Alex Smith said Carrie is a baddie. That she tooked Milo and killed him.'

She swallowed. It was bound to happen. Kids overhearing parents or seeing news reports and adding in everything they knew from fairy tales about stolen children.

'Jacob, pet, it isn't true. We don't know what's going on, but the police don't think anything bad has happened to Milo.' The line between protecting and outright lying was thin, but Marissa had said the guards were reasonably sure the dumped raincoat was a deliberate attempt to mislead the investigation. Meaning Milo was alive.

'Will she come back to mind me? I miss her.'

Jenny could feel her heart squeeze inside her chest.

'I . . . maybe I'll mind you for a while. Won't that be fun?'

He sat looking out the window, saying nothing at all until they pulled into the driveway behind Richie's car.

'Daddy's here!' Jacob squealed, scrambling to undo his car-seat buckle.

'Hold on, I'll do it,' Jenny said, wondering what Richie was doing home so early.

Noise from upstairs drew her to their bedroom. Richie was on his hands and knees, rummaging frantically through a pile of loose pages, torn envelopes and old receipts – the contents of his bedside locker drawer inexplicably upended on their bedroom floor.

'Are you OK?' she asked, making him jump.

'You gave me a fright!' he said, sitting back on his hunkers. His face was bright red, maybe from the effort of whatever this search was, though Jenny had the distinct impression it was because he'd just been caught. But doing what?

'Did you lose something?'

'I . . . it's nothing. It's—'

Jacob ran into the room straight into Richie's arms for a hug, interrupting the conversation.

Jenny put her keys on the dresser. 'What has you home already?'

Richie released Jacob, and they watched as he raced out of the room and into his own, to say hi to Jem.

'Half-day for a rugby match but I cried off,' Richie said, turning back to her. 'It's bloody freezing out there. I said I had a dental appointment.' He grinned. 'Now the three of us can have the afternoon together.'

'Ah.'

'What's up?'

'Well, it's just I had to rush out of work to pick up Jacob. For the fourth day in a row. If you were going to be home early, it would have been handy if you could have picked him up today.'

'Sorry, I didn't think of it.'

She sighed. 'That's just it, Richie – I need you to think of things. Why is it always down to me to pick up the pieces when we have no childcare?'

'Because I can't just walk away from a class of kids – it's not the same as an office job where you can come and go as you please.'

'But I *can't* come and go as I please – my boss will lose patience if we don't sort something soon. But I do it, even if it means I'm in the doghouse, because that's part of being a parent.'

'Working in a school is different.'

'So you've been saying for the last four years.'

'Jesus, Jenny, you never change.'

She couldn't hold it in any longer. '*I* never change? Are you serious? You say you want us to have another baby, and that I'm choosing work over family, but you know what, another baby would just mean twice as much work for me, and absolutely no change for you. So maybe think about that the next time you and your bloody mother have that conversation about how selfish I am.'

She picked up the keys, stormed downstairs, and out the front door, leaving Richie staring open-mouthed after her.

Dammit anyway, Jenny thought, as she drove towards Castle Street and began to breathe more evenly. That was probably an overreaction to Richie's half-day, especially if he'd been looking forward to spending time together. But that was the problem – he thought about the fun bits, not the practical bits. And as soon as her job came up, he seemed to lose all reason. She tried to put her finger on when this attitude towards her job had started. Was it when she'd got the promotion at the start of the summer? It made no sense though, her hours hadn't changed – if anything she had more flexibility, and the salary helped, that was how they'd paid for this year's holiday. Was that it? The salary jump? He'd made jokes over the years about being a lowly teacher with no prospects, but they were always just that – jokes. Weren't they? God. She never, ever saw Richie as petty or jealous. And maybe that was unfair – he was brought up in a house with clear gender lines: men were breadwinners, and women home-makers. And on top of that, he had Adeline Furlong-Kennedy's whispering voice in his ear. *Why is Jenny always working, when is she going to have another baby, poor Jacob at home with the nanny.*

Pulling into the church car park, she paid for thirty minutes' parking, then on second thought, upped it to an hour. She needed time to cool off.

There were posters on the door of the parish hall; Milo's blond hair and cheeky smile beaming out on churchgoers and yoga students and mum-and-toddler groups. The next meeting for search party volunteers was in ten minutes. Jenny looked around – there was nobody there yet. But then, people prob-ably didn't come until the appointed time. She walked out on to Castle Street, and without quite planning to, found herself in Esther's Tea Garden.

It was crowded and there was just one free table, right at the back. Jenny made her way through, eyes down, as whispers wafted up, following her to her table. *The nanny, that's the one she worked for. Imagine.*

Esther was over as soon as she sat, her untamed curls a bird's nest on her head, a wide smile on her warm face.

'Jenny, good to see you,' she said, flipping a notebook out of a hidden pocket in the billowing skirt of her purple dress. 'Can I get you a coffee, and maybe some homemade ginger cake?'

Jenny hadn't had ginger cake since she was a child, but suddenly it was exactly what she wanted. She nodded.

'I'm sure you're tired, I know you've been helping Marissa with leafleting and looking after your little boy and going to work. It sounds exhausting.'

Jenny nodded again, not trusting her voice. Why was it she could keep it together through an argument with Richie but as soon as this almost-stranger was nice to her, she wanted to burst into tears?

'I'll go get those for you now, love,' Esther said, not pushing for the reply that was stuck in Jenny's throat and brimming behind her eyes.

The ginger cake worked its sweet, spicy magic – Jenny felt like she could face anything once she'd finished the last crumb. She'd go home, make up with Richie, and the three of them would snuggle on the couch for a movie night. The local busybodies were tomorrow's problem; she was taking an evening off.

But then her phone beeped with a text from Marissa.

There's news. Please can you come over. I can't do this.

40

Jenny
Thursday – six days missing

A WIND WHIPPED UP as Jenny hurriedly unlocked her car, and one of Milo's posters flapped angrily against the door of the parish hall. The car park was devoid of people. Had anyone turned up for the search party meeting? Castle Street was eerily quiet when she pulled out, though it was still only four o'clock. She switched on the radio to break the silence, just as the news headlines came on.

'Gardaí have not yet formally identified the body found in Dublin's north inner city this morning, but the victim has been named locally as Danny Vaughan, a resident of the house in which he was found. The man's death is being treated as suspicious and an investigation is underway. A post mortem is due to be carried out tomorrow.'

Jenny turned down the volume.

Danny Vaughan.

Why did that name sound familiar? Maybe it was in the news reports she'd read earlier? In her head, she scanned back through the articles. She was nearly sure the victim wasn't named, so why did it ring a bell? She shook her head. It would come.

Pulling into the driveway of Maple Lodge, she spotted a navy car arriving just ahead of her. Not Peter's Lexus or Marissa's

Jeep. The police maybe? Was that why Marissa had asked her to come over? More bad news – the worst news? Her hand shook as she pulled in behind the navy car and got out.

But it wasn't the police – it was Colin, Marissa's business partner. Jenny's stomach flip-flopped and she gave silent thanks.

Colin smiled at her, which felt completely at odds with what had just gone through her mind. She forced a half-smile back.

'Look at us, arriving together – they'll think we're having an affair,' he quipped, and it hung in the air as she struggled to think of a suitable response.

In the end, she was saved by Peter, who opened the front door before the silence became awkward.

'Come in, Marissa's through here,' he said, his face as grey as his hair.

Marissa was sitting at the table, staring at nothing, even more drawn and pale than the night before.

'What is it?' Jenny asked, taking her hand. Marissa didn't react.

'The police still haven't found Kyle Byrde, but they did come up with something,' Peter said quietly. 'A pal of his from prison has just been arrested again, this time for suspected child trafficking. They raided a betting shop – he worked there, I think – and found all sorts of dodgy correspondence on his work computer. He's not the ringleader, just a link in the chain. But still. Child trafficking . . .'

Marissa bolted from the chair and rushed out of the kitchen. Jenny sat, stuck to the seat. Colin stood in the middle of the room, shaking his head. Peter was a granite statue, grey, immobile. The only sound was Marissa throwing up.

'They think Kyle Byrde may be involved in some kind of trafficking ring?' Jenny asked softly.

Peter nodded. 'They didn't say either way. They just told us about the guy they arrested and asked us if we knew him – but I've never heard of him.'

'And they've still had no luck finding Kyle Byrde? Don't they have ways of finding people with PPS numbers or mobile phones or motor tax?'

'Normally, yes, but he seems to have come out of prison and disappeared into thin air. He hasn't claimed social welfare, doesn't have a phone contract – it's like he deliberately stayed under the radar. Which I suppose is exactly what you'd do if you wanted to get involved in organized crime.'

Colin was pacing up and down the kitchen, running his hand through his Tintin hair. 'What about an address? On TV, they always have an address to go to when they leave prison?'

'The only address they have is a place called St Colman's near the city centre. Apparently he grew up there but he hasn't been seen there since he was sixteen, and his mother has passed away. It's a dead end.'

Colin looked crestfallen that his TV-inspired brainwave hadn't panned out.

'Oh!' Jenny suddenly remembered the conversation with Joe Downey earlier that afternoon.

'What is it?' Peter asked.

Crap, crap, crap. This was going to make her look even more incompetent. She took a breath.

'My neighbour Joe told me earlier that he'd seen a man calling at our house from time to time. It might have been Kyle Byrde. I was going to let the guards know.' That sounded lame. Why hadn't she phoned the guards earlier? Too busy arguing with Richie and eating ginger cake. *Damn.*

'You haven't told them yet?'

'Sorry, I had to rush to the school and then . . .' There was no way to finish the sentence without making things worse. Her cheeks burned. 'It might be nothing, and the man who said it is elderly. Joe Downey – he lives with his daughter, Sinéad Downey, the GP?'

Peter nodded.

'He might be wrong about it being Carrie's boyfriend. It could be nothing . . .'

'Surely we should let the guards decide that,' Peter said, ice in his voice.

'Absolutely. I'll call now.'

'I'll do it, I can put you on to explain,' Peter said, taking out his phone and walking through to the sitting room, just as Marissa arrived back in the kitchen. She looked dazed, and pale as a pan of milk.

'Sorry,' she said, slipping into her chair. 'I'm on two different types of tablets and my stomach can't hack it.'

'Don't apologize,' Jenny said, taking her hand again. 'Anyone else would be in a medically induced coma just to get through this, you're amazing. You're really amazing.' And as Colin shuffled, and Peter murmured, and the big kitchen clock ticked ominously on, the two women sat saying nothing at all.

41

Marissa
Thursday – six days missing

DUSK THICKENED TO DARK and the tablets kicked in and Marissa didn't move.

At the blurred edges of her mind, she was conscious of Jenny's departure and Colin's hovering presence.

'Thank you for coming, Colin,' she said after a while. 'How did you hear?'

'How did I – oh, you mean about the guy from the prison?'

'Yes – did Peter call you?'

Colin shuffled from one foot to the other.

'I, ah, no. I didn't know about it actually.'

'Oh, I thought that's why you were here.'

Silence.

Colin cleared his throat.

'What is it?' Marissa asked.

'Look, I had no idea you'd just got more bad news, but I need to get at some files before the audit, so I was calling to ask for your keys.' His cheeks were red, his eyes down. 'Sorry, it sounds like the most unimportant thing in the world with everything you're going through.'

'Not at all, Col. You'll never know how grateful I am that you're keeping things going while all this is happening. You don't have to feel bad for trying to make sure we pass the audit.'

'We'll pass it, don't worry. I know you said you were looking at two files – if I can get those two out of your office and go through them, I think everything else is shipshape.'

'I know the ones you mean, Downey and Fenelon,' she said tiredly, wondering if it was the tablets or plain exhaustion. 'I just don't know where they are. If I give you the keys you could be searching for ever. Look, I'll go down tonight and rummage around, and leave the files out at reception, would that work?'

'Ah, Mar, I can't ask you to do that.'

'It's fine.' She lifted her hand to wave away his objection. 'Peter and I are going back to Pine Valley to knock on doors anyway. It's easy to call into the office beforehand.'

Nodding, thanking her, hands in pockets, Colin loped out of the kitchen and through the front door, no doubt grateful to escape.

Between calls with McConville and an interview with a journalist, it was eight o'clock by the time Peter and Marissa left the house. Irvine and Dobson Associates was in an upstairs office space above a Michelin-starred restaurant and Rayburn Estate Agents. Sometimes the smell of just-cooked food wafted up and made them drop everything for an early lunch, but tonight the smell made Marissa feel sick. She slid the key into the upstairs door that led to reception and walked through to unlock her own office. Standing for a moment in the centre of the room, a tsunami of grief hit her again. Six days earlier, she had walked out of this very office with no idea Milo was gone. Paralysed, she stood, a brittle statue, sure if someone tipped her, she'd crash to the ground and break into a million pieces. A welcome million pieces because then it would be over. But Peter didn't tip her; he put his arms around her and told her it would be OK. And they both knew it wasn't OK and it might never be OK, but she didn't have the strength to argue.

'Is everything all right workwise, do you think – nothing you need to worry about for the audit?' Peter asked.

'It should be fine. The Downey case is tricky because Joe's wife had so many assets in her name only, but I think it's OK. In the Fenelon case, there's just something not quite right but I'd need to go through it.'

'Was Fenelon fiddling the books?'

'I wouldn't put anything past him, but no, probably not. I need to have a proper look.' She stopped, forgetting and remembering all at once. 'Not now though. Sometime . . . else.'

'Right, let's find those files and get out of here,' Peter said.

'Yeah, sorry, they'll either be in my desk or in the filing cabinet, and I think I had printed off some fresh docs – they'll be in the printer out behind reception, or probably in the tray; Shauna would have taken them out since last week.'

She took her filing cabinet keys and started to check the first drawer, while Peter went to gather pages from the printer. After a moment, she heard a grunt.

'You OK?' she asked, putting her head around the door.

Some pages had slipped behind the table on which the printer stood, and he was trying to pull the table out to get at them.

'Yeah, this is more awkward than it looks.'

'Pages are always slipping behind it, it's easier to just get down on the floor to reach them – pull them out that way.'

He did as she suggested and stood back up, looking at the pages. As he did, his face changed.

'Everything OK?' Marissa asked.

Peter looked up. There was something unreadable on his face.

'Yeah. All fine.'

'Right, I've got the two files here – I'll just add those extra pages in.'

Peter nodded. 'I'll do it for you.' He grabbed an empty manila folder and put the loose pages into it, then came over and took the Downey and Fenelon files out of her hands.

'You have a quick look around in case there's anything else you need, and I'll put these behind reception. The sooner we go door-to-door the better – people will stop answering if it gets too late.'

She nodded, thinking how odd it was in their here-and-now; how quickly they'd learned which times were best for knocking on doors, and how to put posters on lamp posts, and what to wear for newspaper interviews.

Back in the car, as they slid on to Castle Street, they sat in silence. Marissa watched as the shops and offices slipped past, gaining speed. Quickly replaced by trees and homes and lights and people whose only worry was whether or not there was fresh bread for tomorrow's school lunches. She sat with her hands clasped, dreading going door-to-door, dreaming of tonight's sleeping pill and blocking all of it out. She couldn't have known – none of them could – that this was the night everything changed for ever.

PART 2

42

Marissa
Friday – seven days missing

THE SOUND OF THE phone was shrill in the silent house, but it took three rings to cut through the fog of sleep. They'd both taken sedatives the night before, and as Marissa opened bleary eyes and felt around for her phone, Peter snored on, oblivious. She couldn't see the screen but managed to swipe the right spot and answer the call. The voice on the other end sliced through the fog like a hot knife through snow. Marissa sat up, wide awake. It was McConville. They had a boy in the station.

A boy who might be Milo.

Marissa couldn't speak – she grabbed Peter's shoulder to wake him and pushed the phone to his ear. On the floor, in a puddle, lay the jeans and sweater she'd worn the night before. She pulled them on as fast as she could, her speed slowing her down as she fumbled with buttons and zips. Peter was up now too, throwing on the nearest clothes he could find. They locked eyes but didn't speak. It was too much. What if it wasn't him, what if it was too late, what if he was injured or worse, and McConville couldn't say on the phone?

Down the stairs and out the door as morning sunlight flickered through the trees that lined the driveway. Into the car,

Peter's car, because there was no way she could drive. In gripped silence, they sped through the backroads of Kerryglen, not daring to believe and still afraid to speak.

Peter reached for the radio as the news headlines came on. Without breathing, they listened. An early morning Post Office raid, a car crash in the Midlands, a renewed appeal for witnesses in the murder of Danny Vaughan, a blip in a peace process in some faraway country.

But nothing about a boy lost and found.

The news became sport and the sport became weather and the weather became a listener competition, and Peter reached out to switch it off because Marissa couldn't move.

At Blackrock Garda station, there was no parking space free. Peter left the car on the footpath, just outside the entrance, and they ran inside, breathless, shaking, but now she could speak.

'Milo. I'm Milo Irvine's mother. Is he here? Detective Sergeant McConville said . . .'

The man behind the glass hatch nodded – to let her know he'd find McConville or to let her know Milo was there, she couldn't. tell. He closed the hatch and walked away, and moments later, McConville opened a door to the side. She beckoned them through. Marissa gulped a breath or maybe a sob, and followed, with Peter close behind. McConville led them to a door, looked at them once, her face inscrutable, and opened it. Inside, on a couch, sat a woman they didn't know, and a little boy they did.

Milo.

Dark hair now, but the face she knew like no other face in the world.

She crossed the room in three strides, falling to her knees to pull him into her arms. Peter was there then too, wrapping

218

around both of them, shaking, sobbing. And she was crying now and finally she could breathe. *Milo.*

They sat together, Milo on Marissa's lap, Peter holding his hand. For a long time, they hugged, and nobody spoke. The woman they didn't recognize stood by the door with McConville. They talked in hushed voices, glancing over every now and then. Marissa put her face in Milo's hair, this new, brown hair that was surprisingly just as baby-soft as it always was, and hugged him to her like she'd never let go. She wouldn't. She'd never let him out of her sight.

Milo was saying something. 'You're not dead, Mummy, I thought you were dead. Carrie told me you had to go away for work, and then you died.'

A well of hate surged through Marissa, so intense it almost pushed her to the floor. And at that moment, she knew if she ever saw Carrie again, she'd kill her. Without hesitation, without regret, she'd kill her with her own hands. She took a deep breath to gather herself.

'Oh my love, I'm not dead. I'm here and you're safe, and nobody will ever take us away from each other again.' She bent her head to look into his face as she said it, wishing she could take a piece of her heart and put it inside him, to convince him, to reassure him. Her eyes searched his face and travelled down to the unfamiliar navy sweater and blue jeans he was wearing. Was he hurt? They'd have told her if he was hurt, wouldn't they?

Reading her mind, McConville spoke.

'He'll need to be examined by a doctor – Dr Downey from the local GP practice is on her way here – but he seems in good health.'

Still reeling, Marissa could only nod to show McConville she'd heard.

McConville was talking again. 'We'll need to ask Milo questions but we can do it in short sessions over time. For now, we
just want to get a sense of what happened last night and where
he was held, so we can try to find the perpetrators before too
much time elapses.'

'But didn't you catch them when you got him? Where
was he?'

'He was found in a locked car on Amersham Park, a residen-
tial street in Sandymount in Dublin 4. A newspaper delivery
man saw him asleep in the back seat and got worried – he
called 999 to report it and waited with the car.'

Marissa shook her head. *Jesus Christ.* Somehow despite everything he'd been through in the last week, the idea of Milo on his
own in a car in the middle of the night was desperately upsetting.

'But whose car was it?' Peter asked.

McConville hesitated but only for a second.

'It was rented by Carrie, under another name.'

'And have you arrested her?' Peter asked.

'No, not yet. We haven't been able to locate her.'

Marissa looked at her son, his small face paler than she'd
ever known it, his eyes drooping with exhaustion, his tiny
shoulders hunched. She wanted Carrie and whoever else had
done this caught. But she wanted her boy home too.

'Do you need to question him this morning?'

The other woman nodded, and Marissa looked at her properly
for the first time. She was tall and dark-haired with a serious face
and big serious glasses. Her cream blouse was buttoned up to
her neck, and her black suit perfectly pressed.

'I'm Sergeant Fiona Sheridan, Mrs Irvine. I have specialist
interviewer training for questioning children so I'll be doing the
interviews with Milo, with you and your husband sitting in, of
course. I know you want to take him home, and that's what we

want too, but I also know that if we're to have any chance of catching the people who did this, time is critical.'

Marissa said nothing, her eyes drawn to the black-and-white clock above the door. The second hand ticked loudly around its circuit, oblivious to the drama beneath.

'The interviews will be in short sessions and in your home if you prefer,' Fiona Sheridan continued, 'but perhaps we can do five minutes now, before you go?'

Marissa looked over at Peter. He nodded. They could do five minutes.

Chairs came from nowhere, as did a small table. McConville and Sheridan sat opposite the Irvines – McConville taking notes, Sheridan recording on what looked like an old-fashioned tape recorder. She stated the time and date and who was in the room, then very gently asked Milo what happened last night.

The answer was the hardest thing Marissa had ever sat through. It took everything she had in her to sit and listen, to stop herself from picking him up and sweeping him out of the room. But she stuck her fingernails in her palm and forced herself to stay, to listen, to live it with him.

'I was in my bed in Carrie's house and a man taked me out of it,' Milo said with a shuddery breath. 'I got a fright because I was asleep. It was dark and I couldn't see anything and I thought it was a monster.'

Marissa squeezed his hand.

'And what happened then?' Sheridan asked.

'He taked me outside and put me in the car. We went in the car and I was crying and asking for Carrie.'

Marissa swallowed and shook her head. How would they ever get past this?

'Did he drive for a long time, Milo?' Sheridan asked, her serious eyes kind behind her huge glasses.

'I don't know.'

She didn't push.

'What happened then?'

'The car stopped. He said he had to meet a bad, bad man and if I get out of the car, the bad man will hurt me.'

Marissa closed her eyes as the room began to move and sway. Her child. This had happened to her child. She gripped Milo's hand so hard, he whispered that it hurt. She loosened but didn't let go.

'And what happened then?'

'I was crying and he told me I had to be quiet or the bad man would be angry. But I couldn't stop.'

'Could you see his face, Milo?'

'No, he had a black cover on it.'

'OK. And what was his voice like?'

'Like a monster,' Milo said in a whisper, and Marissa thought her heart would shatter all over again. 'Can I go home now?' he asked, and that was it, Marissa couldn't go on any more.

'We need to stop, I'm sorry.'

'That's fine, that's enough for now,' Fiona Sheridan said, as she and McConville stood. 'Dr Downey should be here now. I'll need to call in to you tomorrow morning to talk some more, but again it will be only ten minutes. Or you can come here if you prefer?'

Marissa looked at Peter, not sure which was worse. He made the decision for all of them.

'If you could come to the house that would be better for him, I think,' he said, scooping up his son. 'Let's go, Milo-Mouse. The doctor will have a quick look and then we'll get you home where you belong.'

And that was it. For now at least.

43

Marissa
Friday

LATER, MARISSA COULD NEVER quite recall the precise details of that
morning after they got home. A blur of tears and hugs and smiles,
and later, raw, roaring sobs when Milo finally fell asleep and she
tiptoed out of his room to lean against the bannister and let
some of it out. And within half a minute, she was back in the
room because she couldn't leave him, not now, not ever. She and
Peter slipped in and out of sleep, lying beside him, whispering
across his small, newly brown head, while downstairs, their
phones buzzed with messages and calls, all unanswered. That
night, they put on a film in Milo's room and the three of them
lay in his bed, cocooned from the world, at least for now.

The cocoon was split open on Saturday morning when Fiona
Sheridan arrived to interview Milo. Marissa wanted to say no,
to leave him in peace, but of course there could be no peace
until Carrie was caught.

'Ten minutes max,' she said to Sheridan as they sat in the living room.

'Not a second more, I promise.'

Again, she recorded, and this time she took notes. Milo sat on the couch, flanked by his parents. Sheridan sat opposite, smiled at Milo and told him he was a great boy. He smiled back, and Marissa clenched her jaw, waiting for the questions that would make his smile disappear.

'Milo, I'm going to ask you a few things that will help us in a really big way. Is that OK?'

Milo nodded.

'Can you tell us about Carrie's house?'

Marissa tensed at Carrie's name, but Milo didn't hesitate. Describing the house was safe ground, it seemed.

'Carrie has a nice house, and the TV is bigger than the TV in my bedroom here.'

'Was it a big house?'

He tilted his head, considering this.

'A bit big.'

'Bigger than your house?'

'No.'

'Where did you sleep?'

'In my bedroom.'

'In *your* bedroom?'

'In Carrie's house, I mean. She said it was my *new* bedroom.'

'Oh wow, was it nice?'

'Mm hmm,' he said, nodding. 'But 'cept the duvet, it was just boring white.'

'And did it have toys?'

'No.' He looked sad. 'No toys.' Then his face brightened. 'But loads of movies and iPad games. My mummy and daddy don't let me have iPad time during the week, but Carrie said I could.'

'Did you play outside while you were there?'

'No. Carrie said it was too cold and we had to stay in. One day I saw a football – it came over the wall like another kid made a mistake, and I wanted to go out to kick it back but she said no. I was cross about that.'

Marissa watched as Sheridan scribbled notes quickly.

'Did anyone else live in the house?'

Marissa held her breath.

'A man comed one time but then he was gone again. He was apposed to come back but he didn't.'

'What was this man like?'

'He didn't talk to me. He comed in the night to talk to Carrie and I heard him.'

'Did you see him?'

'No, I only heard his voice talking to Carrie.'

'And can you remember what he said?' Sheridan asked, removing her glasses and leaning towards Milo.

'Lots of things. He said something about two more days. And he told Carrie to take my photo.'

'Did she take your photo?'

'Mm hmm.' He nodded.

'Was it a photo of your head or your whole body?'

Marissa froze.

Milo considered for a moment. 'Only my face. I was smiling because you should always smile in photos and she got cross and told me not to, that I can't smile for this photo.'

'Did she say what it was for?'

'No. She said we were going on a long journey. And there would be other children there. I can't remember anything else,' he said, his eyes filling with sudden tears.

Marissa opened her mouth to say that was enough, but Fiona Sheridan got there first.

'That's OK, Milo, you've been the best boy. Can I come back to you tomorrow to chat again?'

'OK.'

At the front door, Sheridan spoke to Marissa in a low voice.

'That was good, he did great.'

'Really? It feels like a needle in a haystack – the house could be anywhere.'

'What he told us about a football coming over the wall tells us it's unlikely to be a remote countryside location – we're probably talking about somewhere urban, possibly here in Dublin.'

Marissa rubbed her temple.

'I feel bad – I don't want Milo to have to answer lots of questions but if he doesn't, you're stuck, yes? There's not much you can do without information from him?'

'Oh, there's plenty, don't worry about that – we're going through CCTV footage from businesses near where the car was found and in the wider Sandymount area.' She took off her glasses. 'But yes, if he says anything at all you think might help, give us a call?'

Marissa said she would and opened the door to show her out, just as Brian rounded the corner and Colin's car pulled up. The cocoon had well and truly burst.

44

Marissa
Saturday

COLIN BOUNDED OUT OF the car and up to the front door like a giant lolloping Labrador and grabbed Marissa into a hug. Over his shoulder, Marissa saw Brian hang back, watching, waiting his turn, though with Brian there wouldn't be hugging, good God no. She smiled at him, rolled her eyes at Colin's ongoing embrace, and immediately welled up. Again.

Extracting herself from Colin, she shooed him in the door, and made way for Brian to join them.

'Milo's in the living room with Peter,' she said to the unspoken question. 'That was the garda interviewer you just saw leaving.'

'Oh my God, they're *interviewing* him? Would they not leave the poor kid in peace?' Colin said, as the three of them stood in the light-filled hall.

'The sooner they can find out where he was held and who else was there, the more chance they have of catching them,' Marissa explained. 'And she's good in fairness – she's very gentle.'

'I guess you guys are asking him questions all the time too,' Colin said, nodding. 'He's probably used to it.'

'No, actually, they advised us not to – they said it's better to let them do it.' It came out sounding prickly.

Colin gave her a funny look. It was almost true. She hadn't quizzed Milo – not so much because she was following orders, but because she couldn't find the words. How do you ask your four-year-old son what it was like being kidnapped?

'Right. And have they been able to find out anything?'

'Not a lot. Carrie brought him to her house, he said. But we have no idea where that is.'

'Didn't someone say she was from a house in the countryside?' Brian asked, frowning. 'Somewhere near Bray?'

'That was all made up, just like her three brothers and her dead parents. It's *insane.*'

'But if she owned a house, the guards can find it – she's hardly managed to buy a house under a false name,' Colin said.

'She might have rented it though, and I doubt she would have used her real name,' Marissa explained.

'But how would she have managed that?' Colin scratched his head.

Marissa threw up her hands. 'Goodness, I don't know, Colin! I'm just going by what the guards have said. And honestly, I don't care, as long as Milo is safe.'

Neither Brian nor Colin said anything to that, but she knew what they were thinking. She was thinking it too. Until the guards found Carrie and Kyle Byrde, Milo really wasn't safe at all.

In the living room, Peter was reading a story to Milo. The brown hair gave Marissa a jolt again, and she wondered how long it would take to grow out. She shook herself. She wasn't supposed to care about that, but somehow, she did – his new brown hair was a constant reminder of Carrie and what had happened.

Colin crossed the room and hunkered down to Milo's level,

starting a conversation about rugby. It was a most innocuous greeting after everything Milo had just been through, but it was perfect. Milo's face lit up and soon he was deep in conversation with Colin.

Peter gently dislodged Milo from his knee and stood to join Marissa and Brian at the fireplace. Marissa watched as he and Brian shook hands and clapped one another on the back in an awkward half man-hug, which was about as tactile as these two ever got. But it was enough – it was more than enough, Marissa thought, it was everything. Her favourite people in the world, all in one room. Nothing could break them again.

It was almost lunchtime before any of them remembered that the youngest Irvine sibling was arriving that evening.

'Oh God yes, where is Lia staying?' Marissa asked, looking up from her iPad. 'And any preference between the Mellow Fig or Indigo Bean for a lunch delivery – I'm going to put in an order now?'

'Lia should stay with Brian, to give us a bit of breathing space after everything,' Peter said.

Marissa hid a smile as she watched Brian's reaction. If he felt there was more than enough 'breathing space' in a three thousand square foot house, he didn't say it.

'Sure,' he said. Then a moment later, he clapped his hand to his forehead. 'Ah, I forgot. I'm getting the house painted, it's going to reek. She'd be better off here, if you're OK with that?'

Peter looked at him for a beat. 'Yeah, sure. We can handle Lia. Of course, I did tell her yesterday there was no need to come now. But she said she's coming anyway, to see Milo.'

'It'll be good to see her,' Marissa said, 'and a good distraction for Milo.'

Peter didn't look convinced, but then he and Brian had always been funny about Lia, talking about her as though she was a troublesome child, not a fully grown adult. How exactly she was troublesome was never quite clear – it was more a sense than anything concrete. *Oh, that's Lia all over*, they'd say, without clarifying what they meant. *That's such a Lia thing to do*, about something that seemed perfectly normal to Marissa, like taking an impulse holiday, or dating someone who didn't live up to the high standards of the Irvine clan – and for 'standards', read 'net worth'. Marissa soon realized there was nothing troublesome at all about Lia – she was quick-witted and droll and quite cutting at times. She smoked too much, had terrible taste in men and fabulous taste in clothes, and she was enormous fun. And that, it seemed, was what worried Brian and Peter more than anything.

'Anyway, food?' Marissa said, looking around at the three men. 'And champagne. At the very least, we all deserve champagne.'

They did, they decided. They all deserved champagne, and really quite excellent sandwiches from the Mellow Fig, and a big pot of coffee, and a raspberry and white chocolate cheese-cake. *Celebrate everything*, Marissa decided, watching as Peter topped up their glasses and Brian handed out desserts and Milo snuggled into her arms. Warm and fuzzy and happy and good. The fuzzy part, however, was less useful when the 'who's picking up Lia' question arose.

'What time are you leaving for the airport?' Peter asked, looking over at Brian.

Brian was standing by the fireplace, frowning at something on his phone. 'Huh?' he said, looking up.

'Isn't her flight in at six – you'd need to be heading soon in case there's traffic.'

Confusion, swiftly followed by understanding, washed over Brian's pale, bony face.

'Oh. I actually can't pick her up – sorry, I thought you were doing it . . .'

Peter's turn to look confused.

'But you . . .' Peter paused. Marissa watched his face. He was struggling to come up with a reason. *But you always do the dogs-body work* didn't sound great.

Peter's eyes went to the coffee cup in Brian's hand.

'You weren't drinking so I just assumed.'

Nice one, Peter. Marissa looked over at Brian, while Milo shifted to snuggle in closer.

Brian looked uncomfortable now.

'I *do* have to drive somewhere, so I didn't have any champagne.'

Silence, as they waited for elucidation. Brian swallowed, his Adam's apple moving slowly up and down, but said nothing.

'I can do it,' Colin said, breaking the silence. 'I haven't had much to drink.'

Peter looked like he was about to accept, despite the fact that Colin had met Lia precisely never, he wasn't a family member, and expecting him to give up his Saturday evening to do a seventy-kilometre round trip to the airport was ridiculous. Marissa jumped in.

'Not at all, Colin, though you're so good to offer. We'll organize something – one of us will get a taxi there and pick her up.'

Peter raised his eyebrows. He knew as well as she did that by 'one of us' she meant him, but he didn't object. Nothing in the world would tear her away from Milo so soon, she'd only just got him back.

45

Jenny
Saturday

EVERYONE IN KERRYGLEN KNEW where they'd been when they heard the news about Milo's return – some of them had seen it on TV, others saw it online, and the ones less attached to their phones had heard it from neighbours and shopkeepers and hairdressers. Jenny had heard it from Marissa, who phoned her during school pick-up on Friday afternoon. She had burst into tears when she put down the phone, sitting in her parked car with great sobs of relief hiccupping out of her chest and up her throat. Jacob got scared, so she pulled him into the front seat and cradled him like she did when he was a baby, telling him the good news – Milo was back.

That night, Richie and Jenny celebrated with a bottle of red and a Thai takeaway, and the next morning, Richie brought her coffee and the papers in bed, and told her to take a rest. It started to seem like things were on the up.

As the sounds of Saturday morning cartoons drifted upstairs, Jenny leafed through the newspaper. There were six full pages dedicated to the Milo Irvine story – what had happened, where was he held, where was Carrie now? More questions than answers, but none of it mattered; Milo was safe. Jenny went online to look for more up-to-date news headlines. A bad car crash overnight, a politician who'd got himself in hot water, and another appeal for witnesses in the Danny Vaughan case. It had come to light that there had been some kind of dismemberment of the body, the report said; his hands had been removed. Jenny stopped reading, her stomach turning.

But something snagged at her memory.

She was sure she'd heard the name Danny Vaughan before. It was like trying to remember a dream seconds after waking up – it kept disappearing, moving further away the more she tried to recall. She scrolled on the iPad, but there was nothing more. And still no news on Carrie's whereabouts, or details of who else had been involved. Meanwhile, online trolls were sharpening their knives.

> Convenient that he was missing for a week then 'found' completely unharmed. Let's see how long it takes the parents to write a book about it or sell their story.

> Something dodgy about the whole thing methinks.

> At the very least, they should be charged with negligence for letting it happen in the first place.

'Letting' it happen. Ouch.

> Watch this space, there's more to this than meets the eye.

Were people really that cynical? *Never read the comments*, she reminded herself, and picked up her book instead.

*

Saturdays often involved a visit to her mother-in-law, but this week Richie suggested they treat themselves to lunch out. Jenny didn't have to think long about where to go. Esther's Tea Garden meant good food, but more than that, she realized she desperately wanted to see Esther, to connect with someone who had lived through Milo's disappearance like she had.

As they were being shown to their table, Esther arrived. She blew in like a south-westerly wind, all tousled and pink-cheeked, and made straight for Jenny as soon as she saw her.

'Oh, I'm so glad to see you, come here,' she said, and pulled Jenny into a long hug that smelled of coffee cake and lavender. 'Well! How are you feeling?'

'I don't really know how to feel. Like, I'm *so* happy he's home, but I still feel terrible that it happened at all.'

'It's an odd one, isn't it? To feel overjoyed that he's safe, and confused too, wondering if we all imagined it.'

'*Yes!* That's it. And obviously I haven't seen Marissa, and I'm reading these horrible comments online and feeling just . . . weird about the whole thing. And still nobody knows where Carrie and Kyle are or why they did it.' She shook herself. 'Anyway, I'm glad I got to see you.'

'I'm only popping in for half a minute to pick up some cake for a friend, so it was good timing.'

'You don't work Saturdays?'

'I come and go. I roster myself for a couple of shifts during the week to keep me out of mischief, but Verena – that's the manager – has everything under control. I'd say she wishes I'd stay out from under her feet at times,' Esther said, her eyes twinkling, and Jenny found herself suddenly wishing Jacob had Esther for a grandmother, instead of Adeline Furlong-Kennedy.

'And how are *you*, young man?' Esther said, turning to Jacob.

'Good, thank you,' he said, lifting Jem's paw to wave at her.

Richie sat, undoing his scarf and unfolding a newspaper in one move.

'Oh sorry, I should have introduced you guys – Esther, this is my husband Richie,' Jenny said, slipping off her coat.

'Lovely to meet you, Richie. Jenny's lucky to have had someone to look after her while she was going through all this.'

Richie looked surprised, then a flash of something else crossed his face – guilt? And whatever way you looked at it, he'd spent more time telling her not to put them in the line of fire than actually looking after her. But it was over now, or almost, and time to move on. Milo was safe, and sooner or later, they'd find Carrie.

As Esther headed behind the counter, Jenny glanced down at Richie's newspaper. Milo's story was the big headline, his smiling face beaming out above the fold. But at the bottom of the front page was an article about the gruesome Danny Vaughan discovery. *Danny Vaughan.* It was driving her crazy now. Where had she heard that name before?

46

Marissa
Saturday

LAZY CANDLES. EMPTY GLASSES. Falling eyelids. Marissa was reading to Milo, stifling yawns and half regretting the champagne, when Lia and Peter arrived in from the airport. She sat up and tried to move Milo so she could stand, but Lia gestured *stay put.*

'He looks so peaceful, don't move him,' she said, in the husky American drawl she'd perfected during her years in the States. Marissa grinned up at her. She looked even tinier than ever, but maybe that was the short black knit-dress and the sky-high heels, huge at the end of legs like twigs. Her dark cloud of just-out-of-bed hair had a similar effect around her pixie face. The trademark slash of red lipstick pulled it all together – she looked like a model or a poet or some kind of New York hybrid of the two.

Lia perched on the couch beside them, very gently touching Milo's shoulder.

'How is he?' she asked in a whisper.

'Better than I expected, but still very clingy with me – understandably.'

'And you?'

Marissa shook her head. 'I don't know how to describe it. I've never been so relieved about anything in my life, but it's all so surreal. Maybe I haven't processed it yet, or maybe we won't relax until they catch the people who did it.'

'Peter said the same. He said the police are certain the nanny person wasn't acting alone? And I guess until you guys know who was helping her, it's impossible to feel safe. It could be anyone!'

Marissa had been working hard to suppress exactly that thought, and hearing it said out loud made her skin prickle. She rubbed Milo's head and kissed it. If she never let him out of her sight again, nobody could steal him. It was that simple. Wasn't it? She kissed him again, without replying to her sister-in-law's statement.

'Where's Lurch?' Lia asked, looking around.

Marissa grinned. 'Be nice. Brian said he had to do something, that's why he couldn't pick you up.'

'Wow, how did he get out from under Peter's thumb?'

'Oh stop, you know it's not like that!'

'Sure, you keep telling yourself that, Marissa. If you weren't here to keep the peace, those two would have come to blows years ago.'

'No, they wouldn't.' Marissa paused. 'Though only because poor old Brian never fights back.'

'True. I don't think he even notices the way Peter treats him – he only has eyes for one person around here,' Lia said with a wink.

'Don't be ridiculous! No drinks for you tonight if you don't behave.'

'OK, I'll be good! Anyway, I come bearing gifts . . .' She picked up a Givenchy faux-fur tote and rummaged inside.

'I love the bag,' Marissa said. 'Is it new?'

ANDREA MARA

'A present from a grateful client,' Lia said. Lia was a trader in a small but up-and-coming investment firm – if investors were giving designer handbags as gifts, maybe Marissa was in the wrong job.

'I'll swap you some of my clients with their by-the-number wills and their so-called amicable divorces for some of yours, how about that?'

'You don't fool me for a second – you've got every one of Kerryglen's secrets in your pocket, you could blackmail the lot of them if you wanted to. Ah, there it is!' She handed a small box to Marissa, and a slightly bigger one to Milo.

Marissa's little blue box was instantly recognizable even without the Tiffany & Co. logo – inside were silver earrings in the shape of an X or a kiss.

'You shouldn't have, but they're absolutely stunning, I love them!' Marissa leaned across to hug Lia.

Milo held his box, a confused look on his face.

'Can you read it, Mummy?'

Marissa removed the card and read it out loud. *'This box is far too small for a big, brave boy like you – your real present is in my suitcase.'*

Milo scrambled off the couch and ran out to the hall, in search of gift-yielding luggage.

'It's a baseball bat and catching mitt,' Lia whispered to Marissa. 'You'll probably kill me when he whacks one of your expensive crystal wine glasses.'

'Lia, that's the first time he's left the room without bringing me with him – you could have brought him a live alligator and I wouldn't mind,' Marissa whispered back. 'Thank you.'

'Happy to help. Now, let's get your mind off the fucking *horrendous* things that have happened – why don't you pour us both a glass of wine, and tell me everything else that's going on in Kerryglen.'

And Marissa did. She poured wine, Peter ordered pizza, Milo played, and Lia sat back on the couch, filling them with New York stories. And for a while, for a little while, they forgot.

Marissa couldn't remember whose idea it was to start on gin and tonics nor what time Peter had said goodnight, but she knew she was beginning to relax for the first time in what felt like a million years. Alcohol was doing its trick, blunting the edges, and she found she was slightly unsteady on her feet when she got up to check the patio doors and put on the alarm. The robotic voice assured her that the system was set, and she reminded herself that there were sensors on every single opening, even the tiny window in the downstairs bathroom. Nobody could get in.

Back in the sitting room, she saw that Lia had kicked off her heels and curled her legs under her on the couch. Marissa flopped beside her.

'So, how's Colin-the-Sheep?' Lia asked, watching her sister-in-law over the rim of her glass.

'You're such a brat! Colin's not a sheep. He's good, he's been brilliant this last week.'

'Oh, I don't doubt it. He's like an eager puppy. You know I dated him once? Disaster.'

Marissa sat up straighter. 'You went out with Colin? I didn't even know you guys had met! He never said a thing!'

'It was a million years ago, and literally one date. Shit, I'm just remembering you did too – back in college, right?' Lia wrinkled her nose. 'Is that weird, knowing we've both dated the same guy?'

'Ew. Kind of. Though it was short-lived, and mostly happened because we were both from here and didn't know anybody else. In fact, so short-lived it doesn't count, so we're good.'

'Peter and Brian once dated the same girl – that's more weird, isn't it?'

Marissa spluttered the swallow of gin she'd just taken.

'Who? Oh my Lord, tell me everything immediately! My goodness, I've never known Brian to date anyone in the whole time I've known him! I can't even imagine him with some-one . . . never mind the same girl as Peter.'

'Has Peter never told you this? It was way back – Brian was in fourth or fifth year and Peter had just started college. Brian was seeing this girl called . . . Sarah, I think, yes, Sarah. Blonde girl, heavy-handed with the bronzer if I remember, and a bit too fond of fake tan. All teeth. Anyway, she and Brian broke up, no idea why, but it seemed amicable.' She took a sip of gin. 'I mean, he wasn't locking himself in his room wailing over mixtapes. But a week later, it was Peter's Debs Ball, and who turns up on his arm?'

'Sarah of heavy-handed bronzer fame?'

'Precisely. The worst thing was, we had a drinks thingie in our house before they all went off to the hotel, so in walks Sarah, stuck like an Oompa Loompa limpet to Peter's side, and Brian's just standing there looking at her with his mouth hang-ing open.'

'He had no idea Peter was bringing her?'

'Judging by his face, no.'

'And did Brian go mad?'

'Nah. He idolized Peter, let him get away with all sorts. Our dad was a useless shit – you know that – and Peter was a kind of father replacement for Brian, though there's only three years between them. Poor old Lurch, always dancing to his big brother's tune.'

'Ah, Brian's a good guy, he's been amazing during – well, you know.' As she said it, Marissa heard a snap from outside, like someone stepping on a twig. Her head swivelled, her eyes on the bay window at the back of the sitting room. The heavy cream curtains hung open, the outside world a stripe of tar-coloured paint between them.

'Are you OK, honey?' Lia asked.

'Did you hear that?'

'Hear what?'

'I thought I heard something. I'm being silly. It was probably an animal,' Marissa muttered, getting up and crossing the room. She reached across the antique daybed to draw the curtains, shutting out the black.

'We don't usually bother to close them,' she said to Lia as she sat back down, her voice a little shaky, 'but somehow I feel better knowing nobody can see in.'

'You don't think she'll come back, do you? Carrie?'

Marissa shrugged. 'I have no idea. Without knowing where she is, or why she took Milo, it's impossible to guess. It seems like she was part of some sort of gang – it was a man, not Carrie, who threw Milo's jacket off Killiney Hill, so she definitely wasn't acting alone. It's possible they kidnapped him as part of—' She swallowed. It was still hard to say it out loud. 'Some kind of child trafficking ring, and I don't know if that means they'll try to get him again. So yeah, I'm scared she'll come back.'

'Oh God, you poor thing. Look, wherever Carrie is hiding out, she's not outside your window. Nobody would get through those huge gates, it's like Fort Knox. And even if they got through the gates, Brian would loom out of the darkness and frighten the life out of them.'

Marissa smiled in spite of herself. 'Ah, be nice, he's always been very good to us.'

'Oh, I know. Peter only has to click his fingers and Brian stands to attention. But hey, we're being devastatingly boring now, talking about those two. Tell me about work and all the juicy secrets of Kerryglen.'

Of course, Marissa didn't, she couldn't, but somehow they talked long into the night and it was exactly the distraction she needed. As she tiptoed into Milo's room to kiss him goodnight, light-headed on gin and chat, dark windows and strange noises pushed from her mind, she rubbed his cheek and smiled. It was over.

47

Marissa
Sunday

It didn't feel 'over' the following morning when Fiona Sheridan arrived at nine on the dot, ready to interview Milo. Marissa knocked back two coffees and Peter's offer to cover the interview supervision – she needed to be there too.

'Hi Milo, do you remember me?' Sheridan asked, smiling.

Milo nodded.

'Great. I have a few more questions but I'll only be here for a very short time – does that sound OK?'

He nodded again, his eyes huge with apprehension.

'This is an easy bit – do you remember the day Carrie collected you from school?'

Milo frowned, deep in concentration, then his face cleared.

'Yes! I was apposed to go on a playdate to Jacob K's house.'

'And when you came out of school, what happened?'

'Carrie waved at me to come over.'

'Good. And then what happened?'

He looked confused.

'When you walked over to Carrie, what happened next – did she say something to you?'

'No, she taked my hand and we walked down the road.'

'Great!' Sheridan said, as Marissa exchanged a look with Peter. Dear God, how easy it had been to walk away with their child.

'Did you ask her where Jacob was?'

Milo thought for a moment. 'No, but she told me that we had to go in a car because my mummy and daddy had a work trip.'

'Can you remember the colour of the car?'

'Red, like a tomato. And inside was dark grey. And a bag was beside me in the back, it was blue and white with handles.'

'Milo, that's great!' She turned to Marissa. 'He has a good eye for detail – clever boy!'

'He's very smart, yes. Especially when it comes to numbers and colours. Sees things differently to how we see them. Hopefully it'll help with this . . .'

'Oh, it will. Any tiny detail might be key.' She turned back to Milo.

'Where did you go in the car?'

'To Carrie's house.' His face lit up. 'She showed me the TV and she gave me Skittles and Coca-Cola. My mummy doesn't let me have Skittles.'

'And Milo, this bit is important. When you got to Carrie's house . . .' She waited for him to nod in understanding before going on. 'Before you went inside, what did you see?'

Milo screwed up his face, in what Marissa recognized as a dramatic display of thinking hard rather than any actual thinking.

'Milo,' Sheridan said gently, 'how about closing your eyes and thinking back to it, then tell us what you see?'

Closing his eyes and snuggling into Marissa, he started to talk.

'Yellow flowers, yellow like Saturday.'

'You mean it was Saturday when you arrived? Not Friday?'

Marissa intervened. 'No, he sees some words in colour. To him, Saturday is yellow. Go on, Milo, what else?'

'Yellow flowers and a red house.'

'Good, what kind of red – red like a tomato?'

He laughed. 'No! Red like this house is at the bottom.' He put his hand over his mouth and opened his eyes. 'Bottom,' he mouthed at Marissa.

She smiled. 'Close your eyes again,' she mouthed back, and looked over at Sheridan. 'He means red brick,' she whispered. Sheridan took a note and carried on with the questions.

'Does it look big or small, Milo?'

'Small. There's no upstairs.'

Sheridan sat forward. She kept her voice neutral though Marissa could hear anticipation bubbling underneath.

'Are you sure, Milo? No upstairs?'

'I'm sure.' He nodded emphatically. 'I asked Carrie where the stairs is when we were inside and she said there's none.'

Sheridan scribbled quick notes.

'Can you remember the colour of the door?'

'White.'

'And were there steps up to the door?'

'One grey step.'

'Milo, I think you could be a detective when you grow up, what do you think about that?'

A shrug. 'Can I go play with my new baseball bat?' he asked Marissa, and she nodded, shooing him off the couch.

'Was that any help?' she asked Sheridan as she walked her to the front door.

'Definitely. We're fairly certain at this stage – based on CCTV – that Carrie's car came from somewhere inside Sandymount that night, so the search is heavily focused there. Now we can focus on red-brick bungalows in the area.'

Marissa turned that over in her mind. All week she'd been picturing some kind of desolate farmhouse or miserable basement or worse – a ferry going somewhere far away and impossible to find. But Milo had been less than ten kilometres away, in a pretty, affluent suburb, just like Kerryglen.

48

Irene
Sunday

IN A SLIGHTLY LESS affluent but almost as pretty suburb just east of Kerryglen, Irene was eating sausages, trying to block out the sound of Frank eating his.

'Well, at least they found him,' he said for the twenty-fourth time in twenty-four hours, his mouth full of toast.

She didn't answer. She'd been turning it over and over since they heard the news. What did it mean for her story – would Faye Foster's editor still publish it? Was it less valuable now the boy was safe? But looking online, all focus had turned to Caroline – where was she, who was she working with, what made her do it, was she a victim too? The story mattered just as much as it ever did. Surely. And then there was the other thing people were asking – had the Irvines paid a ransom on the QT? For all Irene knew, Caroline might be a millionaire now, sitting pretty on her big pile of money. Hats off to her if she was, that kind of thing took balls.

Some people were saying the Irvines had set it all up themselves, for publicity. To sell their story. Jesus, how much did people think they'd get for selling their story – the few grand she was likely to get would be a nice little bonus, but it was hardly worth staging a kidnap for. And anyway, the Irvines were already millionaires. She drummed her fingers on the table as she thought about that. Would Peter and Marissa Irvine be interested in meeting Caroline's mother maybe? She looked at their picture on the cover of the Sunday paper. Beautiful smiling Marissa with her handsome husband, people who'd always had it easy. Maybe there was a way to get some of that pie for herself.

'Irene?'

'What?'

'I was asking you if the guards had been in touch again? I presume we won't be left in peace till she's found. It's over for the Irvines but not for us,' he said, mournfully staring at a piece of sausage on his fork. 'At least nobody in the bank knows about the connection, that's something.'

'True,' she said, with only the tiniest twinge of guilt about what was coming. Anyway, if Frank had just increased her housekeeping, none of this would have happened. She popped a last bit of bacon into her mouth and folded the newspaper.

49

Jenny
Sunday

BACK IN KERRYGLEN, JENNY'S Sunday morning had started well with a strong coffee and a long run. On her return, she found Richie on a high stool at the breakfast bar, reading the Sunday paper. Marissa and Peter's faces were splashed all over the front page along with photos of their house and of Milo. The story had everything – the wealthy couple, the safe return, the photogenic faces, the ongoing speculation about the evil nanny.

'Speaking of nannies . . .' Jenny said, as Richie looked up.

'Were we?'

'Well, everyone else is,' she said, pointing to the paper. 'But yeah, we need to do something about childcare. I'm going to have to start doing full days again soon.'

'I could ask my mother to help out?' Richie said, and after a beat, they both burst out laughing.

'Yeah, um, maybe not. I guess we need to start interviewing childminders again.'

He sighed, and she felt every inch of it. Neither of them could stomach the thought of going through that process again – now with the added worry that each of the candidates would secretly be a psychopath.

'Is there anyone we know who could recommend someone – take the unknown element out of it?' Richie said.

'I'll ask around at school.' There probably wasn't, but it was a way of putting off the decision. 'Where's Jacob?'

'In the playroom.' Richie hopped off the bar stool. 'You get your shower, I'll make us brunch.'

In the playroom, Jacob was in his usual spot on the floor, Jem by his side, playing with Magformers. She bent and kissed his head, then walked over to the chalkboard. The names of his classmates were still there – *Aleks Smit, Andru Murfe, Shan Otool, Milo Rvin, Dani Von*. Milo's name gave her a lump in her throat. How odd to think of all that had happened since Jacob had put it there. About to turn away, she stopped.

Something was hovering at the distant edges of her memory.

She looked back at the board and read the names again.

Dani Von.

Danny Vaughan.

A chill crawled across the back of her neck.

'Jacob, love, see this name you wrote here? Is he a friend from school?'

He looked up and shook his head. 'I think Carrie's friend. She said his name lots of times on the phone.'

She forced herself to keep her voice even. 'OK, love, that's fine – you keep playing.'

She needed to call McConville.

50

Marissa
Sunday

THINGS SHOULD HAVE BEEN starting to feel more normal, but they weren't. Marissa sat watching Milo play, not five feet from her spot on the couch; he hadn't left her side all day. Lia's words kept coming back to her, poking at the protective layer she was trying to build. *Until you guys know who was helping her, it's impossible to feel safe. It could be anyone.*

Her phone beeped. Another message from Ana. Marissa had called her on Friday to tell her the good news, and since then Ana had left three tearful voicemails asking when she could come over to see Milo. But Marissa wasn't ready to babysit the babysitter. She needed time with just family.

And right now, she needed air.

'Milo, will we go for a walk in the garden? Call over to Uncle Brian?'

'I don't want to go outside,' he said in a small voice. God, how was she going to get him to go to school tomorrow if he wouldn't leave the house today?

'That's OK, sweetheart. I'm going to go out for a walk myself – you wait here and I'll see you when I come back.'

He was on his feet before she finished the sentence.

'I'll come,' was all he said, as he slipped his small hand into hers.

The afternoon sun was dipping low as hand in hand they roamed the garden, chattering about easy stuff – TV and friends and school. At Brian's house, they knocked and waited, then knocked again. When he eventually answered, there was a flicker of something in his expression – surprise or maybe irritation? That didn't seem like Brian. He had never been the warm and fuzzy type, but never unwelcoming either. Just as quickly, the look disappeared and he smiled his awkward, bony half-smile, and invited them in.

Marissa hadn't been inside Brian's house in a long time – theirs was the bigger house, where the family dinners and parties took place. Brian's house had originally been a gardener's cottage, renovated and extended when they bought Maple Lodge. And nice and all as it was, it was just somewhere Brian went when he wasn't with them. She looked around the kitchen with fresh eyes. White cupboards, white floor tiles, white walls. Black countertop, like a slash of ink through the middle. An island at the centre of the room, with three chrome bar stools. No kitchen table. But then why would he need a kitchen table, it was only ever him. Her eyes swept across the countertop as Brian scooped some brochures into a drawer. House brochures. Was he thinking of moving? She turned that over in her mind. Brian couldn't move! They were a trio, Brian, Peter and her. And they all lived together on the grounds of Maple Lodge, that's how it had been since day one. She watched as he took down cups. No, Brian wouldn't leave them. It was probably a client's brochure, someone thinking of buying an investment property.

Idly, she examined the counter. Kettle, coffee machine, nothing else. Not even a toaster. No photos or artwork on the walls, completely at odds with her own kitchen where images of Milo, or the three of them together, smiled out from every surface. And for the first time ever, the contrast caught her. Was he lonely? She observed him as he poured coffee, his angular shoulders jutting through his pale blue shirt, and wondered if he was happy in his minimalist bachelor home.

Milo had finished inspecting Brian's downstairs and was clambering to get up on her knee.

'You have no toys,' he said to Brian, as though Brian couldn't possibly already know this.

'Sorry, Milo, do you want my phone?' Brian said, passing it over, and handing Marissa a cup of coffee at the same time.

'The place is looking fab,' she said, because it's the kind of thing you say, even when sitting in a room with zero personality and nothing to say for itself.

'It does the job, easy to maintain. How's he doing?' he asked, nodding towards Milo who was engrossed in the screen.

As she started to tell him, something nagged at her – something about Brian, but she couldn't put her finger on it. He asked about Lia, and she kept talking, filling the air, but suddenly feeling self-conscious and odd. Because she hadn't been here in so long? She saw Brian a lot, but in *their* house, and it was different. He was part of the furniture. Here, in his domain? It was . . . well, somehow strange. She drank her coffee faster than usual and told Milo they needed to go.

'Let's give Uncle Brian back his phone and we'll go home to see Daddy and Lia,' she said, taking the device from his hands. In lieu of finding any games to play, Milo had ended up in Brian's messages. Hopefully he hadn't sent a whole heap of emojis to one of Brian's contacts, as he often did on her phone. She handed it back and popped Milo off her knee, feeling more than seeing Brian's frown as he looked at the screen.

'Sorry, I think he went into your messages.'

Still frowning, Brian shook his head. 'It's fine,' was all he said, before walking them to the door.

As she stepped out into the dusk, she grabbed Milo's hand.

'Let's run!' she said, and he laughed, and they did, because suddenly more than anything she needed to be back inside her own warm, bright, familiar home. She was halfway across the garden when it hit her.

Brian had said he couldn't have Lia stay with him because he was having his house painted. Yet in his house just now, there was no smell of paint at all. Why would he lie?

Twenty minutes later, Marissa was curled on the couch in her living room, with Milo playing on the floor beside her. She had pushed aside questions about Brian's house – maybe he'd made up the painting story to avoid having Lia come to stay. And indeed, Lia was probably much happier in the main house – right now, she was at the other end of the couch, scrolling through her phone, bare feet tucked under her. Peter was in an armchair, reading the Sunday papers. Marissa had lit the fire, and some candles too. In a bit, she'd make hot chocolate for Milo and something stronger for the grown-ups.

'Anyone fancy a cheeky Sunday evening G&T?' she asked.

'No more gin after last night,' Lia said with a groan. 'I need a palate cleanser. Ooh!' She sat up. 'How about margaritas?'

Peter's phone rang, cutting across the conversation, and Marissa's heart suddenly clenched, afraid of bad news. But Milo was home, there could be no more bad news.

Peter frowned.

'Work?' Marissa mouthed as he answered the call.

He pursed his lips in a gesture that meant *not sure*.

She went back to her own phone, to answering good wishes on the *Find Milo Irvine* Facebook page.

Thanks be to God he was found, poor little mite, said one.

So happy he was found safe, well done to the guards, said another. Only the guards didn't really find him, Marissa thought, swiping past; the kidnapper had inexplicably left him in the car and failed to return. Had something happened to him after he walked away from the car? Maybe the man he was meeting had done something to him? She shivered and scrolled on.

Hope the parents keep a better eye on him now, said another commenter. Marissa rolled her eyes and deleted it. She wasn't giving one inch of her time to keyboard warriors, not now, not ever. She glanced at Peter as he stood up from the armchair, still holding the phone to his ear. He hadn't said anything since the initial hello. She watched his face, trying to read his expression. Annoyance? Anger? She sat up straighter on the couch, and mouthed, 'All OK?'

He held up a finger and nodded, then left the room to continue the call. Probably work. It didn't matter. Milo was here, no one could touch them now.

'Oh God, nothing has changed in Kerryglen.' Lia yawned, stretching her pipe-cleaner arms above her head. 'I've just looked up a whole heap of old schoolfriends on Facebook – they're all having babies, and all the babies look the same, but they can't stop posting photos as though the rest of us are interested. And then, they have one night out and put up a hundred photos because they're so damn excited to be "out-out", like they're the first people ever to have gin cocktails. Yawn.'

Marissa nudged her with her toe. 'You say that now, but in a few years, you'll be the same.'

'No chance. Not for me the world of diapers and sleepless nights and pushing my progeny on an already overpopulated world.' She grinned at Marissa, sweeping a strand of hair out of her eyes. 'Obviously I love *your* kid, but he's genuinely the cut-est one.' She scooched across the couch and held out her phone to show Marissa. 'Look at these morons and their posts though. A baby. Another baby. A baby with a baby. Don't they have any-thing else going on in their lives? What happened to politics and culture and discussions about books?'

'They're too damn tired.' Marissa sighed, reaching down to rub Milo's cheek as he played. 'Look,' she pointed at Lia's phone screen, 'there's a photo of normal people having a normal night out, right?'

'Yes, but like I said, a hundred photos of the same night and the same people taking badly judged selfies, eyes red from the flash and the gin. It's just so . . .'

'So Kerryglen? So un-New York?'

Lia rolled her eyes, just as Peter walked back into the room. He was staring at his phone, an odd look on his face.

'Is everything OK?' Marissa asked, reaching instinctively to rub Milo's head.

Peter looked up, his face grey. He opened his mouth to say something but closed it again.

'Hey, look at this one – isn't that the Sheep?' said Lia, oblivi-ous to the exchange. 'Marissa, that's Colin, right? Behind the losers on their out-out night?' She held the phone up to show Marissa. In the foreground, a group of eight or nine people grinned at the camera. They didn't look like losers to Marissa, they looked like tired parents having a blast on a long-awaited night out.

It wasn't the group that interested Lia, it was the person in the top left of the photo, at a high table *behind* the group. The gangly shape, the blond Tintin hair, the earnest puppy-dog look – even in side-profile, it was unmistakably Colin.

But that wasn't the most surprising thing about the photo – that wasn't what grabbed Marissa's attention as she pulled the phone out of Lia's hands and pinched the screen to zoom in.

What grabbed her, what gripped her heart and squeezed it so tight she almost couldn't breathe, was the person sitting opposite Colin.

Because that person, with her long red hair and eyelinered eyes, was undeniably, undoubtedly Carrie.

51

Marissa
Sunday

DIZZY AND SICK AND confused, Marissa stared at the phone. Colin didn't know Carrie – Colin had never met Carrie. How could he be sitting opposite her in a bar? Not just sitting opposite – smiling at her, gazing even. And Carrie – quiet, introverted Carrie – was clearly in the middle of some kind of animated conversation, hands up, as though telling a funny story. The most normal photo in the world really, just two people in the background of someone else's shot. Only not normal. Not normal at all.

'What's up?' Lia was saying. 'You look like you've seen a ghost.'

Marissa held the phone up, first to Lia, then to Peter, but no words were forming.

'What is it?' Peter asked. 'What's wrong?'

'It's her,' she managed finally. 'Carrie.'

'What? She's in the photo too? With my friends?' Lia asked, squinting at the screen.

'Not with your friends,' Marissa said quietly. 'With Colin.'

Lia moved closer, staring at the photo.

'Oh my God, what the hell is she doing with Colin? Did you know they knew each other?'

'No.' Marissa looked over at Peter, who was standing open-mouthed by the fireplace. 'Did you know? Have I missed something?'

He shook his head. But slowly. Not quite committing.

'Peter, what is it?'

As she watched, he worked his mouth towards saying something, but still didn't speak.

'Peter, you're freaking me out now – did Colin know Carrie? Did you know they knew each other?'

'Only since I got that call two minutes ago, and to be honest, I didn't believe it. Jesus.'

'What do you mean, who was on the call?' Everything was spinning now and she realized she'd been waiting for a credible explanation, anything that meant her business partner of ten years, her friend of almost twenty, hadn't lied to her.

Peter crossed the room and sat on the arm of the couch.

'Hey, Milo-Mouse, will you go play in the den for a bit? You can take the iPad if you like,' he said. Milo got up and picked the tablet off the side table, already engrossed in searching for games as he walked out of the room.

'Who was on the call – what's going on?'

'I don't know who it was,' Peter said heavily. 'An older lady, well spoken – she said she didn't want to give me her name or make a fuss, but that we'd "want to be careful" around people we know. That someone close to us, as she put it, is "in cahoots with the nanny".'

'Oh Jesus.'

'Yeah. I thought she was a crank, a busybody looking for

attention. I told her if she really knew something, she should go to the guards. She said that was up to us, and that it might mean nothing but someone very close to us had been seen with Carrie. That was all she'd say.'

'Could she have meant Ana? Since we know they spent time together in the playground?'

'No, she said it was a man, and not to leave Milo alone with anyone, even if it's someone we trust. I didn't believe her, but now . . .' Peter ran his hand through his hair. 'What do we do?'

'Tell the police? Get them to trace the call?' Marissa said, still trying to grasp what was happening.

'We could try . . .' Peter said doubtfully. 'Can they do that after the call has already ended? Jesus. Colin Dobson.'

'Let's not get ahead of ourselves,' Lia said, 'there might be an innocent explanation . . .'

Marissa shook her head. 'I can't believe this. How could he not have said he knew Carrie? With the police looking everywhere and Milo missing and Ana bawling her eyes out over playground trips, he never thought to say, "Oh yeah, I was seeing Carrie"?'

'You don't know they were *dating*. What if he just met her in a bar that night – what if he'd had a few drinks and didn't even remember what she looked like after?'

Marissa stabbed at the phone screen. '*Look at him*. He's not falling around drunk. He's gazing into her eyes like a lovesick puppy. Colin, of all people, I just can't believe he'd do this to me.'

'I can,' Peter said. 'I knew a guy like him in college. Acting clueless, playing a kind of bumbling Hugh Grant character, and getting away with things because everyone thought it was cute. Colin's like that.'

'I don't know that Colin's playing a part,' Lia said. 'I think he actually is kinda clueless. Cute, yes, but clueless.'

'He's not,' Marissa said. 'He's very, very good at his job – a mind as sharp as a tack underneath all the bluster. But Peter never really liked him, did you, Peter – I thought it was because I went out with him once.'

'I don't care who he went out with, I just don't trust the bumbling-idiot act. And turns out maybe I was right.'

Marissa picked up her phone. 'Only one way to find out,' she said, hitting Colin's number.

'Are you really up to this?' Peter asked. 'He's just going to deny it anyway.'

The point was moot. The phone went to voicemail. She didn't leave a message.

'I'll try again in a bit, and either way I'll see him at work tomorrow. And unless he has a very good explanation as to what the hell is going on, I'm calling the police.'

Silence, for a beat.

Then Lia spoke up. 'Well, we can't do anything about it tonight. Is now a bad time to bring up those margaritas again?'

Peter grinned. 'Is now a bad time to tell you we don't actually have any tequila?'

'You guys! You're so . . .'

'Un-New York?' Peter said. 'Tell you what, I'll go out and pick up a bottle and whatever else goes into margaritas.' Lia rolled her eyes, presumably at her brother's lack of cocktail knowledge. 'And I'll go one better – I'll get us takeout burritos from Green Taco to go with it.'

'I always said you were my favourite brother.'

'You never said that in your life,' Peter said, picking up the keys. 'Text me your orders?'

Lia picked up her phone to search for the menu. Marissa just sat. Margaritas and Mexican food were all very nice, but she couldn't get it out of her head. Colin, her friend of twenty years, had known the woman who kidnapped her son. And he hadn't said a word.

52

One month earlier

THE FLICK OF THE eyeliner felt good. She'd spent so long as pale, watery Carrie Finch, she'd almost forgotten how satisfying it felt to put on a new face. Now, foundation hid Carrie Finch's freckles, mascara changed the colour of her lashes, and deep red lipstick promised fun. She stepped back from the small bedroom mirror and appraised her work. A little out of practice, but not bad at all. Her blow-dried hair swirled around her shoulders in salon waves, the colour a hint darker thanks to a wash-in-wash-out tint. Her brows, usually almost translucent, were pencilled in, deep brown now instead of light gold. The top, one of Jenny's expensive, sparkly AllSaints t-shirts, fitted the third-date bill perfectly. Not too dressy, but nothing like Carrie Finch's boring check-shirt uniform. Leather trousers, pencil thin. Sliding a holdall from under the bed, she rummaged inside for heels. Colin was at least six foot three, she reckoned – she picked the highest shoes she owned and slipped them on. God, it felt good to be Lena.

The music thrummed low and constant as she perched at a high table near the bar. A busy waitress flashed by to take her order, depositing a vodka and Coke minutes later. The waitress didn't ask for payment. Carrie had never been to a bar that didn't demand cash on delivery. But of course, this was Kerryglen – the residents probably didn't run off without paying for their drinks. She glanced at her watch, a cheap digital thing she'd picked up before moving in with the Kennedys. He wasn't late – yet – she was early. She sipped her drink, welcome warmth spreading down her throat, and examined the people around her.

At the next table, a group of thirty-somethings passed around a bottle of prosecco. She watched as the last person in their party poured just a dribble into his glass and raised his hand to order another bottle. Raucous laughter followed something he said, and glasses were downed in one. They were giddy and loud, though it was still only five to eight. She recognized one of them from Jacob's preschool – Carrie had only ever seen the woman in gym gear and trainers, hair scraped back in a pony-tail. How different she looked tonight in a black lace shift dress, her blonde hair framing a perfectly made-up face, her head thrown back laughing. Did Jenny know her, she wondered? Would Jenny recognize her if she came in? Would Jenny recognize Carrie Finch tonight? She didn't think so. She smiled to herself and looked up, just as Colin walked through the door.

And suddenly, out of nowhere, a rush of fear hit her like a rock to the chest. What if this was a mistake? What if it all went wrong? What if they got caught . . . or worse? Because despite everything Irene used to say growing up, there were worse things than getting caught. She closed her eyes to push the thought away. Everything would be OK. She smiled and stood to accept Colin's kiss.

53

Marissa
Monday

THIRD TIME. STILL NO answer. Marissa waited, phone pressed to her ear, even though at this point it was abundantly clear Colin wasn't going to pick up. He'd messaged Shauna that morning to say he was sick, and that in itself was a sign something was up – Colin was never sick. But how could he know she'd seen the photo of him with Carrie? On Peter's advice, she hadn't tried calling him a second time last night – *that's a conversation to have face to face*, he'd said, and she knew he was right. How would she even start? *So, Colin, how's the love life – been dating any kidnappers recently? Not just any kidnapper now, but the one who took my son?*

She bashed the phone down on the desk and sat back, unsure what to do next. She was a week behind on work, but all she could think of was Colin and Carrie, and Milo going into school that morning. Letting him out of her hug and into his classroom had been even harder than she'd expected. But when she'd called Tara for a psychologist's take on things, she'd said they should be guided by Milo. *Let him go in if he's happy to go in, don't force him if he's not.* And Milo *was* happy going in – despite clinging to her and only her all weekend, he'd woken on Monday morning excited about seeing his friends again.

Tara had arranged counselling with a colleague of hers – for all three of them, though Peter said he didn't need it. Marissa would talk him round. The sooner they could deal with what had happened and move on, the better.

Even with Carrie still out there. Somewhere.

Marissa swallowed, her throat suddenly dry.

Shauna knocked and stuck her head in.

'I'm going out for coffees – latte?'

'You're an absolute darling, yes please. Shauna, can I ask you something?'

Shauna nodded.

'Do you know if Colin's been seeing anyone?'

Shauna's eyes widened. Clearly not the question she was expecting.

'Um, I'm not sure. I . . .' Shauna started, and stopped just as quickly.

'I know it's an odd question, but I promise it's for a good reason.'

'OK,' Shauna said. 'I came here one night a few weeks ago because I forgot my phone, and when I came up the stairs, the main door was unlocked. I knew I'd locked it before I left, so I got a bit of a fright. But when I walked in, I realized why – there were voices coming from Colin's office. I could hear him and a woman too. I thought it was a late appointment, but I realized pretty quickly it wasn't like that.'

Shauna lowered her voice, though there was nobody else around.

'They were giggling and kind of . . . well, I suppose it was flirting, though I couldn't exactly hear the words. But you know – that kind of conversation. Definitely not a client.'

'Right. And could you make out any details – anything about the woman?'

'It's hard to see through the rippled glass and it was quite dark, but there was a desk lamp on in the office. I could see she was wearing something bluish-green and had long hair.'

'Could you see the hair colour?'

Shauna gave Marissa an odd look, wondering maybe if she'd lost the plot now, or at the very least crossed the boundaries of a business relationship.

'It's important, I promise.'

Shauna screwed up her eyes.

'Long hair definitely, darkish, but not black. Brown or red maybe?'

Marissa nodded, her expression neutral as a cold feeling settled in her stomach.

'Did you see her here any other time?'

A pause.

'I never came back here after hours again – not deliberately or anything, I just didn't need to. But once I'd seen them that time, I started noticing little things.'

Marissa nodded. 'Go on?'

'Like, once or twice, the outer door wasn't locked when I came in, though I'd locked it the night before.' Her cheeks flamed, but she kept going. 'And I noticed used wine glasses in Colin's office when I was dropping in post. And once when I came in early, all the stuff from his desk was on the floor. As though they'd . . . as though someone swept all the things off the desk to . . .' Poor Shauna looked like she wanted the ground to swallow her up.

Marissa nodded, putting her out of her misery. 'Got it. Anything else?'

'I suppose just general signs of disturbance, once I started to look out for them. Glasses and cups, paper on the floor beneath the printer table, even though I'd tidied up the night before – like someone had been printing after hours. Which of course is perfectly fine,' she added hurriedly. 'I don't mind tidying up.'

'Anything else?'

'Well . . . just that he had seemed a bit stressed over the last few months, but then recently he looked like the cat that got the cream.'

When Marissa finally let Shauna go, she heard her racing down the stairs to get the coffees, relieved, no doubt, to escape her boss's bizarre line of questioning. Marissa tried Colin's number again, but still it rang out. Next she phoned the school, to check on Milo – all good, the secretary reported back, Milo was in great form, like nothing had ever happened. Marissa called Peter then, but he was in a meeting. She sat looking at her phone. Was it time to tell the guards about Colin and Carrie? Even before she'd had a chance to get the story from him? Was it a police matter? Supreme lack of judgement, yes, in not telling her, but hardly a crime. Marissa drummed her fingers on the desk, restless and unsure. Maybe if Colin had told them he knew Carrie, the guards could have questioned him and got more information about her – maybe they'd have found Milo more quickly. Fresh anger bubbled up inside. Colin probably thought he had nothing to tell – maybe he felt duped or betrayed by Carrie – but still he should have said something. She picked up the phone.

McConville gave nothing away as Marissa passed on the story, and halfway through, she realized it could sound as though she thought Colin had somehow been involved.

'I don't mean to suggest Colin's done anything wrong, but he may have more information on Carrie that could be of use to you? Like Ana, things he doesn't think are relevant, but might help you catch her?'

'We'll interview Mr Dobson, can you give me his address?' McConville said, and at that Marissa's anger disappeared, quickly replaced by guilt, as she passed her friend's contact details to the detective sergeant.

Shauna dropped in a latte while Marissa was saying goodbye – scurrying back out of the office before her employer could ask any more questions – and Marissa decided she better do some work. Flipping through her diary, one thing stood out – the upcoming audit. She'd need to get back to the Downey and Fenelon files, and iron out those last discrepancies before next week. And now with Colin sick, she'd have twice the work to do. She tried to remember where she'd been at with the audit prep but it seemed like a million years ago. She'd start with the Fenelon file, she decided. The estate showed some figures that didn't add up, but it surely wouldn't take long to figure out if she focused on it. She got up to look for the files, belatedly remembering she'd left them at reception for Colin when she and Peter had come in on Thursday night.

'Shauna?'

Shauna's head jerked up, her face a picture – clearly wondering what her nosy boss was going to ask this time.

'Do you know where Colin put the Downey and Fenelon files on Friday?'

'Oh, he wasn't in on Friday.'

Marissa frowned. 'Strange, he said he was coming here to work on the files before the audit.'

'If he did, I didn't see him. Ah, here they are,' Shauna said, holding up two folders. 'Downey and Fenelon.'

Marissa took them from her outstretched hand, nodded thanks, and lost in thought, walked through to her own office. Why the urgency to get these files from her, if he hadn't bothered turning up on Friday to look at them? Something didn't add up.

The sound of her ringing phone cut through her thoughts as she sat down at her desk. Seeing 'School' appear on screen, she scrambled to answer, her skin flashing cold.

'What is it, is Milo OK?'

'Mrs Irvine, it's Mr Williams here. Milo's fine, don't worry, but he did get a bit upset during yard-time.'

'What happened?'

'It was strange. He was playing with the others, and then he suddenly stopped stock still in the middle of the yard – it was like when you see those nature programmes where a rabbit hears something and freezes, you know?'

Marissa nodded into her phone.

'I went over to see if he was OK. He just stood there, frozen, not saying anything but he looked scared. Like something had frightened him.'

Oh God, poor Milo, they should never have let him go in.

'I brought him into the sick room,' the teacher continued, 'and got him a drink of water and tried talking to him. He didn't say anything, he just sat there, frozen. I left another teacher with him so I could come and phone you.'

'I'll be there in ten minutes. Thank you,' she added, as she ran down the stairs.

Nine minutes later, she was sitting in the school sick room with Milo on her knee. He was starting to thaw out, his hunched shoulders dropping slowly, his clenched jaw softening. But his eyes were still like saucers, wide with fright.

'What do you think it was?' Marissa asked Mr Williams.

'I don't know, it was like the noise of the yard was too much for him?' Mr Williams said, tilting his head to one side. 'I know you're busy with your work and so on, but maybe today was too soon to come back.'

Much as she disliked the patronizing tone, Marissa wondered if perhaps he was right. Standing up, carrying Milo, she
thanked the teacher and headed for home. One thought kept
niggling though. Even if it was too soon to go back, something
had triggered Milo's reaction. What had he seen that had caused
him to freeze?

54

Marissa
Monday

WHEN FIONA SHERIDAN RANG the doorbell at four o'clock on Monday afternoon, Marissa could not have known the sequence of events that would follow. In fact, she considered sending Sheridan away after everything that had happened earlier, but as Sheridan walked into the sitting room, Milo got up from his toys and sat on the couch, ready to chat.

'Now, Milo, I have a few more questions today, is that OK?' Sheridan said.

Marissa hovered on the edge of the couch, ready to whisk him away if he wasn't up to it, but Milo nodded.

'Can you tell me about your hair, Milo? Did Carrie put something in it?'

Marissa tensed. Milo hadn't said anything about his newly brown hair, so neither had she. But Milo didn't hesitate.

'She putted a shampoo in it to make it clean but a funny thing happened, it made it brown instead! She said I was a little robin because my hair is brown like a bird now.' He laughed and pointed at his head.

'Oh! That must have been a magic shampoo,' Fiona said, smiling back. 'And Milo, you remember you told me she took your photo? I want you to think hard – was that with your new brown hair, or before, when your hair was blond?'

'After,' he said emphatically. 'She had to dry it quickly with a hair dryer to make me ready for the photo. She put a red coat on me and said, "Now you're a proper robin," and she taked a picture.'

Marissa looked over at Fiona, who was taking notes. What on earth was all this robin stuff?

'And when she put the red coat on you, was that to go outside somewhere?' Fiona asked.

'No.' Milo's mouth turned down. 'She said no going outside.' He stopped for a moment, as if remembering something. 'I *heard* the outside though, through the window.'

'You did?' Fiona sat forward.

'I opened the top bit of my window because I really wanted to play outside. It was too small to fit, but I heard the noise of outside. Carrie didn't know.'

'And what was the noise of outside?'

'It was like today.'

Fiona looked from Marissa to Milo. From the kitchen came the clattering of cups and spoons as Lia made coffee. In the sitting room, nothing stirred.

'Like today?'

'Like yard-time. The sound of playtime at school.'

Things moved fast then. Fiona Sheridan was up and out in the hall on her phone. This was good, she told Marissa when she came back; it meant the house was more than likely near a school. That narrowed things considerably.

'What about all this stuff with the hair dye and the red coat?' Marissa asked, pulling Milo on to her knee. 'And the bird thing – is that a bit creepy?'

'I'm not sure yet – if this news about the nearby school means we can find Carrie, we can ask her directly,' she said, nodding at the two of them. 'You did great, Milo, you're a big, big help.'

She left, telling them she'd be back at four o'clock the following afternoon.

'Is she going to come every day?' Lia asked, coming into the room with a coffee for Marissa.

'Until they catch Carrie, I guess,' Marissa said, 'and whoever was in on it with her.'

It was close to six when the doorbell rang again; this time Marissa knew who it was – DS McConville had phoned to say she'd call by. To ask Milo questions about the sound of the schoolyard, she said, and to update Marissa and Peter on the case. She spent no more than five minutes chatting to Milo, then asked if Milo and his Auntie Lia might be able to play in another room for a bit.

Marissa nodded, exchanging a glance with Peter, as Lia took Milo's hand and left. Suddenly, her heart was pounding – was this it, had they found Carrie? Peter sat forward. McConville waited until Lia closed the door.

'You may or may not have heard this on the news last week, but a body was found in a house in North Wall – we didn't give out an official ID, but the papers got hold of the name Danny Vaughan?'

Peter nodded. Marissa had only the vaguest memory of it – something gross about hands being chopped off.

'Your friend Jenny realized yesterday that her son had written the name Danny Vaughan on a chalkboard in his playroom. Spelt phonetically as D-A-N-I V-O-N so she didn't realize at first.'

Marissa stared at McConville, trying to understand where this was going.

'What does this have to do with Milo?'

'When Jenny asked Jacob about it, he said he'd heard Carrie say the name on the phone. A number of times.'

Marissa felt sick. She had a sudden urge to check on Milo and rushed over to open the door. Lia and Milo were in the kitchen, sitting at the island, looking at photos on Lia's phone. She closed the door and let out a breath.

'Wait, so Danny Vaughan was involved with Carrie in some way – part of the gang? Is he the one who dropped Milo's jacket over the edge of Killiney Hill?' Peter was asking.

'After Jenny Kennedy told us there was a connection between Carrie and Danny Vaughan, we sent a team back to search the house again. They pulled up floorboards in Vaughan's bedroom this time, and found a stack of old letters, all addressed to Kyle Byrde. Some of them are from Carrie, sent to Byrde when he was in prison.'

'So, what, Byrde and Vaughan knew each other? Were they old cellmates?' Peter asked.

McConville shook her head.

Marissa understood.

'They're the same person, aren't they?' she said. 'Danny Vaughan is Kyle Byrde.'

'Yes,' McConville said. 'Once we found the letters, we showed the old photo of Kyle Byrde to Vaughan's housemates and they confirmed it's the same man. He was using a fake name when he left prison, which explains why we haven't been able to track him down.'

Marissa and Peter sat staring, trying to work out what it all meant. McConville continued. 'We couldn't fingerprint the victim, because as I'm sure you heard on the news, he had been partially dismembered. His hands had been removed after he was murdered, and his face was very severely beaten.'

'To stop you being able to ID him?'

'We assume so. Although if someone wanted him to disappear and never be identified, they'd have removed the body.'

'Unless they couldn't move the body on their own?' Peter said.

Marissa's head spun trying to catch up. 'So, what – you think Carrie got Kyle to help with the kidnap, and then killed him once it was done?'

McConville looked between Peter and Marissa. 'We think it's very unlikely that Carrie would have been able to do this. Not on her own, anyway.'

Marissa paled as she caught on to what McConville was really telling them. 'There's a third person involved – not just Carrie and Kyle, someone else again?'

'Yes,' McConville said, standing up and smoothing down her coat. 'And we still don't know who that person is.'

PART 3

55

Irene
Tuesday

IRENE FIZZED WITH EXCITEMENT even before she opened her eyes. Long before Frank's alarm went off for work. Today was the day. Her newspaper debut. The quotes were good, Faye Foster had said, and the pictures great. It wouldn't be online until tomorrow, only in the paper version for now, and Irene couldn't decide if that was a good thing or a bad thing. It meant a bit more time to breathe before Frank would see it – he didn't buy tabloids. On the flip side, she'd have to get up and go to the shop to actually read it, which meant waiting for Frank to go to work. And she needed to chase Faye Foster about the money. Being famous and in the news was all very well, but she hadn't done it for the good of her health – she needed that cash.

Frank was so slow that morning, like some ancient slug, pottering around the kitchen, sipping his tea, tying his shoes. He was surprised to see her dressed before he left – 'Dentist appointment,' she told him, pointing at her teeth. 'They're looking a bit yellow.' That last bit was true – she'd noticed it when she was getting ready for the photographer. No matter, plenty of cash for teeth-whitening coming her way.

'Do you need a lift? I can drop you on the way to the bank?'

'No, it's not till ten,' she said, *and I only need to get to the shop on the corner*, she didn't add.

Frank kissed her goodbye and pulled the kitchen door after him. Like a greyhound in the traps, she hovered on the seat of the chair, waiting for the sound of the front door closing. What was taking him so bloody long?

She heard it open.

Then voices.

Frank's, and someone else's. The postman? God, this was going to take for ever if they got chatting – the postman could talk the hind legs off a table, not to mind a donkey. Straining to listen, Irene realized Frank's voice had gone up a notch – it didn't sound like the usual rumble of weather-this and traffic-that chatter. And was that a woman's voice too?

Standing up, Irene walked to the kitchen door and opened it. At the front door, she could see Frank, his hand covering his mouth. Outside stood a man and a woman – the woman had a microphone in her hand. Journalists? TV maybe?

Dear God, it was happening. Her story was out. And Frank would lose it – in his own reined-in, thin-lipped way. But who cared; her story was out, and they all wanted to talk to her. This was her moment. What did they say – everyone gets fifteen minutes of fame? Well, she was bloody well having more than fifteen.

Irene glided towards the front door. Ignoring Frank, smiling serenely at the man and woman on the doorstep, one sentence went around and around in her head.

I'm ready for my close-up.

To her left, Frank was saying something. She was just about conscious of his horrified expression, his hand still covering his mouth.

'Irene, my God, Irene.'

She ignored him.

Outside, someone else was coming through the gate – another journalist, another microphone. A man with a camera. Heady with excitement, Irene smiled at her audience. Everyone started to talk at once; a camera flashed in her face. She raised her hands in a *one at a time* motion she'd seen on *House of Cards*. Never had she felt more queenly. She really was ready for her close-up.

Then, out of the corner of her eye, she saw someone else at the gate. Detective Sergeant McConville, the prissy bitch who was so condescending when she interviewed her. And that lanky Breen fella. Well, fuck them, she hadn't broken any laws by talking to the press. Faye Foster had said something about not profiting from selling stories about criminals, but Caroline wasn't a criminal – nothing had been proven. Faye was sure she'd get the budget. *Certain.* And as long as Irene got the cash before Carrie was convicted of anything, she wasn't giving it back. No bloody way, she'd have it spent. She folded her arms and smirked at the approaching gardaí.

As McConville neared the doorstep, the journalists stepped aside, and the babble of voices dissipated. Gormless fools, bowing down to this one with her uppity attitude. Well, Irene wasn't going anywhere. She stood, arms still folded, glaring at McConville. Ready for battle.

But McConville didn't look ready to fight back. There was something else on her face, something she was trying to hide. Irene had seen it before – back when Rob left her, when her mother died, when Caroline ran away.

It was pity.

'Mrs Turner, may I come in?'

And suddenly, Irene knew this wasn't about selling her story. She stepped aside, conscious, but only just, that Frank had his hand on her lower back. The four of them – Breen at the end, closing the door on the journalists – walked through to the living room and sat.

'What's going on?' Irene asked.

'Mrs Turner, I'm very sorry to have to tell you this, it's about your daughter Caroline.'

'She's been caught?'

'I'm afraid she's dead, Mrs Turner.'

Whatever Irene was expecting, this wasn't it. Years of memories and thousands of thoughts and worlds of emotions toppled down on her in that moment, crashing around her, pulling her in every direction, crushing her. The girl who'd been nothing but trouble, the whining, the stealing, the fighting, the nagging. The stress. The *relentless* stress. The girl who'd become a criminal, the teen who'd run away. And good riddance. She didn't care anyway. Why should she care? Caroline had never cared. She hadn't seen her in nine years. She was nothing but trouble. *Nothing.* She should never have been born. If she had her time again, she wouldn't have had her. Irene's legs felt suddenly weak. She reached out to touch the wall, as the bomb inside her continued firing memories. The girl, the poetry, the journals, the angry red pen. The fiery red hair. The baby. The tiny hands, wrapped around her finger. Something huge welled up inside Irene's chest, something she couldn't name, as memories kept coming. The baby in her arms, the toddler at her side, the photo in the scrapbook. The time shared, the time not shared, the words never said. *Too late.* The words never said. Over. *All over.* And for the first time in her life, Irene found herself dissolving into tears for her child.

56

Marissa
Tuesday

MARISSA PICKED UP HER phone, tensing when she saw McConville's number flash up. Had they discovered who else was working with Carrie?

'This is Marissa,' she said, unease sharpening her tone.

'Marissa, I have some news to pass on to you and your husband, I wanted to catch you before you see it in the media.'

A chill settled across Marissa. But Milo was safe. Everything was OK. Whatever McConville was about to say, it couldn't hurt them.

'Did you catch her?'

'We found Carrie Finch's body.'

Marissa sagged against the kitchen counter. Of everything she had imagined, she wasn't prepared for that.

'What happened? Where?'

'In the house where she was keeping Milo, in Sandymount.' McConville paused. 'She was found in bed, and obviously the post mortem still has to take place, but . . . well, you're going to see this in some sections of the media anyway, it's likely she was smothered with a pillow.'

Marissa felt sick. McConville was still talking – about

narrowing the search to houses near schools, about the red-brick bungalow, just like Milo said. About what they found inside, and some pictures McConville wanted to show her. She tried to take all of it in, but even after McConville said goodbye, she stood with the phone pressed to her ear, still struggling to cut through the blur and wondering how exactly to process this piece of news.

Carrie is dead.

Smothered in bed, her body left to rot. The woman who'd taken her child had been murdered. And it was impossible to separate that from the next thought – Milo could have been caught up in it too, if he hadn't been found. Milo had spent time with people who thought nothing of holding a pillow over a woman's face, leaning down on it until her kicking stopped. And what of Carrie – what did she feel for her? Marissa turned it over in her mind. Nothing. She'd taken Milo, she didn't deserve pity or sorrow.

It was over.

Marissa got up to go to Peter's home office, ignoring the little voice that told her it wasn't over, not until they knew who had helped Carrie.

Peter looked up when she came in, pointing to the telephone receiver at his ear.

'Client,' he started to mouth, but at the look on her face he told the person at the other end he'd phone back.

'McConville just called.' It came out in a hoarse whisper. 'Carrie's dead. They found her body last night.'

'Jesus. How? What happened?'

Marissa swallowed. 'She was smothered in her own bed. They don't know who did it.'

'Bloody hell.' Peter looked as shaken as she felt.

'I don't know what to think. Like, am I glad she's dead? I

don't think so – not that I feel sorry for her or anything, but she should have to go to jail and answer for it. Answer to us.'

Peter nodded. 'Did McConville say anything else?' he asked. 'Have they any leads on this third person?'

'None so far, I think, but I didn't really ask, it was all a bit of a blur.'

Peter picked up the phone, stared at the receiver, and put it down again.

'I feel like we should be doing something, but I don't know what. Do we just wait? Even though that other person is still out there?'

'What else can we do? We need to focus on Milo. The main thing is, he's safe. Though *how* exactly he's safe might be a mystery for ever with Carrie dead – who put him in the car?'

'God, it feels never-ending.' He put his hand on top of hers. 'We should get out of here. Go somewhere warm and sunny and forget all about it, at least for a while. What do you think?'

'I can't think of anything I'd love more. The apartment in Marbella?'

He nodded, as his mobile started to vibrate. He frowned at the screen.

'All OK?' she said.

'Yeah, just one of my least favourite clients.'

'Dermot Downey?' Marissa guessed, smiling – Peter was irrationally irritated by the developer, though didn't mind taking his commission from Downey's substantial investments.

'Am I that obvious?' Peter said with mock surprise, as Marissa stood.

'I'll leave you to it. I'm going to phone the school to check on Milo then pop into the office for a bit,' she said as she shut his office door.

Milo had skipped in that morning, but Marissa was bracing

herself for a call as yard-time approached. *It'll take time*, Tara had said, when she called her yesterday evening, *don't rush him, follow his lead*. Sensible advice, but hard to navigate in real life.

And then there was Colin.

Still no sight or sound of him. Jesus, Colin wouldn't know yet that Carrie was dead. Marissa sank to the bottom step of the stairs as the low hum of Peter's conversation rumbled in the background.

It was time to face Colin.

57

Jenny
Tuesday

JENNY WAS NABBING A five-minute break at work when she heard the news. The police didn't tell her – why would they, she supposed afterwards, though Richie thought it was bad form. The news had come as most news did these days – on the internet. She clicked into headlines in between finishing a conference call and running to a meeting, and there it was.

Kidnapper Nanny Found Dead in Dublin 4 House

Jenny stared at Carrie's unsmiling photo, the one they'd used throughout the search, trying to get her head around it. The girl she'd trusted to look after her son. A kidnapper. A liar. Dead.

Dead because she made bad choices? Or because she was caught up in something she didn't choose at all? It felt better to imagine that someone had a hold over her or a knife to her throat. But that didn't explain the engineering, the fake family, the fake references. Jenny shook her head at the screen.

Richie didn't pick up when she rang but he called back a few minutes later.

'I just saw it online,' he said. 'God.'

'I know. In a weird way, taking in that she's dead seems even bigger than taking in that she kidnapped someone.'

'Or is it just that we got used to that over the last week, and this is a new shock,' Richie said, and he was probably right, Jenny thought, clicking from one news story to the next.

'The talk online is all about who killed her, and the comments are *disgusting*,' she said. 'People saying she deserved it.'

Silence. She could almost hear Richie's shrug down the phone line.

'Nobody deserves that, Richie. Prison, yes, but not murder.'

'I suppose. One way or another, it's over now and we can move on.'

'Well, yeah, except that we need to figure out how to keep the news from Jacob, and we still need a new childminder.' *And possibly hours of expensive therapy*, she added, but only in her head.

'I guess if we keep him away from TV for a few days, it'll all die down? And we can explain Carrie's gone away and we need a new nanny?'

'You're right. I'll get on the childminder search.' With a heavy sigh, she said goodbye and logged into Nanny365.ie, the website she'd used when she first started looking for childcare.

A minute later, she sat back, remembering.

Nanny365 had sent five or six candidates, but none of them was exactly what she wanted. One couldn't drive. Another lived way over the other side of Dublin, and much as she swore she'd be in Kerryglen by eight every morning, Jenny couldn't see how she'd manage it. She thought back to the blur of faces, the women she'd discounted, before sticking ads up in the tennis club, in Esther's Tea Garden, and in Jacob's preschool. Carrie had answered one of the ads, though Jenny had no idea now which one – maybe she'd never known. Jenny sat up straighter, casting her mind back to the ad. Did she have the wording somewhere? She clicked into the 'Childcare' folder on her email and searched. There it was, the text she'd used to print up the little cards she'd put on the noticeboards.

Childminder Wanted May 2018
One four-year-old child to be minded in own house (Kerryglen) – finishing preschool, starting in local National School in September: childminder needed for breakfast and school drop, pick-up and afternoons. Live-in or live-out optional. We are looking for someone kind, with full, clean driver's licence. Experience desirable but not necessary. References (for childminding or other work) required.

Jenny sat back, staring at the email. If Carrie had applied based on the ad, she knew Jacob was starting Junior Infants in Kerryglen National. Could she have engineered all of it to target Milo? Maybe it wasn't an opportunistic crime prompted by Ana's talk of big houses and flash cars – maybe Carrie had been scoping out the Irvines for far longer than any of them realized? And she and Richie had put up their ad, opened their house to Carrie, and made all of it possible. She picked up the phone and called McConville.

Jenny had managed to avoid the Coven at pick-up, but as she and Jacob walked into the pharmacy on Castle Street on Tuesday afternoon, her heart sank. There at the till, her blonde hair glinting under fluorescent lights, was Sarah Rayburn. Jenny considered sloping back out, but before she could, Sarah spotted her.

'Jenny, how *are* you? Unreal about Carrie, isn't it?'

Jenny screwed up her face and pointed at Jacob, but Sarah either misunderstood or chose to ignore.

'It's hard to believe she's dead,' she went on, 'but at the same time, if you hang out with criminal gangs, that's what happens I guess.'

'Uh, yeah, we're doing our best to keep things normal for the little guy, you know?' Jenny said, over-enunciating the words in universal parent-code for *read between the lines*. In her head, she added the lesser-known *you dick* – that one was just for Sarah.

Sarah clapped her hand over her mouth, full of faux regret.

'Sorry, sorry, *of course*. But then he's bound to find out, isn't he?' she whispered. 'It's all over the news. Unbelievable. What kind of people was she hanging out with? You'll have to take care the next time – don't use EvilNannies.com! Or When Good Nannies Go Bad – that could be a TV show!' She grinned, baring shark teeth. 'Anyway, I better run.'

'Mummy, is Carrie dead?' Jacob asked, as Sarah sashayed out of earshot.

'I . . . we'll chat about it later, pet, don't worry,' Jenny said, rooting in her handbag for her prescription, until somehow the bag slipped out of her hands and the contents spilled all over the floor.

'Mummy, tell me – what happened to Carrie?' Jacob was saying, as Jenny got down on her knees to grab at rolling coins and loose tissues.

'Are you all right? Can I help you with something?' the pharmacist called from behind the counter, with a tinge of irritation. No, she was most definitely not all right. How was she going to explain Carrie's death to Jacob? She reached under a make-up stand to grab a rolling lipstick and shoved it back in her bag. *Bloody Sarah Rayburn and her big mouth.*

'Ah, now, who do we have here, it's never Jacob Kennedy

looking so big and smart, is it?' came a voice from somewhere above. Jenny looked up to see Esther smiling down at Jacob.

Jenny stood, frazzled, cheeks hot, sweating.

'The other mummy said Carrie's dead,' Jacob said, looking from Jenny to Esther. 'Is it true?'

Jenny stood, mouth open, with no idea what to say next. Esther looked at Jenny with an unspoken question, and Jenny nodded. Whatever Esther was about to say, it couldn't make things worse.

Esther hunkered down to Jacob's height, her navy tea dress billowing around her.

'Jacob, you know the way sometimes very old people die?'

Jacob nodded.

'Well, very rarely, it can happen to people who are not old. Carrie is one of those people who died even though she wasn't old. And it's OK to be sad about that and to ask questions.'

Jacob nodded again.

'Do you have some questions for me right now?'

He thought for a moment. 'No,' he said, and looked up at Jenny and smiled. 'Can we go to Esther's for cake?'

Jenny mouthed 'thank you' to her as Jacob ran over to look at some toys.

'No trouble. I wouldn't normally intervene, but you looked like you had enough on your hands with yer one with the teeth.'

'Thank you,' Jenny said again, out loud this time. 'We were going to try to stop him from finding out but he seems absolutely fine.'

'Kids are funny, they're often better at acceptance than we are. I remember it from when mine were small.'

'Oh, I didn't know you had kids. They're all grown now?'

'Yes, two in London, and four foster children as well, all here in Dublin.'

'Ah, do you still see them?'

A shadow crossed Esther's face. 'Three of them, yes. With the other, it's . . . well, it's complicated. But enough about me,' she said brightly. 'How are *you*?'

It was the same question Sarah had asked moments earlier, but with a world of difference. Empathy in place of gleeful Schadenfreude, and not for the first time, Jenny wanted to hug Esther.

'I'm grand, it's all still a shock. And we still have to find a childminder for Jacob, which Sarah Rayburn thinks is a great topic for her impromptu stand-up comedy act.' Jenny rolled her eyes.

'It'll work out, I promise you. Good things don't always happen to good people – sadly – but I have a strong sense you're due some luck.'

She whirled out the door, without buying anything at all. Jenny stood in line with her prescription, hoping fervently Esther was right. But she couldn't help feeling on edge. There was more to this story, bubbling just under the surface, like a volcano waiting to explode.

58

Marissa
Tuesday

COLIN'S HOUSE WAS CONSIDERABLY larger than Marissa expected – wider than the usual new-builds around the area, homes that sat so close to one another, you couldn't fit a cigarette paper between them. This house had a decent bit of space out front – parking for three cars, and side passages separating it from its neighbours. The house itself was pristine, as if someone had taken it from a box and planted it as is, on a neat patch of grass.

Marissa and Peter hadn't been here before, though Colin had lived here for over a year, and as they walked up the steps, Marissa wondered about that – had Colin not invited them, or had she not thought to visit?

There was no sign of movement as she rang the bell and waited. Maybe Colin really was in his sickbed. Though that didn't explain the unanswered calls.

'Did you hear back from McConville, do you know if she interviewed him?' Marissa asked Peter as they waited.

'No, I forgot to ask – she said she would though, right?' Peter said.

Marissa nodded. 'I bet he won't answer, he's probably seen it's us.'

But as she said it, the glossy black door swung open. Colin stood in the hall, head bowed like a naughty schoolboy. He was wearing tracksuit bottoms and a hoodie, not a look Marissa had seen him go for before. His feet, long, white and narrow, were bare on the thick grey carpet, and somehow that unnerved her – she really didn't want to see his feet. On his grey hoodie, she spotted something yellow – egg? Mustard? This was a far cry from the well-groomed man she was used to seeing at work every day. And still he stood there, chin to chest, saying nothing.

'Colin, I think we need to talk,' she said in her coldest voice, and it was her tone, she reckoned, not her words, that got his attention.

He looked up, and quickly looked down again, unable to meet her eyes. Stepping back, he gestured for them to come in.

His hallway was like the hallway in a show house – plush carpet, light grey walls, gleaming white woodwork. Maybe it *was* the show house – Marissa couldn't imagine Colin decorating it on his own, the man hardly knew how to make a cup of tea. They followed him through to a gleaming kitchen – grey, of course, everything was grey these days – and took seats at his slate-topped island, also grey. Colin stood against the worktop, head in hands.

'I've been trying to reach you since Sunday,' Marissa said. 'Why haven't you answered my calls?'

'I was sick, sorry,' he mumbled into his hands.

'And what else do you want to tell me?'

Suddenly she felt like she was talking to Milo, getting him to confess to a stolen biscuit or a scribble on the wall.

Colin's shoulders started to shake. Oh good God, was he

crying? Colin? She'd never seen him cry, not once. This didn't feel quite real.

'Colin,' Peter said, stepping in, perhaps correctly guessing that she was going to cave at the tears, 'we know you were seeing Carrie. Why didn't you tell us? Or the police?'

Finally, Colin looked up.

'I was embarrassed,' he said forlornly. 'I'd fallen for her and I had no idea what she was really like. When I finally recognized her photo on the news and realized what she'd done, I was afraid you'd think she used information I gave her. You know, to help plan the kidnap.'

'And did you?'

Colin lifted his hands in a helpless shrug.

'Not on purpose.'

Marissa let out a shaky breath.

'Right, spill,' Peter said, still in charge. 'What happened?'

'It was in a bar. I was meant to meet this girl I'd met online but she didn't show. This other girl was sitting just down the bar from me. She smiled over, and said, "I got stood up too," and raised her glass in a salute. That's how we got talking.'

Colin paused, and Marissa tried to picture Carrie in a bar, starting up a conversation with a stranger. It didn't tally at all with the quiet childminder Jenny talked about. But then again, that quiet childminder had turned out to be a criminal, so maybe it wasn't the most accurate benchmark.

'Go on,' Peter said, folding his arms.

'We talked for hours. Lena – that's what she said her name was – told me she was a writer, writing a book set in a fictional wealthy town in south Dublin. She was here in Kerryglen to get a taste of local life, she said.'

'Wait, so she never said anything about being a nanny, or living with Jenny?'

Colin shook his head. 'No, nothing. She said she lived with her aunt, so couldn't bring me back there. We always came here, or . . . well, yes, here.'

'I know about the office,' Marissa said flatly.

Colin looked away. 'Sorry.'

'OK, so what did you tell her – what information were you afraid we'd think she used to kidnap Milo?'

Colin glanced at her, then back at his still-bare feet. Marissa's eyes were drawn there too, and despite the seriousness of the conversation she couldn't help wishing he'd put on shoes.

'She said she'd heard about Kerryglen au pairs and nannies literally raising the kids while parents were off on holidays. I said you guys would never go away without Milo – that you bring the nanny on holidays with you, so you've help while you're over there. She started asking more about you then, and . . . look, I know I shouldn't have, but she was interested and I suppose I was showing off a bit. I told her about the house and the cars and the kitchen that cost forty grand. And older stuff too – Celtic Tiger stuff, like when you used to go to New York with your friends for Christmas shopping,' he said, nodding at Marissa, 'and the two weddings and the helicopter on standby and the taxis everywhere and—'

Peter shook his head. 'Jesus Christ, between yourself and Ana, you may as well have made a documentary called *How To Find Your Ideal Kidnap Target*. What were you thinking?'

'I wasn't thinking, I'm sorry. She was gorgeous and she was paying me attention and God, guys, I never thought she was going to use the information to do what she did.' He looked pleadingly at them. 'Obviously I wouldn't have said a word if I copped what she was doing – I'd have *called* the cops.'

Marissa was still trying to picture Colin with the straggly-haired, pale girl she'd seen on the news and in the papers and on social media – everywhere in fact, apart from that one photo on Lia's Facebook.

'Roll back a sec, Col. When you say she was gorgeous – she doesn't strike me as your type, to be honest. You normally go for a more high-maintenance kind of girl.'

'She *was* gorgeous.' He nodded emphatically. 'That photo on the news didn't look like her at all, I don't know where they got it from. Here.' He pulled his phone out of his tracksuit pocket and scrolled. 'This is what she really looks like.'

He handed the phone to Marissa.

The woman smiling at the camera had glossy auburn hair swirling around her shoulders, framing a beautifully made-up face – professionally done, Marissa reckoned, or by someone who was well-practised in the art of make-up. But the smile was what caught her attention – a confident, almost *sensuous* smile that said *I'm in charge*. She looked nothing at all like the person Jenny had hired. In fact, anyone searching for the girl in the newspaper photos would have walked right past the woman on Colin's phone.

'Good God, she played two completely different people,' Marissa said. 'I can't imagine the effort that must have taken. Carrie, the quiet, mousy nanny, and Lena, the glossy, made-up girlfriend. Literally *made up*.'

The three of them stood in silence, then Marissa turned to Colin again.

'I can't believe you didn't tell me any of this after Milo was kidnapped.'

'Jesus, Mar, I didn't know! I didn't realize it was her – I knew her as Lena, and she looked nothing like herself in that photo that was on TV. But then later in the week there was a new photo in the paper where her face was shown really clearly, and I nearly fell off my chair. I'd been trying to reach her for a few days and got no answer – I thought she'd dumped me. I didn't know what to do. I'd already seen you guys at that stage – on Saturday and again on Tuesday, remember?'

Marissa nodded, though she didn't really know – the whole week had been a blurry nightmare.

'It was late Thursday night when I saw the new photo in the paper and I just froze. You were out of your mind with worry, and telling you I'd been seeing Carrie was only going to make it worse – I needed to think.'

'But it might have helped the guards find Milo – how can you not see that?'

'I know, and I decided I'd go down to the garda station on Friday morning to tell them everything, but then Milo was found and it was over.'

He looked at her, eyes beseeching. Was he telling the truth – was he really planning to go to the guards? She locked eyes, trying to read him.

'I promise you, Mar. I don't know what I can do to convince you.'

Silence as she searched his face. Jesus, she wanted him to be telling the truth. And maybe he was – looking at the photo on his phone compared to the badly taken photo they'd seen on TV all week, it was possible he hadn't realized. And who suspects their girlfriend of being a kidnapper? It's not the first thing you think when your calls go unanswered. But there was something not quite right with the whole thing, and she couldn't put her finger on it.

Peter stepped in, breaking the silence.

'You still should have said something. Even though Milo was safe, the police were looking for Carrie, and we couldn't relax till we knew she was found.'

Shoulders slumped again, head down. 'I know. I'm sorry. I

was just so worried you'd think it was my fault. Or the cops would think I was in on it.'

Peter barked an empty, sad laugh. 'Colin, I don't think they'd have imagined a baby-faced Kerryglen solicitor as a member of a child trafficking gang somehow. You were on safe ground there, mate.'

Child trafficking gang. Marissa shivered. With her thumb, she rubbed at a tiny white spot on the breakfast bar.

'And now Carrie's dead . . .' Colin said in a small voice. 'Where do we go from here? With Irvine and Dobson, I mean?'

Still rubbing, not looking up, Marissa shrugged.

'I don't know, Col. Obviously we're business partners and that complicates things. I need time.' She looked up. 'You know?'

He nodded. 'Well, I can look after the audit if you want to take time at home with Milo, and . . . and see how you feel about all of it?' Hopeful puppy was back.

'We're going away actually, a few days in Marbella to escape all this. I'll be in better shape to plan next steps when I get back.'

It was so odd to be talking to her old friend like this, like a disappointed parent. Odd and uncomfortable.

'That sounds brilliant, Mar, and I'll keep the ship running while you're gone – or sailing I should say, right? I'll do the audit, keep everything shipshape. Too much of the old sailing analogy there now,' he said, ending with a burst of awkward laughter. They did not join in but pushed back their stools and rose to leave. Colin straightened up, rocking back and forth on his feet, eager for them to be out of his house no doubt. It couldn't be easy facing the two of them, Marissa realized, with a small pang of sympathy. And seeing him crying – that was nearly the end of her resolve.

She looked over at him as she said goodbye, and that's when she realized what had been bothering her.

There were no tears in his eyes, none of the redness that comes from crying. On autopilot, she waved and followed Peter out the door, thinking back to the shaking shoulders, the head in hands, the contrite but dry-as-bone eyes. Was it all an act?

59

Jenny
Tuesday

WHAT WAS SHE EVEN doing here, Jenny wondered, as she rang the bell of Maple Lodge. It's not like she and Marissa were going to stay friends now it was all almost over – if anything, Marissa would surely want to run a mile from any reminders. How weird to think only six nights earlier, they had been calling door-to-door in Pine Valley, desperately seeking information on Milo. Now he was tucked up inside his own four walls, safe as houses. Why did people say that actually – safe as houses? Houses weren't all that safe; it depended who was in them, she thought, as Marissa opened the door.

'Jenny! Darling! So glad you could make it – I wanted to thank you properly, and just, well, sit down for a coffee now it's all over?'

Jenny smiled and followed her through to the sitting room. Like the kitchen, it was oversized, with high ceilings and a sense of air and space. Her mother-in-law's house was of similar proportions but stuffed with every piece of furniture Adeline had ever owned. This was light and airy and calming, even on a Tuesday night in November when everywhere else felt dark and hemmed in. The dove-grey sofas were covered with mustard-yellow cushions, and a broad, glass-topped coffee table held a coffee pot and some cups. Another woman came into the room as Jenny sat – a tiny, twig-like woman with a mass of jet-black candyfloss hair and bright red lips. She flopped down on the adjacent sofa and eyed up Jenny.

'Lia, this is my friend Jenny – one of the mums from the school. Jenny, this is Lia, Peter's sister. She's home from New York to keep an eye on us all and is terrifically good at making margaritas.'

Jenny smiled hello, mildly embarrassed at how delighted she was at the word 'friend' and grateful that Marissa hadn't mentioned the Carrie connection. If Lia knew, she didn't show it.

'I've heard so much about school-gate moms and bitchiness and comparing whose kid's best, but you look decidedly nice,' Lia declared, nodding at Jenny.

'Honestly – although there are a few notable exceptions – most people are absolute pets,' Marissa said, pouring three cups of coffee, 'and too busy running around after their own kids to pay attention to what anyone else's kid is doing.'

An image of Sarah Rayburn flashed through Jenny's mind, her beady eyes hungry for drama.

'Pour a cup for Peter as well,' Lia said, 'he's on his way in.'

'And Brian?'

'No, he had to go out somewhere.'

'Oh,' Marissa said, glancing at the carriage clock on the mantelpiece, 'where's he going?'

Lia shrugged, and Jenny remembered what she'd seen on her way home from Pine Valley that night – was it Brian going into the house in the new development, or just someone who looked like him?

Peter arrived into the room, nodding at all of them, showing no annoyance that Jenny was there – maybe she was forgiven.

'So, Lia, you've met Jenny, the woman who had the misfortune to hire the kidnapper.'

Ah. Not forgiven. Jenny's cheeks flamed.

'Peter! Honestly! Let's not get into this again,' Marissa said, glaring at him.

'Oh look, water under the bridge,' Peter said, 'it could have just as easily been Ana – we thought it was at the start. You never really know what's going on with people.'

'Exactly,' Marissa said, sitting beside Jenny. 'Look what Colin was doing behind our backs.'

Jenny looked around at the three faces. Was she supposed to know what Colin was doing?

'Screwing the nanny,' Lia explained. 'Didn't think to tell anyone.'

Jenny's jaw dropped. And somewhere deep inside, in a part she didn't like, she was a tiny bit glad. If their friend Colin was involved with Carrie, it shifted something in the blame dynamics.

'In his defence,' Peter was saying, 'not that he deserves a defence, he didn't realize it was her until the new photo went out on Thursday, and then Milo was found that night.'

'Hmm. I think there's more to it.'

Everyone turned to look at Marissa.

'You surely don't think he had something to do with the kidnap?' Peter said, putting his coffee cup on the mantelpiece.

'No, not with the kidnap directly of course, but just something . . . I can't shake the feeling he was playing a role when we called over to his house this afternoon. Playing the contrite friend who screwed up. Talking off a script.'

'Like Carrie,' Jenny said. It came out hoarse, and she cleared her throat, reddening slightly as three faces turned towards her. 'She played the quiet mouse so well – it was like she picked a role and immersed herself in it.'

303

'Exactly,' Marissa said. 'And you should see the photo Colin had on his phone – this gorgeous, sexy woman who looked nothing like the nanny you hired.'

'Which one was the real Carrie, I wonder,' Lia mused. 'Maybe we'll never know.'

'True,' Marissa agreed. 'She'd been estranged a long time from her mother apparently, so the only one who really knew her was the boyfriend, Kyle whatshisname, and now he seems to be that dead body that turned up last week – Danny Vaughan.'

'Is it definitely him?' Jenny asked, a fresh wave of nausea rolling through her stomach as she pictured Jacob writing his name on the board.

'McConville phoned earlier and said it's definite – I guess they used dental records or something. Isn't that how they do it?'

Three heads nodded and Jenny smiled inwardly – they'd all seen the same TV shows then.

Her phone pinged twice, and as the others continued to chat about Kyle Byrde, she checked it. A pointed text from Richie asking if she'd be home to see her son before bed, and one from Mark asking if she was going to a conference in Luxembourg next week. Crap. She'd forgotten about the conference. How was she going to go with no childcare? She replied to Mark to say she wasn't sure, told Richie she'd be home in ten minutes, and stood to say goodbye.

At the front door, Marissa hugged her, then stepped back to look at Jenny, her hands still on her shoulders.

'Is everything OK? You seem on edge.'

'Oh, no, I'm grand! Just husband stuff and work stuff, and the two not going quite hand in hand.' Why was she telling her this? Marissa had enough going on.

'Ah. Like childcare being your domain regardless of the fact that you work? That's how it is here, anyway. I work full-time, and still do most of the childcare logistics. And notes for school. And PE gear. And signing homework. All that?'

Jenny nodded, quietly surprised to find this common ground. In the end, she supposed, it didn't matter how much money you had – someone still had to remember PE gear.

'I shouldn't complain. Richie is great usually, but since the start of the summer, he's been very distant and—' She shook herself. 'What am I like! Standing on your doorstep, letting the cold in, giving out about my husband!'

'All the more reason to do it in a warm cocktail bar, very soon,' Marissa said, hugging her again. 'And until we can arrange that, I'm here, any time you want to talk.'

As Jenny stepped outside, with the promise of cocktails ringing in her ears, she wondered if friendships founded on trauma are cemented in stone for ever or doomed before they start.

60

Jenny
Tuesday

TWENTY MINUTES AND TWO bedtime stories after arriving home, Jenny flopped on the couch beside Richie, who was busy grading papers.

'All OK in the ivory tower?' he asked, putting down his pen.

Jenny grinned and elbowed him. 'Be nice. But yes, all grand.'

'Was the brother there?'

'Brian? No, not tonight. Why?'

'Just curious about what he's like. Seems a strange fish.'

Jenny sat up straighter. 'Do you know him?'

'No, not at all, but I saw him driving past earlier. I've seen him around here recently, mostly at night. He always strikes me as a bit of an oddball.'

'Maybe he was calling in to the Downeys? I think they're clients of his?'

Richie shrugged, unconvinced. She thought about telling him what she saw – about seeing Brian in the show house when he was supposed to be in the Swan – but something stopped her. A loyalty to the Irvines, maybe? Or just the ongoing disconnect with her husband.

Her phone beeped – another message from Mark, asking

which hotel she was booking for the Luxembourg conference. Richie watched as she replied.

'Everything OK?' That was Richie-speak for *would you ever put away your phone for five minutes*. She put it on the coffee table, face down.

'Yeah, I just need to figure out what to do about this Luxembourg trip. I really need to be there, but what do we do about Jacob?'

Richie looked at her with an odd expression.

'I mean, we need a plan anyway, so maybe the conference is the push to sort it out?' She nodded towards her phone. 'I have to book the hotel before it gets booked out.'

'You do whatever suits you, Jenny, you always do.'

'What's that supposed to mean?'

'I mean, don't let me or Jacob get in the way of your precious job.' He said it so calmly, the words and the tone completely mismatched. Stung, she stared open-mouthed at him.

'Is that what's wrong? The fact that I got promoted, that I'm earning more than you? God, Richie, I never took you for a misogynist. The apple doesn't fall far from the tree.'

He shook his head and picked up his pen to continue grading. That irritated her more than anything. Why couldn't he bloody well have it out? She stood, hands on hips.

'Don't ignore me! This has been going on for months and we need to sort it. I'm sorry if my promotion is causing problems for your self-esteem but bloody hell, Richie, I was hardly going to turn it down in case I hurt my husband's fragile ego. It's not 1952, for God's sake.'

Quietly and calmly, he continued to grade papers.

'Richie!' She grabbed the pen out of his hand.

He looked at her.

'Who was the message from, Jenny?'

Blindsided, she hesitated. He reached for the phone but she got there first.

'Why don't you want me to see?'

'It's my phone, why would you want to see my messages?'

'If it's no big deal, then just show me,' he said, standing now too.

Goddammit. Why did he want to see it, and why did she care? It was a work message, nothing she needed to hide. Except of course it was from Mark, and somehow that didn't sit right any more. Or maybe it had never sat right.

She looked at Richie, ready to do battle, but stopped when she saw his eyes. Wide and sad, no fight left at all.

'I *know*,' he said, and without another word, he left the room.

61

Marissa
Wednesday

FALLING OUT WITH COLIN had a rather unexpected upside, Marissa discovered, climbing the stairs to the Pilates studio. Time to herself. Ana was collecting Milo from school, and for the first time in a long time, nobody needed Marissa to be anywhere in particular at all.

The Pilates instructor greeted her like an old friend, and soon she was on the floor with nothing on her mind but holding the plank for as long as she could. As she collapsed on to her mat, her eye was caught by a movement in the hallway. Alex Fenelon emerged from the small room used for one-to-one classes. She turned on her side, lifting her leg off the mat as instructed, and watched Alex lace up his trainers. He didn't strike her as the Pilates type, but maybe he had something medical going on. She'd been sent after Milo's birth and what happened afterwards. She shook her head, chasing away the memory. Unconsciously, her finger went to her chin, rubbing the tiny scar that remained no matter how much oil she used on it.

Alex stood to check himself in the mirror, turning this way and that, examining his face from all sides. Marissa smiled. It was always interesting to see what people did when no one was watching. And as her instructor told the class to switch sides, that was the thought that stuck.

The things people did when no one was watching.

The file on the Fenelon estate loomed large in her mind. What had he done? There was something not quite right, and she'd been nearly there when Milo went missing. She turned on to her back for bridge, listening to the little voice that told her to leave it, and the louder voice that said, *No, sort it out. Something's not right.* And that's why once she left the studio, she marched up Castle Street towards the Irvine and Dobson office. Time to sort it out.

Shauna was on her own in the office – Colin hadn't shown up. Still sick, Shauna assumed. Still dying of embarrassment, Marissa guessed. So much for steering the ship in her absence. She closed her door and began to pore over the Fenelon file.

Three hours later, she was none the wiser about who did what, but one thing was clear – the figures didn't add up. As far as she could tell, rummaging through an unnecessarily complicated web of transactions, there was €360,000 missing from the estate. Had Alex found a way to hide some of the money and avoid inheritance tax? Or steal from his father's business before he died? At five o'clock, she picked up her desk phone and called Lia to ask if she could take over from Ana. Peter had a client event and she really needed to stay put and figure this out. At six, Shauna stuck her head around the door to ask if she could head on.

'Of course,' Marissa told her, barely looking up.

'Are you sure? Is there something I can do to help?'

Marissa looked up properly and smiled. 'Not at all, you go on.'

'Don't work too late,' Shauna said, perhaps uncomfortable

leaving before her boss, 'hopefully Colin will be back to give you a hand before the audit.'

With a last wave, she pulled the door shut after her.

Marissa sat back in her chair, listening as Shauna locked the outer door behind her. The audit. If Alex did something, it would show up there, no doubt. But how could he have done it without Colin noticing? Colin had dealt with the Fenelon estate, and unless he'd sat back and done absolutely nothing, there's no way Alex could have hidden €360,000.

She sat up straight.

That was it.

She leafed back through the pages in the file, starting at the beginning, but with a new perspective, and twenty minutes later it was abundantly clear.

Alex didn't take the money.

Colin did.

Jesus Christ, her partner had stolen from their client.

She tried Peter's number but it went straight to voicemail – he'd be at the client event until late. She stared at her phone, wondering who to try next – Colin? No, it had gone way beyond that, she had nothing to say to him now. No wonder he was so keen to deal with the audit in her absence. She thought he was being kind, promising to keep the ship sailing or whatever he'd said – when all along, he was trying to hide what he'd done. Jesus Christ Almighty.

That's when the next hideous thought struck.

Colin had asked for the Fenelon and Downey files – those were the two she'd been looking at the day Milo disappeared, the two that were posing problems. Had he done something with the Downey estate too?

The file was thicker than the Fenelon file and it took a while to go through it, but now that she knew what she was looking for, it was clear as day. €200,000 missing. And with Joe Downey mourning his wife, and Sinéad and Dermot busy with their own lives, were any of them really going to notice, especially when the estate was so big? And of course they'd trusted Colin. Why wouldn't they; people were supposed to trust their solicitors, that's how it worked. Anger boiled up inside. He'd taken their money and broken their trust and ruined her business in the process. Her earlier misgivings about talking to Colin gave way to white-hot rage. She grabbed the receiver and stabbed out his number on the keypad, ready to roar down the phone at him. But it went straight to voicemail. He was still hiding. After the beep, she took a quick, calming breath and neutralized her tone.

'Colin, would you mind calling down to the office when you get this? There's something important we need to go through.'

Carefully, she put down the receiver to disconnect the call, then picked it up again and slammed it hard. That was better. He could bloody well come down and explain himself now. Fucker.

Another hour ticked by as she made notes, realizing halfway through that she was subconsciously writing them for the police. There was no way around it, she'd have to report him, no matter what excuses he came up with.

She tried his phone again but still it went to voicemail. Lia had messaged to say Milo was asleep, and to take her time coming home.

At ten, she stood to stretch, then stopped, caught by a noise. A door – the main door to the street? She tilted her head, listening. Had Colin arrived?

There it was again – the door closing this time.

And the creak of the first step of the stairs.

Silence then. The next two steps never made a sound; it was

the fourth that was loudest of all, she knew that from years of climbing up to the office.

There it was, the creak of the fourth step.

Another short silence.

The seventh step.

Why so slow?

Tenth step.

Why hadn't Colin called her back, to say he was coming in or to ask what it was about?

Twelfth step.

Marissa stood frozen, staring at the rippled glass.

62

Marissa
Wednesday

ANOTHER SOUND.

The outer door – the one to reception. The handle turning down. Her mind raced. Had Shauna locked it? Yes, she was almost certain she'd heard Shauna lock it as she left. She held her breath and listened.

A key in the lock. Turning. Fuck. On instinct more than any kind of rational thought, she clicked off her desk lamp. What was she doing alone in the office at ten o'clock at night, standing in the dark? Why hadn't she kept trying Peter or phoned the police or gone home like any normal person would have done? *Fuck.*

The outer door clicked open.

Marissa sucked in a ragged breath. Through the glass, she could see nothing – it was too dark. But she could hear. He was in reception and coming towards her office. Without thinking, she dropped to the floor and slid under her desk.

More sounds.

The handle turning.

Her office door creaking open.

Slow, calm, careful footsteps.

Across the office floor. Towards the desk.

She held her breath.

A click. He'd turned on the lamp. Digging her nails into her palm, holding her breath clenched deep inside her stomach, she waited. Fucking hell, it was *Colin*, for God's sake, not some psycho, what was she doing hiding?

But still she didn't move. Didn't breathe as she heard the sound of papers swishing. The files on her desk. A tapping, gathering noise as he straightened the papers. Then nothing. What was he doing? Reading? Listening? Listening for her? Her mobile was on the desk. Would he see it? *Please God, don't let Peter or Lia ring.* More sounds. A click. Darker now. Soft footsteps on carpet. Slow. Deliberate. But moving away from her. The door opening. And the creaks of the stairs, now in reverse order.

Twelve. Ten. Seven. Four. One.

Silence.

Marissa let out a breath and clambered from under her desk. She couldn't bear to turn on the light, in case he was still outside. Feeling around on the desk yielded nothing but smooth Formica.

The Fenelon and Downey files were gone.

She shook her head. That wasn't going to save him. Was he that dumb? Everything was saved on the case management systems too; it wouldn't take long to prove that Colin had siphoned off money from both estates. Shaking with adrenaline and anger, and grief too for a business lost and a friendship gone, she waited five more minutes, then locked up the office and made her way quietly to the car park below.

The next morning, Marissa was deeply asleep when the clock radio came on, and for a fleeting moment, she forgot what had happened. Then it all came flooding back, and her heart plummeted at what lay ahead.

'Peter,' she whispered to her snoring husband, shaking his shoulder.

'Mmm,' he replied, still half asleep. She shook him again.

'Colin's been stealing from clients. At least half a million, maybe more.'

That did it. His eyes sprang open and he sat up, staring at her.

'What did you say?'

'I went into the office and was there till late last night going through the files. There's no doubt about it – I'd have seen it sooner, only everything happened with Milo and I stopped looking. And . . .' She paused, picking at the piping on the duvet cover. 'And I guess in a million years, I didn't think Colin would do something like this.'

'Christ. Are you sure?'

'I'm sure. I've been over and over the figures. And it makes sense now – how did he afford that house? It's not like we're coining it. You've seen what I bring in.'

Peter looked baffled. 'I just . . . I know we were talking the other night, saying he's smarter than he makes out and puts on an act, but I meant the bumbling-idiot thing, I never thought he'd do something like this. Or be *able* to do something like this without getting caught.'

'Well, he did get caught. And now I have to figure out what to do.'

'Bring the paperwork straight to the guards, that's what you do.'

'I can't.' She swallowed, anxiety flaring up inside as she thought back to the late-night visit. 'He came to the office last night and took the files. I was hiding under the desk.'

'*What?*'

'I heard him coming and suddenly got a bit . . . well, I didn't want to confront him. It's awkward.' It was only a white lie. It sounded better than *I was suddenly scared out of my fucking mind.*

'Jesus, Marissa. Why didn't you tell me any of this last night?'

'I didn't want to call you at your client event, and I fell asleep before you got home. And . . . I'm annoyed at myself for not confronting him. I can't believe he has the bloody files now.'

'Doesn't matter. You can still go to the police. Do you want me to go with you?' He looked at his watch. 'I've a client meeting at nine but I could get Brian to take it? If I can reach him, he's always bloody busy these days.'

'That's OK, I can do it. I'll get Milo to school and do it then.'

He nodded and lumbered out of bed, while she lay back on the pillow, staring at the ceiling.

On the radio, the news headlines had just come on. A political spat, a double murder in Sandyford Industrial Estate, and confirmation that the body thought to be that of Danny Vaughan was in fact Kyle Byrde, one-time boyfriend of kidnapper Carrie Finch. Jesus, Marissa thought, was all of this really happening? She switched off the radio and picked up her phone instead, clicking into Facebook for some light relief. A new friend request caught her attention. Irene Turner. Why did that name sound familiar? She clicked into the user's profile. That's when she saw the message.

> *Hi, you don't know me, but I'd like to talk to you about our stories, because we're two victims of the same woman. Carrie was my daughter. We could do a newspaper story together or a tv program? I think the media going 2 b very interested and I have lots of dirt to dish from her childhood. What do u think?*

Sitting up straight, Marissa started to type a furious response. None of this would have happened if Irene had been a better

317

mother. Carrie didn't turn out the way she did for no reason – and yet here was Irene trying to make money out of it, instead of questioning where she'd gone wrong. What kind of mother was she?

Marissa stopped. Oh God, she was just as bad as the online trolls who were blaming her for what happened to Milo. The 'what kind of mother' brigade. She wouldn't stoop that low. She wouldn't engage with Irene at all. She deleted her draft and blocked Irene Turner, then flopped back down in the bed and let her phone slip to the carpet below.

Roll on the trip to Spain – it couldn't come fast enough.

63

Irene
Thursday

IRENE STARED AT HER phone. The bitch had blocked her. For Jesus'
sake. Here she was, just trying to let Marissa Irvine in on the
action, and she'd actually gone and blocked her. Fuck it anyway. She'd find other ways to string out the story and make
some money. She just needed to decide if she was the grieving
mother of an innocent murder victim, or the victim herself.
Both maybe, in different papers, if she played it right. Faye
Foster had said something about not talking to other journalists, but she could hardly stop her, could she? And anyway,
Faye hadn't actually come through with any money yet,
so she had no right to be telling Irene what she could and
couldn't do.

As she sat staring at the phone, it began to vibrate in her hand.
Incoming call, landline, not someone in her contacts. No good
ever came of calls from unknown numbers, but out of curiosity,
she answered.

'Mrs Turner, it's Detective Garda Breen here. Do you have a
moment?'

She rolled her eyes. This eejit. She should have known better
than to answer.

'What is it now?' she asked.

'We were wondering if the name Sienna Watkins means any-thing to you?'

Irene blinked. Where was this going?

'Why?'

'If you could just answer the question . . .'

Irene thought fast. Was Rob's new girlfriend in some kind of trouble? Linked to Caroline and the kidnap in some way? Wouldn't that be a turn-up for the books. Irene grinned.

'Yeah. She's Carrie's father's new girlfriend. As far as I know, she's moving to Ireland with him. Is she in some kind of trouble?'

'Can you tell me anything else about her?'

'She's blonde, from London, has a kid around four or five. There's a picture on Rob's Facebook, she's the one in the stu-pidly big sunglasses. Was she in on it? The kidnapping?'

'Thanks for your help, Mrs Turner. We'll be in touch if we need anything else.'

He disconnected the call and Irene sat thinking. If Sienna Watkins was in trouble, that was no bad thing. But if she was involved in the kidnap, did that mean Rob was too?

64

Marissa
Thursday

ON THURSDAY EVENING WHEN McConville arrived unannounced, Marissa wasn't surprised. It had been rattling around in her head all day – Colin dating Carrie, Colin stealing money, Carrie taking Milo. Coincidences happen, but not like this. The more she thought about it, the clearer it seemed – there was more to the story. Peter had finished work for the day, grumbling about trying and failing to reach Brian, and Ana had gone home. Lia took Milo through to the playroom, leaving McConville with Peter and Marissa.

'It's about Colin Dobson,' McConville said, taking a seat at the kitchen table.

'I knew it,' Marissa said, shaking her head.

'What?' Peter asked.

'It sounds insane, but I think he had something to do with the kidnap,' Marissa said, her voice catching on the last word.

Peter looked at McConville, her impassive face as usual giving nothing away.

'It's more than that, I'm afraid,' McConville said. 'Colin Dobson was found dead this morning.'

Marissa clapped her hand over her mouth. And everything was gone – the suspicion, the betrayal, the stealing, the lies. All she could think of was Colin, her friend of twenty years. Dead. Tears welled up.

'Please say it wasn't . . . was it suicide?' She went cold thinking of the harsh, accusatory way she'd last spoken to him.

But McConville was shaking her head.

'No, he was murdered. Alongside another man, identified as Rob Murphy, Carrie Finch's father.'

'What?' Marissa took her hand away from her mouth. None of this made sense.

'We are investigating of course,' McConville said, with what sounded like a small, hidden sigh. How many times had she said those same words in this same room in the last two weeks? 'But it seems likely Mr Murphy shot Mr Dobson, who then managed to shoot back, before bleeding to death at the scene. The autopsy results will give us more.'

'What?' Marissa said again, unable to think of anything else to say. Colin shooting someone? Her Colin?

Peter just stared, grey and confused.

'I know it's a lot to take in. There was evidence at the scene to suggest a handover of some kind. Money.'

'But what does Colin have to do with Carrie's father and . . .' Marissa trailed off, trying to make sense of it. 'Wait, do you think this was all about the kidnap?'

McConville gave the tiniest nod. 'Too early to say but it's possible.'

Jesus, the woman never gave an inch.

'Was the money for a ransom?' Peter asked.

'But there was no ransom,' Marissa reminded him. 'We were never asked for money.'

McConville cleared her throat. 'There are other ways to make money from taking children unfortunately, and we're looking into that.'

Marissa looked down at her hands. She couldn't go there.

'We also don't know which of them brought the bag of money – we haven't found any fingerprints,' McConville continued. 'Marissa, when did you begin to suspect that Mr Dobson was skimming from client estates?'

'Only yesterday. Before that, I thought there were mistakes on the files – I was looking into them but obviously dropped everything when Milo was taken.'

She stopped as it hit her.

Peter looked over, realization scrolling across his face too.

'Did he do all this to stop me finding out what he'd done?' She looked at McConville. 'As soon as Milo went missing, Colin took over my work – he came here one night specifically to ask for the Fenelon and Downey files. Oh my God, did he take Milo to avoid getting caught?'

'It would be an extreme response,' McConville said doubtfully.

'Yes, but facing prosecution and jail would be . . . I don't think Colin would stomach that. Maybe he cooked it up with Carrie, maybe he knew Carrie would look after Milo well, and nobody would come to any harm?'

'Until something went wrong,' Peter said, 'and someone killed Carrie.'

'You think Colin Dobson was capable of murder?' McConville asked, eyebrows raised.

'No!' Marissa said, and yet, even as she said it, she wondered. She hadn't thought him capable of kidnapping or embezzlement either.

'Could it be Rob Murphy who killed Kyle Byrde?' she asked, because she wanted to know, and maybe because she wanted to hear that it wasn't Colin. 'Maybe Kyle killed Carrie and her father was getting revenge?'

McConville shook her head. 'That doesn't fit – Kyle Byrde was killed before Carrie.'

None of it fitted, but maybe that didn't matter. The four people involved with Milo's kidnap – Colin, Carrie, Kyle Byrde and Rob Murphy – were all dead now. Marissa got up and walked to the kitchen door. She leaned her head out to listen for Milo. He was playing something with Lia, a guessing game of some kind. None of it mattered, as long as it was over. A prickle of unease snaked over her skin. Was it over?

65

Irene
Thursday

IRENE WAS STILL SMARTING over the distinct lack of cash in her bank account as she ate a solitary dinner in her silent kitchen on Thursday evening. Faye Foster had been full of apologies. The legal team had overruled her editor, she said. Even though Carrie hadn't been convicted of anything, and may have taken Milo under duress, they still couldn't pay her for her story. Profiting from crime wasn't allowed, apparently. Irene could feel her blood pressure going up as she went over it again. It wasn't *her* crime, for Jesus' sake, it was her daughter's. Why should she miss out on making some money? She'd have spat at Faye Foster if she'd had the chance, though of course she didn't even come in person to tell her. She didn't even phone. She texted. Irene shook her head, dunking bread into watery tomato soup. Well, she'd get her own back. She might not be able to sell her story, but she'd still get it out there. And if she got enough publicity, she could do something with that – write a book or start a business. Maybe sell slimming tea. And she was going to be on TV! That'd show them. The researcher had been on the phone this afternoon, booking her in for a night-time current affairs show. What would she wear? Something black, to show that despite everything, she was still a mother mourning her lost child. Or blue, because blue brought out her eyes. She'd wear black to Caroline's funeral of course. Something flattering. An image of Rob flashed up – the new Rob, the version she'd seen on Facebook. Tanned, craggy, handsome. He'd be there, she could feel it in her bones.

There was the key in the door now. Frank had tried to insist on staying home with her, but Frank had never won an argument yet and it wasn't about to start now. The last thing she needed was him hovering as she fielded calls from journalists and researchers.

But you're in shock, he'd said, *you've lost your daughter and you're not processing it yet.* She'd nearly sprained an eyeball at that – he'd been watching too much American TV.

Through the closed kitchen door, she heard his voice, but he wasn't calling her – he was talking to someone else. A woman. A familiar voice. One of the journalists? Frank's voice again. She couldn't make out what they were saying at first, but then she distinctly heard one word – Rob. Why would a journalist be talking about Rob? Frank wouldn't like that. God, Frank was such a ninny. What would he and Rob make of each other? She smiled at the thought. The funeral would be interesting. And . . . who knows. A little fizz of excitement bubbled up inside. She wiped a smudge of soup from her leggings, smoothed down her hair, and got up to open the door.

66

Jenny
Thursday

JENNY PUT HER KEY in the door and braced herself. The cold impasse hadn't thawed an inch since Richie's withering *I know* on Tuesday night. You know *what*? Jenny wanted to yell. But instead she ignored him completely. Maybe this was it – the growing apart thing that people talked about. Life and kids and work taking over. Phones taking over. No time to talk. Then nothing left to say. All of this was running through her head when she arrived in from work on Thursday evening, glad at least that she'd been able to do a full day. Adeline wasn't her first choice of babysitter, but any port in a storm.

She walked into the kitchen and stopped dead at the sight. Adeline, daintily sipping tea at the counter, Richie by his mother's side, a wary look on his face, and Jacob running towards her, tears streaming down his cheeks.

'What happened?' Jenny asked, scooping him up. 'Is he hurt?'

Richie cleared his throat but Adeline spoke first.

'Not a bit. See, that's more of it. Crying over a toy. It's not good for a boy his age.'

'What is it, love?' Jenny asked Jacob, ignoring her mother-in-law.

'Granny throwed Jem in the bin,' he sobbed.

Jenny stared at Adeline, her mouth open.

'I did it in his best interests. You indulge him, Jenny. He'll be called a sissy at school if they know he still holds on to that teddy bear.'

'Oh my God, Adeline!'

'It's OK!' Richie put his hands up. 'I got him out and he's in the washing machine.'

Jenny looked from Richie to Adeline, then down at her son.

'Jacob, Jem is going to be OK. The washing machine will make him nice and clean again, and when he's dry, we'll take him to Esther's for cake. How about that?'

Jacob nodded, wiping his eyes.

'Now, will you go into the den for a few minutes – you can put on the TV.'

Jacob nodded again and left the room. Jenny turned back to her mother-in-law.

'Adeline, he's so attached to Jem, how could you just throw him away?'

'That's precisely it, he was too attached. Goodness, it's just a ratty bear. He'll be teased.'

'He won't, but if he ever is, it's up to us to sort it out – by listening and talking, not by throwing away his favourite toy.'

'A little bit of thanks wouldn't go amiss, Jenny. I looked after your son all afternoon and instead of being grateful, you're getting petty about a silly bear. He's my grandson, I have a say in his upbringing, you know.'

'You . . . what?'

Adeline cut her off. 'If you were here instead of gallivanting, you'd have time to look after this kind of thing yourself. It's all about priorities.'

Jenny could feel the explosion coming from deep inside her chest. But when it came, it was from Richie.

'Mum! You can't talk to Jenny like that. She's a brilliant mother, she's been with Jacob every day since all this happened, and, bloody hell, she's right! You absolutely shouldn't have thrown away his teddy!'

Jenny took a step back, eyes wide. She'd never heard Richie roar at his mother like this.

Adeline looked like she was going to keel over. Without another word, she put down her cup, picked up her coat, and marched out of the room. They waited until they heard the front door slam, then turned to one another. Richie put his arm out and without thinking, she hugged him.

'I'm so sorry she did that,' he said . . .

'Jem will be fine and Jacob will be fine. I'm furious with her but after everything else that's happened, it's not the end of the world.'

They stood together, closer than they'd been in a while, but awkward too, Tuesday night's fight hanging between them. The sound of *PAW Patrol* drifted through from the den. Nothing else stirred.

'Richie,' she said after a while, 'I understand that it's tough adjusting to my new job, but I wish you'd talk about it instead of clamming up and pushing me away. I'm proud of what I've achieved and I'm sorry I'm earning more than you, but I'd never have an issue if it was the other way round.'

She paused, wondering if that last bit was a mistake – hammering home that it *wasn't* the other way around. He stepped away from her. Dammit, she'd done it again.

'Is that what you think?' he asked, his eyes wide and sad.

She threw her hands up. 'I don't know! But you've been distancing yourself from me ever since I got the promotion.'

'It's not the promotion, Jenny, it's Mark.'

What? Where was this coming from? A trickle of unease slipped into her belly. 'Mark?'

'I saw the messages.'

'What messages?' The words came out slowly but her mind was racing. Mark texted a lot, but it was usually about work. Or to check in on her. An image of that night in Nantes flashed up. She'd done nothing, but still. She'd had a drink with a colleague who turned out to like her as more than a friend. Maybe 'doing nothing' wasn't enough.

'The texts at night – why doesn't he just email like a normal person? And why is he checking in on you? And flirting.'

'You read my messages?'

Richie's colour rose.

'Jacob was playing with your phone and he went into your messages. I saw them when I took it off him.'

'But Richie, they're nothing. Yeah, he says hi every now and then, but he's just a work colleague.'

'If he's just a colleague, why was he calling here when I was at work?'

'*What?*'

'He was here, in our house.'

She stared at him.

'No, he most certainly wasn't! What are you on about?'

'You were *seen*.'

Simple words, cutting the air like a knife. And in some kind of parallel universe, she could see how this played out. Him the cuckolded husband, her the cheating wife, caught in the act. And somehow she knew it wasn't enough to go with her gut reaction – surprise, irritation, a good flounce – Richie really believed this to be true and the burden of proof was on her.

She took his hands and spoke as calmly as possible. 'Richie,

I don't know who's been saying what, but Mark has never been here.'

She looked him in the eye, certain that if she was lying that's exactly what she'd do too, but there weren't many other options.

He pulled his hands away.

'Richie, who saw what – tell me.'

'Joe next door said he saw a tall, dark-haired man going in when I was at work.'

'Richie, that was Kyle Byrde, calling for Carrie. You can't seriously have jumped to the conclusion it was Mark?'

There was something else going on, she could tell by his expression.

Eventually he spoke. 'I got notes.'

'*What?*' She was starting to feel like a stuck record.

'Notes from someone telling me to watch what my wife was up to when my back was turned, that someone from work was calling here when I was out. That the trips to France and Luxembourg weren't strictly business.'

'I feel like I'm in an Enid Blyton book – are you seriously telling me someone sent you anonymous notes? Can I see them?'

For the first time, he looked less sure of himself.

'They're gone. I kept them all in an envelope in my bedside locker but they disappeared – that's what I was looking for when I came home early last week and you arrived in.'

'So, like actual paper notes? Were they written from letters cut out of the newspaper?' She tried and failed to suppress a smile.

'No, typewritten. It's not funny.'

'I know. Sorry. Where did you find them?'

'On the hall floor but not sent by post – no stamps. Just my name on the envelope, in block capitals.'

'Richie, you can't be telling me you took them seriously? It's obviously someone trying to stir trouble. If there was really something going on, wouldn't whoever it was have spoken to you in person, instead of hiding behind anonymous notes?'

'I don't know, I didn't know what to think,' he said helplessly. 'And then I saw your messages and Joe Downey said someone was calling . . .'

'When did it start?'

'August, just after I got home from the conference in Scotland. I thought maybe while I was away . . .'

She thought for a moment, belatedly remembering to shake her head, to tell him nothing happened while he was in Scotland. Only something *had* happened – she'd accused Carrie of hitting Jacob. And then got drunk in an attempt to bond and make up.

'Richie, when did you last get a letter?'

'The week before you went to Paris, to tell me it was for more than just work.'

'Right, and when did the notes disappear?'

'I don't know,' he said miserably. 'I put the last letter with the others in my bedside locker, but when I went back last week, they were all gone. It wasn't you, was it?'

She shook her head.

'But who else would have been in our bedroom?' Richie asked.

'The week before Paris? Carrie.'

'You think she stole the notes?'

'Not just stole them. Wrote them in the first place.'

Richie raised his eyebrows. 'What would Carrie know about Mark?'

Jenny looked down at her hands, then back at her husband. 'I swear on my life, nothing ever happened with Mark. But he has been paying a lot of attention, and I may have told Carrie about it over a bottle of wine one night.'

Silence.

'Richie. Nothing happened. I told her about it because we were drinking and talking and bonding. And look, I was flattered by Mark's attention. But *nothing* happened.'

'Then why would Carrie write the notes?'

'I don't know, but remember when you came back from Scotland, I told you I'd frightened the life out of Carrie, shrieking at her to stop when I thought she was about to hit Jacob? Only she was swatting a fly?'

He nodded.

'She was mad as hell at first – holding it in, but I could see she was raging. The following night we had the wine, and I suppose I was trying to get on her right side again. I ended up telling her about Mark. And you got the first note when you came home.'

Richie looked sceptical.

'Think about it – her job was to look after our son, and I had just jumped to the conclusion that she was about to wallop him. Even though she acted like everything was OK, I know she was left smarting. She had all the ammunition she needed when I told her about Mark. Maybe she decided to write that first note to you then, to get back at me.'

Richie said nothing but still looked unconvinced.

'It adds up. She was – as it turns out – a criminal, possibly a psychopath, and at the very least, not a nice person. She lived in our house, had access to every room, every corner, every drawer . . . and who knows what kind of conversations she was listening in on. She might even have been checking our phones. You said the notes were never posted, always just on the hall floor.' She paused, remembering coming downstairs to find Richie stuffing something in his back pocket, while Carrie sat innocently in the kitchen, making breakfast for Jacob. 'God, Richie, it would have been so easy for her to write them and leave them there for you, laughing up her sleeve no doubt at the trouble she was causing.'

'I don't know . . .'

'Richie, which makes more sense? That me, the wife you've known for fifteen years, is cheating on you with a work colleague, or that Carrie, the childminder who turned out to be a deranged kidnapper, was stirring trouble to get revenge?'

She took his hands again. This time he didn't pull away.

67

Marissa
Friday

THE DAY EVERYTHING CHANGED again had started out with a
sense of relative normality. School drop. Pilates. Coffee with
Lia. And until the doorbell rang at four o'clock that afternoon,
Marissa had forgotten Fiona Sheridan was coming by to interview Milo again. *Even though everyone involved is dead?* she'd
asked. They still didn't know exactly what happened, Sheridan
told her, and they needed Milo to fill in the gaps.

Lia was upstairs packing to go back to New York, and Peter
was in his office working, so it was just Marissa and Milo in the
living room with Sheridan when she switched on her recording
device.

'Milo, do you remember what colour hair Carrie had?' Sheridan
said, beginning with what seemed to Marissa an odd question.

'Orange but then she maked it yellow like the sun. When I
put the shampoo to make mine brown.'

'She dyed her hair?' Marissa asked Sheridan.

'Yes. When she was found,' Sheridan whispered, glancing at
Milo, 'she had short blonde hair.' She raised her voice again.
'And Milo, I want you to think back to the last night you were
there, can you do that?'

335

He screwed up his eyes, making a good show of casting his mind back.

'You went to sleep, but then you woke up – can you tell me about that?'

Marissa squeezed Milo's hand as he began to talk.

'A bad man waked me. He taked me out of the house, it was really cold. I was outside in my *pyjamas*.' He shook his head, as though this was the real crime.

'OK, and were you standing on the ground in your pyjamas?'

'No, the man was carrying me. He put me in the car and put on a seat belt.'

Marissa let out a slow breath. This was only the second time he'd talked about that night. She kept a tight grip of his hand as he continued talking.

'I think he went into the house again, then he drove the car but only for a small bit.'

'Good, and then what happened?'

'He said he had to meet a person. He said his boss was a bad man and if I got out of the car, his boss will hurt me. I was crying.'

Oh God. She pulled him close, wrapping her arm around him. Sheridan glanced up at her, an unspoken *don't interrupt the flow*. She loosened her arm but only just.

'And did you see his face?'

'No, it had a black thing on it.'

'Like a mask?'

'Not a Halloween mask. Like a black cover with a space for eyes.'

Sheridan wrote something and Marissa read it upside-down. *Ski Mask/Balaclava.*

'And then what happened?'

We already know this bit, Marissa wanted to say, *please can we stop now?*

But Milo kept talking.

'He asked me my name and address.'

Sheridan leaned forward.

This was new.

'And did you tell him?'

'Yes. Milo Peter Brian Irvine. Maple Lodge, Dublin. Did I get it right, Mummy?' Milo asked, turning to her. She smiled and nodded.

'What happened then?'

'He closed the door and he was gone.'

'OK, Milo, do you want to go and play while I chat to your mammy?'

He slid off the couch and ran for the den.

'I love the way four-year-olds run everywhere,' Sheridan said, smiling after him, like they hadn't just been talking about his kidnapping ordeal. Desensitizing must be part of the job.

'I'm just delighted to see him leave a room without me – he mostly won't leave my side! Anyway, why do you think the man asked Milo his name and address?' Marissa asked. 'And do you reckon it was Rob Murphy?'

'Or Colin Dobson.'

'No, there's no way Colin would have done something like that, I just don't . . .' She stopped. There were too many things she didn't think Colin would do. 'And what about the dyed hair – she was disguising herself, getting ready to leave the bungalow?'

'We think so. There were wigs and lots of make-up found at the scene too, and clothes that look like the kind of thing you'd wear to a smart night club, not the shirts and jeans Carrie always wore.'

Marissa thought back to the photo on Colin's phone, the woman who looked nothing like Jenny's childminder. The many faces of Carrie Finch – how easy it was to change hair and make-up and look like someone else entirely.

'Do you know where she was planning to go?'

'We found passports, one in the name Sienna Watkins. We know from speaking to Irene Turner that Sienna Watkins was the name of Rob Murphy's girlfriend. The passport has Carrie's picture – but with her hair in a blonde bob, coloured contact lenses, and make-up that hid her freckles. She looked nothing like herself.' Sheridan clicked into something on her phone. 'Here's a photo.' She passed the phone to Marissa, who pinched the screen to zoom in. The woman in the passport photo looked like a cross between Marilyn Monroe and P!nk. She could walk down Grafton Street, with everyone in the entire country searching for Carrie Finch, and not one person would look at her twice. Jesus Christ, it was so easy to do. She passed back the phone.

'It looks like she was going to call herself Sienna Watkins and take on a new identity,' Sheridan said.

'Right. And you said there were passports *plural*?'

Sheridan hesitated. 'Yes. This is the other one.' She scrolled on her phone and handed it to Marissa.

This time the passport was for a little girl called Robin Watkins. The photo showed a serious-faced child with shoulder-length brown hair, a hairclip pinning it back. You could just about make out the top the child was wearing – a yellow t-shirt with butterflies.

Milo.

'Oh my God, I can't believe how easily she did that – if everyone was looking for a blond boy called Milo and she was travelling with a brown-haired girl called Robin . . . if she'd got away with it, we might never have found him.' Her voice cracked but she kept it together. 'Where was she taking him?'

'We don't know.'

Marissa waited but that's all Sheridan was going to concede. Something else came to mind.

'Was her phone there? Maybe there's something on that to tell us where they were going?'

'No. It certainly seems she was surprised in her sleep and whoever did it left everything as is, except her phone – assuming she had one – that's missing.'

There seemed to be nothing else to say, and as Marissa walked Sheridan out, she wondered why it mattered at all, but somehow it did. In the end, it wasn't enough that Milo was back and the people who took him were gone – she needed to know the *why* as well as the *who*.

Walking back towards the den after saying goodbye to Sheridan, Marissa stopped and stood still to listen.

Something was different.

Upstairs, she could hear Lia clacking around the spare room, still packing. From Peter's office drifted the sound of a client call. The difference was an absence, an absence of sound from the den. She started walking, picking up her pace. No strains of TV, no clatter of toys. He was probably paging through a book, or colouring. Faster now, she reached the den and looked inside.

No Milo.

Her eyes skittered around the room – strewn LEGO, toppling piles of picture books, but no Milo.

Bathroom maybe? She called out, and again, because Milo didn't always answer the first time.

Nothing.

The bathroom door was open, nobody inside.

Kitchen? She ran through, feeling foolish and panicky all at once. The kitchen was quiet and empty, no sound but the ticking of the giant clock over the back door. That's when she felt the breeze, quiet but distinct. The French doors to the patio. One of them was open.

'Milo!' she shouted, rushing outside. The garden was in almost-darkness, and icy cold. Where was he? Why would he go out-side? Another thought gripped her heart but she pushed it away. The people who took him were gone. And lightning doesn't strike twice. 'Milo!' she shouted again, running past the swing and the giant oak, to the back of the garden.

Nothing. Nobody.

She turned back towards the house, just as Peter appeared at the patio doors.

'What's up – is everything OK?'

'I can't find Milo,' she called back, trying to keep panic from her voice. Was this her future? Freaking out every time he wasn't precisely where she'd left him?

'I'm sure he's fine, I'll check upstairs,' Peter said, going back inside.

'Milo! Where are you? Milo!' she kept calling, as she skirted around the side of Maple Lodge, towards Brian's house.

Brian's windows were in darkness, but as she looked, she spotted a small glow in the front room, like the light of a phone.

And suddenly everything shifted.

The paint job that produced no smell of paint. The late-night disappearing acts. The house brochures hidden in the kitchen drawer. Everything Lia had said about Brian – doing Peter's bid-ding, living in his shadow. Something wasn't right.

She started to run.

68

Marissa

Friday

IN DARKNESS, THROUGH SHADOWS, she raced to Brian's house. The smaller house. The bit on the side. The second best.

'Milo!' she shouted, hammering on the front door. 'Are you in there?'

A light came on in the hall, and the front door opened.

Brian stood in front of her, and behind him, Milo.

She hunkered down, arms outstretched. 'Milo! You gave me a fright!' She tried to hide it, but her voice shook.

Like an eel, Milo slipped past Brian's legs and into her arms. She lifted him and stepped back, facing Brian.

'What's going on, Brian? What were you doing?'

'What?'

'Why was Milo here?'

'He came over and knocked on the door, said he was scared of bad dreams about the bad man.' Brian looked perplexed. 'I take it he's just been interviewed by the guards again?'

'Why didn't you bring him back?' She pulled Milo tighter.

Behind her, Peter approached.

'Cheers for the call, mate,' he said to his brother, 'we were wondering where he was.'

Marissa's eyes went to the phone in Brian's hand, and to the one in Peter's.

'He didn't want to go back till the guard was gone,' Brian said, to her more than to Peter. 'So I figured I'd call you rather than pushing it. Marissa, he's fine, it's OK.'

'No, it's *not* OK. Nothing is OK.' She knew she was being irrational, but she couldn't stop. 'Why did you lie about getting your house painted and where have you been sneaking off to?'

A look she couldn't decipher crossed Brian's face.

'Brian,' she said, her voice low and tight, 'what is going on?'

'Oh God. I should have said something sooner . . .' He stopped, looking down at his feet. Suddenly he looked shy. Marissa couldn't remember ever seeing him shy. Or anything really, he was always just Brian.

'What is it?'

'I didn't want Lia staying here because I'm not always . . . here myself and I didn't want anyone to know.'

Marissa shook her head, exasperated. 'What on earth do you mean?'

His eyes went down again and the answer was a mumble she could barely make out.

'I'm seeing someone. It's . . . complicated.'

Stunned silence. In all the years she'd been with Peter, Marissa had never known Brian to date anyone. And yet, why wouldn't he?

'Tell you what,' Peter said, reaching for Milo. 'This might be something for grown-up ears. You come with me, Milo-Mouse, and Mummy will fill me in later.' He took a reluctant Milo from Marissa's arms, threw a grin at his brother, and headed back across the dark garden. Brian pulled the door wide and gestured for Marissa to come in.

'Brian, I'm sorry. You must think I'm quite mad,' Marissa said, stepping into the shadowy hallway.

'Ah, I should have told you instead of all the sneaking around. But she's engaged to someone else, and I didn't know how you'd react.' He raised his hands in a *what's a guy to do* gesture. 'But I'm mad about her, so here we are.'

Marissa's racing heart slowed to normal with the change of conversation and a surge of affection for Brian came over her.

'I get why you were nervous about telling us. Are you sure it's wise?' she asked gently, hugging herself against the cold breeze coming in through the open door.

'No, it's not wise at all. But I need to live a little. Look at me, working with Peter, practically living with you two. I think I needed to break away, even if it means some questionable decisions.'

'Is that why you had house brochures? You want to move?'

He laughed. 'No! The woman I'm seeing works for Rayburn Estate Agents, she forgot them when she was over one evening.'

'She's been here?'

'Not often. We usually meet somewhere else.'

'Hardly her place if she's engaged?' Marissa was being nosy now and she knew it.

'She has keys to other places, because of her job . . .'

'Oh my God!'

'Not houses where people live,' he added hastily. 'Show houses in new developments . . .'

'Brian Irvine, you dark horse!' She stepped towards him and reached up to give him a hug. 'You know what, I'm delighted for you. If she's the right one, she'll leave her fiancé. And if she's not, so be it.'

Smiling with surprise, reeling with relief, and resolving never again to visit the dark thoughts that had been running through her head, Marissa left Brian and walked back to her house.

An hour later, having waved Lia off to the airport, Marissa was tucking Milo into bed.

'I'm sorry you had to do that interview with Fiona today, was it hard?'

Under the duvet, his shoulders hunched.

'The bad man can't get me now, can he, Mummy?'

She pushed his hair back from his face and kissed his forehead. 'No, he can't. You're safe.'

'He had a monster voice. You told me monsters aren't real.'

'Not the kind you see in books. But sometimes bad people can seem like monsters, even though they're human. And I promise you, Milo, most humans are good and kind and nice.'

He thought for a moment. 'He was a bit nice in the end.'

'Who was?'

'The bad man.'

'Oh yes?'

'Before he went away, he said, "Don't cry, Milo-Mouse, it's going to be OK."'

69

Marissa
Friday

MARISSA STARED AT HER sleepy son, a cold trickle of dread whispering over her skin.

'Can you say that again, lovey? What the bad man said?'

'He said, "Don't cry, Milo-Mouse, it's going to be OK." Like the way Daddy does when I hurt myself.'

'He called you Milo-Mouse? Maybe you're getting mixed up?'

A pout. 'I'm not. He said it. Can you bring me up a glass of water?'

'Sure, pet,' she said, kissing him, before slipping out the door.

She made her way downstairs in a trance, images and memories flashing through her head. How would Rob Murphy know to call him Milo-Mouse? Or was it Colin after all, would he have heard Peter say Milo-Mouse? Would he have noticed? With everything she had in her, she tried to push away the other explanation, because it couldn't be that. It couldn't.

Peter was in the sitting room, reading the paper. She sat beside him on the couch, perched on the edge, rubbing a thumb over her clammy palm. Peter said something but it was like trying to listen through glue. She closed her eyes and opened them again. *Focus.*

'Peter, why do you think the person who put Milo in the car asked him to repeat his name and address?'

She made herself watch his face. She wanted to see nothing – mild curiosity, disinterest, fatigue. But there was a flicker. Just a small flash of unease. He shrugged and turned the page of the paper.

'It's almost like the man was trying to make sure he'd get safely home,' she continued, 'in case he was found by a stranger who didn't realize who he was.'

Peter folded the paper and stared at her for a moment before answering.

'Assuming it was Rob Murphy, maybe he wanted Milo to be safe. Just because he's a kidnapper, doesn't make him a killer.'

'But he had just killed Carrie, his own daughter.'

'We don't know that.'

'I think it's pretty clear that whoever took Milo out of the house killed Carrie.'

'Maybe she was dead already. Either way, she got what she deserved.' His voice was hard, but these were thoughts she'd had too. Carrie hadn't earned their sympathy.

'Peter.'

'What is it?'

She was on the brink now, on one side of a fault line. If she said it, she could never take it back. If she didn't say it, she'd never know. The fault line opened up, the earthquake was hers to make. Or leave. *Walk away.*

'Milo says the man called him Milo-Mouse. You are the only person who ever calls him that.'

Silence. She wanted to look at his face but she couldn't. She couldn't bear to see what might be there. She wanted him to say something, anything. And then she wanted to turn back the clock, just five seconds, enough to undo what she'd done. But she couldn't. His stare was on her, boring into her. She could feel it, cold, heavy, drenched. Peter didn't say a word, and that scared her more than anything.

She didn't hear the padding on the stairs. The first she knew was when Milo pushed the door and walked in.

'Mummy, you forgot my water,' he said. She made to stand, but Peter put a hand on her shoulder. Gentle pressure. Pressure all the same.

'I'll get it, you come with me, Milo,' Peter said.

Together they walked through to the kitchen and returned moments later, Milo drinking from his favourite cup.

'Go on up, Milo, I'll be up to tuck you in soon,' she said, her voice shaking.

'I think he can stay up a bit later tonight, it's Saturday tomorrow. And we three have had enough time apart recently,' Peter said. 'Milo, you sit there on the armchair and you can have my iPad.'

She wanted to object, to say he needed to go to bed, but her voice was stuck in her throat. And part of her wanted Milo near, where she could see him.

Peter placed the iPad on Milo's lap and put headphones on his ears.

'Now we won't be interrupted by *PAW Patrol*, isn't that right, buddy?' He kissed Milo's forehead. 'Hang on, let's make you a bit more comfy,' he added, taking an oversized cushion from the daybed at the window. He tucked it behind Milo's head, kissed him again, and moved back across the room to sit beside Marissa.

She forced herself to speak.

'Peter,' she whispered, 'what the fuck is going on?'

He took a deep breath. 'It started at the playground.'

'What started?'

He sighed. 'I was at the playground one afternoon, the small one down in Dún Laoghaire, outside the bagel place. Milo was going on about colours again, talking about numbers and the days of the week and what colour they are – Monday is orange, Tuesday is green like grass, all that. Part of that condition he has, the synaes—What's it called again?'

'Synaesthesia.' A big name for a harmless condition. She looked over at Milo, lost in his TV show. *Two is red, three is light brown. Wednesday is purple, Saturday is yellow.* Milo adamant that that's how he saw things and surprised that nobody else did.

'I spotted this girl staring at us,' Peter was saying. 'She was drinking a coffee at one of the tables outside the playground. Just sitting in the sun like everyone else, except she kept looking over. After a bit, she came in and I think she was talking to Milo, but I didn't notice straight away. Then she said to me, "I know you, don't I?" I said no. Up close, she looked a bit rough. I thought she was going to ask for money. I genuinely didn't realize at first.'

'Realize what?' Marissa whispered.

'Who she was. She stood looking at me, tilting her head, like she was examining my face. I took Milo's hand and turned to leave. I really thought she was just some weirdo, or a druggie. Then she asked if I was Peter Irvine. That made me turn to look at her properly. And then I recognized her. Suddenly it was clear as day, and I couldn't believe I hadn't clicked. But then again, I hadn't seen her since the crash.'

'Oh my God.' Marissa closed her eyes to the dark, dark time she never, ever wanted to think about. Peter kept talking.

'She looked different, obviously. Back then she was all bandages and drips, just like you were.'

'Carrie was the driver of the other car?'

Peter nodded. And everything slipped into place. The accident just after Milo's birth, the days she spent unconscious, the surgeries, the skin grafts, the driver she never met, the constant reminder in the scar on her chin. Peter had told her the other woman got off lightly, physically anyway, *cuts and bruises mostly*. Bandages and drips didn't sound like cuts and bruises mostly.

'Was she badly hurt? You told me she was OK?'

'She was in a medically induced coma for three or four weeks. I didn't want to worry you at the time, you were in such a state when you came around. You can understand that, can't you, Marissa?' She could hear pleading in his voice.

Oh Christ. Carrie.

'What did she say in the playground?' Marissa whispered.

'She started talking to Milo again – trying to engage him, teasing him – she said Monday is blue, not orange. He laughed and said Monday is definitely orange. I just wanted to get away from her, she seemed not quite there. A bit touched. I picked up Milo and told her to leave him alone, but she kept talking to him, and she followed us when we moved outside the playground and down into the underground car park. I got angry then, anyone would.' He looked at her. 'I had to send Milo ahead to the car – honestly, Marissa, she seemed unstable. Then I kind of . . . pulled her by her shirt and told her if she didn't leave us alone, I'd call the guards on her. That it was harassment and that I'd tell them she was trying to extort money from me and she'd be arrested. I told her I have friends in the courts and the gardaí and she'd be inside for as long as I told them to keep her. She looked petrified. I nearly felt bad. But it worked, she backed off. And that was it. Or so I thought, until she managed to find us.'

'Wait, she got a job as Jenny's nanny so she could get close to us? But why?'

'Because of what happened. Because of what she lost in the accident.'

He didn't use the word. They never used the word. But it was enough. Now Marissa understood.

70

Four years earlier

CARRIE WALKED INTO THE visiting room, her eyes roaming across the rows of seats until she found him. Gaunt and hollow, Kyle looked even paler than he had the week before, as though the six-month mark was some kind of turning point. His face and body giving in to prison life. All around them, people hugged and kissed, but Carrie just sat. She couldn't. Not yet. Maybe not ever. Kyle reached a hand across the table, faltering halfway. Maybe he couldn't either. Maybe they were both broken. Maybe they'd always been broken.

'All right?'

'Yeah.'

What else was there to say?

'Annie being all right to you? I know she's my cousin, but you can be honest – she's a bit of a pain.'

'She wants me to move out.'

At least that gave them something to talk about. Anything other than the accident.

'What do you mean?'

'Yer man's moving in – her fella. She said I'll have to go in two weeks.'

'Fuck.'

'It's fine. I'm going to England to stay with my father.'

'What?'

She almost laughed. He looked so stricken.

'Kyle, you're in here anyway, what does it matter whether I'm living in Dublin or London?'

'But I see you when you visit – you won't be able to visit if you go over there.' The hurt was there in his voice, in his eyes, in the set of his mouth. But she couldn't. She couldn't mind him and mind herself at the same time. She couldn't mind herself at all. Jesus, she couldn't do anything. She couldn't even keep her baby alive. Their baby. Her throat tightened. She gripped the sides of the hard, plastic chair and swallowed.

'It won't be for long. I'll be here when you get out, I promise.'

How could she tell him the truth? *You remind me of him. I can't bear to look at you.* Four days she'd managed to keep him alive, just four short days, and then he was gone. Kyle wouldn't understand. Maybe Kyle would never get it. He'd never seen the baby at all. The baby with no name. Turned to dust, one cold and frosty morning.

71

Marissa
Friday

BECAUSE OF WHAT SHE *lost*. Marissa closed her eyes at Peter's words. They'd never talked about it, never used the word 'baby' because neither of them could cope with the memory. It was an accident, a terrible, tragic accident, and nobody was at fault – that's what the inquest had found. An icy morning, a narrow road, just one of those awful things. The baby who was lost – she couldn't use the word 'died' – hadn't suffered. That's what they'd said. And Marissa, to her shame, had pushed it deep inside, into the black place where her parents' deaths lived, not to be looked at ever.

On the armchair, Milo was deeply engrossed in *PAW Patrol*, oblivious to the unfolding story. Marissa sat with her head in her hands, still trying to make sense of it.

'Jesus Christ. Carrie Finch was Caroline Murphy? And she took Milo to make up for the son she lost?'

Peter nodded.

'And Colin – he helped Carrie take Milo? It had nothing to do with the audit and distracting me from the Fenelon and Downey estates?'

Peter laughed, and it didn't seem right, not with Colin dead.

'Poor old Colin. He had nothing to do with kidnapping Milo.'

Marissa stared. Things started to slip away again.

'What do you mean? The police said he was involved.'

'Oh, he's not blameless – he stole all that money, and he was desperately afraid you'd find out. And he was seeing Carrie. But he never had any involvement in the kidnap. She targeted him, just like she targeted Ana.'

Marissa let out a breath as everything slotted into place.

But wait.

Not everything.

'Peter, how do you know all this? How did you find Milo?'

Peter paused. And to her astonishment, he smiled, a wide, smug grin. This was his big reveal, Marissa realized, he was about to show her how clever he was.

'Because Carrie forged a reference from Colin's computer – on the headed paper in your office – to rent the house in Sandymount. Colin told me he used to bring her up to the office sometimes, and once or twice she sent him out to get wine while they were there. It would have been easy for her to print it off once he was out of the office.'

'But I still don't get it – how did you know?'

The smug smile again.

'Because I found a copy of the reference. The night we were in your office looking for the Downey and Fenelon files – a copy of the forged reference had slipped behind the printer. It had the address of the house in Sandymount on it. I'm guessing she just printed it a second time, without realizing there was a copy stuck behind the table.'

Marissa remembered now – Peter frowning at the page he'd found in her office.

'And you went there that night, to the address on the letter.'

'Yes. You'd taken your sleeping pill and you were out for the count. I didn't take one that night – I waited till you were asleep.'

'To rescue Milo.'

'Yes.'

'But why did you leave him in Carrie's car, why didn't you bring him safely home?'

'I hated leaving him there, you have to believe me, Marissa. But if I brought him home with me, the guards would have known I'd been inside the house in Sandymount. I could hardly say I'd just found him roaming the streets. I'd have had to explain Carrie.'

Carrie. Marissa swallowed. She couldn't say it. She had to say it. She glanced over at Milo. He still had the headphones on, and his eyelids were drooping.

'Peter, what happened to Carrie?'

He threw up his hands. And in that gesture, in that throw-away, oh-so-Peter gesture, her world blew apart.

72

Four years earlier

ON HER FIFTH NIGHT in London, Carrie told her father about the accident.

'Are you sure they won't prosecute?' Rob asked. 'How did it happen?'

She closed her eyes, as a million images flashed through her mind. Headlights. Too fast. Too close. The terrifying realization. The too-late swerve. The crunch of metal. The blackness. And then worse than anything that came before, the waking up. The sympathetic face of the nurse. Their questions. Was there someone they could call? Her questions. *Where's my baby?* The nurse's eyes, wide and brimming. Someone else taking her hand. The words she didn't want to hear. But they said them anyway.

Hours later – or was it days? – him. His face, leaning over. His lined, tanned skin. His three-day stubble. His tight greying hair. His breath stale with hospital coffee. His voice, low. Emphatic.

We're not going to prosecute, he'd said. *You've been through enough. My wife doesn't want to put you through a dangerous driving charge.*

And she was grateful. Through the fog of grief and drugs, she was grateful.

She never told Kyle about the money. What use was it to him, stuck in jail. *To help you get back on your feet*, Peter Irvine had said, slipping an envelope into her hand. *Have a fresh start, in another country. Where nobody knows what happened.* And again, she was grateful. She used it to pay for the funeral, and to buy the ferry ticket to Holyhead, and the train ticket to London. Her father met her at the station. Wary at first. What did she want? Was this Irene's idea? No, she told him, she hadn't seen Irene in years. You can't stay long, he told her, just a few nights until you get on your feet. She bit her lip and nodded, too numb to be hurt any more.

On the fifth night, he asked how her search for a flat was going. That's when she told him. And that's when the softening came. The man who'd never been her father – not really, not in any true sense of the word – hugged her for the first time. Grieving for his lost grandson, maybe grieving for all of it – the lost years, the lack of everything, the broken girl with nowhere to go.

'Are you sure they won't prosecute?' he asked again, opening two bottles of beer.

'He said they won't.'

'Did he sign anything?'

She stared at her father. How could he think she'd have the power to ask the man to sign something? Men like Peter Irvine told other people what to do, and they did it. That's how it worked.

She didn't go back for the inquest. They must have looked for her, but the Caroline Murphy who had lived with Kyle's cousin

Annie in East Wall in Dublin 3 was long gone. Disappeared. Maybe even dead. Lena Byrde, living under the radar in Brompton, London, was an entirely different person.

It was Rob who spotted it – a small report in an Irish newspaper he still read every day. He passed his iPad to her, stabbing the screen with his finger.

'Open verdict. Do you see that? Jesus, Caroline, it wasn't your fault.'

She took the iPad and scanned the article, then read it a second time, more slowly.

'Maybe . . . maybe because I didn't show up for the inquest? They didn't have all the facts?'

Rob shook his head. 'I don't think so. If they thought it was your fault, they'd be coming for you.' He looked up at her. 'Tell me again what he said in the hospital?'

'He said, "We're not going to prosecute." '

Rob let out a long breath. 'He let you think it was your fault, but there's nothing at all here to suggest that.' He stabbed the iPad again. 'Bastard.'

Carrie said nothing.

'Look what they've done to you – running away, hiding out here, leaving your fella behind, your whole life behind. And the guilt, thinking you killed your own child!' He shook his head. 'That's sick. He's a fucking scumbag sicko. I've a good mind to . . .' He sat staring at the inquest report, then slammed his fist down so hard on the screen she thought it might smash.

Still she said nothing.

Minutes ticked by as he nursed his hand, reading and re-reading the report.

Finally he looked at Carrie. 'It means you can go home, if you want to?' he said, his voice softer now. 'You don't have to.

You're welcome to stay here. Whatever you decide, at least now you have a choice.'

Carrie couldn't speak. But inside, a dark cloud formed, curling and expanding like thick, black, poisonous smoke.

73

Marissa
Friday

'I COULDN'T TAKE THE chance that Carrie would try again, Marissa. If she was put in prison, she'd be out in five or ten years.' Peter was speaking so matter-of-factly, as though he was explaining a no-brainer investment to a client. 'We'd never be free of her. She blamed us for losing her baby – people like her always look for someone else to blame. She was determined to take Milo in his place. And she was completely unhinged; I found a gun under her pillow. She might have been planning to shoot us. Who knows? I had to end it.'

She closed her eyes. *This cannot be happening. Her husband cannot have done what he seems to be saying he's done.* She put her face in her hands. There was no way to come out the other side of this. The earthquake she should have left alone.

Peter continued as though he hadn't dropped a bomb on their lives.

'Carrie was going to bring him up as her own son. Her father was helping her. They were going to live together in West Cork, like a family. He'd told his sister he was coming home with a fiancée called Sienna.'

Sienna Watkins, the name on the passport Fiona Sheridan

had shown her. Were they utterly insane? She listened as Peter kept talking, her face still in her hands.

'There wasn't anything incestuous going on, it was just a good cover. They'd live as a family, then somewhere down the line have an amicable separation. And eventually they'd move again, and Robin-the-girl could be Robin-the-boy.'

She jerked as his hand touched her wrist, pulling it away from her face. She looked into the eyes she thought she knew and shook her head.

'How do you know all this – their plans?'

He kept his hands wrapped around her wrists, rubbing the thin skin with his thumbs as he talked.

'Because Rob fucking Murphy tried to blackmail me.'

'What?'

Another sigh. 'Murphy heard on the news that Milo had been found, and when he couldn't reach Carrie by phone, he went to the bungalow. And obviously found her dead. Kyle Byrde was already dead at that stage, and Murphy knew absolutely nothing about Colin, so he figured it must have been me who smothered Carrie.' *Smothered Carrie.* Just like that. Marissa thought she might be sick.

Peter was still talking. 'Carrie had told him about our encounter at the playground.'

'And he came to find you?'

'He called my mobile on Sunday night – the call I said was from some busybody telling us to watch out for someone close to the family?'

He stopped, waiting for her acknowledgement. Jesus Christ. This had all been going on under her nose. How easily Peter had lied about the call.

'He phoned and asked for money or he was telling the guards. I couldn't let that happen.'

The room was swimming now because she knew what he was going to say, and yet it seemed utterly impossible that this was happening.

'The money. Colin.' Her voice was a hoarse whisper.

'I was afraid Rob Murphy wasn't going to be happy with money, he might want revenge for his daughter's death too. And Colin owed me, so to be on the safe side I sent him to bring the money to Rob.'

To be on the safe side.

She swallowed. 'How did Colin "owe" you?'

'I covered for him – about the money he stole from your clients.'

'You knew about that? Oh my God, why didn't you tell me?'

'No, no, I didn't know at first. But when I found the forged reference behind the printer in the office, I knew there was some connection between Colin and Carrie, and then when Lia found the photo of them on Facebook on Sunday night, that cemented it. Rob called just before you guys found the photo, and Colin started to look like a very handy scapegoat.' To her disgust, he let out a small chuckle. 'It was nearly funny – Lia kept saying he was a sheep, and I was thinking, no, more of a goat.'

Marissa bit her lip, trying and failing to find a response. Peter kept talking.

'So when I went out to get tequila and Mexican takeout on Sunday night, I went over to Colin's house and told him I knew he was involved in kidnapping Milo. I said I'd kill him if he didn't tell me everything. He actually cried. He swore he didn't have anything to do with the kidnap, but I kept pushing, said he was a child trafficker and a paedophile, and that's where he got the money for the big house, and if he didn't tell me, I'd strangle him with my bare hands.' Peter smiled, and Marissa died a little inside.

'If he had any sense, he'd have known it was an idle threat,' Peter said. 'But he was too scared to see that.'

Marissa shook her head, trying to take it in. Just a metre away, Milo had fallen asleep on the armchair, the iPad lying on his lap.

'He told me everything then – the house was from the proceeds of his skimming from wills. He'd been doing it for years, small amounts at first, but the Fenelon and Downey estates were so big, he could get away with more.' Peter leaned towards her and kissed her forehead. 'He doesn't deserve your pity, Marissa, he brought this on himself when he stole from you.'

She blinked back tears. Whatever Colin did, he didn't deserve this.

'When we went to his house on Tuesday to confront him about stealing, he knew we were coming, you'd already got him to confess? It was all an act?'

'Yes. I told him on Sunday night that I'd cover for him because you'd been through enough. That I'd book us a trip to Spain and leave him to fix the accounts before the audit.'

Jesus, even the trip to Spain was part of this web.

'But he owed me for covering it up, I told him. I said I needed some cash handed over to a client who was reluctant to leave a paper trail. I don't know if he believed me or not, but he was too scared to argue.'

She could picture Colin, the overgrown schoolboy, the man who liked to coast through life without thinking too deeply about anything at all, with everything crumbling around him. Petrified of being found out, for the things he didn't do and the things he did.

'What did you do to Colin?' she whispered.

'I didn't do anything. I sent him to the industrial estate to

363

meet Rob Murphy on Wednesday night and waited to see what would happen. Colin was there early—'

Marissa cut across him. 'Wait, that's not possible – Colin was in our office Wednesday night, taking the Downey and Fenelon files. I was there, remember, hiding under the desk.'

'That wasn't Colin,' Peter said with a look that was almost sheepish. 'That was me. Sorry you got a fright, I genuinely didn't know you were there till you said it the next morning.'

She sat, speechless, as Peter continued.

'I figured if I took the files, it strengthened the case against Colin, made it look like he was desperate to cover up what he'd done.' He shrugged. 'Then I drove to the industrial estate and hid out of sight to watch. Exactly as I predicted, Murphy ambushed Colin, thinking he was me. Marched around the corner, walked straight over and shot Colin in the chest before the poor dumb fuck had a clue what was happening. I bloody knew it, I knew that's what Murphy was going to do.' Peter folded his arms with a triumphant look on his face, happy to be proved right. 'Then when Murphy was unzipping the bag to count the money, I did the last bit. I didn't know if I could do it, Marissa, it was the scariest thing I ever did in my life. At least with Carrie, she didn't see me coming, and I couldn't see her face. But Murphy looked up, saw me, and I had to keep going anyway. I had to finish it. And I did. I shot him. With the gun from Carrie's house. I've never shot anyone before, it was odd.' He was quiet for a moment. 'Then I wiped the gun down, made sure Colin's prints were on it, and dropped it beside him. It was neat. For the police, I mean. All four kidnappers dead.' The triumphant look was back.

Marissa could barely breathe. This could not be happening.

'I did it all for us, Marissa, for you, me and Milo. Carrie would have taken him away again, she'd have chased us all our lives, we'd never have been safe.'

'Did you know it was her all along? As soon as Milo was taken?' she managed.

'No, I didn't realize until the guards showed us her picture on Saturday, the day after she took him – that's when it clicked.'

She stared at him. It was all wrong, all of it, but more than that, there was something else that didn't make sense.

'Peter. Why didn't you just tell McConville? When she showed us Carrie's photo on Saturday morning, and you recognized her as the other driver?'

For the first time, he looked confused. Lost for words.

'I . . . I knew I could deal with it.'

'What?' Her voice rose. They both looked over at Milo, but he was sleeping deeply now. 'What the fuck are you talking about? Our son had been kidnapped and you knew who had taken him and why, but you said nothing? Are you out of your mind? And why didn't you send the police when you saw the address on the reference?'

'I knew what I was doing.' Stubborn. Defiant. He pressed his thumbs into her wrists as though impressing his logic straight through her skin and into her veins.

'Peter, it makes no sense. At that point, you'd done nothing wrong – if you'd told the police, they might have found Milo more quickly, and none of the rest needed to happen. Colin stole, sure, but he didn't need to die. And Carrie, she should be locked up, but what you did . . .' She started to cry. And for the first time in all this, she felt something for the woman who took her child, the girl who lost her own. Whatever she'd done, Carrie hadn't deserved to die. And she'd been kind to Milo. She hadn't hurt him or mistreated him. She'd treated him like . . .

That's when it clicked. A dawning realization she tried with all her might to push back into the darkness.

Through her tears, she looked at Peter.

'The synaesthesia. The way Milo sees words in colour.'

'What about it?'

'Carrie had it too, from what you're saying about that time you met in the playground. You told me she was chatting to Milo, saying "Monday is blue".'

'So what?'

'I read up on it. I thought maybe the crash had caused it, some kind of trauma effect, but it's genetic. Not always, but often.'

She looked over at Milo, her sleeping son, her only child, the love of her life.

'Peter. Whose . . . whose baby died in the crash?'

74

Seven months earlier

CARRIE SQUINTED AT THE man in the playground. Was it him? She pushed her chair back, stomach churning. Remembering. His face, leaning over. His hospital-coffee breath. The authority in his tone. The relief at his words.

We're not going to prosecute. You've been through enough. My wife doesn't want to put you through a dangerous driving charge.

And now there he was. Peter Irvine. No more than ten feet away. In front of him was a little boy. Milo. She knew his name, she'd read it in the newspaper reports. Not then, not when it happened. Later, when her father had searched online and shown them to her.

Blond hair, down to his shoulders. A tiny frame, a tiny nose. The lightest scattering of freckles. A dimpled chin. And something more. Something she couldn't quite name. She pushed her chair back further, metal legs scraping on concrete ground, and stood. With her hand above her eyes, shading them from the sun, she stared at the man and the boy. At the smile. At the crooked little smile that pulled her closer to the playground. One foot moved in front of the other as she reached to unlatch the gate and step inside.

'Hang on a sec, Milo-Mouse,' Peter Irvine was saying, 'I need to reply to this.'

Head in phone, not looking at Milo. Not looking at Carrie.

'Don't be always working, Daddy, we're in the playground!' Milo said, hopping from one foot to the other.

'Yes, Milo.' Peter sighed, without looking up from the phone. 'I know we're in a playground but it's three o'clock on a Tuesday afternoon, and Daddy has to work.'

Carrie stepped closer, mesmerized by the little blond boy.

'Tuesday is green, isn't it?' Milo said to his dad. 'Like grass. And three is light brown.'

'Milo, I need to reply to this email. Can't you just go on the slide?'

His face falling, Milo moved towards the climbing frame, and sat on the ground beside it.

Carrie followed and crouched down beside Milo.

'For me, Tuesday is green too,' she said, smiling as he turned to look at her.

His face lit up, that smile she somehow knew. Her stomach churned. How could she know that smile?

'Yes! And Monday is orange.'

She shook her head. 'For you, Monday is orange. But I see Monday as blue. It's different for everyone.'

'Really? My daddy thinks the days don't have any colours.'

'I used to draw the days of the week in my journal, all in their own colours. I remember I used to tell my mam that Monday was blue but she didn't understand what I meant. Do you see letters in colour too?'

Milo nodded. 'Is it magic?'

'It's a kind of magic. We sometimes get it from our parents. It has a big long name. Synaesthesia.'

'My mummy told me that word!' Milo said, scrambling to his feet. 'But I can't say it, it's too big.'

'That's OK. The main thing is, it's fun, isn't it? Seeing words in colour? Does your mam see Monday in orange too, or in a different colour?'

His smile fell away again.

'No, she doesn't see any colours. It's only me.'

A noise began to whirr inside her head. White noise. Blurred lines. Crooked smiles. Dimpled chins. Bright colours dancing, making her dizzy. She reached out to grab the climbing frame. *Tuesday is green.* Milo. Kyle. Crooked smiles and dimpled chins.

'What's going on?'

Peter was standing over them, shoving his phone in his back pocket.

She stood. Stomach churning. Deep breath. Calm words.

'I know you.'

'Milo, we have to go.' He took the little boy by the hand and started towards the gate.

'I know you, you're Peter Irvine,' she said, following.

Peter stopped and turned to look at her. Realization. And something else. Fear.

He turned his back again and picked up pace, pulling Milo towards the entrance to the underground car park.

Still she followed.

Inside, in the dark, she watched as Peter fumbled for his ticket, swearing under his breath.

'You're Peter,' she said, drawing close. 'And this—' She pointed at Milo, swallowing, trying and failing to make the impossible words come.

Peter found his ticket and jammed it into the machine, tapping his card against the sensor. Ignoring her.

'I know what you did.'

Milo looked from his dad to her, his face creased in a frown. There was no question now. It was all there. In his eyes, in his mouth, in his cleft chin, just like Kyle's. *Tuesday is green.*

'Milo, can you be the biggest boy, and take the keys to see if you can open the car all by yourself?' Peter handed him the car key and pushed him gently away from the ticket machine. Silently he stood, watching as Milo skipped towards the stairs to the lower level. Carrie blinked, frozen, as the little boy disappeared from sight. This couldn't be happening. She sucked in a breath, searching for words.

But before she knew what was happening, Peter's hands were on her shirt. Pulling, grabbing, shaking. Her head flew back, hitting the ticket machine. Once. Twice. A third time. Slamming against the metal. Pain searing. Tears threatening. Peter hissing.

'Don't you *ever* come near me or my family again.' His face so close to hers, she could feel his breath, see inside his eyes. White-hot rage. 'I'll have you arrested so fast, you won't know what hit you. Or you'll be found dead in a ditch. One less druggie to worry about, nobody will even notice you're gone.' He slammed her head against the machine again. 'Do you understand me?'

She blinked yes. Blood trickled from her lip and down on to her shirt. With a final thrust, he flung her to the cold, concrete ground. And left. Left with Milo. Just like the first time.

75

Marissa
Friday

INSIDE HER HEAD SHE begged him, screamed at him to answer. To tell her she'd got it wrong. To tell her it was a coincidence that Milo and Carrie both had synaesthesia. To remind her not everyone inherits it from a parent. But he said nothing.

No words. No comfort.

She looked again at her sleeping child and her heart smashed into a million pieces.

She stood and walked over to Milo, awkwardly scooping him up. His arm slipped down, his head lolled.

'You need to leave,' she said as calmly as she could.

'They'll take him away from us if they find out.' His voice was gentle, belying everything he'd just told her. 'Sit down and let's talk.'

She sat back on the couch, still holding Milo, smelling his sweet skin, rubbing the top of his back.

'I didn't intend for any of this to happen,' Peter said, standing up and moving towards the kitchen. 'Let's have a drink and talk it through.' He returned with two glasses of white wine, as though they were about to discuss holiday plans.

She shook her head and he set the wine on the mantelpiece.

'The crash was the worst thing that ever happened, we both know that,' he said. 'Carrie was on her way home from the hospital, with her newborn baby, when we were on our way back in, for his check-up – God, he was so tiny.' He nodded towards Milo, as though he'd forgotten what all of this meant, that this child in her arms was not with them that morning at all, and she thought she might throw up.

'The roads were icy, the light was bad, it was nobody's fault.' He looked at her pleadingly but she already knew this.

'And then the crash. You were unconscious and I was panicking. The other driver was unconscious too. And I saw . . . the car seat on the road and . . .'

Don't say it, she screamed inside her head, *don't say our baby died!*

'I took him out, and I did everything, Marissa. I begged him to move, to breathe. But I knew. I knew by looking at him. It was too late,' Peter said, his head bowed. 'Then I heard a noise, a baby crying, and at first I thought I was wrong but it was her baby, the other driver's. I managed to get his car seat out of the wreck. I unbuckled him and held him to calm him down – it was the right thing to do, I was trying to help.' He looked at her, begging, and she nodded.

'I was alone in all this wreckage. And . . . I don't even know what I was thinking, or if I was thinking at all, but suddenly I found myself putting her baby down, and picking up Milo. I kissed him and told him we loved him and I . . . I put him in the other car seat, and pushed it back into the wreck. Then I called the ambulance. When it arrived, I had her baby in my arms. They assumed he was mine and I just . . . didn't correct them.'

Everything crashed around her, as though all along the world was made of glass. Her life in tiny shards, too small to piece together. There was no coming back from this. Grief swept over her. Grief for the child she lost, grief for Milo then and Milo now, and for her and for Carrie. One wrong assumption, one horrific lie. Two families destroyed.

'Marissa, now that you know, you can see why I didn't tell anyone – when I worked out where Carrie was holding him, I mean. We can *never* tell the police, because they'll take Milo away. And now that Carrie and Rob Murphy are gone, we're safe.'

She looked over at him, this man she thought she knew. She felt no sadness – not yet – there was only horror and repulsion and disbelief.

'Marissa, talk to me,' he pleaded.

'I will fight to my last breath to keep him,' she whispered eventually, 'but we can't live this lie, Peter.'

He stood by the fireplace, shaking his head. Belligerent now. Defensive.

'Think about it, Marissa. If her intentions were pure, why didn't she just call the police? She was going to blackmail us or ask for a ransom. No doubt.'

Marissa let out a breath. 'If it was me, I'd have called the police, gone through legal channels to get him back. But I'm a well-off, well-educated solicitor in a nice part of town. It would be easy for me. Carrie'd been in and out of trouble all her life, dumped by her ex-con dad, ignored by her useless mother, a runaway, an outsider who was brought up to believe the system lets you down. Neither she nor Kyle would ever have trusted the law would be on their side.' She pulled Milo closer. 'In her shoes, I honestly don't know if I'd have done anything differently.'

A minute went by. Or maybe a lifetime.

'Peter, I think you should go.'

He looked shocked. How could this be a surprise?

'Go where?'

'I don't know. But I can't get my head around what you've done, and I can't be with the person you are now, and . . . I can't have you near Milo.'

He shook his head.

'I'm not going anywhere. You're my wife, this is my house, and Milo is my son. You think I'm going to walk away after everything I did for us?'

'Everything you did for us? Peter, you've destroyed our lives – you've destroyed other people's lives – you've committed murder!'

'That was Carrie's fault. Not. Mine.' Every word enunciated, firing like bullets. 'If she hadn't taken Milo, none of this would have happened.'

'*Carrie's fault?* Oh my God, it's not Carrie's fault, Peter, it's not anyone's fault but yours! Four years ago you—' She stopped, unable to say the words. 'What you did that morning of the accident was the worst thing imaginable. And everything that's happened since is down to your actions that day. This is nobody's fault but yours.' She paused briefly to steady herself. 'And if you're not leaving, I am.' She tried to stand, but Milo was too heavy.

'Where will you go? Where will you stay?'

'To the police. And I'll figure the rest of it out after.'

'Marissa,' he said softly, hunkering down beside her. He was so close now, she could feel his breath on her face. 'If you go to the police, they'll take Milo. You'll never see him again. Is that what you want?'

She tried to answer, but the words wouldn't come.

'I might go to jail,' he continued, 'or I might not. I have friends who can help. But one way or another, I think we both know I can handle jail time better than you can handle losing your son.'

'You surely don't believe we can go on as though nothing has happened?'

'Why not? That's why I did all this. Don't you see? It's done now, and we can do exactly that – go on as we did before all this.'

All this. He said it as though it was an inconvenience, something that was done *to* them, like a fender bender or a broken window. As though four people weren't dead. As though he didn't steal their son from his grieving mother.

She couldn't do this.

She moved on the couch, shifting forward so she could stand, holding Milo in her arms. She walked to the mantelpiece and lifted her phone. She looked at Peter one last time and went to Recent Calls. She pressed McConville's mobile phone number.

76

Seven months earlier

ROB WAS SCEPTICAL AT first, until Carrie sent him photos – a picture of Kyle from before he went to prison, and one of Milo she'd got from a newspaper feature on the Irvines' house. The resemblance was plain as day once you looked at the two side by side – in the eyes, in the smile, in the dimpled chin. And Rob's scepticism was quickly replaced by fury. Who were these Irvines, thinking they could get away with stealing a child? Carrie had to talk him out of coming over straight away, guns blazing. They needed a plan, she told him. Not a smash-and-grab that would see them both in prison. A plan that would work in the long term and keep her son safely with her for ever. Eventually, Rob stopped ranting and began to listen.

Kyle was less enthusiastic when she told him what she wanted to do.

'I don't know, Carrie . . .' he said, flicking ash over the side of the balcony, 'I'm only six months out of the Joy. I'll top myself before I go back behind bars. Look, I'm doing OK on the building site, I'm moving out of Annie's next week to a house-share in North Wall, things are coming together for me. I don't want to rock the boat.'

'But he's your son!' she hissed, mindful of Annie inside the flat. Didn't he want to move heaven and earth to get his son back?

'What kind of life would it be though? You want to take him away from the only family he knows, to go on the run?'

'We won't be on the run. My father has a house in West Cork. He's telling people he's moving there with his fiancée and child. That'll be me and Milo. You can visit. Or move down too.' She shrugged. 'Or don't be involved at all. I only asked you because I thought you'd bloody care. He's your son, Kyle. Our son. And that man took him.' Her voice cracked, and the last words came out in a whisper. 'He just took him.'

In the end, Kyle didn't really agree to anything, but he didn't stop spending time with her either, and bit by bit, he pitched in. He helped her trawl the internet, gathering information on Peter, Marissa and Milo Irvine. He helped her sift through dozens of 'Nannies wanted' ads online and on shop noticeboards, until they found the right one: a child starting Junior Infants in Kerryglen National School. He helped her pack up her stuff when she moved out of the hostel and into the Kennedys' house. He visited her there when the Kennedys were out at work. And when she said she needed a random address for the fake playdate, he suggested 14 Tudor Grove.

Why? she asked. *Because the woman who lives there once fostered my old cellmate,* he'd said, *and by all accounts, she's kind. Marissa Irvine should end up somewhere kind when her world falls apart.* Sap, Carrie thought, but she didn't say no.

Kyle never said much about his son, or how he *felt* about what she was planning, but then, he'd never seen the baby at all. It wasn't the same for him. It wasn't the same for anyone else but Carrie.

77

Marissa
Friday

'MARISSA?' MCCONVILLE SAID A second time. 'Is that you? Is everything OK?'

Marissa laid the phone on the mantlepiece and switched it to speaker. She looked at Peter. He didn't look scared. He looked serene. Unperturbed. Milo shifted in her arms, nuzzling into her neck. She felt his warm breath on her skin, his soft body velcroed on to hers. She inhaled his small-boy scent, and briefly closed her eyes.

'Yes,' she said, 'everything is fine. I . . . I just wanted to know if there was any news about anything . . . about Kyle Byrde maybe? Do you know who killed him?'

Peter smiled. A smile that said he knew exactly what was going to happen. And as McConville talked – something about a car parked near Kyle Byrde's house – Marissa nodded as though she was listening. Peter was still smiling. He passed the glass of wine to her again. Mechanically she took it. Milo let out a small, sleepy breath. Peter raised his glass and clinked it against hers. McConville said something about calling over, to check in on them, now that it was all over.

'That would be nice, thank you,' Marissa found herself say-ing. 'And yes, it feels good to know it's over.'

As good as her word, McConville called by the following morn-ing. Peter led her through to the sitting room, where Milo was on Marissa's knee, playing with her phone. Peter was jovial, offering tea and coffee, and the pear and walnut scones he picked up while out for a run earlier that morning. Marissa felt like she was outside her body, floating above – looking down at a beautiful family in a beautiful house. People she didn't know at all.

McConville was saying something to her.

'Oh, sorry, I was miles away, I missed that?'

'I might fill you in on the final details of the case, but it's not for *little ears*?' McConville mouthed the last bit.

Marissa knew this was her cue to send Milo off to play. She hadn't let him out of her sight since last night. She'd slept in his bed and had been stuck to him since he woke. Role reversal. Everything reversal.

She glanced at Peter – charming, smiling Peter – and sent Milo out to the den.

Peter closed the door and sat beside her on the couch. McCon-ville was on the armchair opposite.

'You wanted to tell us about Kyle Byrde? Please say Colin didn't murder him too?' Peter said, with what was so clearly feigned horror. Marissa stiffened. How was McConville not seeing through this? But then she hadn't either.

'No, not Colin,' said McConville. 'A car registered to Rob Murphy was clamped in the vicinity of Kyle Byrde's house that night, so our working assumption is that Murphy killed Byrde. When we found Rob Murphy's body, his face had a deep scratch, and there were other scratches on his neck. DNA tests should show if this was due to an altercation with Kyle Byrde.'

'Why so vicious though? Why batter him and cut off his hands?' Peter asked.

'We're not certain, but now that we know about the scratches on Mr Murphy, we suspect he may have been worried about DNA under Kyle Byrde's fingernails.'

Kyle Byrde. Marissa thought of the photo she'd seen on the news. Now that she knew, she could see the resemblance. Milo's father, murdered by Milo's grandfather. Jesus Christ.

'Why did he do it though? Why kill Kyle?' she asked.

'We're not entirely sure yet, but Kyle's flatmate said he was drunk a few nights earlier and shouting about going to the police to report something. We suspect he may have threatened Rob Murphy, told him he was going to turn him in, although we don't know why he would do that – it's not the kind of thing career criminals do, believe me.'

Was Kyle trying to protect Milo, Marissa wondered, trying to get him safely back to the only home he'd ever known?

Dizzy and sick, she put her head in her hands.

'Are you OK, Marissa?' McConville asked, leaning forward in her chair.

Marissa looked at the stranger beside her and back at McConville.

'She's still reeling from all of it,' Peter said, putting his hand on hers. Tight. Squeezing so her rings dug into the sides of her fingers, hurting her. 'We're just relieved to have Milo back. We're never going to let anyone take him again. We'd both do anything for him, wouldn't we, Marissa?'

Her eyes filled with tears, and she nodded.

For Milo, she'd do anything.

78

One week later

WATER, STILL AS BLUE glass, glistens under winter sunlight, and white sailboats bob against the horizon. The East Pier is busy for a Friday morning, walkers making the most of the dry, bright day.

Marissa and Jenny hug for a long time. It's the first time they've seen one another all week. Jenny's been at work, and Marissa's been picking up the pieces of her life, little by little. But now Jenny's got a morning off, and they're walking Dún Laoghaire Pier.

'Did you find childcare yet?' Marissa asks, because that's easier than all the other things they will talk about.

'No, not yet. I just want someone I know, someone who's kind and caring and likes children, who isn't my mother-in-law. That's not too much to ask, is it?'

Jenny laughs and Marissa joins her, but it's sobering. And she feels guilty because she still has Ana. This is a minor guilt in the realm of all the things she feels guilty about right now, none of which she can confide in Jenny.

'So, how are *you*?' Jenny asks, as they stroll down the pier, coffees in hand. They look like all the other pairs of women strolling down the pier, the women who are talking about work and kids and what they watched on TV last night.

'Oh, you know,' Marissa says, flashing her a smile, 'one day at a time. We have counselling for Milo, and family therapy for the three of us together.'

She doesn't add that Milo has been distancing himself from Peter. Asking for bedtime stories from her and her alone, ducking away when Peter tries to kiss or hug him. She wonders if he has subconsciously worked out who 'the man' was that night, and the thought makes her sick.

'I'm glad you're getting professional help, it's too much to manage on your own,' Jenny is saying. 'And if you ever need a coffee and a walk, or those cocktails we talked about, I'm here.'

'Thank you, I mean it, you've been utterly amazing through all of this.'

They stop in unison at a bench and sit, looking out at Dublin Bay.

'Have you had any further contact from Carrie's mother?' Jenny asks after a while.

Marissa grimaces. 'No. I see she's been all over the TV and papers.'

Jenny nods. 'She doesn't look like she's grieving too much, does she? Keen to distance herself from how Carrie turned out but eager for the attention all the same.'

'She certainly doesn't seem to have been fond of Carrie. God, poor girl.'

Jenny looks at her in surprise. 'You're a better person than I am, I don't think I could have sympathy for her.'

Marissa shakes her head. There is nothing she can say.

Irene dusts off her second-favourite dress, her *TV*-dress as she likes to think of it, and lays it out on the bed. Frank's words are ringing in her ears. Two options, he'd said. *Stay here, keep going on TV and talking to the press, but if you do, it's over between us.* He wanted nothing more to do with it. Any of it. Option two: move to Bristol with him. The transfer was happening, the Bristol branch had already assigned him an office. Smaller than his office here, but still. He was going, with or without her. He needed a clean break, he said, and they could keep their heads down over there.

'But what about my *opportunities*,' she'd said. 'I set up an Instagram account today and I already have four thousand followers!'

Frank had given her a withering look. He wasn't for turning.

She picks the dress off the bed and folds it. She puts it in the suitcase. Bristol might not be so bad.

Esther sits at the corner table, buttering a scone. Around her, customer chatter is louder than usual. A week on, there's still only one story in town. Colin Dobson. How shocked they are, the last thing anyone expected. A murderer and kidnapper in their midst. Scratch the surface, they're saying, and you never know what's going on beneath. Maybe it was all him – maybe Carrie was forced into it, maybe she wasn't such a bad person after all. Maybe Jenny Kennedy hadn't put her own son and every child in town in mortal danger when she hired Carrie.

As the babble of chatter continues around her, Esther picks up her phone to type out a text.

Dear Jenny, if you're still looking for someone to mind Jacob after school, and only if you think I'm what you're looking for, I'd love to do it. Take your time to think about it. I promise I won't feed him chocolate brownies every day. Esther.

She presses Send and stands, pocketing her phone in her billowing dress. With practised futility, she smooths down her hair, looks around the bustling cafe, waves at Verena, and walks out into the November sunshine.

Brian Irvine sits on his side of the bed. May is still asleep on her side. *Her* side. Not really though, since her actual bed is somewhere else entirely. Is she ever going to leave him? Brian realizes it's not that important. The last few weeks have put things in perspective. Life's too short. He leans over to kiss her and gets up to make coffee.

Adeline Furlong-Kennedy sits at her writing desk in her dark sitting room. She sifts through the bundle she took from Richie's bedside locker, smiling. The guards are gone now, and nobody is searching anywhere for anything. She switches on her computer and starts to type. Satisfied with her words, she prints off a new note and puts it in the envelope. She marks it with Richie's name. Block capitals, so he doesn't know it's her. He'll never know it's her.

79

Six months later

Irish Businessman Dies Suddenly in Spain

WELL-KNOWN businessman Peter Irvine has died suddenly while on holiday in Marbella. TheDailyByte.ie understands that Mr Irvine was taken ill after accidentally ingesting food that contained traces of shellfish. According to local news reports, Mr Irvine had a serious shellfish allergy, and went into anaphylactic shock on Tuesday night while eating dinner in his holiday apartment. His wife, Marissa Irvine, immediately called emergency services but could not locate her husband's EpiPen.

It is understood that Mr Irvine had prepared dinner using locally bought ingredients, including a stock cube containing traces of shellfish. Mrs Irvine, who does not speak Spanish, is believed to have purchased the stock cube without knowing it contained shellfish.

Mr and Mrs Irvine came to national attention late last year when their young son, Milo, was kidnapped. He was subsequently found unharmed in a car in Sandymount, Dublin 4.

Speaking from Marbella, Mrs Irvine made a brief statement:

'We are heartbroken. I would like to thank the emergency services for their quick response, and all those who have supported me at this very difficult time.' Asked how her son was doing, she explained that he wasn't in Spain. 'Thankfully, Milo is not here, and didn't witness what happened,' said Mrs Irvine. 'He is safely at home in Dublin, being cared for by his wonderful nanny.'

Acknowledgements

First and foremost, thank you to Diana Beaumont, my incredible agent, without whom none of this would have been possible. Thank you to all at Marjacq Scripts, and also to Roz Watkins for the chance conversation in Harrogate that led to a serendipitous meeting that in turn led to this.

Thank you to my amazing editor, Natasha Barsby, who with such ease and wisdom made *All Her Fault* so much better. Thank you too to Claire Gatzen, Vivien Thompson, Josh Benn, Imogen Nelson, Beci Kelly, Becky Short, Ella Horne and Ruth Richardson, and all at Transworld and Penguin Random House who helped get this book from my Word document to bookshop shelves.

Thank you to my early readers: Sinéad Fox, and my sisters, Nicola, Elaine and Deirdre. This book is dedicated to Nicola, and because of the unwritten-but-set-in-stone rules put in place in childhood, there must be more books and more dedications, because there are more sisters.

Thank you to Allen and Stephen who were kind enough to give up their time to answer my questions on Garda procedures in a case like this. Apologies for bending things a little here and there to suit the story, and for never giving my fictional Gardaí any time off work.

Likewise, thank you (and similar apologies) to Catherine

Kirwan and Sinéad Fox for helping with solicitor questions. Marissa and Colin could learn from you, I think.

Thank you to Kevin Mitchell and Dónal Rooney for answering my unusual questions without raising an eyebrow. Thank you Cormac O'Keeffe for the quick responses to my newspaper questions and this is a note to say that real journalists are (almost all) much more ethical than Faye Foster and her editor.

To Nicola Cassidy, for always being at the end of a Facebook message, a WhatsApp, a Twitter DM, or if we're being really old-school, a phone call.

Thank you to the writing community for the cheerleading and the company: I'm not going to risk listing names because I'll definitely forget someone, but between championing books, sending quotes, posting on social media, turning up at launches (ah, launches . . .), sharing posts, and DM'ing your wisdom, you are all wonderful.

Thanks to my parent blogger pals who have been amazingly and continually supportive since the career pivot from financial services to (fictional) murdering started, and thank you to all the fabulous book bloggers who are endlessly generous in their support.

Thank you to OfficeMum readers, you are where it all began.

To my oldest friends, the Sion Hill girls, you are simply amazing. To my newer friends at the school gate, thank you for being absolutely nothing whatsoever like any of the school-gate characters in *All Her Fault*. This book is a work of fiction!

To my Kennedy aunts, who have always been there for us, and who have made the last year so much more fun. To Eithne, for all the support.

To Dad, thank you for the stories you used to tell when we were small, especially the one about the magic clock.

ACKNOWLEDGEMENTS

To Elissa, Nia and Matthew, thanks for all the help with plotting and for keeping your rooms tidy so I have more time to scroll Twitter. I mean write books.

To Damien, for not just accepting the career change, but actively encouraging me, and never losing faith even when I sometimes did.

And finally, thank you to *you*, the reader, for reading this book!

About the Author

Andrea Mara is an *Irish Times* Top Ten bestselling author, and has been shortlisted for a number of awards, including Irish Crime Novel of the Year. She lives in Dublin, Ireland, with her husband and three young children, and also runs multi-award-winning parent and lifestyle blog, OfficeMum.ie. *All Her Fault* is her first thriller to be published in the UK and internationally.